An Argumentation
of Historians

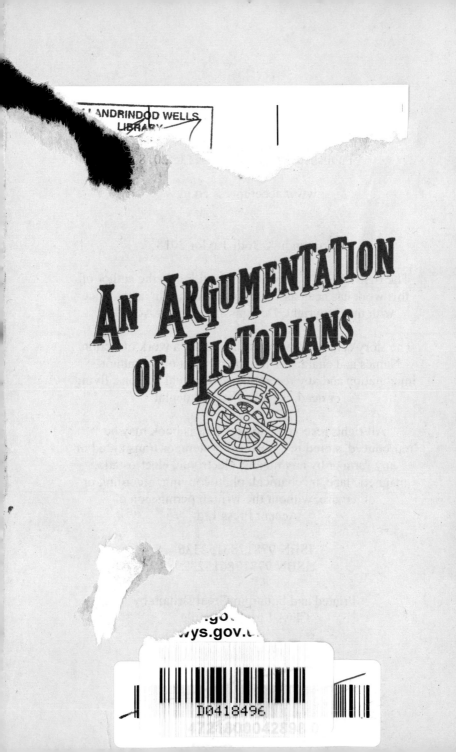

Published by Accent Press Ltd 2018

www.accentpress.co.uk

ISBN 9781786152336
eISBN 9781786152329

Printed and bound in Great Britain by
Clays Ltd, St Ives plc

Author's note

When we put together *The Long and Short of It*, I thought I'd write an introduction to each story, telling how and why it came about, what was the thinking behind it and the circumstances under which it was written.

I personally thought this brief glimpse into my thought processes would frighten the living daylights out of normal, intelligent, charming people – i.e. my readers – but not so. The intros proved to be nearly as popular as the stories themselves, and that's not hurtful at all, is it?

Anyway, I was struggling away at the typeface when the command came down from the cloud-cloaked Accent Press penthouse.

'The intros went quite well. It might be a good idea to do one for the next book. Only a suggestion, of course.'

As an author, I know on which side my bread's buttered. As an *Accent Press* author, I know on which side the electrodes are lubricated, and made haste to comply.

'Oh, and for God's sake make the book a bit more cheerful this time,' was the supplementary command, relayed by a sweating minion. 'Your last effort traumatised so many readers we had to set up a counselling group.'

While on this subject, I've been asked to say that for anyone still suffering the after-effects of that fine book *And the Rest Is History*, a few places still remain on the Accent Press sponsored '*Oh For God's Sake Get Over It and Stop Being Such a Baby'* Support Group. Sessions are held every Wednesday and are open to all. To enrol, please bring either the deeds of your house or your first-born – whichever can be most easily translated into cash.

So, here it is, the next Chronicle. *An Argumentation of Historians* – and yes, it is, I think, a little more light-hearted. There are no fewer disasters, but everyone is very cheerful about them because, of course, I'm not lulling you all into a false sense of security at all, am I?

Anyway, to bang on with the intro: there are certain time-travel scenarios I never wanted to get involved with. For instance, the one where the heroine goes back in time and is swept off her feet by a handsome contemporary who, inexplicably, falls in love with a woman with no land, no fortune, no skills and no important male relations either to protect her or give her status. Never mind that she looks strange, speaks even more strangely, is entirely ignorant of the world around her and seems not to have any idea of her proper place in it. Despite all that their love would cross time itself – she would abandon everything for his sake – and they would live happily ever after.

No heroine of mine – I said – would *ever* fall in love with a contemporary and, inexplicably, abandon hot baths, chocolate, antibiotics, dentists, central heating, universal suffrage, contraception, tea, toad-in-the-hole, bras, soap that doesn't strip your skin away, Lycra, books, and the safe removal of a volatile appendix, to live in a cold, damp, draughty castle with no plumbing – indeed no comforts of any kind – no matter how handsome and romantic the hero.

And then I thought: well, what if the hero wasn't romantic at all? In any way. And neither was the heroine.

What if they could barely communicate? What if their mindsets were worlds apart? What if he found her behaviour inexplicable? What if, despite all her best efforts to fit in, she lurched from one crisis to the next, astounding and frightening those around her? How long would she last?

Everyone has their own place in time. They may not like it. It might not be pleasant. But it's their place and it fits them perfectly and to leave it is always to court catastrophe.

THE CHRONICLES OF ST MARY'S

THE CHRONICLES OF ST MARY'S SHORT STORIES

ALSO BY JODI TAYLOR

Dramatis Thingummy

Talk about a cast of thousands. Have you seen how many characters there are in this book? What was I thinking? My next book will have only three characters in it, two of whom will die at the end of the first chapter.

The Institute of Historical Research at St Mary's

Dr Edward Bairstow	Director of St Mary's. But for how much longer?
Mrs. Partridge	PA to Director. Muse of History.
Dr Peterson	Shiny new Deputy Director.
Lisa Dottle	Thirsk's representative at St Mary's. Suffering a massive crush on Peterson.
Malcolm Halcombe	The leprosy's cleared up. Shame.
Kalinda Black	St Mary's representative at Thirsk. Does not do sympathy.

History Department

Max	Head of the History Department.
Mr Bashford	Dazed historian.
Miss Sykes	Psychotic historian.
Mr Clerk	Calm historian.
Miss Prentiss	Even calmer historian
Mr Atherton	Nice historian.
Miss North	Stroppy historian.

Angus   Historian of the genus *Gallus gallus domesticus*.

Technical Section

Leon Farrell   Chief Technical Officer.
Mr Dieter   Another Technical Officer.
Mr Lindstrom   Quiet and shy. Poor boy.

Medical Section

Dr Stone   Still inexplicably getting his own way.
Nurse Hunter   Is she or isn't she?
Nurse Fortunata   Lying her socks off to the Time Police.

Security Section

Mr Markham   Head of Security.
Mr Evans   Security guard.
Mr Cox   Another one.
Mr Keller   And another one.
Mr Gallacio   And another.

Research and Development

Professor Rapson   The GREAT Professor Rapson as he prefers to be known.
Doctor Dowson   His partner in crime.
Miss Lingoss   You might want to keep your eye

	on her.
Mr Swanson	Making a welcome return from Book One.
Mrs Enderby	Head of Wardrobe. Unexpectedly devious.
Mrs Shaw	Dr Peterson's assistant. Brings him biscuits.
Rosie Lee	Max's assistant. Brings her grief.
Mrs Mack	Kitchen Supremo.
Mrs Midgely	The housekeeper. Possessed of a piercing scream. Very protective of her towels.
Hammy	A tragic story. Sensitive readers should skip that bit.

Time Police

Captain Ellis	The nice one.
The Pursuit Team	Bunch of sick perverts.
The Clean Up Squad	They do what they say on the tin.

Retired

Ian Guthrie	Still giving good advice.

From the future

Mikey and Adrian	Still on the run ... but not for much longer.
Clive Ronan	Still being naughty.

His associates	Should know better.
Lorris	Expendable.
Rigby	Also expendable.

Note to self: this is exhausting. Write shorter books.

Historical figures

Greenwich 1536

| Fat Harry | Henry VIII – about to come a bit of a cropper. |

A big fat horse for a big fat king.

Assorted jugglers, acrobats, musicians, knights, and townspeople.

A would-be time-traveller with a spectacular girlfriend.

Persepolis 330BC

Alexander the Great	Nothing more to say, really.
Ptolemy	Future King of Egypt. Very open to manual persuasion.
Thaïs	A little minx. A dexterous little minx.

Palace guards, slaves, officials, the usual.

Residents of St Mary's 1399

| William Hendred | Marshal of St Mary's |
| Walter of Shrewsbury | Steward of St Mary's |

Sir Hugh Armstrong	Lord of St Mary's manor and all pertaining thereto.
Margery Daw	Washerwoman and a fine figure of … something.
Little Alice	Her assistant.
Roger and Edgar	Kitchen boys.
Wymer and Cuthbert	Stable boys. Chasing anything in a skirt and terrified that one day they'll succeed.
Dick and the other one	Scullions.
Fat Piers	The original foul-mouthed chef.
Ranulf	Village priest.
Rowena	His 'housekeeper'.
Joan of Rouen	Never remembers to have a dock leaf handy.
Owen	Guard and alibi.
Tam the Welshman	William's second in command.
Onion Man	Professional runt.

From the village

Pikey Peter	Poor boy.
Eadgytha	His mum.
William the Carpenter and his family.	
Margaret Brewer	Runs the pub.
Big Alice	Her assistant.

From medieval Rushford

Guy, Lord Rushford   A villain.

Jerald   His brother. Just fractionally unstable …

The infamous yellow horse.

Robert Sutton. Or Sugden. Or Sutton. No one knows.

His servant.

Female stall holder   Drives a hard bargain.

From 19th-century Rushford

Street urchin   Thieving little git.

Portly gentleman with a stick.

Sundry irate citizens.

Tombstone teeth man.

His associates.

A conifer tree that doesn't deserve what is about to happen to it.

Prologue

It's not all about battles and death and violence, you know. Yes, battles and death and violence do tend to be epoch-changing events but, sometimes, just occasionally, some seemingly unimportant event has massive consequences. Ramifications which spread down the centuries affecting everyone and everything. Very often people aren't aware at the time and it's only with the benefit of History and hindsight that the importance of the event is revealed.

Take, for example the year 1536.

In particular, take the 24th January 1536, Greenwich Palace. A holiday. A nice day out for the kids. Take a picnic. Enjoy the show. Thrill to the spectacle of a Tudor jousting tournament. Catch a glimpse of the king and his court. Nobody would die today. But thousands of people would die as a result of today. Because 24th January 1536 was the day when everything changed.

I'd like to say we were all back together again, but that was no longer true. We would never all be back together again. Helen Foster was dead and I missed her every day.

Ian Guthrie had been so badly injured he would never return to the Security Section. He and Elspeth Grey were leaving to start a new life just as soon as he was well enough. They had a plan, he said, and no, he certainly wasn't going to jeopardise its chances of success by telling an historian.

Markham had recovered well. Well enough to enjoy all the sympathy and admiration, anyway. His tale of saving lives, being blown up and surviving a dramatic crash landing in Constantinople grew more detailed and more dramatic with every telling.

Hawking Hangar was repaired. The roof was back on and, thanks to the heroic efforts of the Technical Section, we had a few working pods. Enough to get us back in business, anyway. It takes a lot to keep St Mary's down.

For his own safety, Matthew, our son, was living in the future under the guardianship of the Time Police. The supposedly temporary arrangement was stretching on and on and I should be doing something about it but, at the moment, I had my hands full with Leon. By mutual agreement, Matthew would stay with the Time Police until we'd managed to apprehend Clive Ronan. I still wasn't sure how I felt about that and Leon wasn't happy at all, but since St Mary's had been out of commission for more than six months, we'd had to leave capturing Ronan to the Time Police. I couldn't understand how he was continually eluding them, but he was. Useless bloody lumps. But the good news was that Matthew was due for a visit in a few weeks and we'd take it from there.

And Leon. Yes ... Leon.

He'd been with the Time Police, undergoing a series of operations and was finally back at St Mary's, having been detained at their pleasure. For medical reasons, he always hastens to add, not legal ones. He tells people he's a lot more law-abiding than his wife and I suppose some people who don't know him very well might believe that.

He'd been away a long time, though, and there were certain adjustments to be made. On both sides. I think my spectacles came as a bit of a surprise to him – even though they do make me look both intelligent and sexy. He made haste to agree.

'And,' I informed him as he undressed for bed, 'absolutely brilliant for identifying who you're in bed with.'

About to pull his T-shirt over his head, he paused and looked around.

'Who else has been in here?'

'Well, that's the point I'm trying to make, isn't it? Could have been anyone. We'll never know.'

'I had no idea so many people were trying to get you into bed.'

'Neither did I, but, thanks to the miracle of modern optics, those days are done.'

2

'I'm not sure I find that quite as reassuring as you intended.'

'Who said I intended to be reassuring?'

Joking aside, his recovery had been slow. Rather like his current top speed, as I remarked one day. We had just returned from breakfast and I was about to make him comfortable on the sofa, prior to shooting off to the 1536 briefing.

'I'll see you at dinner,' he said, parking his walking stick against the coffee table.

'Shouldn't you be setting off now?'

He sighed. 'What are you talking about?'

'Well, at the speed you move these days, if you don't set off now it'll be tomorrow by the time you get there.'

I was instructed to go and join all the other idiots in the History Department.

I settled him with a coffee and handed him his newspaper already folded open at the familiar headline – "ENGLAND SLUMP TO MASSIVE DEFEAT" – a headline that could refer to any England performance since 1966. Just to cheer him up I pointed out how difficult it is to find an article describing our football team's performance which *doesn't* begin "ENGLAND SLUMP TO MASSIVE DEFEAT".

He humphed, so I hastily refolded the paper to the science pages and handed it to him. Not a good move. There was talk of the Mars Project being delayed again.

'They'll get there,' I said, as he pointed this out.

He humphed again. 'I'll believe that when I see it.'

'I'm wondering if I should stop you drinking coffee. It's making you very grumpy.'

'Haven't you gone to work yet?'

3

'On my way,' I said, whisking myself out of the door. 'Play nicely with yourself.'

'I think you mean "by yourself".'

'I know what I mean.'

At some point in the day he would make his way down to Hawking, lower himself painfully onto a chair, and preside over whatever it is techies find to do in there all day long. We would meet again for dinner. Often, Peterson or Dieter would join us and we would all chatter bravely, but none of this disguised his slow recovery. He was bored and frustrated.

We all work for the Institute of Historical Research at St Mary's Priory, situated just outside of Rushford. Our main function is to investigate major historical events in contemporary time, although not recently. Our attempts to apprehend the renegade Clive Ronan had gone disastrously wrong and his revenge had been swift. An hour later, Helen Foster was dead and he'd kidnapped our baby son, Matthew. Leon had got him back eventually, but that hadn't been the end of it. Ronan had set off an enormous explosion that had nearly destroyed Hawking, wrecked most of our pods and caused some very serious injuries. You wouldn't think one person could do so much damage but I think we had all been guilty of underestimating him. It's when he's cornered that he's at his most dangerous. Anyway, the combined efforts of St Mary's and the Time Police to capture Ronan had proved unsuccessful. He was still out there somewhere.

And we were all here. Peterson, slowly recovering from Helen's death, was our shiny new Deputy Director; Markham had been made Head of Security; and I was back on the active list after injuring myself in Constantinople. As Peterson said, we were all very staid

4

and respectable now, as befitted our advancing years. Our days of rocketing around the timeline enjoying ourselves and evading death by the skin of our teeth were over and done with. Our lives were about rules, regulations, paperwork and standing back to let the next generation have their turn.

I'm sorry – I don't know why I'm laughing.

'Right you lot,' I said. 'Greenwich Palace, 24th January, 1536.'

A stir of anticipation ran around the room.

We were in my office, settling down with the tea and biscuits that would have been provided by my assistant Miss Lee, if she had even the faintest idea of what her job entailed.

'The rule of three again,' I said. 'Three pods with three people in each. Dr Peterson, Mr Markham and me in Number Eight. Mr Clerk, Mr Evans and Miss North in Number Five, and Mr Bashford, Mr Cox and Miss Sykes in Number Six.'

Bashford stirred. I was taking a bit of a risk sending him and Sykes out together. Their already bizarrely informal relationship had been strained past breaking point by the discovery that Bashford had been unfaithful to her. After a spectacular pub crawl one evening, Bashford had somehow become separated from the pack and found himself on the wrong end of a large group of inebriated young men. Fortunately, Angus had turned up. The two of them had fought together and bonded. Angus was now BBF – Bashford's Best Friend – and slept every night on his wardrobe, both of them oblivious to Sykes' loudly uttered complaints.

In the same way we have asymmetric warfare, Bashford and Sykes could be described as an asymmetric couple. Basically, he hadn't got a clue what was going on, although, as Markham had said, since he was usually unconscious for at least half the day, it didn't matter much anyway.

Sykes now threw Bashford a look that, had he noticed, would have curled his toenails. Being Bashford, however, he was entirely unaware of his peril. I could only admire his unconcern. She wasn't known as Psycho Psykes for nothing. I resolved to keep an eye on them and, if things got sticky, I'd swap North for Sykes to keep her and Bashford apart. I sighed. Life never used to be this difficult. On the other hand, I did have a certain amount of sympathy for her. It can't be easy, sharing your man with a chicken.

Atherton and Prentiss would stay behind on this one. Just in case. We'd discovered the hard way that it's really not a good idea to send all your people off on the same assignment because then you don't have a rescue team. If – when – this one went tits up, the two of them, together with as many of the Security Section as we could herd into one pod, would be our back-up and our rescue.

So, I had historians down one side of the table, bashing away at their scratchpads, the Security Section down the other, pretending to look cool and fooling no one, with Miss Dottle at the foot and –no surprise there – as close to Peterson as she could get.

Her former boss, the idiot Halcombe, was still on leprosy leave, being treated for an illness we all knew he didn't have, leaving his less than faithful lieutenant to hitch her wagon to the St Mary's star. She'd enthusiastically participated in several jumps – at least

6

two of which had been unauthorised – and had settled down at St Mary's as Thirsk's representative on earth. She could frequently be seen scurrying around with armfuls of files looking busy and important and happy.

Gone was the mousey, dumpy Dottle with the slightly protruding front teeth, the badly styled hair and the droopy cardigans. This Dottle had cut and coloured her hair and wore make-up. She no longer spent her evenings alone in the bar reading romantic fiction about voluptuous young women barely able to keep their clothes on in a crisis, but could frequently be found with the younger historians and techies, clutching a spritzer, flushed with excitement and wine and thoroughly enjoying herself. I often wondered what would happen if – or more probably when – her boss, the idiot Halcombe, came back.

She still had a bit of a thing for Peterson – understandably, he said. He was only surprised that it didn't happen more often. Since her passion for him was in much better taste than her passion for the unspeakable Halcombe, people let it go and just grinned when she blushed furiously every time he spoke to her. Or walked past her. Or was even in the same room as her.

As to his feelings for her – I had no clue until the day Markham, Peterson and I had bumped into her on our way out of the dining room. Markham was carrying the tea, I had the chocolate, and Peterson had a plate of chips. I can't remember what we were doing that afternoon but it was obviously something requiring a great deal of strenuous mental effort.

She bumped straight into Peterson.

Markham and I exchanged knowing glances.

'Oh, I'm sorry – are you all right?' she said, covered in confusion.

7

'Yes,' he said faintly, 'but I think you might have crushed my chips.'

It was just a joke – something any of us might have said – but she shot him a look from the corner of her eye, said mischievously, 'Oh, is that's what they're calling them these days?' then looked horrified, blushed scarlet and shot off in some disarray.

Peterson watched her go.

Markham and I looked at each other.

'Shut up,' said Peterson, not even looking round.

We said nothing.

'I mean it,' he said.

We said nothing.

He sighed in exasperation. 'You two are so childish, you know ...'

We said nothing.

'Oh, for heaven's sake.' And he stamped off in the direction lately taken by Miss Dottle.

'She's well and truly crushed his chips, hasn't she?' said Markham, and we continued with our afternoon.

Anyway, back to the briefing.

'Something interesting to celebrate our return to normal working,' I said, bringing up a few images. 'The infamous jousting tournament at Greenwich Palace. The one possibly held to celebrate – if that's the word I want – the death of Henry's first queen, Katherine of Aragon. Things are going quite well for Henry – the inconvenient wife has died, his current wife, that's Anne Boleyn, is pregnant and this could be his longed-for heir. However, as we know, the king comes a massive cropper and, for him, nothing is ever quite the same afterwards. He incurs a serious head injury which, supposedly, leads to a complete personality change.'

'Debatable,' said North. 'If you're going on to say he developed tendencies toward extreme paranoia and cruelty, it's only fair to say he had all those before the accident. Remember, he's already executed Thomas More and his harshness to Queen Katherine and Princess Mary was well documented long before he fell off his horse.'

'I don't agree,' said Sykes at once. Well, she wouldn't, would she? The two of them never agreed over anything. 'All contemporary reports say the king was sporty, fit, popular and generous. He was generally reckoned to epitomise all the kingly virtues. It was only after his accident that he started to develop tyrannical tendencies.'

'Wrong,' argued North, and we all sat back to let them get on with it. 'He certainly didn't enjoy perfect health. He's already survived bouts of smallpox and malaria. There's a possibility he might even have been suffering from syphilis.'

'There's no proof of that,' Sykes said, scornfully. 'He wasn't exactly rotting away in front of people, was he?'

'His leg wouldn't heal.'

'It was a varicose ulcer caused by wearing his garters too tightly,' countered Sykes, the light of battle in her eye. 'They don't heal quickly even today.'

'It wasn't the first accident he'd suffered. He'd sustained a previous head wound on another occasion when he forgot to lower his visor.'

'He didn't lose consciousness on that occasion, though. For this one, he was unconscious for over two hours and when he woke up everyone agreed his personality had changed. He became grasping, covetous and ...'

'He's a Tudor,' North said scornfully. 'He was all that anyway.'

9

'Experts agree he definitely exhibited signs of brain damage when he believed those ridiculous stories about Anne Boleyn's adultery.'

'Really? Well, she was no better than she should be. Suppose – just suppose for one minute – that the stories are true. Desperate for an heir, Anne has an affair. And who better than her brother?'

'Keeps it in the family, I suppose,' said Sykes nastily.

'Well, *he's* never going to betray her, is he? Yes, I know the prevailing view is that she was innocent, but this is the woman who refused to settle for being his mistress, held out for marriage, had no qualms when Henry divorced his wife – whom she had served as lady-in-waiting, by the way – or when he broke with Rome, or when he executed one of his closest friends, *and* she played a major part in Wolsey's downfall. All she has to do is produce a male heir and her position is secure forever. Is it too much of a stretch to imagine that with so much at stake, she wouldn't stoop to a little adultery?'

'Enough,' I said, before they climbed over the table and started having a go at each other.

I often wonder if other professions have this difficulty. I mean, do you ever get a geologist shouting, 'I tell you, it's oolitic limestone, you idiot.' And his colleague yelling back, 'No, it's not. Surely any imbecile can see it's an ultramafic, ultrapotassic intrusive rock dominated by mafic phenocrysts in a feldspar groundmass. Are you a complete moron?'

I once mentioned my theory about non-historian debates to the Chancellor of the University of Thirsk and I could hear her laughing all the way down the corridor.

'Yes,' said Clerk, leaping into the breach, bless him. 'Well, it's a bad year all round. His first wife dies, his second wife miscarries that vital heir, Cromwell finds evidence of adultery, there's all the scandal of the trial and Henry's virility is mocked in court, he executes Anne Boleyn, his illegitimate and only son Henry Fitzroy dies, the Pilgrimage of Grace kicks off ... it just goes on and on.'

'Katherine's death wasn't a bad thing for Henry,' objected Sykes.

'It was for Anne Boleyn,' said North. 'She was Anne's protection. Even Henry VIII couldn't take a third wife with two still living.'

'Be that as it may,' I said, dragging them back on track again. 'We will, with luck, be able to form an opinion as to his physical state, if not his mental one. I want details of how he's received by the crowd. Is he still popular? Do the common people love him? We know Anne Boleyn's not there, which is a shame, but Miss North and Mr Clerk, you'll be opposite the royal stand and I'd like you to pay particular attention to what happens there. Is Jane Seymour present? Does Henry single her out in any way?'

They nodded, bashing away at their scratchpads.

'Miss Sykes and Mr Bashford, I'd like you near Henry's pavilion. We need to know if they take him straight to the palace after the accident, or whether they take him to his tent first. What sort of condition is he in? Will you be able to see if they administer any medical treatment? I expect they'll try and take off his helmet – not a problem since there weren't any neck or spinal injuries – so try and get a good look at him then.'

'Dr Peterson and I will concentrate on the accident itself. We'll be on the stand side because I'm betting that's the side Henry will choose – he's very vain and that's where people will get their best view of him.

11

'Regarding costumes – we'll be our usual middle-of-the-road selves – too prosperous to kick but not rich enough to rob. Ladies: woollen dresses; linen undergarments. Belts with pouches for anything important. Rules regarding hair are beginning to relax, but cover it anyway, just to be on the safe side. Gentlemen: woollen tunics; knee trousers; stockings and shoes. You know the drill. Report to Mrs Enderby later today, please; she is expecting you. Any questions?'

They shook their heads.

'In that case, thank you everyone. Report to Hawking at 10:00 Tuesday.'

I assembled my teams outside Number Eight and we checked each other over for forgotten jewellery, inadvertently acquired tattoos, wristwatches etc., because it was some time since we'd done this. I was actually quite nervous. There was a lot riding on today. According to Dr Bairstow, the equivalent of the Third World's debt had been spent on us and we'd better prove we were worth it.

Looking around, Hawking seemed almost back to normal. Exploding pods had gouged great lumps out of the walls, but that had all been smoothed over. The crater in the floor had been filled in and the permanent roof was on. All the electrics, together with what Dieter had insisted on referring to as 'the fiddly bits', had taken considerably longer, though, and we still had only four working pods. Number One had been cannibalised to repair the others. Number Two was almost back together again. Number Three was still u/s but not for long. Number Four had been blown out of existence and was being completely rebuilt, as was TB2, our transport pod. The jury was still out over whether Number Seven could be saved. Numbers Five, Six and Eight were ready to go.

All the pods had been or were in the process of being upgraded and enlarged, because over the years we'd changed the way we staffed our assignments. When I first arrived at St Mary's the norm had been short assignments staffed by two, possibly three people, usually historians. These days, our assignments were often longer and more complex and the inclusion of the Security and Technical Sections where appropriate meant we needed larger pods. Numbers Five, Six and Eight had been redesigned and could now hold anything from five to eight people. We had comfortable seats. Well, we had slightly less uncomfortable seats. The locker space was better designed and, in an effort to combat the hot, dry and frequently uncomfortable atmosphere, the ventilation system had been upgraded. Obviously, there had been a certain amount of grumbling over these changes – historians are by nature conservative and resistant to modernisation – although the retention of tea-making facilities, the introduction of even more cup holders and a specifically designated area for the biscuit tin had gone a long way towards soothing ruffled feathers. Before anyone asks, they – the pods, I mean, not the historians – do still stink of cabbage with an underlying smell of defeated air freshener, and the toilets still don't work properly. I'd complained about all this to Leon who had responded that, for reasons which escaped him, the priority was getting historians there and back safely and you can't have everything.

I took a final look around Hawking and spotted Leon in his office, frowning at a set of blueprints. I waved. He smiled for me alone and waved back.

'OK, guys, let's go.'

We climbed inside our pods and stowed our gear.

Mr Lindstrom gave the console one last check. 'Ready when you are, Max. Good luck.' He closed the door behind him.

14

I sat myself down, wriggled my bum in the unfamiliar seat, and checked the readouts. Here we go.

'Computer, initiate jump.'

'Jump initiated.'

The world went white.

And here we were. Bang on the nose. Greenwich, 1536. Fat Harry's *anus horribilis*.

The place was heaving. That's not a particularly historical term, but very accurate. There were people everywhere, all streaming in the same general direction. The noise was incredible. People shouted to each other, street hawkers bellowed their wares at the tops of their voices, women shrieked for their children to come here and for their husbands to go away. Dogs barked madly. The occasional horn sounded, as important people tried to shoulder their way through the solid mass of suddenly uncooperative people. Arguments broke out all around us. And the smell could strip paint.

We stood together in a tight group outside Number Eight, getting our bearings and waiting for our sense of smell to shut down. Occasionally someone would stagger as we were buffeted by those trying to get past.

'OK,' I said. 'Everyone knows where to go and what to do when they get there. Communal link. Look out for each other. And, for God's sake, try to stay out of trouble.'

I don't know why my gaze fell on Bashford at that moment. It just did. He gazed reproachfully back. Sykes nodded understandingly.

'Good luck, everyone.'

They dispersed and I found myself with Peterson and Markham grinning at me.

'The Dream Team,' said Markham happily.

That wasn't usually the phrase that described us, but I was so happy to be as nearly back to normal as we could ever be that I didn't argue. And, besides, it was surely just coincidence that no one else ever wanted to be on our team. We were the equivalent of the puny kid with specs and the funny rash who always gets picked last.

There was no question of getting lost – we only had to follow everyone else through the narrow streets. I would have liked a little time to study the architecture – which in this case would have consisted of wondering how these houses were still standing, so warped were the timbers, but I had to watch where I put my feet. Not only were the streets deep in the usual Tudor debris, but such bits as *were* paved were covered in greasy, ankle-turning cobbles. We linked arms and allowed ourselves to be carried along with the crowd. Everyone seemed very cheerful, no doubt looking forward to the colour and spectacle and excitement and probable bloodshed and, on top of all that, we'd get to see the king. *The* king. The legendary Henry VIII. Fat Harry himself.

We found the lists with no trouble. A large, level area of grass that had been roped off, with a wide, wooden, stepped stand, festooned with crimson, gold and purple bunting set up to run along one side. In the centre of the stand, two magnificent canopied chairs had been set up. One was very much larger than the other. One for the king and one for the queen, although we knew she wouldn't be here today, and nor were we sure whether Henry would preside over the tournament before taking part.

A central barrier – the tilt – ran down the length of the field. It was designed to keep the horses straight and give the riders a better chance of hitting each other. A thick

16

layer of sand covered the ground on each side. I couldn't decide whether it was to give the horses a better grip or to soak up the inevitable blood.

The lists were surrounded on three sides. Nobles and royalty sat in the big stand – lesser mortals, dogs and historians stood around the other two sides, using their elbows to get to the front for a good view. The fourth side was a mass of brightly coloured tents – or pavilions, I suppose, would be a more accurate term. Each pavilion was decorated in the livery of its owner. Front and centre was Henry's pavilion, easily distinguished not only by the royal arms hanging limply overhead, but because it was twice the size of anyone else's.

'A spot of overcompensation, do you think?' muttered Peterson. 'That and the infamous codpiece, of course.'

Behind the pavilions, an army of armourers, blacksmiths and farriers were working overtime on last-minute repairs. I could see the glow of braziers, bright on this grey day, and hear the metallic beat of hammer on anvil. Caparisoned horses were being led around, snorting with excitement and kicking out at anyone they didn't like the look of. Some of them had a very nasty look in their eye and most people were giving them a wide berth.

'I'm not going over there,' muttered Markham, never at ease with anything in the animal kingdom. 'Look at the size of the feet on that one.'

Entertainers, conjurors, ladies offering a few minute's affection for a really very reasonable fee, musicians and pie men were working their way through the spectators, their shouts adding to the considerable din. People laughed and money changed hands. A considerable number of casks of ale had obviously been broached – because that's always helpful when trying to keep public order, isn't it? – and I could see and smell various animals roasting on spits.

I caught a glimpse of a muddy mongrel racing past with a lump of part-cooked meat in its mouth, closely pursued by two or three other, larger dogs. His little legs were going like the clappers and I hoped he made it to safety.

Even the weather was fine. It wasn't warm – England in January is never warm, but it wasn't raining and there was no wind. Pennants hung limply in the still air, but it wasn't unpleasant. No frost covered the grass on which we were preparing to picnic. More importantly, the sky was flat and grey. There was no sunshine to dazzle riders and ruin their aim. An equal advantage to all.

And still the crowds were pouring in. I palmed my recorder and got what I could. We were surrounded by people from all walks of life. Townspeople, merchants, tradesmen and their families, locals and those who'd made the journey from outlying villages. There was colour everywhere. Especially in the stands where the nobility sat in comfort, being served wine and sweetmeats. You didn't catch *them* sprawling on the cold ground like us.

When I judged they'd had enough time to get themselves into position, I called the others. Clerk reported his team was well situated, directly opposite the stand, and that he could see us and I should pull my skirt down.

I grinned and told him his codpiece was slipping.

'We've a good view from here,' he said.

'Well, keep your eye on Norfolk,' I said. 'I especially want footage of him racing off to break the bad news to the queen.'

'Copy that,' he said calmly, and closed the link.

Sykes reported that she and her team were exactly where they wanted to be, which was within a stone's throw of the king's tent. Bashford was still conscious and there were no chickens around so she was hopeful of a successful outcome. I could hear his indignant 'hey', in the background.

We'd brought packs and baskets with us and so, just like everyone else, we were having a bit of a picnic. The usual St Mary's staple fare – thick brown bread, a giant wedge of cheese, and apples, all washed down with water. It would have to keep us going all day, too. With that and all the running I do, you'd think I'd be as thin as a rake, but I'm not. I just can't understand it. Oh, and there was a large slab of fruit and nut chocolate hidden in the bottom of the basket, because I need to keep up my sugar levels.

Munching a piece of cheese, I was panning around and getting some great footage of people and what they were wearing. Most people had doublets and dresses inclined towards russet and brown, especially the poorer people, because the dyes were cheap and easily obtained. The middle classes – merchants and the like –wore long gowns of dark, rich colours. The Sumptuary Laws laid down very strict rules as to which fabrics and furs which class of people could use.

For the more expensive reds, greens and blues, you had to look to the nobility in the stands. Beside me, Peterson was dictating details of the appearance and composition of the common spectators and I was busy recording details of the high-born ladies in the stand – their long, full sleeves and ornate headdresses. One or two of them looked almost exactly like the queens in a pack of playing cards. Some hair was visible, especially among the younger women. There was a great deal of fur worn – white, cream, dark –

and obviously mostly for show because, even in January, most women wore their cloaks thrown back so people could admire their dresses. They would be wearing their best clothes for the occasion. I wondered how many had dressed to catch the king's eye. Anne Boleyn was pregnant, but some reports suggested that the king had begun to tire of her already. Speaking of which ... I craned my neck to see if I could spot Jane Seymour in the chattering stands. We'd all studied the Holbein portraits and sketches before setting out, but I wasn't that confident of recognising her even if she was here, so we would get a record of everyone here today and sort it out when we got home.

It's a funny thing about Holbein's sketches of Henry's wives. To my modern eyes, only Anne of Cleves looks even remotely pretty. I suppose that's the changing face of beauty. No wonder women can never catch up. I myself would probably have been extremely desirable about twenty thousand years ago, when the only competition would have been from a shaggy mammoth or a toothless old hag of fifteen.

Just as we were finishing our lunch, the warm-up crew appeared, parading around the arena, playing instruments, singing and dancing. We packed away our picnic and got to work.

Minstrels – all men – stood in the centre. Some had stringed instruments, others played pipes or what looked like recorders. They were actually very good. Around them whirled dancers and acrobats – all men – jumping and tumbling in time to the music. The crowd was eager to be pleased and clapped and cheered every one of them. As did we. They left the field to great applause.

Peterson turned to me. 'All right?'

I nodded. I was. I was dry and comfortable and enjoying myself. As was everyone else. It was good to be back at work. I'd missed this, but we were up and running again. Hawking was repaired. We had our pods back. Leon was recovering and Matthew was safe. We would work something out with the Time Police. It had been a bad year but it was over now. I could look forward to the future.

All around me people were craning their necks. They were waiting for the king. We were all waiting for the king. We were waiting for Henry Tudor, by the Grace of God, King of England, and France, Defender of the Faith, Lord of Ireland, and of the Church of England in Earth, under Jesus Christ, Supreme Head. If you ask anyone who is England's most famous king nearly everyone will say Henry VIII. Not Henry V – although he's my favourite. Or Richard the Lionheart – a right royal plonker, if ever there was one. Or mighty Edward III – hero of Crécy and Poitiers. Or Edward II – the worst king ever in the entire history of kinging. Or Charles II – who was sex on legs apparently. It's always Henry VIII – man and monster combined. And we were about to see him. There was a huge air of excitement and anticipation. And that was just me.

We had speculated on whether the king would open the tournament and then take part, or whether he was already suited up for the opening bouts and would delegate the opening ceremony to someone else. The atmosphere was electric. A crowd this size could never be completely silent, but there was certainly a hushed air of expectation.

Of course he opened it himself. This was Henry Tudor and if there was one thing he loved above everything it was attention. To be the centre of the spectacle ... to have

21

all eyes on him … to have the admiration of men and the adoration of women …

Trumpets sounded in the distance. He was coming. We scrambled to our feet. I had my recorder ready. 'OK, people, this is it. Good luck everyone.' My words were nearly lost in the huge roar of approbation and excitement. He was here.

The trumpets sounded again – closer this time. The crowd was parting. And here he was at last, leading the parade into the arena.

Trumpets blared again and the crowd went into overdrive. And he knew how to work them. Heading his entourage of brightly coloured courtiers, he paraded slowly around the ring, waving graciously and smiling at the pretty girls.

Shouts of 'Harry for England', and 'God save His Grace', rang out around us. This was it. Here he was. Right in front of us. This was Henry VIII – Henry Tudor himself. Here. Not twenty feet away. Close enough for me to see the fine detail of his tunic and the feather in his hat. He wasn't yet as fat as he would be – he was nowhere near that yet – but he was still heavier than most. He was a big man – well over six feet – and his physical presence was bigger still because he dressed to impress.

He wore a doublet of deep vibrant red with a thickly padded red and gold fur-lined short coat over the top. Rather dashing scarlet gloves were setting a new fashion right at this very moment. A soft hat concealed most of his hair but, yes, he was a ginger, just like me. Yay! I shouted, jumped up and down and waved like any star-struck teenager drooling over a boy band, and for one moment – just for one moment – he looked directly at me.

Oh my God, Henry Tudor looked at me! I grabbed Tim's arm.

'Tim, he looked at me. Did you see?'

'Steady on, Max. You are a married woman, you know.'

'The king looked at me. Markham, did you see?'

'Of course not,' he shouted over the roar of the crowd. 'I'm doing my job and watching your backs, not falling about like an hysterical groupie. Seriously, Max, I'm ashamed of you.'

I didn't care. 'But the king looked at me.'

'The king looks at every woman under seventy,' said Peterson, severely. 'There's nothing special about you.'

I still didn't care, but one of us should get on with the job, so I palmed my recorder again and got stuck in.

His clothes today were not as laden with jewels as those in his portraits, but he wore a large ruby in his hat and a magnificent golden chain around his neck. Jewels studded his garters as well, which were cutting tightly into his legs. The garters were very smart but they were known to be the cause of many of his problems. He had good legs. Actually, he had very good legs and he showed them off with tight-fitting stockings with even tighter garters to hold them up. He wouldn't want to spoil the effect by having his stockings bunched around his ankles. But those garters would give him – and possibly had already given him – the varicose ulcers that would plague him throughout his life and play a large part in turning him from man to monster. Jewelled garters aside, everything he wore was designed to catch the eye and invite admiration.

He was still extraordinarily handsome – in his youth he must have stopped traffic – but he was just beginning to be jowly. I suspected he was extremely vain – although he had good reason to be – but watching him now as he paraded around the crowd, basking in their adoration, it was easy to imagine the dismay his increasing weight and lack of physical attractiveness would cause him. Maybe dismay was too mild a word. Anguish maybe? Despair? To have been the most handsome prince in Christendom, the best at everything, to come first in everything, to be admired and envied, and then to deteriorate into the bloated paranoid wreck of a man he would become, lashing out at friend and foe alike. Indeed, no longer able to distinguish one from the other ... what must he have seen when he regarded himself in the mirror? Or did the massive self-confidence dwindle into self-delusion so that he always saw himself as a young, virile, handsome king?

He was a big man. In every sense of the word. He stood head and shoulders above those around him. The crowd was cheering and he was lapping it up. Judging from their reactions to him, at this point in his life he was still hugely popular. He was everyone's idea of what a king should be.

'Not sure there's a lot of hair under that hat,' said Peterson, himself the proud possessor of a hairstyle frequently resembling a windblown haystack. And, as the king moved on and the glamour faded, I could see he limped slightly.

'The leg,' I said in excitement. 'He already has the leg ulcer.'

He was really enjoying himself, waving to the crowd, eyeing up the women, tossing sweetmeats to children. Well – actually he stood, head thrown back, legs spread wide in that famous stance and several lackeys threw sweetmeats for the kids, but the thought was there.

24

Those in the stand rose to their feet as he entered. There was another fanfare; the crowd fell silent in anticipation, the king took his position, gazed majestically around him, raised his handkerchief, paused dramatically and then let it fall. Another huge roar went up and, to yet another brassy fanfare from the trumpets, we were off.

The first event was an archery competition. Designed, I guessed, to give the king time to nip off and climb into his armour. We watched several heats. One was between a team of professional soldiers against the locals. Each flight was cheered or booed depending on which side of the ground you were standing.

The locals lost their bout to a great deal of good-natured heckling. A small purse and a keg were presented to the winners. And then – this was it.

They were bringing up the horses. Grooms led them between the tents. It took two grooms per horse just to hold them back. Riders were climbing into their saddles and lining up for the parade.

We joined the general surge forwards. We didn't have a lot of choice, actually. We were packed in tighter than sardines. The crowd was very obliging. Those at the front sat on the ground so those behind could see. Pedlars passed among the crowd selling last-minute sweetmeats and souvenirs and generally standing on people.

There were six riders. Two teams of three. Each man would fight all those on the other team. Nine bouts altogether. Not that events that afternoon would get that far. I looked at the excited faces around me. This would be a good afternoon's entertainment for them – the excitement of the joust and the presence of the king himself. I wondered how much of his courtship of Jane Seymour was popular knowledge. Perhaps we weren't the only ones craning our necks for a sight of his new girlfriend and possible future queen. Yes, everyone was looking forward to an afternoon of fun and excitement. And apart from us, no one knew what would happen today. How it would all end. How everything would change.

The riders paraded around the ring. Henry's team, which he obviously captained, was known as the Challengers. One of the permanent members was Charles Brandon, Earl of Suffolk and the king's brother-in-law. He was generally reckoned to be the best jouster in the land and was always very careful to lose to Henry – but not by too much. Henry had a temper even before his accident. Brandon wasn't here today, hence the teams of only three instead of the usual four. I guessed the other two would be Nicholas Carew, and Henry Bourchier, Earl of Essex. The heralds had announced their names but the noise was so great I couldn't make them out.

The composition of the other team, known as the Answerers, was unknown to us. There's no record of the combatants, but we would record their liveries and check them on our return.

Henry was easily the biggest man there and easily recognisable in his magnificent armour. The popular picture of a war horse, or *destrier*, is of some colossal lumbering beast, capable of carrying a man encased in heavy armour, and that is true – they were immensely strong, but they were also highly manoeuvrable. They had to be. No one would go into battle on a horse too big to move at faster than a trot. None of them were even as big as modern shire horses. Except for Henry's horse, which was huge and, I suspected, was fed on red meat. He was a magnificent black beast, currently raring to go, frothing at the mouth and working up a heavy sweat. It was typical of Henry that he would ride a horse that took three grooms to control. The horse was drawing nearly as many admiring glances as the king, which, as Peterson said, was all very well, but when you knew this horse was going to be crashing down on top of him at God knows what speed ...

Henry opened the batting, magnificent in his ornate armour which glinted gold even on this dull day. His horse, guessing the moment had come, was rearing and plunging. There were now four men hanging off him. Henry sat easily in his saddle. The crowd was going mad with excitement. As were we.

I don't know who was his first adversary – his badge was quartered with black chevrons on a white background. He stood to our left – the king was on our right. They took up their lances – drums rolled and the trumpets sounded – Henry's horse half reared, scattering grooms in all directions – and they were off.

It was over in seconds.

The two great horses thundered full tilt towards each other. No one held back. Their enormous hooves flung great divots of mud and sand high into the air. The earth shook beneath my feet. I mean *really* shook. And I'm married to Leon Farrell so I know earth shaking when I feel it. As the two riders levelled their lances, I found I was holding my breath.

Necks outstretched, ears laid back and foam flying from their bits, the two horses met at the middle of the tilt – the central barrier – with an almighty great crash. The rider on the far side of the tilt tumbled backwards over his horse's rump to sprawl on his back, unmoving. First blood to Henry and his team. Most of the crowd cheered wildly, jumping up and down and waving their arms. A few groaned and made rude gestures, possibly concerning their favourite's ancestry. Or lack of.

Men ran towards the fallen body and heaved him to his feet. He stood, swaying gently. The crowd applauded politely. He raised his arm to the king, presumably either to acknowledge defeat or possibly to check it was still attached. Henry, meanwhile, was doing his lap of honour, graciously acknowledging the cheers of his subjects. Would he pause at the stand and search the crowd for one face in particular?

Nope. He just swept on past, visor up, waving and smiling, basking in the admiration.

The next bout was already lining up as Henry swept from the lists. I watched him dismount fairly easily from his horse, clap someone on the shoulder, accept a goblet of wine and stride off to watch.

There were very short intervals between each joust. Just enough time to drag away those unable to move under their own steam and put fresh sand over the blood.

The king's team won the next bout as well. I could see Peterson meticulously recording events in the arena while I followed the king as he sat outside his tent, drinking and laughing. Sykes would be down there somewhere doing the same, and Clerk's team would also be covering the action. Double coverage. Belt and braces. And the security team, I knew, would be watching our backs.

They lost the next one. The horse on the king's team – nervous before it even entered the ring and sweating heavily, veered sideways at the last moment. The crowd roared in disapproval. This was Failure to Present – a serious offence. The crowd – all of them experts in a field in which they could never compete – booed loudly and, at the entrance to the arena, the Knight Marshal recorded the foul on his wooden board and indicated a rematch.

Both sides pulled up with difficulty, turned around, settled their lances and set off again. I think the king's rider must have been concentrating too much on his horse, because he was unseated easily, flying through the air and hitting the ground with enough impact to bounce.

'Ouch,' said Peterson, wincing.

The rider was dragged, unconscious, to his tent and two men scurried up with more buckets of fresh sand.

His horse, the cause of all the trouble, was fleeing around the ring, reins trailing, until cornered against the high-fronted stand. Someone flung a sack over its head.

'They're not going to shoot him, are they?' said Markham anxiously. I think that despite every horse on the planet having him on their hit list, he's actually quite fond of the species in general.

'Doubt it,' said Peterson, shaking his head and checking his recorder. 'He's only young. Probably his first time out. A mistake to bring him today but maybe his rider wanted to catch the king's eye. Which he has done but for all the wrong reasons.'

Indeed, we could see the rider being carried into his tent.

'Who's next?' said Markham.

Well,' I said, 'if they keep to the same order, it's Henry again. And if it is, then this is the big one.'

They did and it was.

There was a lot of cheering as Henry emerged from his pavilion, accompanied by some half a dozen favoured acquaintances. The king himself appeared to be in excellent form, tossing a remark over his shoulder that made them roar with laughter. He accepted another goblet of something from a page whose hair he ruffled so vigorously that the lad staggered. He tossed back the contents in one go and, with some assistance, heaved himself onto his horse who, despite the massive weight on his back, skipped sideways and appeared to be making every effort to dump his sovereign lord into the mud. There was a great deal more laughter. Apparently, this was not unusual behaviour.

The laughing group accompanied the king to the arena. Shouts of encouragement and good luck followed on behind him.

I wondered if Henry ever thought about what might have happened if he'd let that final bout go. What would have been different? If Anne Boleyn did not miscarry. If she was delivered of a healthy son. If their marriage somehow survived. Mary might not have been queen. Nor Elizabeth. And Edward might never have been born at all. Jane Seymour would probably have lived – it was Henry's obsessive care of Jane that caused him to order male doctors to attend the birth and they missed the piece of placenta left lodged inside her. Men, in those days, were not experts in childbirth – it being an area best left to women – whereas any competent midwife would have sussed it immediately and probably saved her life.

The ramifications went on and on. I foresaw a massive game of 'What If?' over a margarita or two that evening.

Henry's challenger was a big man – although not as big as the king. I wondered what might he have done if he hadn't been king? With his talents and physical presence would he – could he – ever have played second fiddle to his older brother, the shadowy and little-known Arthur?

His opponent this morning rode a thick-set brown horse – very big around the hindquarters. Peterson spent a couple of moments describing his livery – we'd try and identify him when we got back because there's no record of the king's unlucky opponent – and I stayed with the king.

The horses were already straining at their bits, tossing their grooms around like so many straw dummies.

The marshal had the sense not to keep them waiting. The thunder of cheering and shouting drowned out the drums and trumpets and I never heard the signal, but someone must have given it because the big brown horse was already moving. A fraction of a second later, and from a standing start, so was Henry. They galloped furiously towards each other. The noise was tremendous.

And then for Henry, for Queen Anne, Mark Smeaton, George Boleyn, even Jane Seymour, everything went wrong. Everything went very, very wrong.

Off to my left, there was a scuffle in the crowd. Even over the clamour, I could hear men shouting. I turned for a

31

better view and as I did so I heard something that to me sounded very much like the crack of a gunshot.

Henry's horse shied sideways.

Everything seemed to happen in slow motion.

His opponent's lance hit Henry's helmet with a tremendous crash that pushed him out of the saddle. He began to topple to one side. His horse, severely unbalanced, staggered sideways, tipping Henry even further. I suspected he was already unconscious because he was, literally, hanging from the saddle. His horse was strong and struggling to stay on his feet, but Henry was a big man and armour isn't light. The king went down first with a metallic clang that reverberated off the stands, and then, with a scream that was dreadful to hear, his enormous horse crashed to the ground as well. Right on top of him. It was a massive fall. And at the speed they were travelling, both horse and rider, entangled together, skidded along the ground for a good twenty feet, gouging a path in the sand and mud.

Afterwards we agreed that probably the only reason Henry survived was that the ground was soft and, to some extent, cushioned his fall. Nothing, however, could save him from the crushing weight of half a ton of thrashing horse on top of him.

For a few seconds after the impact there was a shock of silence and then the screaming began. Turmoil. Panic. People surged around. We were pushed to and fro in the confusion. I was aware someone had hold of the back of my dress, keeping me in place, and hoped it was Markham. I just kept recording and I knew Peterson would be doing the same. That's our job. Markham would keep us safe. That's his.

Women were crying. Children screamed as they were knocked over in the crush and then their mothers screamed too. People were shouting that the king was dead and it was at this moment that I suddenly saw things from Henry's point of view. Yes, people were shocked and horrified at his accident, but now we saw a glimpse of just how precarious was the Tudor hold on England. Henry was only the second of an upstart line. He had no male heir and right now he might be dead. The death of a monarch and the accession of a new one is always a perilous time. I didn't mind betting that the thought uppermost in people's minds was – the king is dead and he has no heir. There would still be people alive who would remember the Wars of the Roses. When Plantagenet fought Plantagenet for the throne. With no clear heir, challenges for the succession would arise. The Scots would sweep from the north; the French would be across the Channel as soon as they could get their anchors up.

This was Henry's nightmare come true. People condemn his efforts to get a son but, without a clear heir, an orderly and peaceful transfer of the crown would be impossible. There would be chaos, certainly. Perhaps even civil war. No wonder people were panicking.

We were on the communal link. I could hear Clerk shouting at someone. And someone shouting back. A full-scale fight seemed to be breaking out around him, but no time for that now. Evans was with him. He'd make sure they were OK.

Up in the stands, people were on their feet. Women were covering their faces. No one had swooned but, then again, women don't swoon half as often as men think they

33

do. Yes, I myself have fainted once or twice, but usually it's been a tactical move.

I jerked my attention back to Henry's horse which was screaming in pain and thrashing around trying to get up. I could only imagine the damage he was doing to his rider. People ran to the fallen king, who lay ominously still.

Two men were dragging at the king's helmet. The field medic in me screamed a silent protest, but there was nothing we could do. Or should do. The records show he hadn't incurred any spinal injuries. Besides, removing the king's helmet gave us a glimpse of his face. Eyes closed and deadly white. His hair was plastered to his head and dark with sweat. I panned in for a close-up, trying to find which part of his head he'd injured so Dr Stone could assess the possibility of brain damage.

Men with sharp knives cut away the stirrups and they dragged the horse to his feet. White-eyed with terror and covered in mud all down one side, he was bleeding badly from several deep gashes to his shoulder and flanks. From the king's armour, probably. Henry's enormous saddle had slipped half way around the horse's belly and a brave man slipped underneath to cut the girths. Two russet-clad grooms led the horse away. He was limping and shying at everything in sight, but seemed otherwise unharmed. I don't know what happened to him.

The king, still in his armour, was lifted onto a board. It took eight men to carry him away and even then, they were staggering with the weight.

I said softly, 'Sykes, he's coming your way.'

'On it,' she said. 'We're right by his tent. There's people racing towards us clutching bundles – possibly doctors – although given current medical procedures he'd

34

probably be better off with a vet. We've set up sound recorders to try and listen to what will happen inside.'

'Good work.'

I closed the link and left them to get on with it.

Everywhere I looked, people were crying. Men and women. Already the cry had gone up. 'The king is dead. The king is dead.' We were only one step away from outright panic. I looked for someone to take charge. To initiate some sort of damage control. To contain the rumours that the king was dead. Because if they didn't ...

Peterson touched my arm. 'Over there.'

Someone was on it. I don't know who. Heralds were making their way through the crowds shouting 'The king lives. The king lives,' but all in vain. No one was listening. If anything, the panic was growing worse.

Already, in my imagination, the Duke of Norfolk was racing to the queen's chambers, to fling at her, without warning, the news that the king was dead. This would be the moment when she too would realise how fragile was the framework of her life. In her arrogance, she had made enemies everywhere and without Henry's protection they would begin to close in. The only thing keeping her safe was that she carried the king's child. In four days' time, she would lose that child. He would have been a boy. The boy that would have solved all of Henry's problems. The boy that might, just might, have saved Anne's life. As it was, she would lose her child and, in five months' time, her head. The king would become engaged to Jane Seymour the very next day.

Around the field, the marshals were vigorously dispersing the spectators, breaking up crowds of gossiping people. Despite our protests – which were lost in the protests of many, we were pushed out of the wrong exit.

35

We were now on the north side of the field and would have to walk all the way around the lists to get back to our starting point. But not yet. There was something I wanted to check out first.

'Come on,' I said. 'We should take a look at what that scuffle was all about while we're at it.'

'Yes,' said Peterson. 'I could have sworn I heard a gunshot.'

'You did,' said Markham, heaving his pack into a more comfortable position.

'In that case,' I said, 'we definitely need to check it out.'

I'd barely got the words out when Clerk spoke in my ear. 'Max, you need to get yourself over here. Quick.'

We have a saying at St Mary's. 'Everything was going really well right up until the moment when it really wasn't.'

My heart sank. 'What's the problem? Is someone hurt?'

'No, we're all fine.' He paused. 'But the Time Police are here.'

Bollocks. Now what?

Our relationship with the Time Police is always exciting. Over the years we've shot each other, fought with each other, saved each other's lives, rescued each other ... We've even collaborated once or twice. You just never know how it's going to go. My historian senses told me the gunshot and the presence of the Time Police were somehow connected. As I said to Captain Ellis once, 'Wherever there's trouble, you find the Time Police,' and he had replied that the Time Police had a very similar motto concerning St Mary's but wouldn't say any more. Their purpose, they say, is to patrol the timeline for anomalies and illegal time travel. Their purpose, *we* say, is to bugger things up as fast as they can go. Their response to most problems is to shoot everyone on sight. And now they were here. And there had been a gunshot.

'Oh swive,' said Markham. 'What the swive could those swiving swivers possibly swiving well want?'

I'd once made the mistake of taking him to the 17th century and he'd seized the opportunity to enrich his vocabulary with contemporary swear words. I think we'd all learned something from that experience.

'Mr Clerk. Please tell me they haven't shot someone.'

'Not exactly. You'd better get over here, Max.'

'On my way.'

We set off, elbowing our way through the crowds who, in the way of crowds everywhere, all wanted to go in the opposite direction from us.

There they were. Four of them, all kitted out in the enveloping black cloaks they think enables them to fit into any time any place and really, really doesn't. I tried not to sigh. One of them turned his head and made a gesture of recognition. Captain Ellis.

They were all standing around something stretched out on the ground. Oh God, was this the victim of the gunshot? Now what had they done? I couldn't see clearly because they and Clerk's team were forming a protective huddle as the crowd swept past, unheeding.

With all the righteous indignation of one who is, just for once, completely on the side of the angels, I glared at Ellis and demanded, 'What did you do?'

'We saved the day, Max. There's been an assassination attempt.'

I knew nothing of this – there certainly wasn't anything in the records. I stared at him suspiciously.

'On Henry?'

'No – his opponent.'

'Who?' I suddenly realised I still didn't know his opponent's name. No one does. Like the Viking who held back the Saxon forces at Stamford Bridge, his name is lost to History. Which begged the question – why kill an unknown man?

So I asked it. 'Why kill an unknown man?'

'So Henry would triumph. No accident. No miscarriage for Anne Boleyn. A son for Henry.'

I asked again. 'Why?'

He shrugged. 'God knows. Do you know how many nutters are out there?' His tone implied there were a good few of them standing in front of him right this moment.

'So your purpose here is …?'

'To protect the timeline, Max. That's what we do. It's not all about St Mary's, you know.'

'But how did you know?' I stared even more suspiciously. 'He's not one of yours, is he?'

'If you mean is he Time Police, then no. If you mean is he from our time, then yes.'

I examined the unconscious figure at our feet. The silly sod had obviously based his homemade costume on the historical epics turned out by the future equivalent of Cutter Cavendish Productions. And don't get me started on Calvin Cutter himself. The man's an idiot. Anyway, here was the loose linen shirt with the flowing sleeves – more suited to Charles II than Henry VIII. Plus a pair of baggy shorts more suited to Elizabethan times, and those ridiculous thigh-length leather boots you always expect to see on red-lipped ladies clad in black and clutching a riding crop. Seriously – what a pillock.

I turned back to Captain Ellis. 'I thought the Time Police had brutally obliterated this sort of thing. Don't tell me you haven't been brutal enough.'

He sighed. 'The odd one does still get through occasionally. And then it's a Class A emergency. We drop everything and here we are – saving the day. The irony is, of course, that without his intervention there would have been no gunshot. Henry's horse wouldn't have shied and there wouldn't have been an accident. Silly sod brought about the very thing he was trying to prevent.'

I nodded. It's not easy changing History. For a start, History doesn't like it. This idiot was lucky to be alive.

Although since illegal time travel was a capital offence – he wasn't going to be alive for very long.

'So you tracked him all the way here with your magic equipment.'

'I'm tempted to smirk and take the credit, but no. Not this time.'

'Then how did you know?'

He sighed. 'The idiot left a note.'

I think I might have reeled. 'He *wrote* to you?'

'Worse than that. He wrote to his girlfriend – wanted to impress her, I suppose, and she reported him to us.'

'What a …' I stopped, unable to think of suitable words to describe his … this …

'Yep.'

'What will happen to him?' asked Peterson.

'It's a Class A felony even to be in possession of an illegal time machine, so nothing good. On the other hand, he didn't actually affect the timeline in any way, and it's a first offence, so they probably won't execute him. Probably.'

'He risked all that to impress his girlfriend? I don't believe it.'

He grinned. 'You should have seen her, Max.'

I stared coldly. 'Why?'

'She's an absolute belter, I can tell you. Those eyes. That hair. And I could definitely see those hips launching a thousand ships. Or in this case one small time machine. Or …'

'Yes, all right. I get the drift. But circling back to my original point. How could this happen? I thought you'd stamped out this sort of thing years ago.'

40

'Well, someone still puts up the occasional "How to Build Your Own Time Machine" website up on the Dark Web. We deal with it but it's often too late by then.'

'Can't you just take the site down?'

'Oh, we do much more than that. I don't know about your time, but in ours, everything is electronic and everything talks to everything else, so we have a rather nasty little bug that affects anyone opening one of these sites.'

'But surely it's too late by then,' I said. 'By the time, you've infected them they've already got the info.'

'No, no. For God's sake, Max, we are the Time Police. Give us a little credit. We're better than that.' He grinned

'What have you done?'

'Ever heard of DDOS?'

'Deedos?'

'Distributed denial of service attack?'

I shook my head.

'We've seen to it that each and every electronic device manufactured carries a little something from the Time Police. Every single device – all over the world – leaves the factory with one of our little presents programmed into their operating system.'

I gaped. 'How on earth did you manage that?'

He shrugged. 'Again, we're the Time Police. There's only the one software provider – you can guess who – and it was just a case of intimidating them into doing what we wanted, which was to build it into their manufacturing process.'

'But ... they agreed?'

He just grinned. 'Again – we're the Time Police, Max. Try to keep up. Anyway, every device is affected. Cars, computers, phones – anything with a chip is vulnerable to

41

the bug. It's quite dormant – not a problem to 99.9999 per cent of users – until someone tries to access these illegal web sites. There's a tiny line of code that's vital to anyone accessing the Dark Web – I won't go into details because you're St Mary's and you won't understand – but the instant the code is read it activates the really nasty virus built into the software and – poof!'

'Poof?'

'Gone,' he said mournfully. 'All gone. Lost and gone forever.'

'You mean their computer?'

'No, I mean everything. The user's computer, car, phone, communication devices, house-management system – you know, security heating lighting – all electronics, cars, bikes, washing machines … their entire life.'

He saw my blank look.

'In our time, everyone has their own personal wi-fi network. And every device talks to every other device on that network. People control their entire lives through their comm device. It's a wonderful thing. Until it isn't. Because the bug just rips through everything. Every system is corrupted. Everything shuts down. Cars will never work again. Security systems are inaccessible and won't let you into your own home. Washers dump water all over the floor. Computers go haywire. You can't even access your own bank accounts and that's when someone's life disappears right down the tubes. Usually that's when we're able to pick them up. Before they get the opportunity to do too much damage. This one moved more quickly than we expected and got away from us slightly. Still – all's well that ends well, eh?'

He kicked the prone figure which moaned slightly.

'So who's after Clive Ronan at this moment?' I asked, reminding him of his priorities.

'No one. He's gone to ground, Max. Wherever or whenever he is, he's staying put and keeping his head down and we can't find him.'

'He could be dead.'

'I hope not.'

'Why?'

'Because we need to know, Max. He's tying up people and resources we can't afford and none of us can get a move on with our normal activities. Dead is no good if we can't actually confirm that. Best-case scenario – one of us shoots him, he makes a full confession, expires at our feet and we take the body back for confirmation. Actually, I'm glad I ran into you this afternoon – I want to talk to you about … something. Can you spare me a minute?'

I nodded.

He began to issue instructions for getting the ex-time traveller back to their pod. 'And find his pod, too. It won't be too far away.' He took my arm.

I said to Markham, 'Back in a minute.'

He looked at Ellis. 'Stay in sight.'

People were still streaming past us but the bulk of the crowd had disappeared. The field was now just a sad space of crushed grass and mud, littered with people's discarded possessions. The stands were empty. I could hear people shouting for their horses.

'Actually, Max, I've been meaning to talk to you and I'm quite pleased to have had this opportunity of a chat without raising any suspicions. Feel free to wave your arms around and give the impression you're not happy with me.'

43

'I'm not happy with you. There's nothing impressionistic about it.'

'I'm not happy either. But I haven't been wasting my time as we've been unsuccessfully chasing Ronan up and down the timeline. If I can quote someone standing not a million miles from here – I've been having a bit of a think. Shall we sit down. Before your Mr Markham becomes over-anxious.'

We sat on the grass and looked at each other.

'Go on.'

'I was thinking,' he said slowly, 'that we need to set a trap for him. We're always chasing him and getting nowhere, but you know what they say – a good hunter works out where his prey will be, goes there and waits.'

'What would we use as bait?'

'You, of course.'

I blinked. 'Wow – that's not a bad idea.'

'Thank you. Just to be clear – you weren't my first choice.'

'Oh?' I said, annoyed. 'Who could possibly be more baity than me?'

'Well, Matthew was the obvious choice, but we felt sure that not only would you not say "yes", but you'd force feed me my own legs while you did so.'

'And then your arms and head. And then Leon would have a go.'

'Yes, if we could please move on from my dismemberment and focus on the trap.'

'OK, what sort of trap?'

'Well, I hadn't really got that far, but I was thinking along the lines of leaving you somewhere prominent, alone and abandoned – you know, something Ronan

44

himself would be comfortable with – and just hide until he comes for you.'

'Hmmm. I see you favour the subtle and complicated approach.'

'Well, obviously there are a few details to be worked out yet.'

'A few? That's Time Police speak for all of them. Besides, he'd never fall for something so obvious.'

'And I suppose that being St Mary's, you'll come up with some ridiculously over-complicated scheme involving a cast of thousands that will go horribly wrong, result in massive destruction, enormous numbers of casualties and permanent damage to the timeline, which we, the always reliable Time Police will have to sort out. Whereas Plan A involves hiding behind a rock and just shooting the bastard on sight.'

'Before he kills me.'

'Well, if possible, of course.'

I shifted uncomfortably on the grass. 'How's Matthew doing?'

'Very well. Excellent progress in mathematics and physics.'

I sighed. 'That'll please his father.'

Ellis looked at me.

'My talents lie in other directions.' I said, defensively.

'Good heavens. Have we finally found something you're *not* good at?'

'Not at all. I was in the top 98 per cent for maths at school. I was less good at physics.'

He smiled slightly. 'Well, he's good at sport. He enjoys his football. He's had a long-suffering mentor appointed to him who, at this moment, is working on persuading him to have his hair cut.'

45

He grinned at me and I grinned back. 'Yeah – good luck with that.'

'He's a good lad, Max. I took him to the Science Museum last week and he enjoyed it so much I was only able to get him out by threatening him with broccoli.'

I smiled. 'Thank you for taking him on.'

'It's my pleasure. He's a great kid. And having been present at his birth it's the least I could do.'

There was a long pause as I sought for a way of asking what I really wanted to know, 'Does he mention me at all?' without sounding needy.

He read my mind. 'He was talking about you yesterday, actually. Yes, he's looking forward to returning to St Mary's for a visit. He's very keen to see Markham and Miss … Lingoss, is it?' I nodded. 'He's made a 3D puzzle he wants to show you and … there was something else. Oh yes. You have good chimneys. Can't remember what we were talking about at the time, so sorry – no context for that one.'

It was beginning to get dark and I needed to get my people back to the pod before the curfew bell rang. I stood up and brushed down my skirt. 'What we were talking about – you know – Clive Ronan. Let me have a think as well and I'll …' I stopped, not sure '… contact you.'

'Dr Bairstow can always get hold of us.'

'Can he?' I frowned. How? How do you contact someone in the future?

'He can.' He nodded over his shoulder, presumably in the direction of the failed time traveller. 'I'm going to have my hands full with Sunny Jim and his illegal pod over the next few days.'

'Why?'

He looked at me directly. 'If you're going to execute a man, Max, you need to make sure the case is watertight.'

'Will you? Execute him, I mean?'

'Well, I won't, certainly. Not part of my duties, thank God. But I doubt it will come to that. And even if it does, he brought it on himself. I don't have to tell you what would have happened had he succeeded today. We'd have had to bring in clean-up squads and all sorts of nastiness ensues when we have to do that.'

I peered at him in the gathering gloom, suddenly cold. 'Does it?'

'Yes, it does, but you don't need to know about that. Go and hatch a masterplan.' He nodded over to where Peterson and Markham were pretending not to listen. 'You should get back to your people.'

'Yes, I should. I have a mission to complete here.'

'I'll wait to hear from you, Max.'

'You will.'

'Trouble?' said Clerk, as I rejoined the others.

'Not for us,' I said, 'but that poor bugger's going to wish he hadn't got up this morning.'

'Serves him right,' he said. 'And where did it get him? He didn't change a thing and he's going to spend the rest of his life regretting he ever tried.'

'If he's lucky,' said Prentiss, sombrely. 'Max, will they really execute him?'

'I don't know,' I said. 'Ellis seemed to think there might be some leniency shown, but certainly he's in for a long, long spell in a very unpleasant place.'

'Clerk is right,' said North. 'If he'd succeeded …'

'I'm not sure he deserves to die,' said Peterson.

'If he'd succeeded, many more people would have died than just him. And it's not as if he did it out of any sort of religious or political conviction – he only did it to impress his girlfriend, for God's sake.'

'Whereas religious or political convictions would have made it more acceptable?'

'That's not what I'm saying …'

'Time to wrap things up,' I said. Historians argue like other people breathe. 'Miss Sykes, how are you doing?'

'We're on our way back to the pod, Max. The king was only here for a few minutes and then they carted him off in a closed carriage. He'll be at the palace by now.'

And the queen would be contemplating a future that was suddenly looking a lot less rosy.

'We'll meet you there,' I said. 'Have we done the FOD plod?'

Foreign Object Drop check is very important. We're not allowed to leave anything behind. There's a corresponding POD plod when we check equally carefully that we haven't inadvertently picked something up. We don't just fling these assignments together, you know.

Back at St Mary's, I made them all wait while the decontamination lamp did its work and then watched them bicker their way up to Sick Bay. I was sitting at the console, shutting things down when Leon entered.

'Hello,' I said, pleased to see him.

'Hello yourself,' he said, elbowing me aside to take over. 'How did it go?'

I decided not to mention Ellis's plan or using me as bait – and certainly not about using Matthew – not until I'd spoken to Dr Bairstow anyway, so I gave Leon the version suitable for nervous husbands.

'It was fine,' I said. 'We watched Fat Harry taking the first steps to paranoia, tyranny and murder, and met the Time Police.'

He finished at the console and turned to me. 'What were they doing there?'

'Apprehending a fugitive. He says Matthew is well and looking forward to his next visit.'

I chased everyone for their reports, including Markham, who seemed to think because he was Head of Security now he didn't have to do that sort of thing any longer, and Peterson, who as Deputy Director thought something very similar. Sykes and North were in the same ward as me and knew better than even to try. It was a bit like pulling teeth, but I got there eventually, signed and initialled everything and bundled it all off to Dr Bairstow, following up with a personal visit on my discharge from Sick Bay the next morning.

Mrs Partridge waved me straight through and I entered his office with the confident air of one whose assignment hadn't gone perfectly to plan but, just for once, was completely blameless.

He was sitting behind his desk. I ran my eye over its polished surface. It's never cluttered, because he doesn't work like that, but the odd file positioned to one side is usually a good sign and gives him something to fiddle with during the difficult bits. A completely empty desk is a very bad sign and always a signal either to:

a) Marshal the appropriate arguments as quickly as possible, or

b) Issue a blanket denial that covers everything that has ever happened since recorded History began and – given the nature of our job – everything that can happen until recorded History ends.

Neither is ever particularly successful.

On this occasion there were two files in front of him. Both mine – so no clues there.

He opened the batting, pointing his beaky nose at me. 'I've read your mission reports, Dr Maxwell. It would seem you encountered an unexpected circumstance.'

'I did, sir. What did you want to discuss first?'

'Let's start with the reason for the jump, shall we? I gather Henry came – how does Miss Sykes phrase it – a bit of a cropper.'

'He certainly did, sir. If you've had a chance to view the footage you'll know it's quite horrific.'

'I agree. Dr Stone is reviewing the files now. A fall of that nature certainly lends credence to the theories of a completely altered personality.'

'Indeed, sir, although I always feel the need to point out he was a bit of a bastard before he fell off his horse.'

Silence fell as he lined up my files with mathematical precision.

'I believe there is something else you wish to discuss with me.'

'There is, sir,' and I described the conversation I'd had with Captain Ellis. 'I haven't actually had much of a chance to think through the implications, sir, and I didn't think I should do so until I'd had a chance to discuss it with you.'

He swivelled his chair and sat for a long time, staring unseeingly out of the window. I suddenly thought how tired he looked. As always, I had no idea what he was thinking, but he obviously came to some sort of a conclusion because he turned back and said, 'Very well, Dr Maxwell, put something together and we'll discuss it another time. There would be a great number of details to work out.'

'Yes, sir.'

I got up to go.

'And Max?'

'Yes, sir?'

'Tell no one. No one at all.'

'Understood, sir. Do I have a deadline?'

'As soon as possible, I think.'

I don't know what made me ask, 'Any particular reason why, sir?' but his answer frightened the living daylights out of me.

'Be aware, Max. It won't always be me sitting in this chair. My successor may have different priorities.'

'But surely, sir, Dr Peterson will be your successor.'

'That is my intention, but it would seem others have other ideas.'

'I can't imagine St Mary's without you, sir.'

'You may have to.'

I stood silently, turning over the implications of his words until eventually he waved a hand, indicating my departure was urgently required, picked up a file and lost interest in me.

I called in at our room to drop off my gear and, to my surprise, Leon was there, making himself a mug of tea. I could see at once it wasn't one of his good days.

'Just passing through,' I said, chucking my grab bag in the corner. 'I thought you'd be down in Hawking.'

He sighed. 'I can't help feeling it doesn't do much for my image when people see me tottering about this place, a broken man.

'Oh, give over. You were a broken man long before Ronan blew you up.'

'Do I gather you don't actually want any tea?'

I watched him struggle. Even the simplest tasks took him ages. I stifled the urge to go and help but I did have to carry the mugs for him. We sat on the sofa and I covered his face with kisses.

'Well,' he said, fending me off with one hand and reaching for his tea with the other. 'This is very nice. Don't think I'm not appreciative, but why?'

'Don't get excited. I do the same to every man who brings me tea.'

'Well, thank God for that. I wouldn't want to think I was a special case.'

I laughed, even though I really wanted to cry for him. I could see he needed to close his eyes and rest, so I told him I'd see him later and pushed off, taking my tea with me.

I headed for my office. Rosie Lee wasn't there, which never surprised me. She was obviously off savaging someone else.

I sat at my desk, cradled my mug of tea, put my feet up and had a bit of a think. It took a while. I had to hit on something that would be a perfectly legitimate assignment – something that would win the approval of both Dr Bairstow and the Chancellor, produce a tangible result, and still give me the freedom to go off and be bait.

I pulled up the outstanding assignments list. Once a year, I lay everything out over about four tables and plan the coming year's assignments. There's the stuff that comes down from Thirsk, which takes priority, obviously, since they're paying. Then there's any uncompleted assignments from the previous year – there aren't usually many of those. Then there's anything we, St Mary's, feel warrants further investigation and, finally, there are people's personal wish-lists. I felt a momentary pang for Ian Guthrie. He was never going to get to Bannockburn now.

I laid it all out chronologically and sifted through, picking up one assignment, discarding it in favour of another, whittling them down until, at last, I thought I had exactly what I was looking for.

I took the file back to my desk, topped up my tea and put my feet up again, assuming the traditional St Mary's thinking position.

Persepolis.

Originally known as Parsa, City of the Persians, Persepolis was the ancient capital of Persia, built in 518BC by Darius the Great to house his greatest treasures. And not just gold. There were literary works by the foremost scholars of the day and fabulous art, collected from all around the Persian Empire. The city and palaces had been greatly enhanced by Xerxes the Great – yes, that Xerxes! – the one who invaded Greece, overcame the Spartans at Thermopylae, and was eventually defeated at Salamis, but not before he had burned much of Greece, including the Parthenon at Athens. Something for which he was never forgiven and would have dire repercussions for Persepolis.

Anyway, that was the city, light, bright and lovely until Alexander the Great – another 'Great'; although to be fair, he did deserve the name – turned up in 330BC, conquered the place and then, for reasons never clearly understood, set fire to it. The most magnificent city in all of Persia became known as The Place of the Forty Columns, those forty columns being all that is left standing.

There's some dispute as to why Alexander, usually a fairly benevolent conqueror as long as no one gave him any trouble, should choose to burn this magnificent city to the ground. Diodorus Siculus says he and his men were all as pissed as newts at a party, and the courtesan, Thaïs, suggested burning the city as revenge for the Persians burning Athens. A fitting humiliation, she said, to have their finest city destroyed by women. Plutarch and the Roman, Quintus Curtius Rufus more or less agree with this account. Arrian of Nicomedia however, maintains Alexander was sober at the time and it was a deliberate act of revenge.

No one disagrees that Alexander did burn Persepolis, the debate has always been about *why*. This was something we might be able to settle.

And – and this would appeal to our overlords at Thirsk – there was always the chance we'd be able to rescue something valuable from the wreckage. By valuable I don't necessarily mean gold and silver. Alexander stripped the Treasury long before he burned it. Apparently, it took twenty thousand mules and five thousand pack camels to carry it all away, but there are other treasures besides silver and gold. It's very possible that records, scrolls, tablets, anything not intrinsically valuable would be left behind as too much trouble to shift, but to us – and to Thirsk – that sort of thing was far more valuable than gold.

We can't remove anything from its own time – neither people nor objects, but some time ago, I'd inadvertently brought back a fir cone from the Cretaceous Period. I hadn't noticed at time because I was being chased by a T.rex – as you frequently are in the Cretaceous, let me tell you. Anyway, when I eventually got back, there was this poor little fir cone, burned and damaged and caught in the lining of my jacket. It seemed that if an object was about to be destroyed – if it wasn't in a position to influence the future timeline in any way – it could be safely removed without jeopardising time, History, or the universe in general. A very useful piece of information that has allowed us to rescue a small part of the library at

Alexandria from the Christians, a couple of Botticellis –
also from the Christians, now I come to think of it – King
John's lost treasure, and one or two other things along the
way as well. Anything like that always makes us very
popular with Thirsk and doesn't do our funding any harm
either. From what I remembered, Persepolis' archive was
famous for holding copies of the Zoroastrian Avesta –
beautifully written on goatskin in golden ink. If even a
smallest fragment of that could be rescued, then it would
be priceless.

So, on the plus side we'd get:

a) A glimpse of the magnificent city of Persepolis
before it burned, although hopefully only in our rear-
view mirror as we made another successful getaway.

b) Possibly a sight of Alexander, his Companions,
Thaïs, and all that merry crew as they danced about
setting fire to everything in sight.

c) The opportunity to rescue fabulous documents
before they were toast.

Really, I couldn't see a downside anywhere. And it
ticked so many boxes.

Dr Bairstow would like it because the Chancellor
would like it and the Chancellor would be ecstatic at the
thought of all those goatskin scrolls. We'd love it because
we might get the opportunity to solve one of the greatest
mysteries of the ancient world. What made Alexander do
it? The chance to find out would keep St Mary's happy.
So, as I said – no downside. It was perfect.

I sat and stared for a while, my brain devising and
discarding all sorts of scenarios, and then I telephoned
Kalinda Black at Thirsk and talked at her for ten minutes
or so.

At the end of it she said faintly, 'Why are you telling me this?'

'You're our liaison officer. I'm liaising.'

'You're giving me a bloody heart attack.'

'Rubbish. Nothing gives you heart attacks. You're a cause of them in others. What do you think?'

'Safe in the knowledge you'll never get it past Dr Bairstow, I think it's a great idea.'

That was all I needed.

I spent the rest of the day on the phone to various people.

I chucked Rosie Lee out of the office and, would you believe it, she took offence and said she had a lot on at the moment, moving subtly to hide her almost empty 'In' tray. 'And who will make your tea?'

I snarled, 'The same person who always makes my tea,' picked up her 'In' tray, thrust it at her and told her to make herself scarce. I've no idea where she went.

I couldn't have done it without Kal. If you're ever planning something outrageous and risky and borderline illegal then, trust me, Kal's your man. Or whatever. We mounted a two-pronged attack and eventually, grudgingly, the permissions came through.

Only for forty-eight hours, though, was the warning. Not a second longer.

Forty-eight hours was fine. If my scheme worked then forty-eight minutes should be enough.

I read my mission plan through again – I don't know why; it wasn't as if I didn't know it off by heart – and then I bundled everything together and went to see Dr Bairstow.

He took his time, reading through my Persepolis notes twice, scanning the pod and staffing lists, the equipment requisitions, twirling my data stacks – that's nowhere near as improper as it sounds – before finally closing everything down, folding his hands and staring at me across his desk.

I grinned at him because I knew what he was going to say.

'Well planned,' he said. 'Detailed, do-able and …'

'Dull?' I suggested. 'Unimaginative? Unoriginal?'

'Forgive me, Dr Maxwell, but I do detect a certain lack of … originality in your scheme?'

I grinned again. 'I hope so, sir.'

He twirled the data stack. 'You appear to be setting up a scenario in which you almost invite Clive Ronan to swoop in and shoot you.'

'Yes, sir.'

'You don't think that's a little – obvious?'

I can't help it. I'm a showman, too.

I brought up the second part of my plan.

He read it through. And read it through again. And read it through for a final time. I waited patiently because every reading was a step nearer acceptance. Finally, he looked over his desk at me.

'I might find it quite difficult to apply the word "unoriginal" to this part of your proposed plan.'

'Thank you, sir.'

'That wasn't a compliment.'

Well, there's no pleasing some people, but it was probably best not to mention that.

'If you could give me the *entire* scenario, please.'

'From beginning to end, sir?'

'If it's not too much trouble.'

'We strip St Mary's of personnel and send everyone off to Persepolis.'

'Leaving St Mary's virtually unguarded.'

'Yes, sir.'

'And in the meantime ...?'

'In the meantime, while we're away, you take delivery of the Crown of the Empress Mathilda.'

'Which just happens to be passing at the time?'

'Not exactly, sir. It's on its way to be exhibited at the British Museum.'

He blinked. 'Why would it pause here?'

'For us to study, photograph, to make a holo – the usual things we do, sir.'

'Why?'

'We have dibs on it, sir. We discovered it. On our land. We generously donated it to the University of Thirsk. This is a gesture to demonstrate their goodwill and gratitude towards us.'

A word of explanation here. A little while ago, seeking to rehabilitate ourselves in the hypercritical eyes of our paymasters, we'd discovered a small number of items supposedly 'lost' by King John in the Wash and turned the whole lot over to them. Part of the hoard was the supposed Crown of the Empress Mathilda.

Dr Bairstow frowned. 'Is the Chancellor aware of the extent of their goodwill and gratitude?'

'I believe Dr Black is apprising her of it now, sir.'

'And while the crown is lodging here?'

'Clive Ronan swoops down and steals it from us, sir.'

He blinked. 'Forgive my asking, Dr Maxwell – are you insane?'

'Certainly not, sir. Dr Stone had me tested.'

59

He sighed. 'Explain to me again, how this scenario will play out.'

'The crown is here, sir, virtually unguarded because everyone is at Persepolis, but actually the building will be riddled with Time Police officers, sir, who will arrest him as soon as he sets foot outside of his pod.'

'Yes,' he said thoughtfully. 'Do please forgive my denseness, but is it likely I would have the Crown of the Empress Mathilda here without an adequate security presence?'

'Not at all, sir. Your detailed and meticulous plans are based on the crown arriving here *after* the security section returns from Persepolis. Unfortunately, the crown will arrive two days early. While we're all still away.'

'Why?'

I must admit, even my ingenuity had failed me over this one. I struck out at random.

'An administrative cock-up, sir. Happens all the time.'

He blinked. 'I look forward to being present when you attempt to explain to Mrs Partridge that everything is about to be her fault.'

'If you don't mind, sir, I'll take my chances with a burning city collapsing around me and leave the more hazardous side of the assignment to you.'

'You don't intend to remain at St Mary's then?'

'Well, I was tempted, sir, but it would rather give the game away don't you agree? Is it likely I'd stay behind and miss this important assignment to Persepolis? And remember – the crown isn't supposed to show up until after our return.'

He nodded. 'An attitude of self-preservation I never thought to witness in an historian.'

'Persepolis will be a far less dangerous environment, sir. And, hopefully, well outside the blast zone of Mrs Partridge's professional indignation.'

He sighed. 'Max ...'

'I know, sir, but I really think it might tempt him. It's just the sort of thing he would go for. A deserted St Mary's and a fabulous crown – his for the taking. It will make us look the most complete incompetents. We'll be in no end of trouble with Thirsk. Our credibility will be blown. All at comparatively little risk to himself. I don't think he'll be able to resist.'

'And we do have to use the real crown?'

'Oh, I think so, sir, don't you?'

'Well ... no.'

'Sir ...'

'We could not, for example, use something slightly less valuable and irreplaceable?'

'It's the bait, sir. I don't think he'd turn up for a ledger of 16th-century household accounts.'

'I mean, Dr Maxwell, must we use the crown itself as bait? Could we not simply place a large rock in a suitable container, clearly mark it "Crown of the Empress Mathilda – Do Not Touch" and let events take their course without in any way imperilling one of the most valuable artefacts in the country?'

'I think we have to use the real thing, sir. We need to make it as realistic as possible. Everyone will see it setting off from Thirsk on its journey to London. It's going to be on TV.'

He looked alarmed. 'And will everyone see it arriving here?'

'No, sir. Just leaving Thirsk and arriving in London.'

'So how will Ronan know of its overnight stay here?'

'I have no idea, sir, but I'm sure he will. Especially when you vigorously deny every rumour that it would break its journey here.'

'You want me to lie to the press?'

'Well, it's not as if they don't lie to us, sir.'

'But …'

'Actually, I want you to lie to everyone, sir. If you don't mind, of course.'

'And where am I supposed to keep this priceless artefact while we wait for it to be stolen from under our noses?'

'I thought we could shove it in a bin labelled "Kitchen Waste" and leave it near the kitchen door ready for collection. No one's going to find it there and *then* we substitute your large rock, sir. We wouldn't want to take any chances with one of the most valuable artefacts in the country, would we?'

He appeared to be temporarily lost for words. I think he suspected me of sarcasm.

I took pity on him. 'And then, sir, you very ostentatiously place the imposter crown in Hawking.'

'Hawking?'

'The safest place. Hawking in lockdown is almost impregnable.'

'Not to Clive Ronan and his pod.'

'Exactly, sir,' I said, beaming. 'We set up a token guard – remember we won't have many security guards because they'll all be at Persepolis because the crown turns up two days early. The Time Police set down one of their big pods – probably where TB2 parks, although that's really up to you and Captain Ellis, sir. They engage their camouflage device and sit and wait. Their pod signature will be invisible amongst our own pods.'

'As will Ronan's.'

'That's true, sir, but if he wants the crown then he's going to have to leave his pod and come and get it and that's when we've got him. You've got him. They've got him. Whatever. I'm certain the Clive Ronan apprehending part of the plan can be safely left to the Time Police. They depart with a chained and manacled Ronan, the crown continues its way to London, and – and this is the beauty of my plan, sir – we return from Persepolis with footage of a burning city and Alexander himself. And, with luck, we'll be able to pick up some good stuff before the fire gets it. It's all good, sir.'

'Apart from the city being destroyed around you.'

I waved aside these normal hazards of an historian's working day and waited hopefully.

Finally, he leaned forwards, picked up the data stacks and files and locked everything away in his filing cabinet.

'Who else knows of this?'

'At the moment, sir, only Dr Black knows of part of the scheme. As per your instructions, I haven't mentioned anything to anyone else.'

'Not even Leon?'

Especially not Leon was the answer to that one. I sought for a non-committal answer. 'As soon as you give me the go-ahead to do so, sir.'

'Very well, Dr Maxwell, you may do so, but it must remain between the four of us for the time being. I don't want to take any chances with this one. I shall speak to the Chancellor and then contact the Time Police to present your proposal. We shall take things from there.'

Which reminded me – this was something I'd wanted to ask him and now seemed an excellent opportunity to do so. I inched forwards on my chair.

'Excuse me, sir, I have to ask. How exactly *do* you contact the Time Police?'

I think I imagined information-laden data streams stabbing their way into the future by means far too complex for my tiny historian brain.

'I write them a letter,' he said, calmly.

I blinked. 'I beg your pardon, sir.'

'I write to them,' he said again. 'By means of the method known these days, I believe, as snail mail. How exactly did you think it worked?'

I said, 'Well, sir ...' and described the whole data-stream fantasy thing which he seemed to find quite amusing.

'Let us assume, Dr Maxwell, that you wish to assassinate me.'

We both paused to contemplate this all-too-likely scenario.

'Suppose you came at me armed with my own paper knife and full of homicidal intentions.'

I picked up his paper knife and mimed coming at him full of homicidal intentions.

'I simply dash of a note –' he unscrewed his fountain pen and mimed dashing off a quick note.

'But, sir,' I said, hovering menacingly with his paper knife and keen to point out the obvious flaw. 'With respect, by the time you've written the note, I've cut out your liver.'

'I just need a stamp,' he said imperturbably, opened his top drawer and pulled out the biggest handgun I've ever seen in my life. And I've seen a few. He levelled it at my face. The barrel was the size of the late and very unlamented Channel Tunnel and there was no discernible safety catch.

I put down the paper knife and sat down slowly.

He replaced the gun, closed the drawer, and my heart started up again.

'Obviously, there are situations which call for a more immediate solution but, in general, if I wish to summon our colleagues in the Time Police, I simply write them a letter, clearly stating the circumstances and detailing the coordinates at which I wish them to present themselves.'

He sat back in his chair, apparently oblivious to the actually quite massive flaws in this scheme.

'But surely, sir, by the time you've finished your written request for assistance and it has arrived at its destination, whatever crisis is occurring has resolved itself. One way or the other. And how on earth do they get the letter in the first place? They're well away in the future. Do they turn up and sort out our great-great grandchildren?'

'It's ...' he paused, obviously rummaging for another phrase, found nothing appropriate, and continued with distaste, '... time travel, Dr Maxwell. By enclosing the appropriate coordinates, I can ensure they present themselves where and whenever I require them to be. I post the letter – well, I believe Mrs Partridge arranges that, but the letter is posted somehow, to be delivered to a discreetly coded PO Box in London.'

'London?'

'Well, the US has ruled itself out, of course, and I don't have to tell you why Moscow or Beijing could not even be considered.'

'So it sits in a post office box in London for years and years?'

'Of course not, Dr Maxwell. The Time Police have instituted a twice-weekly collection. A young person appears, opens the box, records the contents and returns to Commander Hay who despatches her people accordingly.'

I stared at him. I'm certain my mouth was open. Just for once, however, no sound was coming out.

Weirdly, it made sense. How else could you contact someone in the future? Anything electronic would have to go through satellites that hadn't been launched yet. Or even designed and built. Computer data can be lost, hacked or corrupted. So, if you have a threat of some kind, you simply send off the details and the Time Police turn up where and whenever and render whatever assistance has been requested. Or make the situation considerably worse, of course. It could go either way and frequently does.

He was following my train of thought. 'It's a remarkably simple and efficient system. So much so that Director Pinkerton, whom I'm sure you remember, once told me that the Time Police responded so rapidly that she actually had no time to write anything more than "Dear Sir or Madam" before they crashed through her door demanding to know whom she wanted them to shoot. Things calmed down eventually and the situation was successfully resolved. I do believe, however, that in the spirit of scientific curiosity for which she is so renowned, she pretended to forget to complete the request for assistance, in order to see what would happen.'

He paused. Being a showman again.

I obliged. 'So what did happen, sir?'

'Three of them crashed back through her only very recently repaired door and made a strong – a very strong – suggestion that she complete her written request without further delay. Closing the circle, Dr Maxwell. Just because, sometimes, effect comes before cause, does not mean we should neglect the basic rules.'

'No indeed sir,' I murmured from my weakened position as one who neglects the basic rules on a daily basis.

I worked on the fine details for the rest of the day and most of the evening and was roused only by Leon calling me up and enquiring whether I'd left him. I told him yes, I'd found myself a man who could move faster than a three-toed sloth and was better looking as well', shut everything down and shot off to meet him for something to eat.

He was very quiet when I eventually climbed into bed that night and snuggled up to him.

He moved away fractionally, saying, 'Max, we talked about this. You know I can't …'

'I do,' I said, fighting down pity and panic and anger and God knows what else. 'But as far as I know your injuries don't exempt you from all other husbandly duties – bringing tea when required, knowing where my boots are, providing a safe and warm environment to put my feet at night, and putting your arm around me when I've had a long day.'

There was a short silence which I pretended to ignore and then he said, 'Have you had a long day?' and put his arm around me.

I sighed and snuggled. 'Endless.'

I gave him a moment to relax and then found a safe and warm environment to put my feet. There was a small yelp in the darkness and I smiled to myself. Revenge might be a dish best served cold but so are feet in the middle of the night.

Of course, convincing Dr Bairstow was the easy bit.

'No,' said Leon when I mentioned my wonderful scheme to him in the privacy of our own room the next day.

'But ...'

'Out of the question.'

'But ...'

'No.'

And now I had a problem. Strictly speaking I didn't need his permission for this assignment. As Chief Technical Officer, he had no authority over me, the Chief Operations Officer. As my husband – well, he still didn't have any authority over me and, had things been normal, I would loudly and cheerfully have pointed this out to him, but things weren't normal. Not even close. Now was not the moment to remind him that this was something else over which he had no control. In typical fashion, of course, we'd never discussed the elephant in the room – just papered over the cracks and carried on as usual, because that always works, doesn't it?

Dr Stone had said it was a natural result of his injuries and would probably right itself over time. Probably. And to be patient. And neither of us was to stress about it, so we'd dodged the stress by dodging the issue. And now I found myself having to defy a husband who was already considering himself less than he had been.

I said carefully, 'Leon ...'

'Oh, I know,' he said angrily. 'You'll go anyway.'

He flicked on the TV. Tiny figures chased a ball back and forth.

I sat beside him and said, 'Are you telling me not to go?'

'Waste of time. You'd go anyway.'

'Not necessarily.'

He turned to look at me.

'It's simple, Leon. If you *ask* me not to do it then I won't. All you have to do is ask.'

There was a long silence and then he said, 'You know I'm not going to do that.'

'Look,' I said, trying to keep my voice steady because tears wouldn't help at all. 'You've done your bit. You ran him down and you cornered him and he was so desperate he blew us all up. Including himself. Now it's my turn. He's out there somewhere – intent on revenge. We're presenting him with an opportunity that's too good for him to miss. And there will be very little risk for me. I won't even be here. I'll be completely out of trouble.'

'At Persepolis?'

'The city won't be under attack. The population will have a chance to get out safely.'

'Max ...'

'I know, sweetheart, but if this comes off then we get our lives back. We get Matthew back.'

'It should be me.'

'Yes, it should and, after you've recovered, it will be you. But at the moment, it has to be me.'

He said bitterly, 'I can't do *anything*,' and we both knew what he meant.

'Well no, you were in an explosion that blew you back eight hundred years and two thousand miles, Leon.'

'You know what I'm talking about.'

'Yes, I do,' I said carefully.

'You haven't said anything ...'

'You know what Dr Stone said. It's a natural result of your injuries and not to stress about it. So I'm not stressing about it.'

I was treading on such thin ice here. Picking a careful path between not seeming to place too much importance on what he saw as his failure, while not giving the impression I didn't care. Because I did care. The physical side of our relationship was important to both of us.

He couldn't look at me. 'You've never said anything. I wondered – don't you ... want me?'

'Of course I want you, Leon. Shagging you is my favourite thing. After chocolate, of course. And sausages. And my first cup of tea in the morning. And a good book. And anything with Stephen Hawking in it. And a long hot bath ...'

'So according to you, almost everything is more exciting than me?'

'No, of course not. Don't get yourself in a tizzy. There's loads of things more boring than you. For instance, you're streets ahead of broccoli.'

'*Everything* is streets ahead of broccoli. And I've never seen you eat green food in your life.'

'Mint choc-chip ice cream?'

It was a joke too far. He pulled his hand away.

'This isn't a joke to me, Max. I'm trying to tell you that ... that ...'

I hit his arm.

'What? Ow. Why are you hitting me?'

'Because you're so bloody stupid, Leon.'

He opened his mouth but I didn't give him a chance to speak. Always get your licks in first.

'How long have we been married? A bloody long time now and in all that time you've stood by me as I've let you down, disappointed you, got you into trouble, got myself into trouble, worried you sick, been kidnapped ... You name it, I've done it, and you've always been there for me. You've been polite enough not to mention my expanding waistline, my grey streaks and my short-sightedness. You've been the rock on which I've built my life. You've never wavered. Not once. And here you are thinking I don't want you any longer just because you can't give me what you think I want. I know you well enough to know that, whatever happened, you would stand by me. To the end and beyond. And I'm upset – no, actually I'm not upset – I'm absolutely bloody lividly furiously ragingly angry that you think I wouldn't do the same for you. How shallow do you think I am, Leon Farrell?'

Silence in the room. On the TV, the commentator bemoaned yet another England catastrophe in the penalty box.

We sat, side by side, staring at the screen.

After a minute, he reached across and took my hand.

After a minute, I rested my head on his shoulder.

After a minute, he put his arm around me.

After a minute, I curled up on his lap.

After a minute, he pulled the throw over us both.

After a minute, I switched off the TV.

71

After a minute, he kissed the top of my head and we both fell asleep.

Whatever miracles Dr Bairstow, Mrs Partridge and His Majesty's Royal Mail performed, Captain Ellis turned up the next day.

He, Markham, Peterson, Dr Bairstow, Leon – in a technical capacity – and I discussed the plan. There were a few amendments but not many because basically it was simple. We were setting a trap for him to walk into.

Leon was very quiet. He'd said everything he had to say the night before. He took notes, offered up advice or suggestions where needed, and promised to have the pods ready whenever they would be required.

I left him talking schedules with Peterson and Dr Bairstow and walked Captain Ellis outside and back to his pod. We took the long way round because it was a nice day and because we needed to talk secrets.

We wandered out of the front door, around the side of the building and through the car park.

He pointed to some recent gouges in the side of the building and some bare patches showing through the Virginia creeper. 'There's been some damage here. What happened? Not Ronan again?'

'Shrapnel. We blew up a couple of rocks.'

He looked around in alarm. 'You're not doing it again today, are you?'

'No, of course not.'

'Come to your senses?'

'Run out of rocks.'

We turned into the sunken rock garden where it was warm, still and private.

'Well,' I said. 'What do you think?'

He nodded. 'I don't think it's a bad idea. And it's simple. Either he'll turn up for the crown or he won't. It's black or white.'

'Leon will shut down Hawking – you'll have the place to yourselves.'

'If he turns up then we'll have him. We'll wait until he's out of his pod, hit it with an EMP and grab him.'

'Alive?'

'I don't think anyone much cares but yes, if we can. And anyone with him of course.' He turned to me. 'If he shows up.'

That was my fear. That he wouldn't show. I tried to put on a brave face. 'He will, I'm sure. If ever anyone turns up in the wrong place and at the wrong time it's him.'

'Max, I don't know ...'

'Well, if the Time Police had managed to catch him then we wouldn't be having this conversation, would we?'

All my frustration and worry and disappointment – everything I hadn't realised I'd been bottling up came boiling to the surface.

'I mean why? Why does he always escape? How does he manage to get away? Every bloody time. He's in some ratty pod that barely functions and you ... we ... still can't catch him? Anyone accompanying him has a life expectancy of about four seconds and yet every time – every bloody time ... he outmanoeuvres and out-thinks us. How? As the Time Police, you have every resource known to man, a budget of billions, licence to do as you please, and you still can't catch him. Why can't you catch him?'

I stopped, quite aghast at my outburst. I hadn't meant to say any of that.

He took it quite well, really, in that he didn't shoot me.

I could see him bite back what he'd been going to say, take a deep breath and make an effort to answer calmly.

'I don't know, Max. I'm as frustrated as you are, but shouting doesn't help.'

I nodded, staring at my feet. He was right and now, not only was I still angry and frustrated, now I felt guilty as well.

'We *have* to get him, Matthew. We're hamstrung here until we do, and sooner or later someone high up is going to decide we're not worth the effort and expense and that'll be the end of us.'

'Well, let's hope it never comes to that.' He sighed. 'I will take this idea of yours to my boss and talk her into it. And you never know – it might work.'

'It will work,' I said stoutly. 'Just make sure you get him this time.'

'We'll give it our best shot,' he said. 'You know we will. Now I must go. I'll talk to you soon, I promise.'

I nodded. OK. 'Take care.'

'You too.'

He disappeared in the direction of his pod.

I turned away, meaning to take a stroll around the water garden and calm down a little. Fat chance. Because, as if I didn't have enough to think about already, yet another disaster was, even at this moment, hurtling towards St Mary's. As I rounded the first corner, there was Dottle, draped over a bench like a pre-Raphaelite painting and sobbing as if her heart would break.

Wrapped up as I was in my own problems, even I could see something was wrong here.

I stood helplessly. 'Lisa, whatever is the matter?'

There was a lot of snorting and sniffing and nose wiping – like me she's not a pretty crier, but the gist of it was that the idiot Halcombe was coming back. My heart sank. This was the last thing we needed.

'Oh, shit. When?'

She was vague as to the details and there was even more snorting and sniffing and nose wiping.

I plonked myself alongside her. This was not good news. We had Dottle well trained. Yes, she sat in on our briefings, but other than that she didn't trouble us and we didn't trouble her. The idiot Halcombe was another kettle of fish entirely.

On the other hand, maybe he'd learned his lesson, namely – don't mess with St Mary's or you'll spend a year being treated for the leprosy you don't have. Perhaps, once he was back, we could persuade him he'd picked up some kind of flesh-eating bacteria from someone – Markham seemed a safe bet – and pack him off for another six months of painful injections.

I said some of this to her and she gave a snot-filled snort which I chose to believe was a laugh, blew her nose and said, 'I'm sure you're right, but now that he's coming back to St Mary's I'm worried he's going to want his job back again.'

The idiot Halcombe – or *Mister* Halcombe as he inexplicably insisted on being called – was the result of our naughtiness a year or so ago, when Thirsk had finally made good their threat and installed a permanent presence here to keep an eye on us. Miss Dottle had been his slightly oppressed assistant. He'd muscled his way onto the Caernarfon assignment and it had all gone horribly wrong. Nothing too unusual there, but the bastard had pushed off and left them in trouble. He'd ordered a withdrawal and returned to the safety of St Mary's leaving half the team behind, including his own Miss Dottle, and

I'd had to go and get them. There had been a street riot and enormous quantities of pollocks. Yes, I know, the plural of pollock is pollock but the jokes are better if you say pollocks. Especially in the History Department where sophisticated humour and an elegant play on words don't ever happen.

Anyway, we're St Mary's and he'd contravened one of our most important rules – we never leave our people behind – so we'd had to get rid of him as soon as possible, and given that there was a ten trillion to one chance he'd managed to contract leprosy, we sent him off to the leprosy clinic with instructions for them not to bother sending him back.

Alas.

And the timing could not have been more unfortunate. We certainly didn't want the idiot muscling in on the Persepolis jump. This was an unfortunate coincidence that would have to be dealt with. I stared at my feet, lost in thought.

'He's bound to want his job back,' she said, not quite wringing out her hanky but close. 'And I've worked so hard. And I'm good at it. And ...' She stopped suddenly.

And she had the world's hugest crush on Peterson who really didn't help himself by smiling kindly at her whenever she passed. I wasn't too sure of their relationship status and she did seem content to worship him from afar – something the rest of St Mary's would do well to emulate, he always said – but yes, she was right. Halcombe would want his job back and she would almost certainly return to the thankless task of many women – that of being assistant to an idiot.

I really didn't know what to say to her. Perhaps, given her hopeless passion for Peterson, it would be better for her to move on. Forget him and build a life somewhere else. I don't know. My own life is frequently so tangled that I never really feel I'm a suitable person to advise others. And, it has often been pointed out to me, I'm not really a role model for distressed young women. Or distressed young men. Or anyone, actually.

I could see she was in need of a little gentle sympathy and support, however, so I clapped her on the shoulder, told her to buck up Buttercup, and took her in for some tea.

He arrived two days later. Earlier than Dottle had thought he would. Much earlier than Dr Bairstow had bargained for. And worst of all, before we'd got Persepolis out of the way.

I watched him pull into the car park and unload his suitcases. He would need to be got rid of. By lawful means preferably, but if that didn't work …

Somewhere in the depths of St Mary's, a handbell pealed and a voice intoned, 'Unclean ... unclean …'

He made his presence felt almost immediately by falling foul of Psycho Psykes.

Hitting the ground running, and probably wanting to avoid a repeat of his one and only catastrophic assignment he thought he'd instigate a series of risk assessments and method statements. It did not go well.

We were all in the Hall working away. There were files and whiteboards everywhere. There were odd bits of paper pinned to the walls. A couple of data stacks twirled in digital limbo. We had Mrs Enderby with us trying to sort out what we were to wear in Persepolis. Bashford was trying, unsuccessfully, to measure his own inside leg and Sykes was watching him without pity.

'Fifty-two inches,' he announced, so God knows where he'd had his tape measure.

Mrs Enderby ignored him, stared appraisingly at me for a moment and then said, 'I understand you're expecting to be even more than usually active on this assignment, so I've cheated a little, Max. We've run you up a chiton in the Doric style. More room for movement.'

I nodded. Not a bad idea. The Doric tunic was much more modest and less drapey. And, importantly, it was held together considerably more securely than by just a pin at one shoulder, which was all very well if your day consisted of lounging around eating grapes, but was less useful if you were dodging drunken soldiers, burning buildings, and the like.

Legend says that a long time ago in Ancient Greece, the messenger bringing the sad news of their husbands' deaths in some battle or other had been set upon by the grieving widows, who had stabbed him to death with their own shoulder pins. Being a messenger in ancient times was a hazardous occupation – presumably giving rise to the saying, 'Don't shoot the messenger.' Anyway, the authorities, casting a wary eye on pin-wielding widows had henceforth forbidden women to fasten their chitons with pins so the Doric chiton was an altogether sturdier garment. Which was good for me – my chiton was almost a straight tunic and very easy to move around in.

That settled, I turned back to the others who were discussing whether to dress as contemporaries or go in full fire-fighting gear. Clerk was arguing that those who would be concentrating on Alexander could dress in contemporary costumes while only those actually attempting to get into the Treasury would need fire suits. We'd reached the point where everyone was trying to work out the difference between flammable and inflammable and the debate was vigorous because no one knew the answer – when the idiot Halcombe turned up with his latest recipe for catastrophe.

I was talking to Miss Dottle when she peered over my shoulder and said quietly, 'Max, he's coming.'

I turned and the idiot Halcombe was coming down the stairs, scratchpad in hand.

'May I have your attention, please?'

Somewhere at the very back of the Hall, the handbell rang again and an anonymous voice called, 'Unclean ... unclean ...'

Wisely, Halcombe ignored it.

'I have been carrying out a series of risk assessments which, while they will radically alter the way we operate, will, I think you will agree, result in a much higher success rate than this establishment has hitherto experienced.'

'You mean we stick our noses out of the door and then run for home in case it starts to rain?' suggested Clerk, and someone laughed. It had been Clerk's assignment the idiot Halcombe had buggered up and he obviously hadn't either forgotten or forgiven.

'Not precisely,' countered Halcombe. 'But certainly more time will be spent assessing the situation in advance, rather than just bursting out of the pod and immediately finding ourselves in difficulties.'

'We?' said Clerk, obviously determined not to let it go. 'Ourselves? You're surely not proposing to include yourself in our merry little jaunts?'

Halcombe ignored him and soldiered on. 'Perhaps the most important of our new routines will be the exclusion of women on certain assignments.'

The temperature dropped. Like a stone. Everything stopped. Even the walls leaned in to listen. No one said a word.

The idiot didn't even notice. I started to work my way down the hall because I might have to save a life in a minute.

'I'm sorry?' said Sykes, sweetly. 'My tiny female brain was unable to process your last statement.'

Reaching the front, I nudged her into silence. 'Are you saying the type of assignment will determine the gender of those carrying it out?'

'Exactly,' he beamed.

I persevered. It wasn't yet too late for him. 'Are you absolutely certain this is a course you want to pursue?'

'I am. I think you will agree that there are some areas where the presence of women is inappropriate. Battlefields for instance. No one can deny the presence of a female at say, Bannockburn, would not only be distracting and dangerous, but historically inaccurate as well. My proposal is that female historians confine themselves to ... social and domestic issues ... which would free up male historians to concentrate on the more important aspects of history.'

'You mean History,' said Sykes.

'Idiot can't even get that right,' muttered Clerk.

'What is he talking about?' whispered Prentiss to me.

'I'm not sure,' I said, 'but I think he's saying it's a man's world.'

She looked around at Mrs Mack, Mrs Enderby, Miss Lee, Miss Lingoss, Mrs Partridge, Miss Sykes and Miss North. None of whom should be crossed even for a brief second. 'When did that happen?'

'Apparently, about thirty seconds ago.'

'Oh, wow,' said Sykes in excitement. 'Does this mean I'm a plucky little woman struggling to make her way in a man's world. I've always wanted to be a plucky little woman struggling to make her way in a man's world. Please. Pleeeaaaaase.'

'Stop whining,' I said. 'Plucky little women never whine.'

Miss North made a sound indicating that, actually, far from struggling in a man's world, men frequently struggled in hers.

'No, he's made a very good point,' said Bashford provocatively. 'Women are just vessels, you know.'

'That's very true,' said Sykes, smiling angelically at him. 'I myself am a seventeen-thousand-ton Dreadnought class battleship with enough firepower to destroy a medium-sized city.'

Well, no one was going to argue with that.

Halcombe stood his ground and prepared to argue his point. 'I'm simply saying ...' he said.

'I wouldn't,' said Peterson, gently taking his arm. 'I really wouldn't.'

'What are you doing?'

'Taking you to Dr Stone to discuss your apparent death wish.'

He pulled his arm away angrily and stamped back up the stairs. We watched him make his way around the gallery.

'Like a disdainful flamingo with a stick up its arse,' said Markham, quoting someone whose identity escapes me for the moment.

Halcombe's office door slammed.

82

'He's got to go,' said Markham to me, and I would have agreed except that as I opened my mouth, a terrible scream echoed around the building.

I suppose in normal places of employment a terrible scream echoing around the building would produce some sort of reaction. At the very least heads would lift. Someone might possibly say, 'Did you hear that?' and someone else might say, 'I think so,' and there would be vague looking around, as if the reason for the terrible scream would helpfully waft down the staircase and make itself known.

This being St Mary's, none of that happened. Terrible screams are ten a penny here and could range from Markham shutting his finger in a door – you'd think he'd lost his entire arm – to Professor Rapson drinking from a beaker subsequently discovered to be clearly marked with a skull and crossbones and bearing the legend "*Do Not Drink – Deadly Poison*". Just to be clear, on that occasion the scream emanated from his panicking staff, not the professor himself, who, throughout the entire stomach-pumping process maintained his traditional air of slight bewilderment at all the fuss.

Anyway, back to the current crisis – the terrible scream and its dying echoes. St Mary's continued with its normal working day because, quite honestly, if we stopped working for every terrible scream and its dying echoes we'd never get any work done at all. Every organisation has its weak link, however. A door opened and the idiot Halcombe appeared again, this time enquiring who was making that ridiculous noise.

Every person in sight immediately became completely immersed in what they were doing. I sighed. If only they could display the same level of dedicated focus during a normal working day. Given that all I could see was the back of everyone else's heads, any response was obviously up to me.

'No idea,' I said. 'But it seems to have stopped now,' and tried to slide past him to return to the safety of my own office.

Easier said than done. Our housekeeper, the majestic Mrs Midgeley, was descending the stairs, as unstoppable as a glacier on its way to the sea to mate with the icebergs. Actually, I don't know what put that picture in my head but I really wished it hadn't.

We don't see a lot of her. She prefers, she says, to carry out her duties behind the scenes and not, in any way, associate herself with the madness for which St Mary's is apparently legendary.

I remember crossing my fingers as she approached and hoping I was not her ultimate destination. I didn't see how she could possibly want me. Yes, Leon *had* put his foot through a sheet a couple of weeks ago, but he was a firm favourite of hers and she'd let him off with no more than a finger wagging as he stood before her, head bowed in contrition. What she could possibly want with me was a mystery.

She shouldered aside the idiot Halcombe as if he didn't exist – I should be that lucky – and deposited a small pile of towels on the table in front of me and demanded to know, in a voice which rang from one end of the Hall to the other, what was the meaning of this.

I stared, baffled, first at the small pile of six clean white hand towels, and then pathetically around the Hall, seeking assistance from someone. Anyone.

Markham folded his arms and grinned at me. Peterson was apparently engrossed in a file with Miss Dottle and

84

too busy to notice what was going on, and there was no sign of Leon anywhere. You have to ask yourself what is the point of being married if your husband is too busy repairing a pod to rescue his wife from an enraged towel-bearing housekeeper.

'I'm sorry, Mrs Midgeley, I don't understand. Is there a problem with the towels?'

Her not unsubstantial bosom heaved with passion. 'Not the towels, no.'

'Well, what then?'

She peeled back the top four layers to reveal what looked like a puddle of furry raspberry jam with legs.

St Mary's crowded round.

'Oh yuk.'

'What is it?'

Miss Dottle pushed her way through the crowd.

'Oh no – it's Hammy.'

'Hammy?'

'Hamlet'.

I stared accusingly across at Markham who had once appeared in a 17th-century production of Hamlet. He'd understudied Shakespeare after the great man had set fire to himself. On the face of it, however, Markham seemed as baffled as I was.

I said cautiously, 'Hamlet?'

'My hamster.'

We're not allowed pets. Except for Mrs Mack's beloved Vortigern, the kitchen cat, of course. And Angus the chicken. And Markham from Security. And now it would appear Miss Dottle had a hamster. *Had* had a hamster.

'But what,' demanded Mrs Midgeley, not one to lose sight of her target, 'was a hamster doing in my airing cupboard in the first place?'

Dottle sniffed. 'Well, I woke up one morning and he was stretched out in the bottom of his little cage and I thought he was dead.' She sniffed again. 'And I was taking him out to the garden to bury him when I met Professor Rapson.'

She paused to rifle her pockets for a handkerchief.

I sighed and turned to Miss Lingoss. Today's hair was metallic bronze. She looked like a statue of the goddess Athena. 'My compliments to Professor Rapson. Could he spare me a moment please?'

'Righty-ho.' She was gone in a flash, appearing a moment later with the professor who was absent-mindedly patting his pockets for his glasses.

'On your head, Professor,' said Miss Lingoss kindly.

'Really? Oh, so they are. Thank you, my dear.' He hooked them over his ears and smiled at me. 'Good afternoon, Max. What can I do for you?'

'Good afternoon, Professor. I wonder if you could shed any light on this?'

I flipped back the towels as I spoke.

'Oh, my goodness. Is that Hammy?'

I don't know how many dead hamsters he thought there would be in our airing cupboard.

Miss Dottle nodded wetly.

'Why is he so flat?'

Miss Dottle burst into tears and so I turned to the professor for enlightenment.

'Well, I met Miss Dottle and she was very upset because she thought her hamster was dead. As it happens,

86

I had a hamster as a small boy and the same thing happened to me.'

'They thought you were dead?' said Markham, deliberately muddying the issue.

'No, no,' he said seriously. 'I thought my hamster had died but she hadn't. She was just sleeping.'

I stared at him. Yes, all right – you see it written on tombstones all the time – "Not dead. Just sleeping" – but I had no idea that saying originated with hamsters. Tombstone images crashed into my mind. I was sure the day was fast approaching when I was going to need psychiatric help.

'You see,' he said, peering at me over his spectacles, 'hamsters hibernate, Max. If the temperature drops off, then so do they. Apparently, many a hamster has been prematurely interred, as I told Miss Dottle and, obviously, we didn't want that, did we? So I suggested she pop him somewhere warm and see if he woke up. So we put him in the airing cupboard.'

Mrs Midgeley's bosom reared up again, to the peril of all. 'And when exactly did this happen?'

'Last week.'

A lesser woman would have staggered. 'I've had a dead hamster in my fresh linen for a *week*?'

Dottle gulped and nodded.

Trying to keep my voice steady, I said, 'Exactly how long should Hammy's ... period of recovery have taken, Professor?'

'Oh, my dear Miss Dottle, I'm so sorry. I'm afraid there's been a little bit of a misunderstanding. Thirty to forty-five minutes would probably have been sufficient.'

Our heat-seeking housekeeper was homing in again. 'You left a dead hamster in my fresh linen for a *week*?'

Atherton, who's a nice boy, offered her a glass of water.

'No,' said Dottle, still distressed. 'I went to get him out an hour later but he wasn't there. I thought either he'd woken up and run away or ...' she gulped '... he'd died and been taken away.'

I was trying not to laugh. I could just see Dottle peeking into the airing cupboard and assuming Hammy had been wafted up to hamster heaven.

In reality, of course, someone had just unknowingly dumped a load of towels on top of him and if he hadn't been dead before – sensitive readers might want to go with that assumption – he had certainly been dead afterwards. Probably best not to mention that. And certainly not to Miss Dottle who was weeping like the Trevi fountain.

The solution was to take her away for a cup of tea, grovel to Mrs Midgely, remove poor Hammy from his white, fluffy sepulchre, and carry on with our working day so, obviously, this was the point at which Malcolm Halcombe decided to showcase his management skills.

Glaring around, he ordered everyone back to work, including Mrs Midgeley – I tell you, this bloke was living permanently in the shadow of death. Leprosy would have been nothing to this – and to demonstrate his mastery of the situation, demanded Miss Dottle fetch him the file on something or other.

She blew her long pink nose – I noticed suddenly she'd gone back to the droopy cardigans again – and went to scuttle off, only to be prevented by Peterson, the world's kindest man, who said he was awfully sorry, but Miss Dottle was scheduled for a meeting with him which should, in fact, have started some ten minutes ago and was she ready?

She nodded and he took her away for a damp half hour of tea and tears.

Mrs Midgeley shot the idiot Halcombe a look which sadly failed to incinerate him on the spot, and departed with her towels. The rest of us ignored him and after a minute he drifted off whence he came.

I said to Markham, 'You're right. He's got to go.'

Obviously, we tried to carry on as normal. When I say normal, you know what I mean. But the bloke was everywhere. You couldn't have a private conversation without him turning up at your elbow demanding to know what was the subject under discussion. We took to meeting in my office. Rosie Lee would lock the door and pull down the blind and we would hold the meeting in whispers.

We tried everything to get rid of him. We ignored him. We were downright rude to him. Nothing seemed to have any effect.

Two days later there was an all-staff briefing from Dr Bairstow. As if I didn't have enough to do preparing for Persepolis, liaising with Thirsk over the crown, not worrying about Leon or Matthew, and dodging the idiot Halcombe. I kid you not, some days I barely sat down.

I was in the front row with Peterson on one side and Markham on the other, all of us wearing expressions of rapt enthusiasm. Professor Rapson and Dr Dowson were on the end. Our days of sitting at the back and playing Battleships were long gone.

Dr Bairstow opened the briefing.

'I would like, officially, to welcome Mr Halcombe, who returned to this unit a few days ago after a long absence.'

He paused. Traditionally there should have been a round of polite applause. After a moment, when it became clear that, on this occasion, tradition was being ignored, he continued.

'In a not-unrelated item, I should make it clear that from this moment onwards, the practice of walking in front of Mr Halcombe, ringing a handbell and shouting "Unclean, unclean," is to cease forthwith. Have I made myself clear?'

St Mary's swallowed its disappointment and nodded.

I sat back in my chair and watched the dust dancing in the sunlight shafting through the big glass lantern above Dr Bairstow's head. I usually go on to describe how it picked out the highlights in his hair but those days were gone as well. Along with most of his hair, although the little bit around the back was hanging on for grim death.

Peterson nudged me and I lurched back to the here and now.

'... and so,' Dr Bairstow was saying, 'in the light of this recent legislation, it is necessary for you all to present proof of life. In other words, for bureaucratic purposes at least, you need to prove you are not dead.'

Someone somewhere snorted and tried to turn it into a cough.

'Normally,' he continued, 'I would simply request you to present yourselves before me in my office where I could use my own skill and judgement to decide your existential status, but Mrs Partridge informs me that, as with everything government related, things are not that simple. You will, therefore, be required to complete the forms she will distribute at the end of this session and return them to her by 10:00 tomorrow.'

I nodded. I could do that. Easy-peasy.

He raised his voice slightly. 'Together with some form of photographic evidence. I shall then compare photograph to document, keep my inevitable reflections to myself, sign and stamp where appropriate, and forward to the relevant government department where it will be lost, misfiled, challenged, queried, denied, eaten by their computer, lost again, and finally returned to me in three or four years, by which time, no doubt, most of you will have achieved your apparent ambition to end your lives in a flamboyant and spectacular manner, and I shall have to begin again.'

I don't know why he was looking at me, but I beamed anyway, just to reassure him that none of the above was anything to do with me and, for some reason, he didn't look reassured at all.

Markham raised his hand. 'Photographic evidence, sir?'

'Yes, anything will do. Driving licence ...'

Bollocks – by popular demand, I'd cut mine up. There had been a bit of a celebration afterwards.

'Passport ...'

Bollocks – I didn't have one of those, either.

'What about our St Mary's ID cards?' I said hopefully.

'No. Only an official government document is eligible.'

'But I work for the government.'

'Yes, but they don't know that.'

All around me, I could hear the buzz of conversation and much rifling of wallets.

I raised my hand again. 'Would a marriage certificate do, sir?'

He sighed. 'Is there a photograph attached?'

'I could enclose one of me and Leon cutting the cake.'

He stared at me coldly. 'No.'

'Then I might have a problem, sir.'

Several other people said, 'Me too.'

We're St Mary's. Our lives are full of files and forms and paperwork of some kind or another. We see no reason to burden ourselves with even more of it in our private lives.

The buzzing rose to a clamour.

Dr Bairstow held up his hand. 'Mrs Partridge has informed me that those of you unable to comply can get around this obstacle by presenting any photographic image no more than six months old.'

I was surprised the sighs of relief didn't bowl him over but, as usual, he'd left the kicker right to the end.

'These images must be presented to Mr Halcombe, who will, if he feels like it, countersign and date them, thus ensuring their validity.'

Another of the Boss's brilliant moves. Presenting the correct paperwork for anything is always a challenge for St Mary's and when you add photographs as well ... and to a stickler like Halcombe ... the ensuing struggles would keep both him and us occupied for weeks.

I caught Dr Bairstow's eye and grinned. He ignored me.

'And if he doesn't feel like it?' enquired Markham, cautiously, obviously seeing difficulties ahead. Many of the handbell ringers had come from his section.

'Then I suppose you will have to reconcile yourselves to eking out the remainder of your lives in a state of official non-existence. As far as the government is concerned, you will be dead. I'm sure that many of you would be happier if things were the other way around but, as we so frequently discover, this is not a perfect world.'

'Well, that's not so bad,' said Cox. 'I could quite happily live a life of official non-existence.'

Dr Bairstow smiled thinly. 'I should perhaps advise you now that a state of official non-existence will lead to a corresponding state of official non-existence regarding your salary. While, as director of this unit, I welcome and applaud the thought of so drastically reducing the wages bill, as a caring human being,' – he paused but no one seemed willing to challenge him on that point – 'I advise you to approach Mr Halcombe, offer him whatever inducements you feel appropriate, and get it done, Mr Cox.'

He scowled. 'Yes, sir.'

Not that the idiot Halcombe looked any happier at the thought of every member of St Mary's trudging through his door armed with incorrectly completed paperwork, inappropriate photographs and a ton of attitude.

'Moving on. Professor Rapson informs me that what I believe has become known as The Great Battering Ram Experiment will take place this afternoon after lunch. All personnel wishing to participate are to assemble behind the stables at 15:00 hours. I have no doubt that most of you will wish to do so, thus rendering much of what I have said concerning proof of life irrelevant. More prudent members of staff are advised to remain inside, don protective clothing, and stay well away from the windows. Are there any questions?'

We were already getting our stuff together, prior to going back to work. There were never any questions. And then a voice said, 'Actually there is just one thing ...'

The idiot Halcombe was on his feet. 'While we're on the subject of paperwork, I wonder if I might have a word?'

'Of course,' said Dr Bairstow pleasantly, limped down the stairs and seated himself alongside Peterson.

Halcombe took his place on the half landing, fussing with various sheets of paper. Finding what he needed, he held up a blue flimsy. 'What is this?'

We peered. My heart sank. It was blue so it had originated from the History Department. The large blob of chicken shit in the top right-hand corner designated it as one of Mr Bashford's efforts.

'Well,' I said, standing up and taking it off him, 'it looks to me like Mr Bashford's report on the 1536 assignment. Bashford, you don't spell "caparisoned" like that. Learn to use the spell check.'

'Not that. This.'

I peered artistically then took out my specs, carefully wiped off the worst of the greasy fingerprints and peered again. He was pointing at the blob of chicken shit. Obviously, Angus had assisted Bashford with his report.

'I've no idea. Did you sick up something while you were reading it – because that has happened.'

'It's chicken excrement,' he said, outraged.

'No,' I said, astonished. 'Is it? How on earth did that happen? Were you reading it in a chicken coop?'

'Or in the farm down the road?' said Sykes

'Or that dreadful battery place on the other side of Rushford?' enquired Mrs Mack. 'You shouldn't have anything to do with them. We only have free range here.'

A dozen other voices piped up, all apparently eager to solve the mystery of the unexplained chicken shit. The briefing began to deteriorate somewhat.

I think we might have got away with it except that, with the lack of self-preservation for which all of St Mary's is so renowned, Angus chose this moment to wander down the stairs, presumably on her way from Bashford's wardrobe to the stables where she would enjoy luncheon.

Well, I say 'wander', but she hasn't quite got the hang of stairs. The first two or three were fine, as she jumped inelegantly from step to step but, as usual, gravity was not her friend and she tumbled the last half dozen steps, feathery arse over plumy tip, to land with a faint squawk at the bottom.

No one moved.

I cast an anxious glance at Dr Bairstow, but he appeared to be immersed in the file Peterson had opened and, unfortunately, neither seemed aware of circumstances around them.

Halcombe pointed a finger. 'What is that?'

'What's what?' enquired Markham, staking his claim to be first in the ensuing Halcombe-mocking programme. 'Are we still talking about your little pile of poo?'

'That!' He pointed at Angus who had picked herself up, smoothed her ruffled feathers, crooned her love to Bashford and was now sashaying down the Hall en route to the kitchen where she could bum a tasty treat from someone, give Vortigern a serious beaking, and make her way to the stables for a substantial repast.

'What,' said Markham, cleverly peering at the spot where Angus had last been.

'That. That chicken.'

St Mary's began to look up, down, around, in, out, left, right and inventing several new directions that had yet to be named. People began to look under chairs, pat their pockets …

'Have you got the invisible chicken?'

'No, I thought you had the invisible chicken.'

'I had the invisible chicken yesterday. It's your turn today.'

People began to wander vaguely around calling, 'Here, chicken. Here, chickie chickie.'

The briefing appeared to be descending into noisy chaos.

Dr Bairstow closed his file with a snap and stood up. 'Enough.'

The noise subsided immediately.

Unwisely, Halcombe opened his mouth to have another go.

Dr Bairstow began to climb the stairs, pausing long enough to pat his arm gently. 'I'd leave it there if I were you, there's a good chap.' And continued on his way.

With a face of thunder, the idiot Halcombe returned to his office.

Peterson turned to me. 'He's got to go.'

I had a lovely lunch with Leon. We sat by the windows at one of the quiet tables and just for once no one disturbed us. We chatted about Matthew and his impending visit – things we could do together and so on. I enquired whether he would be participating in the professor's little soirée that afternoon and he laughed. 'I'm infirm, not insane. I shall visit Ian this afternoon and we'll watch from the safety of Sick Bay. From where, of course, we'll have a first-class view of all the casualties being carted in.'

The Professor Rapson's Great Battering Ram Experiment – or The Great Professor Rapson's Battering Ram Experiment as he persisted in referring to it – is actually a bit of a misnomer because it wasn't all Professor Rapson's show. At least 50 per cent of it could be laid at Dr Dowson's door and the whole thing was the result of a long running … debate seems too sensible a word for some of the really quite energetic discussions they'd had over the years. Anyway, the whole thing had come to a head during a recent showing of *The Lord of the Rings* trilogy in the Hall a couple of weeks ago.

Because of the Clive Ronan threat, we're not allowed out much these days – to the endless relief of the outside world, says Dr Bairstow – so we have to amuse ourselves. Hence Dr Bairstow giving permission for the battering ram thing this afternoon. Anyway, every other week or so we have a big cinema experience in the Hall, with popcorn and hotdogs and so on. We'd dragged out the chairs, put up our feet and had a *LOTR* marathon. Things had been fairly sedate – for us – until the Battle of Minas Tirith and the appearance of Grond, the battering ram, and the old argument had surfaced again. There had been shouting and arm-waving, a lot of it considerably more dramatic than what was happening on screen. And with fewer orcs, too. Unless you count the Security Section, in which case delete that last sentence.

The argument was this. Modern movies and holos always show the castle gates opening inwards – thus rendering themselves vulnerable to battering rams and the like. Professor Rapson's longstanding and dearly held theory was that all gates opened outwards. Like lock gates, he says, so the pressure from the water or the force from the battering ram simply pushes them even more tightly closed. Dr Dowson was vigorous in his disagreement, although whether that was from conviction or just because he always opposed everything the professor said was unknown.

Anyway, as Dr Bairstow had said, they were about to test their theories on our old barn. No, I know it's not a castle, but it was a substantial structure and possessed two very large, outward-opening wooden doors. According to Miss Lingoss, who had been enthusiastically bending my ear about this for days, it would be an ideal opportunity for the professor to test his theory.

I refrained from pointing out that the last time we'd tested one of the professor's theories we'd had to take cover under the furniture, caused massive devastation to a number of rocks, and very nearly killed a leading member of the British film industry. It had been quite a lively afternoon.

I had mixed feelings about this one. Not the experiment itself – I had a small wager with Peterson that the doors would hold. He was maintaining they wouldn't – but I hadn't been near the barn for some time. Not since Isabella Barclay had shot me there and I'd nearly died. They say that smell is the most evocative of the senses and the familiar smells of wood, earth, oil and straw brought back memories I didn't want to relive, so I made sure I kept my distance. Today, I was planning to make sure everyone kept their distance. When it came to this sort of thing, both Professor Rapson and Doctor Dowson had form.

Under the professor's careful direction, R&D had built a sturdy wooden frame from which, on some hefty-looking chains, was suspended a carefully shaped tree trunk, finished with a pointed metal cap. Someone had painted 'Grond' along the side in blood red paint.

I could see Lingoss trotting around checking various bits and pieces and I thought how much Matthew would have enjoyed this, which brought Leon to mind. I turned and stared back at St Mary's. I was pretty sure I could see Leon and Ian sitting at an upstairs window. I waved and turned back to this afternoon's bone of contention.

They'd mounted whole thing on modern wheels because the point of the experiment was to establish the ram's effectiveness, not its mobility. Twenty or so people, ten to a side, were heaving the contraption across the grass towards the barn. While one or two of them had remained faithful to the medieval aspect of the experiment, wearing chainmail and moderately accurate helmets, the vast majority had gone for the orc look, sporting leather and worryingly realistic warts, scars and metal prosthetics. Sauron would have enlisted them on the spot.

Reaching what the professor referred to as the optimum ramming position – a phrase wilfully misinterpreted by most of the Security Section who had their own inaccurate ideas as to ramming and the optimum positions to be assumed for the purposes of – they ground to a halt – or Grond to a halt, if you like – and stood awaiting further instructions.

Step forward that misguided missile, Mr Bashford, bright and alert for once, who had blagged himself a leading role in the proceedings by acquiring a drum nearly as big as he was and booming out the beat. He had dressed for the occasion by removing his upper garments to grant an unimpressed St Mary's a glimpse of his spindly physique. He looked like a very malnourished Hulk. His beloved Angus perched nearby. I assumed her function was that of mascot. Leon, had he been here, would have said her function was that of Most Intelligent Person Present. She was observing the proceedings with bright-eyed interest and her resemblance to Sykes was quite unnerving, although it would be a brave man who pointed that out to any one of that interesting trio.

For the record, no one had painted themselves blue. As the government is so fond of saying at the press conferences called in the wake of its latest catastrophes – lessons had been learned.

Having achieved optimum ramming position, our stalwart volunteers threw their weight against the chains, chanting, 'Grond. Grond. Grond.' I despair sometimes.

Slowly at first, but with increasingly long swings the tree trunk began to move backwards and forwards until it was scything through the air like something out of Edgar Allan Poe, building up an unstoppable momentum.

'Impressive,' I said to Peterson.

'Disturbingly similar to "The Pit and the Pendulum", isn't it? There will be tears before bedtime.'

'There always are,' I said, 'but today, none of them will be ours. Hang on – this next swing should do it.'

The next swing did do it.

Urged on by worryingly realistic orc war cries and drum beats, the trunk swung forwards one last time, impacting the barn doors with a massive crash.

The doors fragmented into a million flying pieces. Together with the surrounding door frames. And the walls. And the roof. Slowly, deafeningly and with surprising dignity, the entire bloody barn fell down. Massive amounts of dust, chaff and God-knows-what mushroomed into the air, enveloping us all.

'Well,' said Peterson, coughing. 'What do you know? It appears we *can* hit a barn door, after all.'

My first thought was shit – what was I going to tell Dr Bairstow, but as it turned out, destroying the barn was the least of our problems. And there aren't many establishments where you can say that.

I fought my way out of a suffocating cloud of pulverised ex-barn just as Markham, staring over my shoulder, shouted, 'Code Red. Security Section to me. On the double,' and someone else shouted 'Behind you, Max.'

A familiar strong wind stirred my hair.

I turned around, expecting the worst.

I got it.

A twelve-foot-high teapot was standing on the South Lawn.

Again.

9

I stood staring with my mouth open but fortunately, Markham is quite well equipped to deal with this sort of thing. In only a moment, half the Security Section was surrounding the teapot and the other half was racing away for weapons. Although I was pretty sure they wouldn't be needed. I knew who this was. Adrian and Mikey were back.

We'd met them a little while ago when they'd turned up at St Mary's to visit us as if we were some sort of historical curiosity. Or, as Peterson had said afterwards, a major historical event in contemporary time. Anyway, they're a couple of renegade teenagers – geniuses the pair of them – fleeing up and down time in a homemade pod and getting themselves into all sorts of trouble. Their pod – and feel free to disbelieve me – is teapot-shaped, about twelve feet high, amateurishly sprayed in what are supposed to be woodland camouflage colours, and with a hand-painted Union Jack on the side. They are constantly pursued by the Time Police who will shoot them dead if they ever catch them.

Dr Bairstow, greatly taken with the awe and reverence with which Adrian and Mikey had regarded him, had allowed us to restock their pod, mend the radiation leak that was slowly killing them and offered them sanctuary in the future should they ever need it. It looked as if that day had come.

As if in confirmation of this thought, the hatch was thrown open and Adrian's head appeared. He was crying.

'Help. Please help. It's Mikey. Help us.'

Dieter pushed his way through the ring of security guards. 'Toss down your ladder.'

Their heavy wooden ladder thudded to the ground. Dieter climbed up and peered inside their pod, shouted, 'Dr Stone – we have a medical emergency here.' And climbed back down again.

Dr Stone, who'd been with us long enough to know he should turn up at one of Professor Rapson's little jaunts into Practical History with a fully equipped medical team, shot up the ladder and disappeared down into the pod.

Dr Bairstow appeared at my elbow. 'What time is it, Dr Maxwell?'

'Just gone half past three, sir.'

'That pod must be out of here by five at the very latest.'

'Understood, sir.'

Adrian and Mikey were never more than two hours ahead of their pursuers. The Time Police couldn't catch them, but Adrian and Mikey couldn't throw them off either. It was a kind of dreadful stalemate that Dr Bairstow had always suspected would end badly and it would appear that, today, it had.

Mikey was being lifted from the teapot and carefully lowered down the ladder. There was a very great deal of blood, all of it fresh. Adrian, following on their heels, was white-faced and panicking. My heart went out to him. He was so young. And Mikey was even younger.

They laid her on the grass while Dr Stone and the medical team gathered round. Someone organised a stretcher comprising broken bits of barn and an orc cloak and a few minutes later they were all heading towards Sick Bay at top speed, passing Leon on the way.

He hobbled towards us at the best speed he could muster. 'Is this it?'

I remembered he hadn't met our lovable scamps before.

I nodded. 'Leon, we need to get this pod out of here. The Time Police are less than two hours behind and they're not a nice bunch.'

They weren't. Matthew Ellis is the acceptable face of the Time Police. Most of the rest of them are a bunch of homicidal thugs with the IQ of earwax.

Dieter was already disappearing into the teapot. He looked over his shoulder. 'Leon, can you make it up here?'

'I can,' he said, handing me his stick.

I knew better than to say, 'Are you sure?' or, 'Be careful,' contenting myself with, 'Try not to break anything.'

He grinned at me, suddenly looking much younger than he had in ages. And people think he's the respectable one in our marriage.

Dr Bairstow intervened. 'Dr Peterson, I would like you to take care of things at this end. Dr Maxwell, see to our young friends, if you please.'

We both said, 'Yes, sir,' and I set off for Sick Bay.

Adrian was pacing up and down. Up and down. Up and down. Wringing his hands. I didn't know people really did that. Cox and Evans were with him. They were saving their legs by sitting down and watching him pace up and down. Not that Adrian was any threat to anyone at this precise moment.

'Where's Mikey?'

They nodded towards a door with a red light over. 'Prepping for surgery.'

Adrian surged towards me, his long coat flapping around him. 'Dr Maxwell, you have to ... they shot her. They shot Mikey.'

'We'll talk about that later,' I said gently. 'Right now, we're a little preoccupied with saving you both from our friends in the Time Police. Mikey's getting the best treatment there is and we're hiding your pod. All of us are prepared to lie like stink to the Time Police, so there really is nothing to worry about. Now, I need one or two things from you. Firstly, do they know Mikey's a girl?'

'I don't know. It's never come up.'

Evans was grinning at me.

'Right, you two ...' I turned to our trusty security guards. 'I'm taking Adrian with me. The Time Police will be here soon and I need the Security Section to buy me time up here. Don't tell me how you're going to do it.'

I called up Markham. 'I'm going to need you to delay the Time Police for as long as possible.'

'Already on it.'

'Thank you. Mr Dieter?'

'Busy, Max.'

'How long?'

'There's some damage here. Talk later.' He closed the link.

I left them to it.

'Dr Peterson?'

'Everything fine here, Max. A lot of barn-related trauma but all minor injuries.'

105

'What sort of minor injuries?'

'The sort you get when an old barn falls on you.'

'Nothing serious? At all?'

'Not really. Even Bashford's fine.'

'Good God. Are you sure?'

'I know. Sykes reckons he can't have been present when the barn collapsed and only joined us afterwards. The thing is, there's a big patch of blood on the grass where we got Mikey out.'

'Then we need a number of serious casualties to account for all the blood.'

'And you will have them. Step forward, Mr Bashford.'

I said, 'Tim ...?'

'And Mr Swanson, sir, if you would be so good.'

'Tim, don't tell me what you're going to do.'

'Wasn't going to,' he said cheerfully. 'Talk to you later.'

I closed the link and said to Adrian, 'Come with me if you want to live.'

And Markham thinks I don't get the cultural references.

The Time Police were seven minutes late. Peterson tutted. 'Couldn't organise a piss up in a brewery.'

'Don't forget to tell them that. Especially while they're holding their guns.'

Dr Bairstow was nowhere to be seen. He tends to stay back during this sort of thing. I like to think it's so he can bail us out afterwards, although sometimes I have my doubts.

I was back outside at the scene of our recent barn catastrophe. When I'd left, there'd been a very large pile of dusty wood, a lot of coughing and recrimination, and one or two minor casualties. I was now present in a war zone.

The surely much too large to be just our barn heap of wood was partly on fire. Smoke drifted listlessly across a scene of complete devastation. Broken people lay everywhere. Miss Lingoss, Mr Atherton and Mr Lindstrom were half buried under the debris. Miss Lingoss was artistically shrieking with pain. Half her face was smothered in blood. Atherton was ominously white and silent. Miss Sykes was weeping piteously over a felled Bashford who was pumping blood into the ground at an alarming rate.

'If they don't get a move on we're going to run out of blood,' said Peterson, casting nervous glances over his shoulder.

'Dear God ...' I said, appalled at the carnage.

He grinned. 'Good, isn't it. Professor Rapson and Mr Swanson got the casualty make-up out. From our disaster drills. We have broken limbs, fractured skulls, severed arteries, massive internal trauma – the lot. What's one casualty amongst so many?'

A trail of injured and moaning people were being helped to their feet and slowly making their way towards Sick Bay.

And here they came ...

A dramatically large black pod had materialised outside Hawking. The door opened and they poured out. Four of them as usual. I watched them approach, guns at the ready.

I whispered to Peterson, 'I gather Leon and Dieter got the pod away?'

'They did.'

'Don't tell me where.'

'Don't know where.'

'Good.'

'Adrian?'

'With Mrs Enderby.'

He blinked. 'O ... K ...' He turned back to the carnage around us. 'They're here, everyone. Let's go.' He began to stride about, barking orders, a shining example of a Deputy Director in complete control. It was quite impressive if I do say so myself. 'Be careful with those timbers, you don't want to make things any worse. Get those people to Sick Bay. Report to Nurse Hunter. Dr Stone is in surgery. Field medics to Mr Bashford and ...'

'Hey,' said a Time Police officer.

I spun around. 'Oh, thank God you're here.'

He blinked in surprise. I didn't blame him.

I went into overdrive myself. 'Give us a hand lifting these timbers, would you? Do you have any medpacks on you? Miss Sykes, keep applying pressure to that wound ...'

I strode off, issuing a hail of instructions to those around me.

What the officer should have done was pull back, let us sort ourselves out and then hit us hard, but he seemed to be experiencing the sort of disorientation frequently suffered by those encountering St Mary's on one of our more exciting days.

He chased after me. 'Just a minute ...'

I turned in exasperation. 'Look, I don't know why you're here but if you're not going to assist then push off and let me get on with it. As you can see I have other things on my mind at the moment. Tell Captain Ellis ...'

'Ellis isn't here', he said, allowing himself to be distracted.

'Why not? We always deal with Captain Ellis. Where is he? Don't stand in that blood.'

He didn't move. 'This is another matter. I have reason to believe …'

I cut across him. 'Careful how you move Mr Bashford. He might have internal injuries.'

You had to hand it to the Time Police. They don't give up. I felt a slight pang. They'd rescued Leon, Guthrie and Markham from Constantinople for us when we didn't have a working pod to our name. They'd nursed Leon back to health. They were sheltering Matthew for us. Commander Hay was a decent woman. If they could just stop pursuing two rather engaging teenagers up and down the timeline they'd almost be quite likeable.

But that was their job. Pursuing those engaging in illegal time travel. The penalty for which was usually death. Mikey and Adrian had been leading them a merry dance for years, for which, I suspected, they would pay heavily. But not if I had anything to do with it. Too many people had died around here recently.

'It is Dr Maxwell, isn't it?'

I turned impatiently. 'Yes, it is. How did you know?'

'Everyone knows,' he said heavily, and I wasn't sure about that. 'Dr Maxwell, I have reason to believe you're harbouring two fugitives and …'

'We're not harbouring anyone,' I said indignantly.

He carried on anyway '… and it's my duty to search these premises. Immediately.'

And at that exact moment I heard Mrs Enderby in my ear. 'Ready when you are, Max.'

'Of course it is,' I said to him, 'but as you can see, we're a bit busy at the moment. You go on and make a start. I'll catch you up. I'd leave Wardrobe to last if I were you. They've got a bit of a flap on at the moment.'

'More of a flap than this?' he said, gesturing around at the last of the survivors being scooped up for medical treatment.

'Well,' I said, in the full knowledge she could hear every word I said. 'I'm afraid our Mrs Enderby's a bit of a diva.'

I'd pay for that later on. My next jump was Persepolis, but I didn't mind betting she'd get me into a corset and bustle somehow.

I had no idea how Mikey was faring in Sick Bay, but I reckoned I could leave Dr Stone to sort that out. He wasn't Helen Foster but he was certainly Captain Devious from Devioustown in Deviousshire.

They split up – presumably so we couldn't move the fugitives around the building behind their backs – and searched everywhere. And they were very thorough. I was pleased to see they had to search manually. No one was waving tag readers around. It was obviously the pod they followed, not Adrian and Mikey themselves, and the pod was long gone.

But they were good. They had a system and they stuck to it. Every painstaking inch of it. They ignored Mrs Mack's tight-lipped hostility and Professor Rapson's careful confusion. The Technical Section stood outside each pod, arms folded, following their every move. No one was allowed into the pods but all the locker doors stood open and there was obviously nothing to be concealed. I began to hope they'd lose interest and drift away, but they knew they'd injured Mikey. They suspected the two of them had sought refuge with us and although their pod wasn't here, there was no reason they themselves shouldn't be. We were St Mary's after all. Concealing a couple of known fugitives was just the sort of thing we would do.

Mikey was actually very easy to conceal because she was in theatre, covered in sterile cloths, with only a tiny area visible. When asked who the patient was, Nurse Fortunata informed them it was Miss Grey, whom they knew, who had collaborated with them in the search for Clive Ronan. She went on to say that she understood they *still* hadn't found him, and had they considered how much more a chance they would stand if they put some people on that job instead of faffing around getting under the feet of people who had a real job to do, and that the man standing behind them was Major Guthrie whom they definitely did know, and she didn't think he'd take kindly to a bunch of idiots wanting to inspect his girlfriend while she was unconscious and undergoing surgery.

They made a cursory check of the wards which were bulging with casualties suffering barn-related traumas. Ian Guthrie silently and unnervingly watched them every inch of the way and personally escorted them to the door.

They went over every part of the building, found nothing, and eventually we found ourselves outside Wardrobe, which was buzzing like an overturned beehive. People were rushing around with mouths full of pins. I had a brief attack of Health and Safety. Should they do that? Suppose someone fell over? We'd be picking pins out of their tonsils for days afterwards. Others were whirring away at sewing machines. Lengths of beautiful material hung everywhere.

Mrs Enderby got up off her knees, dusting French chalk off her hands. 'Is it urgent, Max? If we don't get these costumes completed today, Mr Cutter will be

111

invoking the penalty clause in his contract.' She apparently noticed the Time Policemen standing beside me. 'What do you want?'

I was soothing. 'It won't take a minute, Mrs Enderby. They think someone's hiding here and we don't know it.'

That wasn't strictly true, but a little bit of misdirection never does anyone any harm.

'This really isn't a good time, Max.'

'I know,' I said, careful not to be too cooperative, 'but it's probably easier if we just let them get on with it.'

She stepped aside. 'Just don't touch anything. Anything at all.'

His squad filed into the room. They began yanking open doors and looking behind screens. No Adrian anywhere. I caught Mrs Enderby's eye. What the hell had they done with him? She winked at me.

'What's through there?' said their leader, pointing through an open archway.

She said in surprise, 'Our fitting room, of course. You can't go in there.'

He set off.

'No,' she said, 'wait.'

He ignored her. I waggled my eyebrows at her and followed him in.

A pleasant scene met my eyes.

Late afternoon sun was slanting in through the windows. A number of dummies against the wall showed a range of Tudor costumes, both male and female. In pride of place, however, was a stunning court dress for the upcoming TV series on Elizabeth I from Cutter Cavendish Productions. Mr Cutter's latest venture into the world of historical fiction involved an apparently thirty-year-old Virgin Queen shagging the Earl of Essex bandy before sallying forth in the *Golden Hind* to lay into the Armada personally. Don't ask. There's History and then there's Calvin Cutter's history.

The dress was gorgeous. And huge. The Virgin Queen didn't mess about when it came to her wardrobe and neither did Calvin Cutter. If we added any more layers we'd have to put the bloody thing on wheels.

The dress was being modelled by a tall figure standing in the middle of the room on a sheet, arms outstretched. They'd obviously reached a tricky point in its complex construction because a team swarmed over the wide petticoats like ants over Mount Snowdon. The heavily embroidered cloth of gold overskirt was flipped up and covered the model's face. Two more people were fitting the sleeves and another was crawling on the floor tacking up the hem.

I stared. The model did seem rather tall and I couldn't think who it could be. We didn't have anyone that tall in Wardrobe.

Beside me, the officer stiffened.

'Well,' I said, cheerily, 'nothing to see here.'

He didn't reply, walking slowly into the room, circling the figure which, at the same time, and by a strange coincidence, was also rotating, in accordance with instructions from the construction crew, and keeping its face well averted.

'Shall we go,' I said, trying to edge him towards the door.

'I don't think so,' he said, slowly.

Shit.

I looked in dismay at Mrs Enderby, still slightly dishevelled from crawling about on the floor. The officer caught us staring at each other and drew an unfortunate conclusion.

'And through here ...' I said, gesturing back towards the archway, and hoping that subconsciously he'd move in that direction.

He didn't. Of course he bloody didn't.

'All of you.' He gestured at Mrs Enderby's team with his gun. 'Step back.'

As one, all those working on the dress stared at Mrs Enderby. No one moved.

'I don't know what you want, young man,' she said, stepping between him and the petticoat-enveloped figure standing on the sheet. The really quite tall figure standing on the sheet.

Again – shit.

'I want you all to step back, ladies – before any of you gets hurt.'

As he spoke, he moved towards the model, transferred his gun to his other hand, and groped around what I shall refer to as the bosom area.

The model uttered a shriek of rage that rang around the room, drew back her arm and fetched him a ringing slap that nearly lifted him off his feet. Before he could pull himself together, he was enveloped in a maelstrom of outraged femininity, all shouting and waving their arms. Words like 'pervert', 'dirty devil', and 'sex maniac' bombarded him from all sides.

His cries for assistance did not go unnoticed.

The other members of his team burst through the archway, guns raised and ready for anything, although they might not have been ready for the sight that met their eyes.

Mrs Enderby, ably supported by Mrs Mack and Mrs Shaw – both of whom had appeared from nowhere – and surely only someone with a mind as evil as mine would suspect they'd been waiting behind the door for this very purpose – were being more than vociferous in their condemnation of nasty rough soldiers who tried to put their hands down other people's bodices.

Technically the three of them were outnumbered and outgunned by the Time Police, but that didn't seem to be holding them back in any way and the Time Police were giving ground under their onslaught. I remembered these three had fought at the Battersea Barricades, stepped back against the wall and let them get on with it.

Chairs and tables were overturned. Tins of pins flew everywhere.

The original officer – the cause of all the trouble – staggered and fell backwards over the person who had been tacking up the hem. The remaining policemen pulled out their guns and shouted to the model to put up his hands.

There was a great deal of flailing around and finally the layers of dress were pulled aside and a dishevelled Rosie Lee emerged, red-faced and furious.

'What the fu ...?'

Half a nanosecond later she had a gun in her face.

Mrs Enderby surged forwards and knocked it into the air. 'Get away from her at once. How dare you attack a member of my staff. And look at the damage to this dress.'

She wasn't alone. Mrs Shaw and Mrs Mack were on either side of her. The rest of her department surged around like so much indignant pin-bearing flotsam and jetsam, jostling bewildered Time Police officers who

115

knew something was going on but couldn't quite put their fingers on it if only all these bloody women would stop shrieking at them.

Their true quarry, young Adrian, green smocked like the rest of them, had abandoned his tacking and was kneeling on the floor picking up pins. We'd kept him on his knees to hide his height.

Back at Ground Zero, the officer was trying to defend himself from three stout, middle-aged women. He was losing on all fronts.

'I thought it was him. She was tall.'

It wasn't often Rosie Lee was able, legitimately, to attack people and she was obviously determined to make the most of it. 'I'm standing on a stool, you pathetic moron.'

'Watch your tone,' he said sharply and unwisely.

I judged it time to intervene – and muddy the issue a little more. 'What in the world is going on in here?' I turned to the officer and demanded, 'What did you do to her?'

Miss Lee burst into noisy tears. 'They tried to pull my clothes off.'

'We didn't. Nothing. I just …'

'It says "No Entry" on the door for a reason,' said Mrs Enderby. 'But they couldn't wait to get in here and start tearing her clothes off.'

'He put his hand down my bodice,' wailed Miss Lee.

'I thought she was a boy.'

'Are you insane?' demanded Mrs Enderby. 'Does she look like a boy? Do any of you actually have any idea what a boy looks like? Would you like me to get one in for you so you can familiarise yourself with people who aren't girls? Or are you just a bunch of sick perverts?'

They'd pulled themselves together by this time, grouping together in a tight clump, guns bristling. One of them must have had a blaster because I could hear the whine of it charging up over the sounds of indignant womanhood. I knew I really should intervene before someone got hurt, but at that moment Dr Bairstow turned up, standing in the doorway and leaning on his stick.

Rosie Lee shut up. Adrian crawled around the back of the dress, well out of sight. Everyone else subsided.

'I have been waiting for your report on this afternoon's disgraceful behaviour for some considerable time, Dr Maxwell. If you thought for one moment that any delay would lessen my…. annoyance … over this unit's reprehensible behaviour then you were mistaken.'

I said, 'Yes, sir,' reviewed what he'd said and amended that to, 'No, sir.' And even then, I wasn't sure I'd got it right.

'Report.'

'A considerable number of casualties, sir, the worst being Miss Grey.' I spared a minute to hope Cox and Evans had had the sense to hide Elspeth under a bed somewhere. 'She is, at present, undergoing surgery. I do not, as yet, have any details but Dr Stone will report as soon as possible.'

'You misunderstand me, Dr Maxwell. I was referring to …' he gestured around him '… this.'

'Sorry sir. Err … as you can see, the Time Police are here. Again. They haven't yet introduced themselves and I'm sure it probably wasn't intentional bad manners and general ignorance that prevented them from making their presence known and formally requesting permission to carry out a search as detailed in the treaty signed after we kicked their arses at the Battle of St Mary's.'

117

Having given him this promising opening, I stepped back to let him have some fun.

Their officer stepped forward. 'Dr Bairstow, we are tracking an illegal pod and our readings show …'

'Where?' he interrupted. 'Let me see these readings.'

There was a muttered consultation with his men. 'The radiation signature is very faint. As yet, we have nothing conclusive.'

'Then why are you here?'

'Our intention is to locate and apprehend …'

'On what evidence?'

There was another consultation and some head-shaking. I heard, 'Echoes everywhere, sir. All over the building, including the roof. Outside on the grass, outside the hangar, all over. Some new – some old. There are even signatures from our own pods from previous visits.'

The officer turned back to Dr Bairstow. 'As at this moment, Dr Bairstow, it is not possible to …'

He got no further.

'So, to sum up, you have arrived this afternoon, in pursuit of something your own equipment tells you might not be here …'

'With respect, Dr Bairstow, this unit has a record of harbouring …'

He might as well have spared his breath. I could have told him that.

'… perpetrate an unforgiveable assault on one of my staff …'

Rosie Lee redoubled her sobs. The entire Wardrobe department crowded around to comfort her

The officer made a real effort to regain control of the situation. 'We are the Time Police …'

Dr Bairstow looked around at the milling crowd. 'I can certainly see that. Tell me, how is the hunt for Clive Ronan progressing?'

'I can assure you that every member of ...'

'And yet you are not?'

'I'm sorry?' he said, stiffly.

'You and your team do not appear to be engaged in what Commander Hay assures me is your primary objective at the moment, the capture of Clive Ronan, though she assures me that she has deployed all her best people to this end. Can I infer from this that you and your unit are not ... how can I put this ... her best people?'

He turned an unlovely crimson. 'Different department.'

'I think that has been apparent to all of us. So, other than having impeded our casualty clearing, stormed our medical centre, compromised the treatment of Miss Grey, turned my unit upside down, sexually assaulted one of my staff and compelled me to leave my duties in order to quell a riot, what do you think you have achieved this afternoon?'

And now his colour was verging on purple. 'I ...'

'Quite so. Mr Markham. Kindly ensure our guests are signed out – you should probably sign them in first – and then escort them to their pod, if you would be so good. Dr Maxwell, my office. At your earliest convenience.'

I said meekly, 'Yes, sir,' and watched the Time Police follow Markham's team from the room.

Thirty minutes later, I was in Dr Bairstow's office. He pulled out a bottle and two glasses from his bottom drawer.

'Report, Dr Maxwell.'

119

'Everything's fine sir. Adrian is still concealed in Wardrobe. He'll sit quietly in a corner, tacking hems, just in case the TP suddenly reappear hoping to catch us out. Mikey's surgery has been successful. The bullet has been removed and she is expected to make a full recovery. Miss Lee has been plied with alcohol and is now feeling comparatively benign, although it might be an idea to keep the Time Police away from her in future. For their own good.'

'Any other casualties?

'No, sir. Every officer was able to make it back to his pod unaided.'

'I meant among St Mary's personnel.'

'Sir?'

He sighed. 'I believe the History Department brought the barn down.'

'Sorry, sir. I'd forgotten about that.'

'You had forgotten the demolition of a substantial wooden structure that has stood on this property for some considerable time?'

'Oh God, sir, it's not listed, is it?'

Wrecking listed buildings leads to all sorts of trouble. Trust me.

'Fortunately, no. That does not mean, however, that I am accepting its loss with a careless flick of my wrist and a light-hearted laugh.'

'No, sir,' I said, trying to imagine him doing either of those things and failing.

'Casualties, Dr Maxwell?'

'Quite light actually, sir', I said, glad to be able to report good news. 'I don't think Mr Bashford even lost consciousness.'

120

'Are you sure? I distinctly saw Miss Prentiss covered in blood and Mr Cox appeared to have an arm hanging off.'

'Make-up, sir.'

'I beg your pardon?'

'Casualty make-up, sir. For when we have disaster practice.'

'We have to *practise* having disasters?'

'Sorry. I expressed myself badly. I should have said we have casualty make-up for when we familiarise ourselves with the correct procedures to be undertaken should we have a disaster. To add an air of realism to our simulations, sir.'

'I congratulate you and your people on the realism of this afternoon's disaster.'

I beamed. He'd forgotten about the barn. Crisis averted. 'Thank you.'

'I thought the collapsed barn was particularly realistic.'

Oh no, he hadn't.

'We do our best, sir.'

I looked at him. The current crisis had been resolved. No one had died. There were no bodies buried anywhere. And the barn could be rebuilt. Probably. And annoying the Time Police always put him in a good mood. There were no Deductions from Wages for Damages Incurred forms on his desk, so I took a chance.

'Tell me, sir, when you first set up St Mary's all those years ago – all that effort and expense – did you ever think it would be like this?'

He poured me a glass of something and pushed it across the desk.

'Dr Maxwell, I expended a very great deal of money and effort to ensure that St Mary's ended up exactly like this.'

I grinned and raised my glass. 'Good job, sir.'

He inclined his head, graciously accepting his due. 'Thank you, Dr Maxwell.'

Obviously, despite all our best efforts to distract him with chicken shit and exploding barns, the idiot Halcombe found out about Persepolis. And he wanted to be included. And then he found out about the crown and insisted on being involved in that, too. I couldn't decide where he would do least damage and took my problems to Dr Bairstow.

'We have to get rid of him, sir,' I said. 'Not just because the Persepolis jump is imminent and the crown is coming, but now we have Mikey and Adrian and that could be a problem as well. At the moment, Mikey is camouflaged among the wounded survivors of Professor Rapson's Great Battering Ram Catastrophe, but Adrian can't sit sewing hems in the corner of Wardrobe forever.'

'No, indeed,' he said, sitting back in his chair. 'Do I understand your efforts to rid St Mary's of this troublesome priest have proved ineffectual?'

'I'm afraid so, sir. He has a hide like a rhinoceros.'

'Hm,' he said, thoughtfully.

'Sir?'

'Please do not regard this as any sort of learning experience.'

'Sir?'

'Come with me, Dr Maxwell.'

There was a hell of a row going on. There often was, these days. Halcombe and Clerk were standing face to face, toe to toe. Clerk was flushed and furious.

'You ruined the Caernarfon assignment. None of us can ever go back there again. We only ever get one shot at anything and you' ruined it. If you think you're going anywhere near Persepolis then you're gravely mistaken.'

He turned to me. 'You put me in charge of the Alexander part of the assignment and I tell you now, Max, there is no way I'll have this pillock anywhere near my pod. And that's final. If he goes – I don't. Everyone knows he turns and runs at the first sign of trouble – and that was just a small town in Wales. God only knows what damage he could do in a burning palace. I won't have him in my pod.'

'Nor me,' said Atherton, surprisingly, given his usual, 'let's all get on together' position. 'The bloke's unreliable.'

'The bloke's an arsehole,' said Sykes, from her position of 'couldn't give a shit'. Arsehole being a technical term frequently used in the History Department.

Halcombe drew himself up. 'I represent the University of Thirsk. May I remind you all that I am here at the instigation of the Senior Faculty because of St Mary's inability to function either effectively or efficiently. Or even legally. Members of St Mary's staff stole a valuable artefact belonging to the university, and if I had my way, many of you would be serving a substantial prison sentence.'

'Well, that's never going to happen, is it?' said Clerk hotly. 'Because you're too busy abandoning people up and down the timeline. If you have your way there soon won't be any of us left to put in prison.'

Swelling with pomposity, Halcombe warmed to his theme. 'I have contacted the Chancellor to inform her that the security arrangements here at St Mary's are in no way adequate for keeping safe such a valuable artefact as the Crown of the Empress Mathilda, and instructing her to cancel all the arrangements pertaining thereto.'

There was a torrent of protest. Shit. This was getting out of hand.

I went to intervene because sooner or later someone was going to thump the pillock, and however commendable I might find that, we'd be in serious trouble. Just as I was taking a breath to calm everyone down, Dr Bairstow put his hand on my shoulder.

'I'll handle this, Dr Maxwell.'

'If you like, sir, but I should point out that the id – Mr Halcombe – really can't be permitted either to go to Persepolis or disrupt our other plans.'

'Of course not,' he said calmly.

Halcombe was attempting to speak again but his efforts were drowned out by the History Department in full flow. Even North was having a go at him. In a dignified and restrained manner, of course, but I'd once seen her attack Herodotus with a wooden tray and lived in perpetual hope of a repeat performance.

She never got the chance. Dr Bairstow thumped his stick on the floor for silence and got it.

Halcombe moved forward to take advantage.

'Ah, Bairstow. I see your control over this rabble has not improved in my absence. With immediate effect, you will ...'

Dr Bairstow regarded him icily. 'All my staff are handpicked.'

'That's quite true, actually,' said Markham, sunnily. 'I've been handpicked many times. Mug shots. Police line-ups. ID parades. People are always pointing at me and shouting, "That's him.".'

I don't think Dr Bairstow even heard him. 'Mr Halcombe, you are here because the University of Thirsk has agreed to foot the bill for our recent damage and we are in their debt. You will, I am sure, remember that on your first, and what, I can assure you, was your last assignment with St Mary's, you not only displayed appalling leadership qualities and a complete lack of a comprehension of the role required of you, but you abandoned half of your colleagues to cope as best they could in a potentially dangerous situation. You contravened our number one rule, Mr Halcombe – you left your people behind. It is perhaps fortunate for you that my staff are far too courteous to indicate the complete contempt in which you are held – to your face, anyway – and so that duty falls to me. Mr Halcombe, you are held in complete contempt. You do not have, as far as I can see, a single redeeming quality of any kind. There are no circumstances under which anyone – anyone at all – will ever get into a pod with you again – and you will, therefore, understand very clearly that, as far as you are concerned, your participation in this or any of our future assignments will not ever happen.

'As far as I can see, your sole function here is to observe what is going on around you, draw the wrong conclusions and report these to a Chancellor who is actively seeking a reason to dismiss you. This frequently happens when one does not have the foresight to attach one's wagon to the correct star. You have no friends either here or at Thirsk, and nor will you ever have. The knives are out, Mr Halcombe, and my advice to you would be to return to Thirsk with all speed and watch your back. Throughout my time as Director of St Mary's, I have always endeavoured to employ the best and brightest people in their fields. I am not sure which particular field you occupy, Mr Halcombe, but I think it is very apparent to everyone that, whichever it is, you are very far from the being the best and brightest in it. I regret to inform you, therefore, that you have failed to achieve the standards required here at St Mary's and I would be obliged if you would, from this moment, consider yourself dismissed from my unit. If you are suffering a lack of comprehension or there are other, simpler words I can use to make the situation clearer to you, please do not hesitate to apprise me of them.'

Wow. In the silence that followed you could have heard a slipper-wearing mouse dance the fandango on a feather cushion.

Dr Bairstow turned on his heel, shot Peterson and me a glance which clearly said, 'Amateurs,' and limped off into Wardrobe. The idiot Halcombe remained uncertainly for one moment and then stormed off to his office. Again, the door slammed behind him.

Peterson, Markham and I grinned at each other. He was gone.

An hour later, Rosie Lee reported she'd seen Halcombe's car trundling down the drive and out of the gates and then took advantage of my jubilation by claiming I'd agreed to give her the rest of the day off. I told her to pull the other one. She spent the rest of the afternoon banging files around and I sat at my desk humming happily, just to get on her nerves.

At four o'clock I sent her down to Wardrobe to enquire about progress on the Persepolis costumes. I could have gone myself, but I guessed she'd be gone for some time and I needed the time to think, because I was having second thoughts. Buyer's remorse, I think they call it. Not about Persepolis – the whole burning-building thing was what St Mary's was all about – but about the other end of things. Suppose, just suppose, Ronan did manage to get away with the crown. Just suppose everything went wrong for us and he actually stole the real crown and we were left with more than egg on our faces. Yes, the Time Police would be here and they'd nail the slippery bastard, I was almost convinced of it, but suppose they didn't …

I think, deep down, when I'd pitched my idea to Dr Bairstow I'd been convinced he'd say no. But he hadn't. And if this went wrong … if Ronan succeeded … there would be no coming back from this. St Mary's would be finished. And it would be my fault.

This doesn't happen very often – usually I can see quite clearly what should be done, even if I don't want to do it – but it was happening now. I needed to talk to someone. I needed a sober and balanced point of view. And because he had enough on his mind at the moment, someone who wasn't Leon.

I tend to stay away from Sick Bay because every time I go near the place they find something else wrong with me. I often wonder if Dr Stone works on commission. I haven't mentioned this before, but Guthrie was still in there, sitting up and looking better as each day passed. I was astonished at his progress but he was bringing the same single-minded determination to his recovery and rehabilitation that he brought to every task he undertook. He was walking every day. Not a lot, but a little further and for a little longer every day. He certainly wasn't so sick that I would feel guilty about troubling him. But first, I needed to bear gifts.

I raced down to the kitchen, braking just in time to avoid colliding with Dottle, who was making her careful way up the stairs with the biggest plate of sandwiches in the history of the world.

She jumped a mile, to the detriment of the top layer. 'Goodness me, Max, you startled me.'

I picked them up and blew on them. They'd be fine. The five-second rule would apply. 'Good God. Are you feeding the five thousand? Or just Markham?'

'I'm working late tonight.'

'You look as if you're working until next Tuesday.'

She smiled shyly. 'Hopefully it won't come to that, but I have to do it.'

'Do what?'

She glanced nervously over her shoulder again, lowering her voice to a whisper. 'I have to do well. Now that *he*'s gone, this is my big chance. I have to show people what I can do. Dr Bairstow. The Chancellor.' She glanced in the direction of Peterson's room, said nothing, but the inference was clear. 'Everyone here is so ... passionate about what they do. I want the chance to be proud of myself and of my job as well. If you were me, you'd do the same.'

'I would,' I said, 'but make sure you don't overdo it.'

'I won't, don't worry. I've made a start by putting some stats together for Thirsk, because I think it will give the Chancellor an argument for increasing our funding.'

I noticed she'd said *our funding*, smiled and stepped out of her way. 'In that case, have at it.'

She smiled. 'I shall. You just wait and see.' She passed on her way, and I shot off, first to the kitchen to pick up a few things, and then on to see Ian Guthrie.

Usually half the Security Section was in there, putting back his recovery by months. Leon too spends a lot of time with him. On this occasion, though, Ian was on his own.

'What ho,' I said, shouldering my way through the door into the men's ward. 'I've brought you a coffee and some of Mrs Mack's apple cake.'

'Oh, excellent – Mrs Mack's cake will go a long way towards reconciling me to your presence. You talk. I'll enjoy the cake and ignore you.'

He looked so much better. His black eye-patch gave him the jaunty air of a pirate and he'd grown a beard which really suited him. Yes, he'd lost some weight and his face was very pale and he still had a cradle over his leg, but compared to the way he'd looked a month ago when he finally came back to us from the Time Police, he was another person. They'd set him on the road to recovery, they said; the rest was up to him.

He was healing well. A tribute to his superior Caledonian stamina apparently. As opposed to all us non-Caledonian wimps and weaklings. He'd been up and walking a surprisingly short time after having his leg reattached, firstly with a frame and then just a stick. He was very slow still and he had bad days, but he was recovering.

Anyway, today he was miraculously alone so I plunged straight in with compliments and good wishes. 'Oh my God, Ian, you have a badger on your face.'

He fingered his beard. 'Looks good, doesn't it?'

'If you're comfortable with that delusion then who am I to argue.'

'What do you want, Max? Why are you here?'

'Major, I have – not a problem – but something I need to talk about.'

He sighed. 'This is the price I'm paying for the cake, isn't it?'

I had sudden second thoughts. He was still an invalid. I shouldn't be burdening him.

'No, the cake is free. And the other thing's not important. How are you feeling?'

'Good. As always.'

Yes, that was what he always said. I got up to go.

'Sit down, Max.' And yes, all right, he wasn't functioning properly and probably never would again and his life would never be the same, but he was still Ian Guthrie and when he spoke in that tone I did as I was told.

'I shouldn't be bothering you with this.'

He finished his slice cake and started on his coffee. 'I wish someone would bother me with something. It's my leg that's damaged – not my brain.'

Good point.

I pulled my chair closer. 'OK – I have – not a problem, but an issue.' I told him everything. My conversation with Captain Ellis, my idea, the plan – everything – and then asked him whether, this time, I'd gone too far. Did the possible favourable outcome outweigh the probable potential for catastrophe.

He sipped his coffee, frowning. 'Have you taken everything into account? Tried to foresee every possible contingency?'

I thought of all my risk assessments. To say nothing of those dodgy moments at half past two in the morning when I lay next to Leon imagining Ronan wandering out of the building with the crown under his arm and laughing his head off. 'Yes.'

'And the St Mary's end of things – that's completely outside your control?'

'Yes, I'm on the Persepolis end.'

'And you have faith in Ellis and his men?'

I nodded. 'I do, yes.'

'And Dr Bairstow?'

I nodded.

'And Peterson?'

I nodded again.

'In that case, Max, let them all get on with it. They have their function – you have yours – concentrate on that. Put everything else out of your head and focus on the job in hand.'

'OK.'

'Tell me you're working closely with Markham on this.'

'I am,' I said.

'And you have complete confidence in him?'

'I do. If I can't have you or Leon then I'd rather have him than anyone.'

He hesitated and then looked around the room as if he didn't want to be overheard. Great – that was two of us at it now.

'Do me a favour?'

'Of course,' I said, thinking he just wanted another slice of cake.

'Make sure he knows that, will you?'

I stared at him.' I don't understand.'

132

'He's having problems.'

'*Markham*?'

He nodded.

'What problems?'

'He's the new Head of Security.'

'Yes, I know.'

'Some people are having difficulty accepting that.'

'In what way?'

He began to brush the crumbs off his covers. 'Well, the thing is, Max, you and I, and Peterson and Leon, we all just walked into our jobs, didn't we? We were the first. There was never anyone to measure us against. Markham is following me. I'm not big-headed, but comparisons are inevitable, aren't they? He's having some problems, which he's ascribing to not being me. He sees himself as not being tall; he has no army rank to give him the authority he thinks he needs; he's aware of his reputation as a bit of a clown – and so is everyone else.'

'Really?' I said grimly.

'No, it's nothing bad. No one is defying him or laughing at him, but there's bound to be a bit of settling down to do.'

'But he's been Head of Security before.'

'He has, but it's always been temporary and short-term. This is permanent. His problem is that he thinks he's not measuring up to me. What he doesn't see is that he doesn't have to.'

'No,' I said slowly, 'I see what you mean. Dr Bairstow knows what he's like – none better – and he obviously thinks he's the best man for the job.'

'Exactly. He could have gone outside the unit for my replacement and he hasn't. The trouble is that everyone here remembers him running into that horse's arse. And falling off the stable roof. And mucking around in that reindeer suit. They don't always remember him saving Cleopatra from the asp …'

'Or the two of you from Ronan last year.'

'Exactly. And I'm tied here and can't do anything.'

'Leave it to me,' I said.

'I knew I could,' he said smugly. 'Leave the rest of the cake will you.'

I got up to go. 'Where's Elspeth today?'

He looked mysterious. No, I mean he looked exactly the same as ever – he just assumed a mysterious expression. I enquired if he needed a laxative. He said having me in the same room was all he needed on that score thank you very much and to close the door behind me on the way out.

Well, that was something to think about, wasn't it? I made my way slowly back to my office, pondering ways and means of putting things right for Markham. Of getting him alone somewhere and somehow bringing up the subject without embarrassing him. Or myself. As it turned out I didn't have to because he was waiting for me in my office when I got back.

I peered closely. There was nothing specific, but now that Guthrie had mentioned it I could see something was troubling him. I kicked myself for not having noticed anything was wrong. He was my friend and I should have noticed. Time for a tactful chat. On our own.

I sat at my desk, picked up a file and said, 'Miss Lee, please could you …' and foreseeing I was about to ask her to do some work, she muttered something and disappeared out of the door. Result.

'What ho,' I said to Markham.

He muttered something and stood staring out of the window.

I waited. Something was definitely wrong. Normally a 'what ho' produces a long lecture on Heads of Departments having to maintain certain standards, although what standards he's referring to is never really clear. It was obvious he had something on his mind and was having some difficulty getting it off again. With Ian Guthrie's words still ringing in my ears, I thought I'd give him a gentle shove in the right direction.

I got up and locked the door. Just to give him something else to worry about. And put the kettle on. We waited in silence as the kettle boiled.

I handed him his tea and said, 'No one cares that you're not Major Guthrie, you know.'

We stood together, staring out of the window.

He said, 'I …'

I said gently, 'I know, but the only person who thinks that is you.'

'But …'

'No, you're wrong. Dr Bairstow chose you over everyone else. He didn't go outside for Ian's replacement – he chose you.'

'I …'

'I know you're not Ian Guthrie. No one is. Well, apart from Ian Guthrie, of course, so stop trying to be something you're not.'

'It's …'

'You have your own way of doing things. You have your own identity. You're Markham. You do things the Markham way.'

'But …'

'Yes, you've messed around in the past. And you've messed up, too. We all have. And yes, you have some giant shoes to fill, but you're Markham. You're more Markham than anyone I know. Be Markham. It's always worked for you before.'

'Max ...'

'I tell you now, with the possible exception of Leon, I'd rather have you at my back than anyone. And I'm not the only one.'

'Actually ...'

'You need to embrace your Markham-ness. Life is really opening up for you. And I speak for Peterson, too. You know, don't you, that if there's anything either of us can do ... we'd do it in a heartbeat.'

'Actually ... I just came to borrow the Persepolis file.'

'Oh.' The room was suddenly very hot. To hide my face, I reached across the desk and thrust it in his direction, too mortified even to look at him. He took it and headed to the door. I continued to stare out of the window in buttock-clenching humiliation. Perhaps in six months' time – when the embarrassment began to subside ... I'd be able to look at him again.

He was flicking through the file, not looking at me. 'But that other stuff was pretty good as well.'

I made an indeterminate noise that could mean anything he wanted it to.

There was a bit of a silence. 'Thanks, Max.'

'You're welcome. And don't lose that file.'

'No, I mean about what you said.'

'Oh ... well ... you're welcome.'

'No, I mean it. Hunter ... well ... things are a bit ... you know ... at the moment.'

I did know. I remembered the panic, the elation, the terror, the overwhelming sense of responsibility ... the knowledge it wasn't just the two of us any longer ...

'How is she?'

'Well, early days yet, but she's fine. Better than me, anyway. Everyone's better than me these days.'

'You're going to be fine.'

He smiled. 'What are we talking about at the moment?'

'Anything you want. You have a great future ahead of you. The Boss thinks so. And Ian Guthrie. And Peterson. And me.'

'Thank you. That means a lot, but sometimes I think ...'

'Well, don't,' I said sternly. 'You know it's not your strong point. Look – it's your section now. You have to do things your way. And your way is ... are you even listening to me?'

He was looking as if Newton's apple had just landed on his head.

'What? Yes, of course I am. Thanks, Max. You're brilliant.'

Well, that was true, but I had no idea what he was talking about.

He thumped me on the arm, unlocked the door and clattered off down the corridor.

The memo came round that afternoon. To all Heads of Departments. Peterson called me up and we had a good laugh over it. He'd changed the Security Section's call sign from 'Hawthorn' to 'Horse's Arse.'

We weren't getting things all our own way, however. We might have escaped having the idiot Halcombe foisted upon us, but Thirsk were still muttering about a presence on the jump, which meant Miss Dottle.

'It's a burning city,' she said faintly, obviously having done her homework.

'No, it's not.' I said, trying to reassure her. 'Well, not to begin with.'

'It bloody soon will be after St Mary's turn up,' said Sykes, which didn't help at all.

'Actually,' said Peterson kindly. 'I wondered if it would it be possible for Miss Dottle to remain here and assist me with the preparations for safe storage of the crown. I could certainly do with an extra pair of hands here. Miss Dottle, I know you're probably itching to be out there with the rest of them, but I really would be grateful ...'

'Yes, of course,' she said quickly. 'I'm happy to help.'

'Excellent,' he said, beaming at her. 'The more the merrier.'

I flashed him a grateful glance. Problem solved.

I stood up. 'Right, everyone. The purpose of this assignment is twofold. To catch a sight of Alexander and his famous Companions as they burn the city of

Persepolis, and to rescue anything we possibly can from said conflagration. This assignment will be considerably less structured than our previous jump to rescue the contents of the Library at Alexandria, because we don't know what the Treasury will contain, or if it will even be possible to get anywhere near it. We are, therefore, going in without a fixed plan of action but the capacity to adapt to any situation in which we might find ourselves.

'Being optimistic, we have already despatched Mr Atherton and Professor Rapson to identify a suitable burial site for anything we do manage to lay our hands on. If you could update us please, Professor.'

'Thank you, Max. Well, we've sourced appropriate containers and material with which to manufacture pitch and we've located a safe refuge in which to bury anything we do manage to rescue. The whole thing is very similar to our jaunt to Alexandria. Goodness me, what a long time ago that seems now.'

He paused, presumably rummaging through his memories, but since a good number of those would involve Clive Ronan and a homemade flame thrower, I thought it best to move him on.

He was pulling up maps and diagrams. I looked at the absorbed faces around me and I too couldn't help remembering our very first search-and-rescue assignment. I suddenly realised how few of us were still left. People had died there. Good people. I remembered Big Dave Murdoch, the gentle giant, and young Jamie Cameron with his shock of dark hair. I don't visit their graves as often as I should because there's one out there for Madeleine Maxwell and it's not an easy sight to see. And one for Helen Foster and that's even worse.

Evans was lolling back in his chair and banging away on his scratchpad. Without looking at Markham, he said, 'Do you want five-minute position checks?'

Silence fell. Everyone looked at Markham who didn't answer. The silence lengthened, almost to the point where it became uncomfortable. People stirred and still Markham said nothing. I held my breath. The situation needed the very lightest of touches. Evans wasn't a bad lad. None of them were. They just needed to realise this new Markham wasn't the old Markham.

Becoming aware of the long silence, Evans looked up and gazed around the table. It took a moment or two and then the penny dropped. Flushing, he sat up straight and said, 'Sorry. Do you want five-minute position checks, sir?'

Markham nodded as though nothing had happened. 'A good thought. Yes, five-minute position checks initially. Once the place is on fire, increase to two minutes, I think.'

All the tension went out of the room. People nodded.

Just to reinforce the point, I said, 'Mr Markham is the one who will call "time" on this assignment. We will take our instructions from him. Is that clear to everyone?'

People nodded, and the briefing continued without a hitch.

'Mr Dieter, I understand work on TB2 is completed.'

Dieter nodded. 'There are still one or two minor tests to complete but I guarantee it will be ready on time.' He sighed heavily. 'Try not to break it.'

'As if,' said Sykes, indignantly.

And he sighed again. The sigh of a man who has been dealing with the History Department for longer than could reasonably be expected.

I coughed and continued.

'The medical team will have their base in our newly rebuilt TB2, along with Professor Rapson, Dr Dowson, Miss Lingoss, and Miss North. Mr Keller will be there to keep order.

'Mr Clerk's team – that's me, Mr Markham, Mr Atherton and Mr Evans, will be in Number Eight. Our priority is Alexander, obviously, but anyone else we can get as well.

'Mr Bashford, Miss Sykes, Mr Dieter and Mr Cox – you're in Number Six. Make your way to the Treasury and wait for any opportunities that may arise. No one is to take any unnecessary risks ...' I was wasting my time there. All risks are necessary according to St Mary's.

I paused, because the next bit was important. 'From the moment the first fires are lit, Mr Markham will have overall control of the assignment. I will say this only once – when he says to move out you will move out. No arguments. We will remain in constant contact. All coms open at all times. No one leaves their group. If anyone is injured then the entire team returns to their pod. No ifs or buts. Doctor Stone will then assess the situation and only if he deems it safe for them to continue will that team return to their assignment.'

I could see Peterson tapping away at his scratchpad. He didn't look very happy. I flashed him a grin of almost manic optimism. He rolled his eyes.

We drew our kit. Fire suits and breathing apparatus for those in Number Six, and loose Persian robes for everyone else. My chiton was a long, loose linen tunic in a dull, browny colour that almost certainly marked me out as a member of the servant class. Over that I would wind a silk stole in vivid reds and greens that almost certainly marked

141

me out as a member of the servant-owning class. According to Mrs Enderby, I could move between the two worlds simply by wearing or not wearing the stole. Nor was I wearing the traditional Persian ladies' light and elegant footwear, settling instead for sturdy leather shoes. Not what a Persian lady would wear at all, but I would be able to run, climb and possibly kick, should the situation call for such measures.

Outside Number Eight, Peterson, who'd come down to ensure we were safely off the premises, surveyed my multi-purpose costume.

'So as usual everyone else will be doing the work and you'll be … doing what, exactly?'

'Oh you know, wafting about the place, bringing colour and excitement to everyone's day.'

'For God's sake, take care, Max. I shan't be around to look after you on this one.'

'I'll be fine,' I said. 'You just keep an eye on that crown. If anything happens to that then burning alive at Alexandria will be the least of my problems.'

We shook hands and he took himself off to the gantry to watch our departure.

I climbed into the pod where the others were already waiting. Leon was giving the console a final check. He turned as I entered and blinked at my costume.

I put my hands on my hips. 'What?'

'Nothing,' he said, in that voice that actually means 'everything'.

'It's functional,' I said defensively.

'It's bright.'

'Says the man wearing orange,' said Markham unwisely.

142

Markham had gone for practical in a loose robe which could easily be discarded for the short tunic underneath. Leon turned and looked him up and down. 'Were you on your way to bed?'

'I don't wear anything in bed,' said Markham, affronted.

Leon grinned. 'Not even a hopeful expression?'

'There's a lot of leg on show,' I said. 'I'm not sure Persepolis is ready for your nether limbs. And I'm certain it's not historically accurate.'

'That's me,' said Markham proudly. 'Always going outside the box.'

'Like a badly house-trained kitten,' said Leon.

Markham turned to me. 'I tell you what, Max, next time you find a bloke lying under a wall in Constantinople, just bloody well leave him there, will you.'

Leon looked him up and down again. 'Says the man held together by staples.'

Checks complete, he picked up his gear and headed for the door.

Everyone tactfully looked somewhere else as we shook hands.

'Take care.'

'I always do,' I said, affronted.

Someone, somewhere, snorted.

'And for God's sake, look after that crown. It'll be a bit of a bugger if we get back only to find someone from the Technical Department has accidentally built it into Number Four.'

'What do you mean, accidentally?' muttered Markham.

Leon sighed. 'Just go, will you?' He smiled for me alone and then the door closed behind him.

'Right, you lot,' I said. 'Everyone set? Computer, initiate jump.'

'Jump initiated.'

And the world went white.

Persepolis is often described as a city, but it was a city in two parts. The main part – the bit we were concerned with – was the ceremonial area; the complex of official buildings such as palaces, throne rooms, audience halls, civic buildings, the harem, the treasury and so on, all set on a massive artificial terrace some fifty or sixty feet high.

Unfortunately, even the most fabulous city in the world needs working bits and pieces to keep it going and, in contrast to the pomp and splendour of the palaces on the terrace, the surrounding plain was smothered in a disorganised and very motley collection of mostly mudbrick, wood and animal-hide structures that provided housing and working areas for all the people who actually made the place work – the masons, metalworkers, carpenters, goldsmiths, artists, sculptors, butchers, bakers, leather workers, grooms, recreational ladies and so on. All the thousands of people necessary to keep the Great King in the luxury he obviously felt he deserved.

Sadly, Alexander's army had been through the place like a plague of locusts. He'd promised his men the city to loot, while keeping the contents of the Treasury for himself, and they'd taken full advantage of the opportunity. That was why they followed him, after all. Alexander might dream of conquering the world, but it

145

was the promise of rich pickings that interested his soldiers.

The structures nearest the palaces had been razed to the ground. Broken, blackened walls stuck up like jagged teeth. The buildings on the outskirts had fared better, however. Whether this was because the poorer quarter had little to offer in the way of hidden loot, I don't know, but about two thirds of the city remained untouched and people, men and women, seemed to be moving around as usual. The presence of Alexander's army with its tents and campfires encircling the city did not appear to be impeding commercial life in any way. The streets weren't thronged with people, but they certainly weren't empty. People still moved around, a lot of them staggering under heavy loads because Alexander had commandeered nearly every pack animal in the northern hemisphere to transport his stolen loot to Susa.

Soldiers stood at every street corner, most of them leaning against the walls and staring at the women. Their spears leaned with them so they obviously weren't expecting any trouble. These were professional soldiers who would fight their way from Macedonia to northern India and there was no showing off in glittering armour or ornate helmets. They were competent-looking men and, in the way of soldiers everywhere, not looking for any trouble unless it came looking for them.

Water cisterns stood at regular intervals, presumably for use by the public and their animals. Periodically, slaves would emerge to damp down the streets with water in an unsuccessful attempt to combat the clouds of dust enveloping everything in sight. A surprisingly considerate idea, although it was likely the slaves' priority was to protect the gorgeous palaces and their even more gorgeous

146

occupants from the thick clouds of red dust mixing with the smoke from innumerable small fires.

Everyone seemed quite calm. There were no bodies swinging from gallows or heads impaled on spikes. No one was being executed or dragged off to prison. In the less gorgeous part of the city at least, life seemed to be much as normal. Alexander was, in the main, a benevolent conqueror. As long as you submitted to his rule, behaved yourself and paid your taxes, then life would continue pretty much as before. He'd help himself to any treasure knocking around, install a puppet government and then push off to conquer someone else. He'd recently returned from an expedition to subdue the mountain tribes, all of whom had surrendered with flattering rapidity, so everyone was in a good mood.

We spent an hour getting our bearings, working out where everyone was in relation to everyone else and just watching Persepolian life. I'd split the screen and we had all the cameras going.

Number Eight was outside the palace complex on the north-west side, about four hundred yards from the Great Stairway and the Gate of All Nations. Yes, it was the main entrance and very grand and very public, and I'm sure there would be other gates as well, but the mudbrick walls surrounding the palace were over sixty feet high with regular towers and look-out posts, all heavily manned, and we didn't want to draw attention to ourselves by going out and poking around for more discreet entrances. Just because no one was actually being publicly executed at this exact moment didn't mean that couldn't change in a heartbeat. No, we'd take our chances at the Gate.

Number Six was – we hoped – safely lost in the maze of miscellaneous outbuildings between the Throne Hall of

Xerxes and the outside wall. We had spread out as much as we were able to, just in case of trouble. One pod inside the complex, one outside and one, TB2, down in the town. Hope for the best, plan for the worst, as they say, and no matter where anyone found themselves in difficulty, there should be a pod not too far away.

As I said, the much larger and harder to conceal TB2 was parked about a quarter of a mile away, all ready to do duty as safe haven, hospital, treasure repository, tea station and so forth. Keller and Lingoss, under the direction of Professor Rapson, would be disguising it with stuff carefully selected from the piles of old rubbish lying around – leaning lengths of charred timber against one side, and scattering around a few broken pots, a rickety old ladder, and a two-legged stool. The real find – a dead dog – had been laid carefully across the threshold, despite the hygiene-based protests of Dr Stone.

'We won't move until just before dusk,' I said. 'Easier for everyone. They're not going to start carousing at half past four in the afternoon. And everyone agrees they were all well and truly pissed when they set fire to the place. Is everyone clear on where and when they should be?'

They were, of course, but it never does any harm to remind people occasionally.

My team were to shadow Alexander, getting as much footage of him they could. There are very few images of Alexander and no one knows for sure what he looked like so anything we could get would be worth its weight in gold to Thirsk.

The other team was to ignore everything going on around them – drunken soldiers, wild carousing, panicking people, leaping flames, stampedes, falling buildings – the little things, as Bashford had said – and get themselves to the Treasury to wait and see. I'd given them the freedom to make their own decisions and act as they saw fit until Markham gave the word to evacuate. I'd spoken sternly about not taking unnecessary risks but to historians there's no such thing.

The sun was a red ball of fire, sinking slowly into the dusty horizon. Street life continued at full pace. I'd wondered if there would be a curfew, but apparently not. If anything, there seemed to be even more people on the streets than when we arrived. Dark shadows crept across the landscape. There's very little twilight in these latitudes. And now it was time to go.

I spared a moment to wonder how things were going at St Mary's and then put it firmly out of my mind. Everyone had a job to do and should focus only on that. Dr Bairstow, Peterson and Captain Ellis were all far more capable than me. They would have everything well in hand there and I should be getting on with things here. I felt my heart lift a little. A chance to see Alexander …

We all wished each other luck and slipped out into the gathering dark.

The air smelled of sweet perfumes, incense, spices, dust, hot people and even hotter animal products. The ends of my stole flapped in the wind and I took a moment to wind it more tightly around my face, covering my mouth against the all-pervasive dust. The sand underfoot was coarse and gravelly and would, I knew from experience, easily and painfully work its way into all my nooks and crannies. Trust me, when you come back from this sort of assignment, there's half a desert in the bottom of your shower tray.

There were no streets as such – just narrow, gritty paths meandering around groups of buildings. Goats and really rough-looking sheep stood or lay silently in makeshift pens. Skinny stray dogs slunk past looking for somewhere to sleep and even skinnier cats were waking up and setting off to see what the night might bring.

With the sun gone, faint stars began to appear. The sky above me was a deep, rich purple, shading to a glowing lavender on the horizon.

I opened my com and called up Bashford. 'All set?'

'Ready when you are.'

'Good luck, everyone.'

We had no difficulty getting into the palace complex. There was a constant procession of people traipsing up and down the Great Staircase and in and out of the Gate of All Nations. We needn't have worried about blending in, either. This was a very cosmopolitan city. There were all sorts here – and all nationalities. Soldiers, traders, minor palace officials, and a massive number of slaves. Everyone was heading in the same direction, too. Under the Persian kings, Medes and Persians had taken a shorter, more privileged processional route to the Great King, while lesser and conquered peoples went the long way around. Now, everyone just piled in. There was some muttering and jostling, but everyone had an eye on the ever-present soldiers and behaved themselves.

We joined the crowd pushing their way up the ceremonial staircase with its reliefs of conquered peoples bringing tribute. In fact, tribute-bringing and homage-paying were recurring themes throughout all the public buildings, presumably in case anyone forgot why they were there. I recorded what I could. Clerk navigated us through the crowds and Markham watched our backs.

Reaching the top, we passed through the massively impressive Gate of All Nations, past a couple of giant bulls I thought would look rather nifty outside the Boss's office, through the Unfinished Gate and into the Throne Hall courtyard where, despite all our careful training, we stopped and gawped like tourists.

Yes, I know, but it was impossible not to be distracted by the magnificence around us. The entire complex was mind-boggling. Gaudy and tasteless and opulent and over-decorated, of course, but just ... mind-blowing in a gloriously overstated way. Ahead of us was the massive Throne Hall of Xerxes, standing so high I had to tilt my head back to see the top. The front was porticoed and the pillars decorated with beautifully drawn lions, eagles and those ever-recurring twin-headed bulls.

Ahead and diagonally to our right stood the Audience Hall of Darius – even more massive and twice as magnificent. Behind the Throne Hall and invisible from this position stood the Treasury and behind the Audience Hall were the palaces of Darius and Xerxes and the Harem. I was gratified to see that everything was exactly where it should be – which is not always something you can rely on in our line of business. I knew where I was. I knew where everyone else was. Time to get stuck in.

We started with the Throne Hall, walking slowly but with great confidence to the portico and staring inside.

I hardly knew where to start. The floor beneath my feet was white marble, gleaming in the hundreds of torches and braziers that slaves were lighting all around us. The flames flickered noisily in the desert wind. An eerie foretaste of what was to come.

I saw towering walls decorated with gold and winking glass. The wooden roof was supported by huge, fat, also wooden pillars, decorated with complicated designs painted in every colour. Bulls still appeared to be very popular – if a touch inappropriate for indoor design. A lot of them were depicted back to back – like bookends – along with lily flowers and lotus blossoms.

Looking up, I could just make out the enormous beams supporting the roof. Had they been cut from the legendary Cedars of Lebanon?

Such doors as I could see were more in the nature of gates – huge, wooden, intricately carved and, judging by the size of the hinges, massively heavy. I wondered how many men it took to open them. Not that a shortage of manpower would ever have been a problem for the Great King.

There was no consistent style anywhere. Nor any consistent theme. Everything was over-painted, over-decorated and over-dressed. These walls, too, depicted their favourite scenes of conquered nations bringing tribute to the King of Kings – just to remind subjugated peoples why they were here.

Once, there would have been rows of guards – the Immortals – those same Immortals who had fought at Thermopylae. Now this vast building was empty and echoing. This was a conquered city. Broken furniture lay shattered or piled up in heaps. Everything had been stripped of its gold and inlaid jewels. Dark fluid – oil or blood – lay pooled on the palely gleaming floor. People had walked – or run – through it and footprints tracked everywhere. We didn't push our luck by going in. The giant Hall was deserted and somehow sad. As if it knew these were its last hours on earth. It occurred to me much later that we were among the very last people ever to see it. We backed out slowly and drew into the shade of a fat pillar. A giant ram frowned down at me. I turned my back on it and called up Bashford.

'Mr Bashford, report.'

'We're at the back of the Tripylon, Max. We've a good view of the northern side of the Treasury. I have good news and bad news.'

'Give me the good news.'

'Not many people around.'

'And the bad news?'

'Not many people around.'

I sighed. That meant the Treasury was empty. There was no point in guarding an empty building.

'OK,' I said. 'Check it out by all means, but be aware that just because you can't see the guards doesn't mean there aren't any.'

'Understood.'

'Stay safe.'

'You too.'

He closed the link.

We crossed the wide courtyard to the other massive building – the Audience Hall of Darius. In contrast to the deserted Throne Hall, there were plenty of people here, all passing through the pillars and disappearing inside. I wondered if all those we'd encountered on the stairs were heading for the feast as well. We'd been unsure whether we'd find a small intimate dinner consisting solely of Alexander and his close friends, or a large public affair, open to all. We'd hoped for the latter, obviously. The more people around the better.

Everyone we could see was streaming through the Hall. And every single one of them was male.

'Shit,' I said, drawing back, although I'd expected this. A treacherous voice said the idiot Halcombe might have

153

had a point about inappropriate women. All was not lost, however. The universe might have a habit of ignoring women in general and women of a certain age in particular, but this isn't always the drawback it might appear.

'Slight change of plan,' I said to Clerk. 'You lot carry on through and I'll nip round the side.'

'We'll *all* nip round the side,' he said, because we're not supposed to split up.

'No,' I said, firmly. 'Because if there's no access to be had there, then only I'll be shut out. Markham can escort me if he likes.'

'Markham will certainly escort you,' said Markham, grimly.

I looked around. A lamp burned nearby, flames flickering. Set slightly apart from the lamp stood a small urn, half full of oil by the look of it. I picked it up. I always try to have something in my hands because it makes it easier to blend in. Markham once served in the army and swears he never did a stroke of work – just walked around all day with a clipboard looking serious. To which Major Guthrie always remarks, 'If only ...'

It took a long time to get myself around the outside of the Audience Hall – it's not a small building – but it would give the others time to get themselves into place. I couldn't see anyone around, but that didn't mean no one was watching me from the shadows.

As with any group of buildings there were the bright, well-frequented public areas, and then there were the dark, silent places where few people venture. Except for historians, of course. Confidence was key. I trod silently but briskly, looking neither to right or left, concentrating on not dropping my urn – just a lowly palace servant on

154

her way to ... do something or other. Of Markham, I could see nothing, but I knew he would be there somewhere. My heart was thumping away with what I told myself was the excitement of getting a glimpse of the great Alexander.

Ahead of me was a wall with an archway set into it through which, in the gathering gloom, I could make out another small courtyard. A soldier stood at the entrance, picking his nose. He showed very little interest in me, but I flourished my urn at him, just in case. He took it off me, checked the contents – for alcohol, I suspected, and then nodded me through.

Once inside, I turned left into a small garden which itself was in darkness, but beyond it I could see lights and hear music. This must be the place. I crept up a flight of marble steps and peered cautiously around a pillar. This was the place. I was looking down into an open courtyard set between what I reckoned was the Palace of Darius on my left and the Palace of Xerxes on my right. Lovely buildings but not the most imaginative names ever.

The area was crowded with couches and tables decked out in brilliant colours. A hundred torches made the space as bright as day. Even from this distance I could feel the heat coming off them. The advantage was that they made the shadows in which I was lurking all the darker. There were people here already, gathered around the courtyard, watching silently. But no women. I eased my way between two slim pillars, clutching my urn with one hand and my recorder in the other.

Clerk spoke in my ear. 'Max, where are you?'

I kept my voice to a whisper. 'West side of the courtyard just behind the red couches. I can see you.'

'I can't see you.'

155

'Good.'

'Markham?'

His voice startled me. 'In position, mid-way between both of you.' I knew better than to turn around to look. I wouldn't be able to see him anyway.

I took a deep breath. 'OK, people – let's get started.'

The whole thing was rather low key. There were no fanfares, no drum rolls, no ringing announcements to indicate Alexander's approach. I heard male voices approaching. Slaves stopped flying around making last-minute adjustments and melted out of sight

Silence fell and fifteen or twenty young men emerged from the palace. They'd recently bathed, their hair was either still wet or heavily oiled. They were neatly but not splendidly dressed in comfortable robes. I craned my neck. One was dressed in the Persian style. That must be him. That must be Alexander himself. His face was turned away from me. He was talking to someone on his right. They weren't raucous but they were boisterous. One or two of them already had goblets in their hands and were drinking thirstily.

Becoming aware of the silence, Alexander looked around and made a gesture for everyone to be seated. Perhaps his army life had left him with a distaste for the formal. There was a great deal of milling around but everyone found themselves a place. Four or five women appeared and perched themselves beside their men. Their costumes were gorgeous and their jewellery magnificent. I was interested to see they had painted their faces. They hadn't bothered covering their heads either, and I could see their intricate hairstyles, interwoven with gold and silver ribbons. They stared boldly around, dark and handsome women, beautifully dressed and presented. Courtesans.

I could see Alexander's profile. I could see his Greek nose, his curly hair, his high cheekbones. He had a very prominent Adam's apple. His bare arms were tight with muscle. He looked young and fit. His eyes sparkled. He was lively and energetic and he couldn't talk fast enough, waving his arms around to make his point. He was laughing, drinking, accessible, on top of his game. It was hard to believe he'd be dead at thirty-two.

With Alexander sorted, we needed to identify his companions. Ptolemy, who would go on to rule Egypt, was easy because he appeared to be wearing the courtesan Thaïs. A rash could not have covered him more closely.

People get the wrong idea about courtesans. They think the word means prostitute, but a courtesan is so much more. Yes, they traded in sex, but they were almost always well-educated and intelligent women, carefully trained in the arts of singing, dancing, conversation, politics and so on. They invariably attached themselves to wealthy and powerful men and, in these times, when marriage was simply a mechanism for acquiring more property or preserving a bloodline, they wielded enormous influence.

There have been some famous names – Aspasia, Theodora, Diane de Poitiers, Nell Gwynn, Madame de Pompadour and many more – all of whom have managed to leave their mark on history. As Thaïs was about to do.

Unseen musicians played. Soft pipe music was almost drowned out under the chatter. There were no dancing girls in diaphanous whatnots flinging themselves around in an unseemly manner. Calvin Cutter would have been bitterly disappointed. But only by the lack of dancing

157

girls. The rest of it was right up his alley. Gaudy and completely over the top.

Servants brought in huge trays of bite-sized food. The long tables were soon smothered in gold and silver dishes. I was interested to see that not only did they recline when eating, but they ate with their fingers, too.

And they drank a lot. The music kicked up a gear, moving smoothly from soft and gentle to something with a much livelier beat. Voices grew louder. Everyone was talking and laughing.

As far as I could see there were about a hundred people attending the banquet, including one or two Persians. They ate silently – not because they were sulking, but because it was their custom. What they thought of these noisy Macedonians did not show in their faces. Another couple of hundred people encircled the courtyard. Whether they were servants or officials or just nosey like me was hard to say. I didn't think any of them were bodyguards. I couldn't see that Alexander even had a food taster. Perhaps he felt he was among friends.

Apart from the Macedonian concubines, there were no women. And certainly no Persian women. All the servants were men. I would have to be very careful to remain concealed but I had a prime position here and I was getting some great material.

Wine flowed like a river. Slaves were continually refilling goblets. The Macedonians' capacity was amazing and they weren't mixing their wine with water in the traditional Greek manner, either.

The food was constantly replenished. Trays came and went. Alexander's liking for Persian ways included desserts. Lots of desserts. I couldn't make out any individual dishes but the smells were enticing.

Everyone was having a great time. No one knew the city was about to burn. That this was its last night on earth. Its last hour, almost. In twenty-four hours' time, it would be nothing but a bed of cooling ash blowing sadly across the sands. They talk about the glory that was Greece and the grandeur that was Rome, but Persepolis deserves a mention as well. And, in a few hours, it would be lost and gone, never to rise again.

My view was quite restricted because I was making sure to stay behind my pillar and slightly apart from the watching crowd, but interestingly, from what I could see, Alexander ate very little. A slave would offer him something sumptuous on a plate, he would look at it, and then someone would say something to him and he'd be off again, talking and drinking in equal measure. There was something almost frenetic about him. His drive and ambition were tangible. Raw energy came off him in waves. It was as if he knew he had to do everything as quickly as possible. Did he somehow know, deep down, that he wasn't long for this world?

I checked around carefully and then called Clerk. 'You still OK?'

'Yes. I've got Alexander full face on, but I can't get a good view of Ptolemy and Thaïs.' His voice had the slightly distracted note of a dedicated historian on the job.

'No problem,' I said. 'You stay with Alexander. I've got those two.'

'Copy that.'

I wondered how long I'd been recording. I'd be the first to admit time does tend to get away from me occasionally. My ankles and back were beginning to ache. These marble floors don't do your feet any favours at all. I

159

was just wondering whether to try for a better position when it all began to kick off.

For the previous five minutes, Thaïs had been whispering in Ptolemy's ear. Judging by the expression on his face, it wasn't sweet nothings, either. He seemed disinclined to listen to begin with, leaning across her to talk to someone else, but she was insistent, resting against him, pushing her breasts into his arm and tickling the back of his neck. He leaned back against the cushions and she whispered some more.

He shook his head curtly and gestured for more wine, but still she didn't give up. With one hand, she pulled some sort of jewelled cloth over his lap and her left hand disappeared.

Now he was listening. What a little minx she was to be sure. And a very skilful little minx, too. In seconds, he leaned back, closed his eyes and sighed.

She, too, leaned back – trust me, butter wouldn't have melted in her mouth – withdrew her hand and reached for more wine. Job done.

She was a very clever woman. She made no attempt to speak to Alexander directly. She worked through Ptolemy who, opening his eyes, took the wine she offered him and, after a significant glance from his girlfriend, began to talk to Alexander. Fast and furious. I had no chance of catching the words, but I could see him gesture around the courtyard. Several times. Those on each side of Alexander stopped talking to listen. Silence spread gradually outwards.

Thaïs leaned back on her cushions, regarding Alexander through heavily made-up eyes. Her expression was enigmatic and I wondered again about their relationship. He was, apparently, very fond of her, although whether because she was his best friend's 'best friend', or whether he'd been there himself would be a subject for endless speculation over a margarita or two when we got back.

The reaction to Ptolemy's words was interesting. Most of Alexander's companions looked appalled. Alexander himself didn't look that enthusiastic. If, at this moment, I'd been asked for an honest opinion, I would have said it wasn't going to happen. Persepolis would remain unburned. Alexander was already turning away and holding out his goblet for a refill.

And now Thaïs spoke. Her voice was harsh, but with an edge of honey. She leaned forwards, her robe tightening around her, highlighting her spectacular charms. I couldn't make out the words but we'd get that sorted on our return.

I tightened my grip on my sweaty recorder. This was really good stuff. Just what we'd come for. And given the absence of screaming and shouting in my ear, things were going well for Bashford at the Treasury, too.

In my own defence, I should say I did retain a grip on common sense. I stayed in the shadows. I stayed quiet. I did nothing to attract attention to myself. I was being the model historian. Discreet, dedicated, watchful and getting the job done. Just so we're all clear on that.

Obviously, I wasn't alone in my little nest between the pillars. There were people everywhere. Slaves, servants, personal attendants, palace officials – it must have taken a small army of people to service even one small banquet, but I was off to one side in the shadows and no one was taking any notice of me at all. I doubted the man on the other side of the pillar was even aware of my presence.

161

In the courtyard, however, things were heating up. Thaïs had stopped talking but others had joined in. There was a vigorous debate going on. I panned from face to face. Because I was at right angles to Alexander, some had their backs to me, but I didn't need to see their faces. Their voices were growing louder. Someone gestured expansively and most of his wine went over the woman next to him. She didn't even squeal.

Alexander was looking thoughtful, playing with his goblet. Suddenly, he swung his legs to the ground and sat up. As if it was some sort of signal, his companions followed suit.

Thaïs herself stopped sprawling all over Ptolemy and crawled over to Alexander who regarded her with a half-smile. Kneeling up and supporting herself with a hand on his shoulder – a familiarity he seemed happy to allow – she whispered in his ear.

The music stopped. Silence fell. I stopped breathing. This was it.

The man who had been standing next to me behind the pillar eased his weight to the left. I was forced to take a step backwards and made a small sound of alarm.

He said, 'Sorry.'

I said, 'No problem.'

And then I realised he'd spoken in English. At the same moment, I realised there was nothing under my heels. Instinctively, I grabbed for the pillar.

He threw back his hood and I found myself looking at Clive Ronan.

162

I wasted a vital second and a half just gaping at him. He wasn't supposed to be here. Why was he here? Why wasn't he at St Mary's getting himself arrested by Captain Ellis and the Time Police? What had gone wrong?

As I said, time wasted. If I'd ever had a chance – that was it. Too late, I opened my mouth to shout and he pushed me hard against a wall and shoved his hand over my mouth. Crushing me against the wall with his body, he ripped off my stole and scrabbled around in my hair until he found my ear. Rough fingers wrenched out my earpiece. I heard the crunch as he trod on it. The whole thing had taken only one second. Maybe two.

He whirled me around so my face was pressed into the wall. I grunted as the breath was knocked from my lungs.

He thrust his face close to mine. I felt his hot breath. 'How stupid do you think I am?'

Not as stupid as me, that's for certain.

Behind us, a great shout went up. The music started again. A jolly tune with a stamping rhythm. I could imagine a Macedonian conga line forming.

Ronan was immensely strong. I, on the other hand, have the muscle tone of lettuce. Somewhere along the way I'd dropped my recorder and my little jug of oil must have been kicked over because I slipped in something and lost my balance.

Someone grabbed me. Not Ronan. Someone else grabbed my legs and I was lifted up and carried away like an old bolster.

I tried to struggle but it was no use. I tried to bite the hand over my mouth but he was pressing so tightly it hurt my teeth. I could barely breathe. I tried to twist and kick and none of that was happening either.

I was carted around the corner back into the small garden behind the Audience Hall. Someone had watered it recently. I could smell the night flowers and wet earth. It was very dark – a tiny empty space. In all this massive palace complex, swarming with soldiers, prozzies, slaves, conquering heroes, cooks, butlers, servers, historians – millions and millions of people – this tiny courtyard was completely deserted.

I was gasping for breath. The large, rough hand was blocking my nostrils. I couldn't breathe properly. I couldn't even manage to squeak for help. I redoubled my struggles.

Many things were happening all at once.

In the distance, I could hear men's voices shouting and the thunder of footsteps. Someone quite close was banging a huge gong. The echoes reverberated through my chest. They were driving people from the palace. Thaïs had triumphed. Persepolis was about to burn. Was this what Ronan had planned for me? Would he leave me here, somehow immobilised as the flames crept ever closer?

They shoved me against a wall. My face bounced off a nicely carved bull and I could taste blood. They spread my arms and legs. I tried to kick out, expecting the worst. I

164

heard a faint electronic beeping as they scanned me. No, not scanned. They weren't scanning me. They were neutralising my tags. So I couldn't be tracked.

I tried to twist my head around. To see what was happening. I could hear men talking nearby, but their voices were drowned out by what sounded like huge crowds of panic-stricken people being driven from the palaces. I could hear men shouting, women screaming and the crash of furniture being overturned. Panic and hysteria were in the air.

Well, that was good. At least Alexander didn't mean anyone to burn. This was a forced evacuation. I don't know if it was my imagination but I thought I could smell smoke on the wind. Already?

And what of Markham? He wasn't here which meant he was dead – something I refused to believe – or injured – which was possible. I refused to allow myself to panic. He wasn't dead. He was Markham. Somehow, he would get back to me. Somehow, he would find a way.

I twisted my head the other way. Only a few yards away, Ronan was talking to someone I couldn't see. As I watched, another group of people charged past, shrieking and colliding with each other in their haste to get out. He reached out and took someone's arm and drew them aside. It was a woman. Her stole had fallen around her shoulders. I recognised that hairstyle. It was Thaïs herself. Well, wasn't that interesting? Thaïs had whispered in Alexander's ear – was it possible that Ronan had whispered in hers? My fears for Markham rushed back a hundredfold and I felt sick. Because, instead of Ronan falling into our trap – we'd fallen into his. I could taste the bitterness in my mouth. I could have lined St Mary's with the Crowns of Empresses, hung Swords of Tristram from the ceiling, filled the Hall with recently discovered Botticellis, littered his path with ancient scrolls from Alexandria – presented him with the Seven Wonders of the Ancient World even, and he wouldn't have taken a blind bit of notice. Because that wasn't what he wanted.

It was a harsh thing to admit to myself, but I'd really screwed this up. I'd misread Ronan and his motivation. I'd underestimated him big time. I really thought he'd go for an undefended St Mary's and the possibility of easy pickings. And he hadn't. Whether he'd guessed it was a trap or whether he was genuinely uninterested, I had no idea. I only knew that, once again, I was in deep shit and, this time, it was all my own fault. I'd been far too complacent and smug for my own good and now I hadn't just endangered myself, but everyone else here. I had no idea whether it was just me he was after or everyone on this assignment as well, but my duty was clear – to put every possible obstacle in his path. I stamped down on fear – because that wouldn't help at all. I should concentrate on what *I* could do, not on what could be done to me. I had no way of warning anyone but I would make things as difficult for him as I possibly could.

Ronan and Thaïs disappeared through an archway. She would want to be getting back to Alexander.

Now. I should act now while his attention was distracted. And I could definitely smell smoke on the wind.

I twisted suddenly and tore one arm free. Pivoting, I fetched a shadowy figure an almighty clout around the head, and the momentum freed up my other arm. Not having a clue where to run, I ducked and headed back the way I'd come. Right back into the fire they'd started in the courtyard where the feast had been held. The couches, the hangings – everything was ablaze. The heat was enormous. Sparks flew in the wind. There was no way out here. I had no time to stop and think. No time even to look around me and get my bearings. I had to move and move fast.

I skirted a wall, trying to get back into the Palace of Darius because from it I could access the Audience Hall, and once there I could hide in its vast emptiness of huge pillars and deep shadows.

Alas for that plan. I got there, but the Audience Hall was burning too. They'd flung oil up and around the wooden pillars and they were all ablaze. Dry wood, covered in paint, soaked in oil and fanned by the strong wind. The flames roared. The heat sizzled my eyebrows. This was *not* a place to be.

I veered away, meaning to run back into the Palace of Darius. From there I'd try for an exit to the Tripylon. I had no idea what I'd do after that. Joining the hysterical crowds as they headed towards the Gate of All Nations seemed the best bet. Get lost in the crowd and re-join the rest of St Mary's – who would know I was missing by now.

Yes. Excellent plan, Maxwell.

I turned and ran full tilt into Ronan.

I saw my death in his eyes. In a flash, I knew I wasn't getting out of this. There would be no rescue for me. But I could take him with me and call that a good day's work.

I launched myself at him in a fury of kicks and punches. Alley cat fighting. I scratched his face. I went for his eyes. I used my knees. I used every dirty trick I'd ever learned from Ian Guthrie. I never let up. I was a whirlwind. I saw Helen and Matthew and Leon and

167

everyone he'd ever injured and I just flew at him. I think I even bit his ear. Something I did made him yell, anyway.

I knew I stood no chance. He was a big and powerful man but the dynamics had changed. I had nothing left to lose. He knew I would do everything in my power to keep him here and fire is an equal-opportunity bastard. All I had to do was prevent him getting away and we would burn together. At that precise moment, I had no problem with any of that.

His foot slipped – spilled oil again, I think, and we both crashed heavily to the floor. He was on the bottom but I banged my elbow and my arm went tingly and numb. The best I could do was to knot my fingers in his hair and bang his head against the marble. I think I was hoping to knock him unconscious before he, probably quite literally, tore me apart.

And then someone yanked me off him. Two people actually. It took that many to hold me as I spat and twisted and kicked.

Someone else helped him to his feet. There were other people around him but I have no memory of how many or what they looked like. My attention was all on Ronan. I never took my eyes off him. I'd done some damage there. His head was bleeding. Scratches ran down one side of his face. And I think he'd hurt his wrist when he fell. Dislocated certainly – broken possibly. He wasn't standing straight, either. He'd encountered the Maxwell knee.

I was struggling for breath, my chest heaving. Smoke drifted past on the wind and I could hear the flames roaring around us. A small part of my mind wondered whether he would kill me now or knock me out and leave me to burn. A larger part of my mind hoped everyone had got away. And if Markham had them out searching for me when we knew the entire complex was about to be engulfed in flames then he'd be encountering the Maxwell knee as well.

He and Clerk would do their best but they'd never find me in time. I had no tags. They wouldn't be able to trace me. They were loyal but they weren't stupid. They wouldn't like it – but they'd get everyone away and jump to safety.

Ronan stood before me, his dark eyes glittering in the firelight.

I said, 'They'll find you. You won't get away forever. You can do what you like to me ...'

'I intend to.'

And he did. I could see it in his face. I was going to die at Ronan's hands here, now, at Persepolis.

I took a tiny step backwards which was all my captors would allow and a huge piece of burning timber fell from nowhere, landing between me and Ronan, hiding him in a shower of sparks, embers and smoke.

I don't know what happened to the men holding me. I only know that suddenly I was free. I didn't hang around. I could hear Ronan screaming, 'Find her. Find her.'

He was still screaming at his people as I ran for my life. I could hear crashes all around me. I remembered the broken furniture stacked up in Audience Hall I could just imagine how that would burn. And hangings, cushions, curtains – all oil-soaked. Everything would burn.

I needed to stay away from the buildings. I was in a kind of no man's land between the huge outer walls and the lower inner walls on my right. If I kept the outer ones on my left then I would eventually emerge near the Gate. I could hear Ronan shouting. He'd taken a wrong turn

169

somewhere and now he was trapped behind the inner wall. My heart leaped. There were no gates or archways in the inner wall. He couldn't get to me. I had a chance – only slight – but I was prepared to seize it.

Now I could hear shouting from those outside the city, too. Sparks were being borne away on the wind. Everything here was a dry as a bone. It wasn't just the palaces that would burn tonight – the town would burn too. The glory of Persepolis was ended.

Smoke caught at my throat and made my eyes stream as I ran along the base of the walls, desperately looking for a way out. Any way out.

And then, faintly in the distance, I heard Clerk shouting my name. Panic seized me. He shouldn't be here. They should all be gone by now. And Ronan couldn't be far off. If I responded I'd be giving away my position. If I didn't they'd keep searching for me.

I shouted, 'I'm all right. Get out of here.'

'Where are you?' His voice was closer.

'With a group of women being escorted through the gate. We're all fine. Go.'

That should reassure him. Enough to get him out of here anyway.

There was a scrabbling noise, some heavy breathing, and a pair of hands appeared at the top of the wall. Shit. The ground must be much higher on his side. Well, it would be, wouldn't it? For defensive purposes. With the massive outer wall behind them, any attackers would be trapped in a kind of pit. As was I.

I heard Ronan's voice through the thick clouds of smoke billowing over the wall, quiet and deadly.

'I'm coming for you, Maxwell.'

Adrenalin was coursing through my system and I was dancing about like a madwoman, all ready to fight for my life. All ready to take him down with me.

'Oh no, you're not.'

Someone grabbed me from behind and a strange voice said, 'Oh yes we are.'

Being grabbed by a stranger never brings out the best in me but on this occasion I stood quite still because – and don't ask me why – I thought it was the Time Police. I mean, it could have been them, justifying their existence for once and helping us bring this night's sorry shambles to a triumphant end. All right, things hadn't gone quite to plan so far but, let's face it, for us they rarely do.

So, like an idiot, I stood quietly until a voice behind me shouted, 'Got her, Mr Ronan,' and I realised I'd got it wrong.

I could hear Ronan's feet scrabbling as he tried to pulled himself up the other side of the wall and then I heard a long, low rumbling sound and everything stopped. I looked wildly round. An earthquake? On top of everything else, were we having a bloody earthquake?

The noise grew louder and then, high above us, the palace walls began to topple. Pieces of burning wood and masonry fell all around us, thudding into the ground.

A voice, cracking with youth and panic shouted, 'We need to get out now, Mr Ronan.'

'No. Wait for me.' As much as he ever could, he sounded desperate.

Something big fell and a shower of sparks and burning rubble fell with it. The heat was intense.

'Mr Ronan, sir, we have to go now.'

For a second there was silence and I wondered if he was dead. Killed by his own desire for revenge and serve him right.

No such luck. He was panting. 'Take her somewhere and kill her. Dump her. Don't tell me where. I don't want to know. Don't tell anyone where or …'

The rest of his words were lost in the clattering of falling masonry.

Behind me, someone said, 'Come on,' and I was dragged away.

I was rather hoping that in the way of minions everywhere, they'd be so desperate to get out of here that if I put up even some small resistance, they'd abandon me to save themselves. Or possibly shoot me, of course, but in situations like this, optimism is usually key. So I struggled, determined to make life difficult for us all.

It was worth a try but they weren't having any of it. A very young man thrust a blaster in my face. 'Move or I'll shoot you.' His voice was wobbling nearly as much as his gun.

I stood stock still.

The other soldier, a much older man grabbed my arm. 'Never mind him. Do as you're told or *I'll* shoot you.'

Something big fell in the distance, causing the ground to shake beneath my feet. Flames danced everywhere. I did as I was told because it's one thing to be held at gunpoint by steely-eyed professionals. They usually know what they're doing and right up until the moment they pull the trigger, you're comparatively safe. It's quite another to be held at gunpoint by a terrified nineteen-year-old who, at one and the same time, is terrified of shooting his first victim but can't wait to shoot his first victim, and is oscillating wildly between those two states.

Ronan's fortunes tended to fluctuate as did the quality of his associates and these two were certainly scrapings from the bottom of that barrel. The older man was experienced enough but was, I suspected, long past the age at which he should have retired. The younger one had barely left his mother. Neither of them was what you look for in a hit squad.

The youngster flourished the blaster again. I had a feeling he got off on doing that. 'Into the pod.'

What pod? They had a pod? Now *that* was more like it.

I think the younger one would have preferred to drag me along, kicking and screaming in the traditional manner, but I trotted along beside them quite happily because they had a pod, for crying out loud. My ticket out of here. And there it was, parked in the angle made by the outer wall and a jutting lookout tower.

So, to sum up. Not everything was going *quite* according to plan, but here was a pod. All I had to do was escape the burning city, overcome my captors, steal their pod, get back to St Mary's, and hand them over to the Time Police for interrogation. I could still be sitting down with a margarita and a full report for Dr Bairstow in no time.

The old man said, 'Now then, lass, we don't want any fuss, do we? Into the pod with you.'

I nodded because I certainly didn't want any fuss. Far from it. I was certain that, sooner or later, they would make some mistake I could twist to my advantage, but for that I had to be alive, because if you're alive then anything is possible. It's being dead that limits your choices.

I raised my hands and walked slowly into the pod. Where my heart sank.

What a state. Yes, I know from experience that they can get a bit ripe, but the smell in this one was ... I can't think of a word, so let's go with 'exceptional'.

I stopped dead, saying, 'Bloody hell,' and got a not very gentle poke in the back. I picked my way carefully around the torn floor covering, unable to believe what I was seeing. Half the locker doors were hanging off. Most of the ceiling panels were held on with duct tape. Acres of duct tape. There were two seats but the one on the left was broken and the one on the right didn't look too sturdy either. Leon and Dieter would have done their respective nuts and I wouldn't have blamed them in the slightest.

The young lad spoke, his voice still jumping with excitement and nerves. I wondered if this was his first important assignment.

'Sit down. In the corner. Hands on your head. Don't even think about it.'

I didn't even think about it. He was a young boy with a gun as big as he was and panting for an excuse to use it. I went and stood in the corner, kicked over an ammo box and sat on it. I had no choice. I didn't want him firing his blaster in here. He'd take out half the pod. I did as I was told and waited for an opportunity. There would be one. There always was.

But not this time, it would seem. The old man pulled out a small handgun and handed it to the lad who reluctantly handed over his blaster. The old man powered it down and stood it in a locker – I think to the relief of both of us.

Not that I was any better off. The handgun wobbled just as violently as the blaster had done. I sat very still.

Partly so as not to set him off and partly so I could use the time to have a look around me.

As I said, the pod was in a terrible state. Untaped wires hung from the ceiling. The console was dark in places and such lights as were on were flashing red warnings. The screen was cracked and blank. The interior was dim because only one of the ceiling lights was working. I didn't even want to see the bathroom. I could feel my bladder shrivelling to the size of a grain of sand just thinking about it.

I was amazed at how calm I was. There was an air of unreality about the whole thing. The seconds were ticking by and taking my options with them. I think I didn't believe this was happening. Surely some chance would materialise. Someone would come and save me. Although they'd better get a move on. I could hear the clatter of falling bricks on the roof. We could find ourselves buried under tons of burning masonry any minute now.

The old man appeared to be consulting a piece of paper, pressing buttons and bringing up crackly displays. There was a muttered consultation during which the gun continued to point my way. Finally, they appeared satisfied.

The old man sat at the console, the other continued to watch me – just waiting for an opportunity. Were we going to jump? What was happening? Another burst of stones falling on the roof reminded us all that whatever we were going to do, we should get on with it.

'Safety,' said the old man.

'But ...'

'Just do it, lad.'

Reluctantly, he snicked on the safety and it was just as well he did because it was the roughest trip I've ever experienced. I swear I felt the pod jump, which really shouldn't happen. I moved, my stomach stayed put – or possibly the other way around – something crackled on the console and then we landed with a bone-jarring thud that even Peterson would be ashamed of.

I sprawled on the floor wondering if I was dead.

'Get up.'

I said, 'Forget it,' into the floor and waited either to die or for my stomach to catch up. Whichever happened first. I really didn't care.

'I said, "Get up.".'

I opened one eye. Perhaps it was all a horrible dream. Nope. He was still there. The gun was still there. And I was still here. Wherever 'here' was.

I lay unmoving, trying to think. I was somewhere that wasn't Persepolis. I was alone. I was at the mercy of two men who, given their ages and the state of their pod, were not in the vanguard of Ronan's shock troops. I remembered his final words. 'Take her away somewhere and kill her.'

'Give her a minute,' said the old man. 'It knocks you back a bit if you're not used to it.'

The young lad laughed. 'Won't matter in two minutes, will it?'

I definitely didn't like the sound of that.

'Come on, lass. Up you get.'

I made a big business of getting unsteadily to my feet, resting my hand on a locker door for support. I think I had some crazy idea about whipping it open and using it as a shield, then going on to overpower the two of them, and hi-jacking the pod back to Persepolis.

Yes, I know, but my options were getting fewer by the moment. For God's sake, Maxwell, think of something.

What did I have to work with? A clapped-out old pod. Two very definitely second-string soldiers. An unknown time and location. And the life expectancy of a politician in a truth-telling contest. He pointed the wavering gun at me. The safety was off again. I had only seconds left.

And then the god of historians, traditionally absent on occasions like this, had a brilliant idea.

I straightened up, sighed theatrically, and said woodenly, 'No. No. No.'

He took a two-handed grip on the gun and set his mouth in what he probably thought was a sneer. 'It's no use you pleading.'

'I'm not pleading, you idiot. I'm advising.'

'What?'

'Well, you're doing it all wrong, aren't you?' Sometimes I just can't help myself.

'I'm the one with the gun. I'll do it any way I please.'

'Look,' I said kindly. 'I'm not saying don't shoot me. I'm just saying don't shoot me in here.'

He grasped his gun even more tightly, which only doubled the trembling. 'Why not?'

'Well, firstly, because it's likely the bullet will go straight through me and hit something much more important and then you'll be stuck here forever. And secondly, kill me in here and you'll have to cart the body outside yourself and believe me, I'm no lightweight. And I'm betting at least one of you has a bad back.'

The old man turned from the console and twinkled at me. 'You got that right. Listen to the girl, lad. She's done this before.'

'You bet I have,' I said, willing to exploit this sudden friendliness.

'Yeah, he said you were a slippery bitch. Warned us not to give you even an inch. Let's stop messing about, shall we?'

He peered at the console, confirming my suspicions that they didn't. have a clue what they were doing. It's bloody typical, isn't it? We historians spend bloody years learning about the timeline, temporal and spatial coordinates, pod procedures and God knows what and these guys are bucketing around the place with the instructions scribbled on the back of a bloody envelope.

'The green one,' I said helpfully.

'Got it. Much obliged.'

The door opened. I saw woodland. Summer green leaves rustled gently. There was a smell of leaf mould and sunshine.

I felt a tiny surge of optimism. All right, I wasn't dead yet. And trees were good. Trees could be hidden behind while I tried to get away. I thought I could see a faint path leading away. Paths could be followed – tracked back to their beginning or onto their end. Once outside I could make a run for it. Get away. Stay alive. And while you're alive anything is possible.

As if he read my mind, the older man shook his head. 'Not a chance, love. Off you go now. Ten paces and then stand still.'

Whatever the status of the youngster was, this man was a professional. Ten paces away was too far away to jump them. And not far enough for the young lad to miss. And nowhere near a useful tree either.

I walked slowly towards the door and out into the inappropriately cheerful sunshine. Birds twittered on, the way they do. Insensitive bastards. As I passed through the door, I turned back.

'Don't stop,' said the boy, gun wobbling even more wildly than ever. He was going to shoot himself in the foot any moment now.

'Listen to me,' I said, quietly. 'Just a friendly warning. Don't go back.'

They both stared at me. 'Why not?'

'You heard what he said. "Just kill her and dump her. Don't tell me where. I don't want to know. Don't tell anyone.".'

'Well?'

'Why do you think he doesn't want to know?'

'You're not important enough?'

'Maybe. But my guess is that he doesn't want to know because he knows that one day the Time Police will catch up with him. They can do what they please to him but he can't tell them what he doesn't know, can he?'

'So?'

'So what do you think he'll do to the only two people on the planet who *do* know what happened to me? He's not going to want you cutting a deal with the Time Police behind his back, is he? So – just a friendly word of advice. Don't go back. You've got a pod. Not a particularly brilliant one by the looks of it – I'd be surprised if you had enough power for the return jump. And don't tell me that's not a coincidence.'

Maybe I was getting through. They both turned and looked at the red-light display that was the console.

'Choose somewhere quiet and peaceful. I'm thinking somewhere rural. Maybe England in the 1920s. The Great War is over and the country's flooded with undocumented men. Do you have any skills?'

The old man drew himself up. 'Soldier.'

'Well, there you are then. What about you?'

The boy shrugged. Once again, the gun went everywhere. I could see the old man trying not to wince. Or duck.

'I'm good with my hands.'

'Well, that's brilliant. Get yourself a job in a garage working on these new-fangled motor cars. You'll be a millionaire by the time you're thirty.'

I wondered if I was getting through to either of them. 'Just promise me you won't go back, guys.'

There was complete silence. Apart from the bloody birds, of course. We all looked at each other. No one said a word.

'OK,' I said. 'I've done my best to save your lives and now I'm going to ask you to do me a favour in return. I don't want to be shot in the back. I'm not going to give you any trouble. I'll walk out of the door, but please – just tell me when, so I can turn around and face you.' I looked at the old soldier. 'Being shot in the back is not good. Even a firing squad looks you in the face.'

I waited, but there was no response from either of them.

I smiled. 'Thanks, guys. Take care.'

Without waiting for a reply, I set off across the clearing, completely forgetting to count my steps because I'm an idiot. I walked very slowly, not making any sudden moves. I just put one foot in front of the other, every step taking me further away. Had I read them right? Was I going to get away with this?

'Hey.'

It would seem not. I was going to die in this sunny clearing on this sunny day.

I let my breath out slowly, turned, squared my shoulders, lifted my chin, and tried to hold a picture of

Leon and Matthew in my mind. I wanted my last thoughts to be of them. I stood still and waited for the bullet. They were both standing in the doorway. The old man had his hand on the boy's arm, pointing the gun downwards.

'Thirteen ninety-nine,' he said quietly. 'Well, that's what we were aiming for.'

It took me a moment or two to grasp the implications of what he was saying and then I had to swallow before I could say, 'Thank you.'

'And you're probably not that far from home.'

I said again, 'Thank you.'

He nodded.

'Please, promise me you won't go back to Ronan, guys. He's going to kill you.'

I didn't wait any longer. I turned and walked slowly down the path. My back felt very exposed. The old man seemed to be well disposed towards me, but it was the young lad who had the gun. At any moment, I expected to hear a shot. Feel the impact between my shoulder blades. Or maybe in the back of the head. In which case, I probably wouldn't feel anything at all.

With every step, I kept thinking, I'm still here. I'm still here. I'm still here. Until eventually, the path meandered away to the right and I was out of their sight.

I felt a sudden wind and knew they'd jumped away. And I was still alive. I was still alive.

My legs gave way. I collapsed in an untidy little heap at the side of the path and threw up. I was still alive.

I sat up, wiped my mouth on a woodland plant, and tried to think clearly. I looked at the trees around me and said, 'You're not out of the woods yet, Maxwell,' and giggled hysterically for longer than the feeble joke warranted before finally pulling myself together.

Right – what did I know? I was in 1399ish. I didn't know where, but that shouldn't be a problem. People might not know in which year they were living – many people reckoned the years by the current king's reign. They would say, 'In the second year of the third Edward's reign.' Or, 'In the seventh year of the second Richard.' – but they usually knew where they lived. They could tell me where I was. If I was in England or Europe, I had a chance. Any of the Scandinavian countries wouldn't be too bad. The Americas were an unknown quantity and if I was in the Middle or Far East then I was doomed. I'd never survive there.

And I was never going to be rescued. My tags had been neutralised – and people would think I'd died in the fires of Persepolis anyway. There was no hope of rescue for me, but I was still alive. For the time being, anyway.

I rested my back against a convenient tree trunk and had a bit of a think. They wouldn't go back. They'd disobeyed Ronan's instructions – they wouldn't dare go back. They'd find somewhere, settle down and build new lives for themselves. Thanks to me. I'd saved their lives. Partly because I'm a nice person – no, really – but mainly because that meant that out there somewhere were two people who knew when and where I was. St Mary's wouldn't let it go. Whatever had happened at Persepolis – and not knowing was tearing me apart – Dr Bairstow would initiate a ferocious search for me, and Leon would tear the timeline apart. For a moment, I felt quite optimistic – and then I remembered again that I had no tags and they had no way of tracing me. And Leon was ill. And Dr Bairstow had a great deal on his plate at the moment. And his priorities would depend on whatever was happening back at Persepolis. I might not be the only person missing. And they would look for me there. If they had the chance to look for me at all. And Ronan had neatly side-stepped our trap. In fact, he hadn't even bothered to show up for it. And I'd been delegated to a pair of second-rate soldiers: a has-been and a raw boy. What a cock-up. What a bloody awful cock-up. I sat in the shade of a giant beech tree and faced the fact that no one was ever going to find me. I was never going home again.

I couldn't sit there forever. I wanted to – but I couldn't sit there forever. I had two choices. I could give up, bury myself in last year's crisp golden leaves, close my eyes and wait to die, or I could follow the path to whatever fate awaited me. And then die. I wiped my nose on my sleeve and tried to think. What did I know so far?

I was in 1399 – always supposing the old bloke hadn't been lying. And I wasn't far from home. His home or my home?

I sighed, heaved myself to my feet, and did my best to look presentable. I smoothed back my hair, wrapped my suddenly much too bright and very conspicuously foreign stole around my head and shoulders, shook the worst of the creases from my tunic and set off along the path. The wood was very quiet. A bird sang somewhere, faint and far off, but the air was heavy and warm. The only thing moving here was me.

I emerged from the woods into cooler, fresher air. I judged it to be late afternoon. The trees were covered in leaves but the colours were still fresh and green. Nothing had that tired, dry look of the end of August. So, late afternoon on a day in late spring or early summer. In 1399.

That was when. What about where?

I stood in the shade of a straggly, moss-covered hawthorn and looked around.

I was on a slight rise, looking down at a small village spread before me. A medieval village. It looked English. European certainly.

I saw a winding, rutted track that was the main road, bordered by small cottages, most thatched but a few tiled. The majority had long back gardens which seemed to be divided up into orchards, livestock pens and cultivated areas.

At the top of village, about a hundred yards straight in front of me stood the village church. Short, squat with its familiar Norman tower.

My heart soared, because if it's one thing that doesn't change very much over the centuries it's the village church, and I recognised this one at once. Yes, there were some ramshackle wooden buildings attached to one side and there were no ghastly Victorian headstones with cherubs or weeping angels. Yews encircled the churchyard instead of the horse chestnuts I remembered but, otherwise, it was amazingly unchanged.

The old man had said I wasn't far from home and he'd been right, but I'd had no idea how close.

I craned my neck, following the main street, no more than a deep track, really, down the slight hill and across the familiar stream at the bottom. There was no bridge – not yet, anyway – but a series of flat, white stones denoted the ford and there, on the other side, silhouetted against the woods, presiding over carp ponds and a dovecote and a poultry house and a water mill and several barns and all the other necessary accoutrements essential to a comfortable 14th-century life – there stood St Mary's.

Not my St Mary's. Or even the St Mary's before that. This was the medieval St Mary's and it was amazing.

I could see a gatehouse with two stumpy little towers built either side of a big wooden gate. The curtain walls were a good fifteen to twenty feet high, so I could only see the upper parts of the buildings they sheltered, but there was a small tower to the north and a corresponding but taller tower to the south. Both towers were overhung by wooden jetties into which modern – for the time – windows had been built. I could see the sun glinting off them, indicating that the upper parts at least were glazed. Between the two towers there was a tiled roof, covered in moss and lichen, indicating a great age. As far as I could see, the hall was in exactly the same position in this time as in my own. And about the same size, too.

The old man had said I wasn't too far from home. I wondered if, given their obvious lack of expertise with a pod, they'd just banged in the easiest set of spatial coordinates they could find. Because this was St Mary's. Not my St Mary's, but St Mary's nevertheless.

I couldn't believe how little it had changed. True, there were no cars, or yellow lines, no village shop, or streetlights, but the little houses were in almost the same place as they were in my day. The pattern of tracks and paths was familiar. I remember reading somewhere that, even today, the street plans of many cities still follow the original paths taken by animals as they went down to drink at the river. Except in those unfortunate places where town planners have had their way, of course, straightening winding roads, knocking down lovely but inconvenient old buildings and replacing them with contemporary statements of concrete and blue plastic. I myself am eagerly awaiting the day when we burn town

187

planners with as much enthusiasm as our ancestors burned witches.

The day was warm and sunny, with a heavy smell of cut grass in the air. Everyone seemed to be working on the land. They were getting the hay in. I could see figures dotted all over the place. I couldn't help contrasting the scene with our modern village when you were lucky to see anyone at all between the hours of eight in the morning and six in the evening.

I drew back under the trees for another think. Because if this was summer 1399 then things were about to get very sticky indeed.

In February of this year, the richest man in all the kingdom, mighty John of Gaunt, Duke of Lancaster, had died and the king, Richard II, taking advantage of the heir's absence, had made his long-planned move to seize the vast Lancastrian estates for the crown – and you really can't do that sort of thing in England. An Englishman's home is his castle etc., etc. Every property-owning man in England immediately panicked. Because if the king could do that to the richest and most powerful man in the country, what could he do to lesser men?

The new Duke of Lancaster, Henry Bolingbroke, exiled abroad, turned out to be not so powerless as Richard had hoped, and set sail for England immediately, with the sole purpose of reclaiming his inheritance. He said. And that might have been true but, when he landed, Henry discovered that Richard, not the brightest king around – and soon not to be around at all – having angered and antagonised every property-owning man in the country, had pushed off to Ireland, leaving his country temporarily unguarded. You honestly have to ask yourself, what was he thinking there?

Anyway, Henry lands at Ravenspur to popular acclaim and, apparently, has the crown thrust upon him in Richard's absence. Reluctantly – 'You want *me* to be king? Oh, but I couldn't possibly … well, all right then.' – he accepts the job. Richard returns, surrenders, and then dies of 'starvation' at Pontefract Castle.

Now, usually, these events are faint and far off and have very little impact on tiny, remote villages like this one. But, as I happened to know, the manor of St Mary's was part of the Lancaster lands and a certain Guy of Rushford, who was some sort of cousin to the current owner, had long cast covetous eyes on this particularly prosperous place. Taking advantage of the political turmoil, he would attempt to seize the manor and make it his own, assuming – probably correctly – that, with everything else going on, the king wouldn't give a toss about a piece of property so tiny and insignificant.

Looking around, it obviously hadn't happened yet because I'd never seen such a peaceful rural scene, but that wouldn't last.

I racked my brains, drawing patterns in the dust with a twig as I thought. Henry would land at Ravenspur at the end of June. The king would return in late July, landing in Wales and taking refuge in … in … I pummelled my brains. Yes, I know you're lost and panicking, Maxwell, but if you don't get this sorted out then you're not going to last for very long. Concentrate. Conwy. Conwy Castle, that was it. There would be negotiations, and Richard would surrender in August. Henry would ascend the throne and Richard would die. And at some point during all that, Guy of Rushford would descend on St Mary's and attempt to take it by force.

It was going to be a lively summer. If I lived that long.

There was no point in hanging around here. I couldn't remember the last time I'd eaten and, after the smoke of Persepolis, I was thirsty too. I needed to step out and meet my fate. Chin up, Maxwell. Shoulders back. No creeping about. Straight down what would one day be the main street, over the ford, up to St Mary's and ... and ... and think of something when I got there.

I made sure not to meet anyone's gaze as I strode down the main street, but from the corner of my eye, I could see heads lift. People straightened, scythes or rakes in hand and stared at me as I passed. I suspected strangers were a rarity and unaccompanied female strangers absolutely unknown.

The smell of cut grass was even stronger as I descended into the valley, along with smoke, hot horses, hot people and something peculiar I later identified as a product of the brewing process.

I paused at the ford and dipped the end of my stole into the cool water. I needed to tidy myself up, wash my face, and try to look a bit more respectable. I couldn't do anything about the smell of smoke or the small brown holes singed into my tunic but, in my experience, most people in History smell of smoke and animals anyway and I couldn't do anything about it, so no point in worrying.

Looking around without seeming to look around, I could see that work had almost come to a halt as people watched me.

I crossed the ford, stepping carefully from stone to stone. I had no wish to arrive dripping wet and an object of ridicule. And then, having come so far, I stopped. I lost my nerve. What on earth did I think I was doing? Where was I going and what would I do when I got there? I think that was one of the worst moments. That was when I realised how truly lost I was. My head swam. I stood by the bank, listening to the water swirling around the stones and breathed. I needed to find a little courage. I needed to be bold. I thought – what would I do if I was at St Mary's? And then I thought – bollocks to that. I *am* at St Mary's. Or I soon would be.

I lifted my chin and followed the path. Straight up the slope to the gatehouse.

The big wooden gate was shut, but there was a wicket set into one side. I caught a glimpse of some cobbles through the open door. The gate was unmanned but a bell hung from the wall. I muttered a prayer to the god of historians – for all the good that would do – and rang the bell. Just once.

For long seconds, nothing happened and I wondered if I should take a chance and just go through the gate anyway. Good manners said I should leave any weapons here and wait for permission to enter, but there was no one to ask permission from. I was lifting my skirts to step through when a man appeared. He stared at me for a moment and then came forward to stand over me, smiling and nodding.

My first thought was that as the guardian of the gate he was a bit of a dead loss. Yes, he was a big lad, but this was not the bigness of a military man. He was flabby around the middle, spotty around the mouth and had the eyes of a child. He grinned amiably, showing more gap than teeth, and mumbled something.

I drew myself up and said in my best Middle English. 'God give you health, sir.'

'Ah,' he said cheerfully. He didn't appear to understand me. I wondered if perhaps I'd got everything

wrong and I was somewhere in another country. Or even –
given my lifestyle – an alternate universe.

I said even more slowly, 'Of your kindness, sir, I seek
shelter.'

He beamed at me.

I beamed back again.

I pointed at myself, then in through the gate, and then
mimed drinking something.

He nodded and smiled but didn't move.

I nodded and smiled and wondered what on earth to do
next.

'Ah,' he said, nodding over my shoulder. I turned
around to see a man approaching at a fast walk, closely
followed by two others. He ignored me completely,
clapped my host on the shoulder and shouted angrily
through the gate. A third man appeared, rubbing sleep
from his eyes. The real gate-guard, I guessed, taking
advantage of the boss's absence for an afternoon nap. And
now, thanks to me, he'd been caught. He threw me a very
unloving look. I sighed. Another friend made. How long
had I been here?

Everyone looked at me. Assuming the new shouting
man to be the boss – correctly as it turned out – I clasped
my hands respectfully and tried again. 'God give you
good health, sir. I seek shelter for the night.'

He didn't move. My heart sank. They weren't going to
let me in. They might give me water – perhaps even a
piece of bread – and then they would turn me away.
Where would I go? What would I do? It wasn't the first
time I'd been thrown out of St Mary's but life in the real
world never goes well for me. This would be even worse.
I might just as well go back into the woods, choose a spot,
curl up there and die.

There were two men standing behind this new man and they both had their hands on their daggers. It seemed a little excessive for one small woman. People usually only want to kill me after they've got to know me better, but these were suspicious times. I wondered how much they knew or had guessed about what was to happen here.

He said something I didn't understand. I do have some medieval English words, but dialects vary from region to region. Even from village to village. It was perfectly possibly that people living as closely as Whittington and Rushford would be unable to understand each other. I'd thought of this, though.

I said slowly, and in Latin, 'God grant you health and long life, sir. I beg for aid and shelter. I am alone and in a strange land.'

He continued to stare at me for an unnervingly long time. No one moved. All around I could hear the shouts of the people calling to each other in the fields. A dog barked somewhere and another replied. The heavy scent of cut grass hung in the air.

The silence seemed endless. They weren't going to let me in. Ronan's men had meant well. They probably thought they'd done me a kindness, but I was going to die here. This time next week I'd be just as dead as if they'd shot me in that clearing and left my body for the forest animals. That could still happen. The forest animal bit, I mean. I sighed. What did it matter anyway? My shoulders sagged – I hadn't realised I'd been so rigid with tension – and I turned to go.

I'd taken no more than three or four steps when he called me back. I turned to face him and tried to wipe the tears off my face with the back of my hand.

He still wouldn't let me in, but there was an old tree trunk half hidden in the grass and he pointed to it. I sat gratefully and smoothed my dress as best I could. One of the men brought me a beaker of water for which I thanked him. He stared curiously and then, at a word, the two of them disappeared again, back to the fields.

I knew better than to gulp the water down. I made myself take small sips. One sip – count to five – and then another and so on. It lasts longer that way. He said nothing the whole time. I discovered later he rarely said anything at all.

I studied him as I drank. I saw a man possibly about my own age but it was hard to tell. I suspected he wasn't as old as he looked. He wasn't dour, but he certainly wasn't someone who laughed a lot. His thick fair hair was mixed with grey. Bright grey eyes flecked with hazel stared unnervingly at me from under thick eyebrows. I suspected he was a fighting man. He wasn't short, but very thick-set and well-muscled. A small scar bisected one eyebrow. It was a hot day and he wore his sleeves rolled up and I could see a very bad scar across his forearm. Whoever had stitched that together must have had his eyes closed as he did it. He reminded me of someone though I couldn't think who. His clothes were a dark russet, clean and well made. Medieval fighting men don't wear studded black leather anything like as often as the entertainment industry would have us believe. I looked down at his boots. Again, they were well made – scuffed, but good quality. His men had been armed but he himself carried only a small dagger at his belt and that he probably used for eating. I was a little puzzled. He was obviously in charge, but he wasn't well enough dressed to be lord of this manor. And he wasn't the steward. This was an outdoor man. More like the marshal. Yes – he was the marshal here, I was sure of it. In charge of the small garrison and in a place of this size, possibly the stables and other outdoor matters. And he was responsible for security. He was the 14th-century Ian Guthrie. Yes, that was who he reminded me of. That same air of quiet competence and complete control. That same air of exasperation. Except this one, just like everyone else, smelled strongly of hay.

'I am William Hendred,' he said quietly and in very reasonable Latin. I wondered if they did speak English here. I know at the beginning of the 14th century everyone who was anyone spoke medieval French. By the end of the century everyone spoke English, but this was a very out-of-the-way spot.

He continued. 'I am the marshal here. What is your name?'

'Joan,' I said, remembering an excursion with Peterson to Southwark some time ago. He'd managed to catch the plague, silly bugger. A huge pang of homesickness stabbed at my heart. I'd been Joan of Rushford then, but that wasn't a good idea here. We were too close to Rushford. He'd be despatching messengers to check and no one there would have the faintest idea who I was. I needed somewhere further afield. I would be Joan of Rouen. I'd been to Rouen. Not for long, but at least I'd be able to describe the market square. And being from France would account for my peculiar accent. Until some fluent medieval French speaker turned up, of course – which, with my luck, would be in about ten minutes' time.

'You are not French.' A statement not a question.

'No,' I said, 'but my husband Leon is – was – from Rouen.'

'Where is he?'

I heaved a sigh. 'Dead.' Never tell anyone anything more than they ask.

'When?'

'I am not sure. A month … perhaps.'

He twisted round to look at me more fully.

'How?'

My voice trembled uncertainly because I was uncertain. If you're going to lie then you should always go for it big time, but this was going to be a whopper.

'We were travelling to England from Calais. Leaving Normandy. The times there are not good. We sold everything. There was a group of us, all going to England. To start again. The crossing was good. We were nearly safe when the weather changed. They made us all stay below deck. Someone saw a light but the ship hit some rocks. Water poured in. They pulled some of us out. I … never saw my husband again. I slipped on the steep deck and fell into the water. I clung to a small barrel. I prayed to God because I thought I would die. But I did not.'

I stopped.

He waited for me to finish. Damn and blast.

'There were men on the beach. With a light.' I stopped again and then said in a whisper, 'They took the cargo and killed the people.'

'Except you.'

I nodded. 'I stayed in the water.'

'You can swim?'

I knew better than to say 'yes'.

'The good Lord protected me.'

'And then?'

'They loaded everything on wagons. People … my friends … were struggling ashore. They cut them down and then they threw them back into the sea.'

'And then?'

There were no clues in his face or voice. I had no idea how this little fantasy was going down.

'The sun came up. I struggled ashore. I didn't know where I was. I wasn't sure if I was in England. And if I met anyone, would they help me or kill me? I walked along the coast until I found a small group of houses. There were nets outside. A woman gave me some bread. Then I walked. For a long time. I found some work at an inn but it wasn't … I didn't … the landlord wanted me to … so I set off again. To look for work. I think I thought I could earn enough to try to take a boat back to Normandy. Although there's nothing for me there. Or perhaps stay here. I don't know …'

He stared at me grimly as I outlined this daft plan. 'And your husband …?'

'Gone forever,' I said, truthfully. It was the first time I'd acknowledged this to myself and the tears poured down my cheeks. I put my hands over my face and, no longer caring whether he believed me or not, I gave way to an overwhelming sense of loss.

I honestly thought he'd push off and leave me – most men do when I cry all over them. I don't cry prettily and there's snot and all sorts of unpleasant substances, but when I took my hands away and wiped my nose on my mistreated stole, he was still there, looking down at me.

I stared damply back again.

More and more people were passing in and out of the gate, returning from the fields and staring curiously as they passed. I wondered how much I cared.

Abruptly he said, 'We can shelter you tonight. Tomorrow we will see. I must speak with the steward.'

Interesting. We had an absentee landlord then. He and the steward would be in charge.

I faltered, 'You are not lord here?'

He shook his head. No resentment. No pretending to be what he was not.

'Abroad.'

'His name?'

'Why?'

'So that I can remember him in my prayers.'

'You owe your shelter to Sir Hugh Armstrong.'

That was useful to know. And he wasn't here. Was he in London? Had he gone into exile with Henry of Lancaster? And if so, was he on his way home?

I said demurely, 'Now I know who to thank.'

He frowned. 'You thank me.'

I bowed my head. 'Thank you, sir.'

He stood up and waited. Apparently, I was to come too.

We entered through the wicket into a good-sized courtyard beyond. As I stepped through, he said, 'Lady, you be welcome,' and I remembered this was a formal world.

I said, 'Sir, I thank you for your kindness and goodwill.'

He nodded and I felt a small relief. I'd got it right.

I saw a range of buildings opposite. A hall – *the* hall, with towers at each end. This was a prosperous place. The main buildings were of stone – there was even some glazing. A number of smaller, wooden buildings were built against the tall curtain wall – a kitchen, a bakehouse, stables, a poultry house, the dovecote – it was all here.

The place was bustling with life. A queue of people waited to draw water at the well, over to my left.

Without pausing he led me across the uneven cobbles and we stepped down into the hall.

I stood on the threshold, blinking. The interior was very dim after the bright sunshine outside but I knew where I was. I was in the Great Hall at St Mary's.

All I had to do was stay alive for the next six hundred and fifty or so years and I'd be home.

16

He left me and disappeared through a door at the far end. I stood with my back to the wall and looked around me.

This hall seemed very slightly smaller than the one I remembered, but the smell was exactly the same. Dust, sunshine, damp stone – I closed my eyes and, in that moment, the History Department swept past me, clutching their mugs and scratchpads and bickering away. Then they were gone, fading into the dusty sunbeams.

I looked up at the enormous cruck roof. The beams were colossal. The windows were shuttered at the lower part and glazed only at the very top. Where they couldn't be damaged. There was a staircase on the far right-hand wall – not the magnificent modern version I knew, but a series of triangular oak steps set in a sturdy wooden frame. They ran up to a first-floor door and then turned and ran up the wall to another door on the second floor.

Under the stairs a small door led down into what I guessed would be the buttery and behind that, the kitchen. It seemed the 14th century had far more idea of health and safety than the modern St Mary's, since the kitchen was housed in a separate building.

At the other end of the hall stood a wooden dais. Household servants were putting together a long trestle table. Similar but less grand tables were being set up at right angles down the hall. They were getting ready for their evening meal.

At first, I couldn't think what was missing and then I could. There was no fireplace. An octagonal hearth stood between the high table and the lower ones, swept and empty at this time of year. I looked up because Professor Rapson would expect me to. No hole in the roof. No louvres. I looked at the smoke blackened beams. Obviously the smoke found its way out through the gaps in the tiles.

The floor was of stone, not tiled as it was in my day. The two doors in the back wall opened into what I suspected was a private solar and would, one day, lead to Wardrobe. William Hendred had disappeared through the one on the left.

I stood quietly against the wall pretending not to notice the curious glances coming my way as they dragged out the benches and made ready for the evening meal. All the servants were men. I had no idea whether this Hugh Armstrong was married or not – even if he was, there would be very few women here. His wife and her maid and that could well be it. There might be a washerwoman – and brewing was traditionally a female activity as well, but all other functions were carried out by men.

I stared down at the shiny stones on the floor and tried not to think about what had happened to me. Or what was happening to me. Or what would happen to me.

William Hendred appeared and gestured curtly. I weaved my way around the servants, up the step and through the doorway.

I'd been right. This was a private room. A very pleasant private room. A small fire burned on a hearth and

201

the shutters were open letting in the last of the afternoon sun.

An elderly man sat at a table carefully positioned to get the best light. Two or three small scrolls lay in front of him and he was very carefully and very slowly inscribing something at the bottom of one of them. The sound of his pen scratching the parchment was very loud in this quiet room. This was obviously the steward. Walter, as I later discovered. Walter of Shrewsbury. And he was making me wait.

I took the time to study him because he was as important as William Hendred. Probably even more so in his own eyes. He wore an old-fashioned robe that reached to his ankles. It had once been a dark red but had faded along the folds and hem. A number of small, leather pouches hung from his narrow leather belt. He wore soft felt shoes – whether because he was inside or because he had bunions I couldn't say, but from the sour expression on his face I would guess the latter. His sparse grey hair hung around his face and I suspected his bald patch was carefully concealed by his soft, floppy hat.

Eventually, he put the parchment carefully to one side. I could see the still wet brown ink catching the light. We looked at each other and I realised how lucky I'd had it up to this moment, because here was instant and mutual dislike. I strongly suspected he was an ancestor of Malcolm Halcombe.

I told my story again and it took a long time because he questioned every sentence. When things got really tricky I took refuge in not completely feigned tears or in pretending not to understand his Latin. Which was actually very good. I was careful to make sure mine wasn't better.

I didn't blame him for being suspicious. These were perilous times. They must be expecting the king's commissioners and official seizure any day now. I wondered if they knew about Guy of Rushford and his unofficial plans.

Time dragged by and all the time the smell of cooking grew stronger and stronger. I hadn't eaten for hours and the little that had been in my stomach was back in the forest. I tried not to think that twenty-four hours ago, I'd been with the Boss and Peterson, putting the finishing touches to the Persepolis assignment, or that twelve hours ago I'd been breakfasting with Leon, or that six hours ago I'd been waiting to see Alexander the Great. And now I was here.

I stood back by the wall while the steward and William Hendred held a whispered consultation. Their dynamic was interesting. They didn't like each other, I could see that easily, but each listened to what the other had to say, considered their words carefully, and then made a measured response. There might not have been liking but there was respect.

I was, according to custom and tradition, entitled to a night's hospitality, but then what? If they chucked me off the manor in the morning – as they were perfectly entitled to do – where would I be this time tomorrow? It occurred to me that perhaps I could trade something of value. Information. Perhaps there was some way in which I could warn them of imminent events without being too specific. Would it help or hinder my cause? Or would History just scythe me off at the knees for doing so?

Ah well, as Markham often says, it is always better to seek forgiveness than permission.

I took a step forward. 'Sir, may I speak?'

Walter looked up and said curtly, 'No.'

'Sir, I have heard some talk about …'

'Be silent.'

Well, that took the decision out of my hands. I was silent. I think Dr Bairstow would have been impressed.

It was William Hendred who said, 'What have you heard?'

I bowed my head respectfully. 'I have heard talk of …'

Walter cut in. 'Where?'

'A tavern, sir, just outside of Rushford.'

'Which one?'

Shit. 'I cannot remember the name. It had a bush outside the door.'

They all had bushes outside the door. That was how you knew it was a tavern. Even today, many pubs continue the tradition with hanging baskets.

Walter made an exasperated sound. 'Tavern gossip.'

William stared thoughtfully but said nothing. The discussion resumed. My ankles began to ache again. It had been a long day.

Eventually, William stepped back. A decision had been made. It would seem that enquiries would be set in hand and I would remain here in the meantime. It was unclear what enquiries they would be making – whether about my imaginative shipwreck or the possibility of any survivors I could not determine. I was also unsure whether I was a guest or a prisoner.

I was dismissed from the steward's presence with a casual flick of the wrist. I turned to go, waited for William Hendred to join me and, when he didn't, I trailed uncertainly toward the door.

The sun was very low now, although it would be light for a little while longer. Everyone was busy in the hall.

Cloths had been laid. The smell of cooking was driving me insane. Everyone had a purpose and was busy fulfilling it.

I stood against the wall and wondered what would become of me.

They put me on the bottom table. The one with its back to the main door and carefully placed to catch all the prevailing draughts. Like modern railway stations. If my status plummeted any lower I'd be out with the dogs.

Servants brought us bowls in which to wash our hands, but whereas they politely held the bowls for their betters and passed them soft cloths to dry their hands with, ours was just dumped on the table and left. Nevertheless, it felt good to wash my hands again.

I had two very elderly men opposite me, whom I suspected were former servants and now retired. I took a measure of comfort from knowing this was a place that looked after its people, even after they were too old to work. There was an old woman next to me. There was a musty smell about her as if she was wearing clothes that had been put away while still damp. She was the only other woman in sight. Perhaps in this society women conveniently died when they became too old to breed or work. If that was the case then this one hadn't read the rules. There was absolutely nothing wrong with her appetite. She ate everything in sight. Her name was Maud – I wondered if that was short for Mathilda – and she was a lady who really enjoyed her food.

We've all read about medieval banquets – boars' heads, swans roasted with their feathers replaced so they look just like the real thing, elaborate desserts and so on. Our meal was nothing like that. Meat was served, but to the top table only. There was no grand procession around the hall as the cook showcased his talents. Just a couple of boys briskly laying out bowls and platters to each table.

A row of chairs had been laid out at the top table, including an elaborately carved armed chair with a small canopy, which I suspected was where Hugh Armstrong usually sat. A smaller chair would accommodate his wife. If he had one. Walter and William sat together at one end. They had meat served to them – pork by the looks of it.

I'm not sure what I was expecting to get. A bone, perhaps, or a bowl of lukewarm sloppy gruel if they weren't feeling very generous, but it wasn't bad. There was some sort of stew. Very thick and quite tasty. No meat, of course, because you don't waste the good stuff on the non-productive members of the community. There was a lot of green stuff in it I didn't recognise – plucked from the hedgerows, I suspected, but it really wasn't that bad. And I was starving anyway.

Believe it or not, the table manners at this St Mary's were better than anything displayed at mine. I had to remember to hold back because good manners were important in this society. I should not speak with my mouth full or speak to anyone while they were drinking. I shouldn't dip my bread in the salt – chance would be a fine thing – it was all the way up on the high table.

I knew that women didn't swear and shouldn't touch men not of their own family. I especially knew that women didn't usually walk anywhere alone. By doing so I had already marked myself out as different.

I had no eating implements – not even a knife – and everyone else had brought their own so I had to eat with my fingers. I used the end of my stole to keep my hands clean. More than ever I was glad I'd brought it.

The old man opposite me, wearing an old and much darned tunic that had originally been brown, offered me his beaker of beer to share. I had no choice but to accept. It was a polite gesture. I smiled my thanks, and sipped at the gruesome contents. When I'd finished, I carefully wiped the rim with my stole as etiquette demanded and handed it back with a nod of thanks. I could see this met with some approval.

While remembering not to shove down my food like a heathen, I tried to listen to the conversations around me and to pick out the odd word every now and then, but the local accent very strong. Making myself a foreign woman had been a good move. Obviously, none of my companions spoke Latin, so, apart from being nudged to pass the jug of beer occasionally, I was left alone. Which was good of them because I could see they were curious.

I filled up on as much bread as I could politely take, chewing it carefully. Breaking a tooth on some medieval grit would not be a good move. Medieval dentistry was to be undertaken only as a last resort.

The food was plentiful but dull. Of course, it was a difficult time of year. Their winter supplies would be nearly used up and the main harvest not yet in. Fruit wasn't ripe yet. But there was enough here for everyone in this seemingly well-organised manor.

Every time I looked up I would see William watching me. Except for the times when he was speaking with Walter. Then they would both turn and look at me. I wondered if they thought I was a spy. I'm certain Walter thought so.

In the absence of Hugh Armstrong, they were the two most important men on the manor. They were talking together a lot. Well, Walter was talking and William was playing with his beaker, turning it around as he listened attentively. I knew they were talking about me.

The meal was finishing. William strode from the hall. Walter, after one last baleful glance at me, vanished through the other door in the wall behind him. Where the library would one day be.

And what of me?

I looked around the hall. Maud had vanished. I was the only woman here and on the receiving end of more than my share of strange looks. The majority were curious – guests usually paid for their board and lodgings with news and gossip from other parts, but no one could understand me. I was better dressed than most, but my clothes were odd, and I was alone. I had no husband or father or brothers. No male relatives of any kind. I wondered how far my story of shipwreck, murder and escape had been accepted.

I looked around. People were pulling out straw palliasses and laying them down, or gathering in groups for a gossip at the end of the day. The hall doubled as a dormitory for everyone not important enough to have their own space. Like me.

I had no palliasse. But I could manage this. All I needed was to set my back against a wall – a corner would be best – and make myself as inconspicuous as possible. I did briefly consider sleeping outside, but remaining with the crowd might be a safer bet. I was the only woman here, but on the other hand, Walter of Shrewsbury seemed to run a tight ship. The laws of hospitality would prevail – I was almost certain of it.

I needed to shift, anyway. That's the problem with beer. It doesn't stay put for long. I followed several people outside, all of us heading in the same direction.

The midden was round the back of the stables. The same gap-toothed lad I'd met at the gate smiled helpfully and pointed. I gathered there was a women's side and a men's side. Well, that was better than I'd hoped for. I made my way to the women's side, made my preparations, closed my eyes to the sights, sounds and smells and hoped for the best. And made a note never again to be without a couple of broad dock leaves in my pocket. I had an idea my traditional historian constipation was going to turn out to be a Good Thing after all.

Making my way back to the hall in the gathering dusk, I reviewed things so far. I wasn't dead. I had a roof over my head for the night. I'd eaten. I'd drunk beer and survived – although I might turn into a man any moment now – and I'd used the public facilities and lived. Tomorrow could take care of itself. At the moment, things were good.

No, they weren't. The marshal was waiting for me.

I tried to bluff it out, smiling and nodding politely and pretending I didn't know it was me he wanted by sidling past him. That didn't work.

He planted himself squarely in my path and said, 'I have a place for you. Come with me.'

I hesitated, weighing the odds. A night in a public place with ten or so men around me or a night in a private place with just one man.

A sudden wave of desolation swept over me. What did it matter? I would probably be dead in a few days anyway. I'd say or do the wrong thing and either they'd chuck me out to die slowly in the woods or hang me for some trivial misdemeanour such as being female. I wasn't Chief Operations Officer Maxwell any longer – I was Joan of Rouen, friendless and penniless and ranking somewhere

209

below the duck-billed platypus on the evolutionary scale. I'd lost my husband, my child, my job, my home, even my own time. What the hell did anything matter any longer?

I turned silently and followed him to the guardhouse. He halted outside the door in the right-hand tower and flung it open, motioning me inside.

No. I stopped dead. One man – maybe. Although probably not – not without buying me dinner first – but the evening's entertainment for a room of soldiers? Definitely not.

I folded my arms, just in case he wasn't familiar with intransigent womanhood.

He stared for a moment and then I think the penny dropped. Or more probably, the groat.

He smiled slightly, shook his head and motioned me inside again.

I took a tiny step forward, trying to convey obedience, modesty, but above all – chastity.

He rolled his eyes. Yes – 14th-century men roll their eyes. You heard it here first. Stepping back from the door he again motioned me inside and managing by this simple action to convey he was being restrained and patient but not for very much longer.

Well, what did it matter? I stuck my chin in the air again and stepped inside.

The passage forked. Left led to the guardroom where I could hear a murmur of male voices. Right was a short passage leading to a flight of stone steps spiralling up into the gloom.

He took an oil lamp from a niche in the wall and motioned me to follow him up the stairs. I paused for a moment and he disappeared around the bend. It was suddenly very dark. I took a deep breath, put my hand on the rough outer wall for guidance and stumbled after him.

The stair opened into two rooms. One was obviously his private quarters. There was a low bed with a wooden chest at the foot. Another chest was placed under a window. Clothing hung from pegs on the wall and several pairs of boots were ranged against the wall. A small stool stood behind the door. Everything was very neat and in its place. The room of a man who fended for himself.

He settled his flickering light on the chest and motioned me through to the second room, which was empty. I don't know for what purpose it had originally been built. There was no window and it was too big for storage and not big enough for a bed. Even I could barely stretch out in it and I'm not tall. I wondered if it had once been a garderobe – there was a narrow shelf around the outside wall wide enough for someone to sit on – and a smell of fresh mortar. Had they blocked up a possible entrance in anticipation of what was to come? Whatever it was, I didn't care. Here was a huge piece of unlooked for luck. Yes, he was between me and the door, but he was also between me and the world out there. It could have been a lot worse. And it wouldn't be the first toilet I'd slept in.

If you don't undress, clean your teeth, wash your face and hands or brush your hair, then preparing for bed takes no time I at all. I lay down on the rough floor and closed my eyes. And then, of course, because the human mind must always have something to worry about, no sooner did I know I was safe-ish for the next few hours, than the events of the day came crashing back with the force of a tidal wave running downhill.

What of Markham and the others? How had they fared at Persepolis? What had happened to them? What the hell had happened back at St Mary's? Had Ronan shown up for the crown? And Leon? How would they tell him what had happened to me? How angry would he be? Would they send a rescue party? Yes, of course they would, but they wouldn't find me. No one would ever find me. I was here in 1399 and things were about to get very dodgy indeed at St Mary's.

And the rest of the country wouldn't be much better off. Henry IV was a usurper and would never be allowed to forget it. He'd fight off rebellions by the various nobles, including the Percys from the north and Owain Glyn Dŵr from Wales, and everything would culminate in the Battle of Shrewsbury in 1403.

I rolled over onto my back. 1403? Why did that date ring a bell? Apart from the Battle of Shrewsbury, I mean. 1403 ... and then I had it. I'd been to 1403 before. My first jump. The solo one that signified the end of my training. I'd been despatched to Shrewsbury, 1403.

I hadn't got there – the pod had been programmed to take me somewhere else. It was the last part of our final exam. To see how we coped alone, lost, in the wrong time and the wrong place with no hope of rescue. I'd worked out I was in no danger, sat back and enjoyed a pleasant few days in the sun with plenty to eat and a couple of good books. I'd still been quite pleased to get home though. I remembered dancing out of the pod trying to be cool and historian-like and failing utterly. But – and I could hardly believe I'd been this stupid – I hadn't asked where and when I'd been. I'd been so relieved to get back that I hadn't asked. I remembered the distant mountains and the sound of the wind sighing in the long grass that definitely wasn't Shrewsbury. But if it hadn't been Shrewsbury then it might not have been 1403. It probably hadn't been. But I couldn't take that chance. Because you can't be in the same time twice. There are a lot of rules and regs about time travel – sorry, observing major historical events in contemporary time – and I'd broken most of them at one time or another, but there's one rule that is unbreakable. You can't be in the same time twice. If I'd already jumped to 1403 and if I was here when 1403 came around – as it surely would in a couple of years – then the result would be catastrophic. No one's quite sure exactly what would happen but even Professor Rapson says it would be very bad indeed and if he thinks it would be bad then trust me – it would be apocalyptic.

So, even if, against all the odds, I survived here – even if I managed to make myself a life and a home – even if everything went well for me and I prospered – once 1403 turned up I could be finished. And there wouldn't be anything I could do about it. One day, in a far corner of the world, a long way from this place, a pod would arrive with me in it and something awful would happen to reality as a consequence.

But, argued the other part of me, that was in a different universe. That might not have happened here.

There are too many similarities, said the first part. Isabella Barclay was shot in both worlds and although it was by different people, the end result was the same. Peterson still incurred that awful wound to his arm. All right, David Sands didn't have that terrible car accident on his way to Rushford and end up in a wheelchair, but only a few weeks later he lost his foot. There are similarities all over the place. You can't afford to take the chance. You

213

have to assume you jumped to 1403. Still, the problem's easily solved, isn't it?

Yep – easy-peasy. All I had to do was ensure I wasn't here in 1403. So either I needed to get myself rescued, or build my own pod and rescue myself, or …

Or end my existence before the worst could happen. I didn't know the specific date I'd landed in 1403, so, to be on the safe side, I should be topping myself as the clock struck midnight on New Year's Eve. Yes, I know there were no clocks here, but allow me a little dramatic licence, please.

And could I do it? When the time came, could I actually do it? If I hadn't been in the original 1403 then I wouldn't have to. I could be ending my own life unnecessarily but could I afford to take the chance? The odds were stacking themselves against me. They often do when you're not in your own time. History doesn't like it.

It was all problematic anyway. I was going to be dead long before 1403.

I curled up into a tiny ball and cried quietly in the dark.

I would have liked at least a few hours to myself, to think about things a little and to settle my mind, but chance would have been a fine thing.

I was still awake when I heard the stir of people beginning to move around outside. I heard William Hendred use his chamber pot, splash some water about, dress, and then the door banged behind him.

No sooner had he departed than I was up and running as well. Has anyone ever noticed how a lot more beer comes out than goes in? It's a fluid that defies the laws of physics.

Keeping my eyes firmly to the front, I trotted round to the ladies' side of the midden, did my business, reminded myself about the broad-leafed plants *again*, shook out my skirts, adjusted my hair and swilled my face in the water trough outside the stables. There are basic historian rules about this sort of thing but it struck me that dying naturally of typhus or cholera would also be a Good Thing and therefore I should make a start.

I stood for a moment looking around me, watching the early morning bustle. And it *was* early morning. A mist lay over the stream and the three great carp pools. The gate was wide open and people were already streaming in and out.

William Hendred strode past and gestured towards the hall. Apparently, I was entitled to breakfast.

Porridge. I quite like porridge. And this wasn't the girlie stuff made with milk and sugar either. This was man's porridge, guaranteed to put hairs on your chest – or in my case, keep me on my feet throughout the longest working day I'd ever known.

I shovelled down a bowlful as fast as I could and joined the procession of people out of the gates and into the fields.

Because it was haytime.

I never before realised the importance of modern machinery in the hay-making process. Giant machines that roar up and down enormous fields, cutting, spreading, gathering, baling, carrying away and stacking, while the driver twiddles a few levers and listens to Radio 4, pausing occasionally for a swift mug of tea and a pack of chocolate digestives.

Bloody hell, I've never worked so hard in my life. And I work for Dr Bairstow!

Someone handed me something shaped like a wooden rake. Someone else pointed to a line of people moving slowly across a patch of land. I joined the end and looked to see what everyone else was doing. This was where my lies would start to unravel. Anyone born into this world would know exactly what was happening. Knowledge was handed down from generation to generation. It was bone deep. In their blood. I hadn't got a bloody clue. And I couldn't pass myself off as a townswoman either. I couldn't cook, sew, spin – all women from the highest to the lowest could spin – tend livestock, rear poultry, brew beer – I couldn't do any of that. I was in deep shit here.

Someone said something on one side of me and I bent to my task. As far as I could see they were raking the dried hay into piles. I looked behind me. A horse-drawn flat wagon with slatted sides was waiting. Right. So, someone had cut the hay. Someone else had turned the hay until it was dry. We were raking it into piles ready for someone to cart it away to be stored in a barn or made into a haystack. I was part of a process but, looking around, only the easiest bit. I looked along the line which was mostly women, one or two of whom were pregnant. Another had a baby tied to her back. There were elderly people on the line as well. And then there was me – the foreign woman, who should show them she wasn't such a useless lump. I set to with a will.

Of course, I hadn't got a clue. Certainly not enough of a clue to tear off a strip of material to protect my hands from the rough wooden handle. Within an hour, I could feel the blisters forming. Not that I was taking a lot of notice because my back was killing me. And the hot sun beating down was making my head ache. And I hadn't had any sleep the night before. And I hadn't had the sense to pace myself because I had hours of toil ahead of me.

This was important to them. This crop – and the one that would come after because there would be at least two cuts – would feed their livestock through the winter and spring. Without winter fodder, they'd have to slaughter most or all of their animals and, without their animals, the next year would be a tough one. I was about to get a glimpse of medieval country life, where everything interlocked and everyone and everything was reliant on someone else doing their job properly. Failure to do so was a lingering death by starvation. And everything was hostage to the weather.

217

So, I went at it with a will – just to show them I wasn't completely hopeless, raking away for dear life, and two hours later I was nearly dead. I looked up at the sun and judged it to be about nine o'clock. Another eight hours at least.

I don't know how I got through it. Children brought ale around at intervals. I drank deeply, peed under a tree, remembered I'd forgotten about dock leaves yet again, and just carried on. I stopped looking up, concentrating only on the square yard of ground in front of me. Rake a small pile, step forward, add to the pile, do it again, and when it was knee high, move on and start again. No one seemed to work very quickly, but they never stopped, and neither could I. I just kept going. It wasn't unpleasant. The smell of hay was wonderful, the birds sang, a slight breeze blew, and all around me people talked. Occasionally someone sang. I thought I recognised 'Symer is icumen in, Lhude sing cucco!' and joined in to the best of my ability. And then, just to show willing, I gave them a quick blast of 'Twice Daily', which I hoped to God they didn't understand. The two women to my right were laughing although whether at me or my song remained to be seen.

Some time before noon, they brought round bread, a little cheese and another kind of pottage or stew. Not so nice as the one last night but I ate it all. I needed the strength because I was knackered and the day was only half gone. I think I thought if I put in a good day's work then they'd keep me on tomorrow. It was a time of year when every able-bodied person was needed. Hence the old, the pregnant, the weak – and me.

We sat for a half an hour under the tree where I'd publicly peed – I no longer cared – and it took everything

218

I had to get back up again. My hands were bleeding, my legs and back had stopped working properly and my head was splitting. Any worries I'd had about what would happen in the future had long since fled because I'd be lucky to make it to teatime, never mind 1403. I'd give my aching right arm for a mug of tea. For a moment, my eyes blurred with tears. Angrily, I blinked them away. I wasn't going to give up on my first day. I'd give up tomorrow.

Fortunately, or so I thought, the afternoon clouded over. The breeze stiffened. Everyone looked up and then redoubled their efforts. It looked as if it was going to rain. Anything not under cover would get wet. The hay would have to dry all over again – even I know you can't stack wet hay because it goes mouldy.

I raked and raked until I couldn't feel my arms any longer. My hands throbbed. I'd finally had the sense to tear off a little of my stole and wrapped it around both hands, but the blood had seeped through and I was pretty sure my hands were stuck to my rake. Pulling them away was going to hurt.

Walter of Shrewsbury appeared several times, casting an expert eye over the proceedings, speaking occasionally to the workers. He particularly barked at a pregnant woman who had stopped to ease her back. I was pleased to see her answer him back. The Black Death had turned out to be a friend to the survivors. Labour was now so scarce that many peasants could almost name their own price. Poaching other people's peasants was unlawful and frequent. If a man didn't like his master he could easily find another. Society was in flux and it was no bad thing. Walter of Shrewsbury was an elderly man. He might well have difficulty adjusting to this newer, more bolshie set of serfs, many of whom were being freed or buying their

219

own freedom. Or just plain running away. Anyway, I don't know what she said to him, but he pursed his mouth and turned away.

An hour later, William Hendred turned up, his shoulders covered in wisps of hay. He'd obviously been working, rather than just standing around pissing people off. He stood for a while, hands on hips, watching what was going on. I did my best but I must have stood out like tits on a bull.

I heard him call something but took no notice until the woman next to me nudged me, nodded in his direction and I realised he wanted me. Reluctantly, dragging my bloodstained rake behind me, I trailed over.

He stared at me. All right, we might have a bit of language problem sometimes, but I'd seen that look before. Teachers, employers, Major Guthrie, Leon in his previous incarnation as my primary trainer – exasperation mingled with amusement. He pulled my rake out of my hands and, yes, I was glued to it with dried blood. I refused even to wince, gritting my teeth and glaring at him. He took my hands, stared at them and then called to the hay wagon coming along behind us. Someone raised an arm in acknowledgement. It seemed I'd been sacked from raking and was now to work at the hay-face.

I trudged over and climbed onto the back of the wagon. They forked up great armfuls of hay and I and two others unloaded it onto the cart. This work was slightly easier although it soon became apparent I hadn't a clue here, either. You can't just chuck it on any old how. It has to be carefully stacked so as to get as much as possible on the wagon without it all sliding off again.

I was covered in hay in no time. And I was hot and sweaty. My scalp prickled under my stole. When the smell

220

of hay wore off I was going to be rather unpleasant to be downwind from. Although, of course, so would everyone else.

It took a long time to clear the field. I suspected they were getting it done now because it might rain in the night. And ours wasn't the only field being cleared. All around, every patch of grass in sight had been cut. The common grazing all around the village, patches of land belonging to various cottages. Everyone, everywhere, was getting the hay in. Two or three wagons were slowly trundling towards the barns, the big one up by the church and the two even bigger ones outside St Mary's. At least the crop wouldn't be ruined if it did rain.

At last, when it was almost too dark to see, they called a halt. Either that or I was going blind with fatigue. Everyone climbed onto the cart and we slowly trundled home.

I felt too tired to eat, but that wouldn't be a good idea. This wasn't my time, where a missed meal could be compensated for with a giant breakfast the next day. There was never any guarantee that food would turn up tomorrow. I should eat now. Always sleep, eat and spend a penny when you can. You never know what tomorrow will bring.

Most people had dispersed back to their own cottages. I sighed. I had public dining to contend with and a stone toilet to sleep in. What I wanted was a bath, a gallon of tea and one of Mrs Mack's McBurgers. What I got was a thick stew that actually wasn't bad. No meat again, but quite tasty nevertheless, with some kind of flat unleavened bread, speckled with green herbs and grit. I soaked it carefully in my stew and set to, secure in the knowledge that I'd done a good day's work. Well, a day's work, anyway. Everyone chattered around me. No one else was on the point of exhaustion. I was such a wuss.

I washed it all down with half a beaker of beer, nodded politely to my elderly companions and wandered out to the midden before bed. Squatting, deeply contemplative, and staring up at the stars, it struck me that what wasn't unpleasant now on this warm summer night would be bloody awful on a sleety night in winter.

Still, looking on the bright side, I'd almost certainly be dead by then.

When I arrived at William Hendred's penthouse suite, the door was closed. I stopped, wondering what to do next. Enter? Knock and enter? Go away? Did he have a woman in there? I didn't think he was married – he didn't have the look of a married man, but he might well be indulging in a little light entertainment to round off the day. Or perhaps last night had been a one-off and I was now back in the public domain. I hesitated and while I stood undecided, he opened the door and motioned me inside.

The stool sat in the middle of the room. He pointed sternly and I sat down before I fell down. Crossing to his wooden chest, he rummaged for a while and then pulled out a cloth-wrapped bundle which he carefully unwrapped. Inside, were three small wooden boxes, each made of a different wood. He picked up the smallest and opened it, releasing a pleasant, almost pepperminty smell. The box contained a pale green salve.

He held out his hand for mine. I was too tired to argue. He carefully peeled off my makeshift bandage, examining the raw patches carefully. I remembered how important it was not to get an infection in this time. Tiny wounds that

222

could safely be ignored in my time could be very dangerous in this.

No. I had to remind myself. *This* was my time now. *This* was when I lived. *This* was my life. Get used to it. True, as a member of St Mary's, all my jabs were up to date, but we needed to renew them regularly and that wouldn't happen now. I needed to watch for sepsis, tetanus and God knows what else.

While I'd been thinking about this he'd carefully cleaned the wounds and anointed them with a tiny amount of salve which tingled slightly but not unpleasantly.

He did the same with the other hand. To my surprise, he handed me back the bloodstained strips of cloth. Of course – everything had value. I could wash them out and use them again. Protection for my hands. To tie up my hair. Anything. I would never throw anything away again. I was the woman who had nothing. Not even a comb for my hair. And sooner or later the period-preventing injections I had every six months would wear off and that would be something else to cope with.

But, other women managed – so would I. I could find a stick to keep my teeth clean. And I could bathe in the stream. And wash my clothes there, too. I would survive. Somehow.

Until 1403 anyway.

The second day was a repeat of the first. Except that I was on the hay wagon all day. And we only worked for half a day because the rain came down after lunch.

Back at St Mary's, I didn't know what to do with myself. Everyone seemed to have some function or purpose. Everyone scuttled busily to and fro, finding something to do and I had nothing.

I stood uncertainly in the gatehouse doorway, watching the rain run down the roofs and splash into the muddy yard below. The midden continued to steam, even in the downpour. The chickens had taken cover. People splashed back and forth, calling to each other. I was just turning to go back upstairs when there was a shout from the other side of the yard. Walter and William wanted to see me. I knew better than to keep them waiting.

I hoisted my skirt and galloped across the yard, dodging the deeper-looking puddles. It's no problem getting wet if there are hot baths and dry clothes at the end of the day, but getting wet and having to live in those clothes for the next twenty-four hours is no joke.

Under Walter's close scrutiny and even closer questioning, I repeated my story. They'd obviously been mulling it over between them. As far as I could see from their body language, Walter was still deeply suspicious of me.

224

William Hendred spoke first. 'You will remain with us for the time being.'

I bowed my head. 'God's blessings be upon you both.'

Walter snorted. I pretended not to hear. 'You will work for your keep.'

I nodded, channelling strong, sturdy, medieval womanhood. I would have preferred to be an honoured guest, but an unpaid servant was better than nothing. I would have food on the table and a roof over my head. Well, William Hendred's roof over my head.

I think, somewhere, someone had decided I wasn't making any meaningful contribution to the haymaking process and the next day I was put on what, initially, I thought were light duties.

I was up with the sun, waiting in my room for William Hendred to finish his ablutions so I could begin mine. I soon learned not to drink anything after late evening. Beer goes through me faster than a politician through his expense account.

Once he'd banged the door behind him I was off, dock leaf in hand to avail myself of the latest thing in public facilities, a quick splash in the water trough and then, closing my mind to the lack of Leon bearing tea, I was ready for anything.

First up were the chickens, feathery and malevolent at the best of times – all of whom were grumpy at being woken so early and would take it out on me. I could see why the poultryman had embraced delegation with enthusiasm – an extra half hour in bed and the prospect of getting through the rest of the day unbeaked.

I would chivvy a large number of disgruntled birds out into the fresh air – rather like my old games teacher cattle-prodding thirty unenthusiastic schoolgirls into sub-zero temperatures for a refreshing bout of bloodstained hockey – feed said chickens without losing a leg or an eye, and then, while they were busy, nip back into the hen house to collect the eggs.

I'd take the eggs to the kitchen for the head cook – a massive, tow-headed, red, sweaty, man who was generally known either as Fat Piers or That Bastard, depending on how his day was going. Hands on hips, he would hold me responsible for the disappointing number of eggs reposing on his table. In the first week, I stood meekly, head bowed, and then one day I caught a couple of the scullions smirking at each other and cottoned on.

Next morning, I presented the eggs and stood and grinned at him. He shouted – I grinned some more – he paused, things hung in the balance for a moment, then he too grinned gummily and made a 'get out of my kitchen' gesture. I dumped the basket and ran.

I would draw endless buckets of water for the washerwoman Margery Daw, a brawny woman with forearms like hams and fists to match, who was sporadically assisted by a waif named Little Alice, who was barely tall enough to see over the vats, so I was the one doing most of the heavy lifting. Occasionally, I think as some sort of reward, I was allowed to stir a vat of scummy water.

Then I was off for a breakfast, usually of porridge and then back to help the two of them spread their washing over the bushes to dry in the sun.

The next task was to take a midday meal up through the village to Father Ranulf, the elderly priest, now half blind and his even older and frailer 'housekeeper', Dame Rowena.

226

It would seem that he and she had been together for years. I suspected he was the younger son of a good household and that either just before or just after his ordination there had been some Rowena-related scandal, and he'd been despatched to this remote place. Out of sight and out of mind. I think it had been a stroke of luck for all concerned and he'd arrived here as a young priest, bringing his 'housekeeper' with him, and the village had been the gainer because he was a conscientious and compassionate man with slightly less hair than Dr Bairstow – which is to say none at all. I was lucky – his Latin was excellent. Many local priests had virtually no Latin at all. They'd learned the services by rote years ago and were sometimes unintelligible.

Rowena had been beautiful – you could see it in her fine bones and patrician profile. The poor soul was crippled by arthritis these days, her fingers twisted into uselessness. Hence me taking them up their midday meal and making the return trip with the used dishes from the day before.

I would also take the opportunity to sweep around their house, tidy a little, and empty their pots for them, and in return they taught me a few useful words and phrases in the local dialect. Weather permitting, we would sit on a bench against the church wall and talk in a strange mixture of medieval English and Latin, with me relapsing into modern English and mime under stress. They laughed a lot. I think they thought I was hilarious. Sometimes they poured out beakers of something apple-flavoured and then things became even more hilarious and I often had trouble getting back down the hill.

In the afternoon, I would sweep my room, William Hendred's room, and the gatehouse stairs, often meeting his men-at-arms as I did so. They always stepped aside politely, which surprised me. I wondered if they thought I was his property and were therefore keeping their hands to themselves. I tried to feel that this was a Good Thing.

After I'd tidied our rooms, it was back to take in the washing for Margery who herself was often incapable by this time of day. There was never any sign of Little Alice at this hour. I had no idea where she took herself off to.

Out of kindness, Rowena had given me a drop spindle for which she had no more use because her fingers couldn't cope any longer. She'd spent a couple of hours trying to instil the basics and when I felt I was well enough advanced I thought I'd have a go in public, I sat on the bench by the gatehouse door and practised my spinning. I was rubbish. To this day, I'm convinced the stupid thing was defective.

Sitting in the sun, I assembled my bit of practice fleece, hooked on the spindle, let the fleece rest over the back of my left hand as she'd shown me, and cockily gave it a twirl. A nice thread appeared and, greatly encouraged, I teased out a little more of the fleece and gave it another go. I'm not sure what happened – I think I overspun. Or possibly underspun – let's face it there's only two ways it could go. Anyway, the yarn parted and the spindle dropped heavily to the ground. Presumably, that's why it's called a drop spindle. Although in my case, thud spindle would be more appropriate.

I sighed and reached down to pick it up, caught a movement out of the corner of my eye and looked up to find William Hendred, hands on hips, watching me from a few yards away. I gave him my 'Yes? Can I help you look?' but he just shook his head and walked away.

I practised constantly. I had to – this was not an age when women sat around and did nothing – if they weren't ploughing a ten-acre strip with a teaspoon while eight months pregnant, or delivering a breeched calf in a thunderstorm, or brewing something dark, bubbling and unspeakable, or shrieking at their countless children, then they were spinning. And you didn't catch *them* scowling in concentration, or cursing under their breath or grappling with yarn that looked like a string of badly stuffed sausages. These women sat, coiffed heads close together, their tongues as busy as their fingers, chatting, watching their children over their shoulders, and doing a hundred other things at the same time.

They were friendly – I was sometimes invited to join them as they sat outside Pikey Peter's house, waiting for their bread to bake in the public oven.

Pikey Peter was the enormous lad who had greeted me at the gate on the day I arrived. He'd been a big, strong and handsome lad – the apple of his widowed mother's eye – until the grave he was digging one day had collapsed on him. He had been working alone and by the time they got him out he'd been buried for too long. Now he was capable of only the very simplest tasks and his great strength was not the blessing it had once been. But people rallied around. He was given work to do – lifting and carrying – and his exhausted mother, Eadgytha, earned a little extra in the way of an egg or two or a small bundle of firewood by minding other people's bread as it baked in the oven outside her house. I sometimes hid a wrinkled apple or two in the bottom of my basket as I toiled up the hill and left them on her doorstep.

Anyway, I sat with them if I'd finished my tasks early and occasionally – out of polite exasperation, I think – one of them would take my spindle and twirl it expertly for me, and sorting out the tangle I'd managed to get myself into. Mostly I just listened, picking up words and phrases and listening to the gossip.

Interestingly, no one liked Walter of Shrewsbury – he was generally reckoned to be a hard man. William Hendred they seemed to like. I once asked if he was from Castle Hendred across the county, but either they didn't know or more likely my accent defeated them. Hugh Armstrong was an unknown quantity. He'd never spent much time at St Mary's. As a young boy, he'd gone into service to John of Gaunt's son, Henry Bolinbroke – soon to be King Henry if he wasn't already – and had remained with him ever since, sharing his exile. I gathered from their talk that news of Henry's landing at Ravenspur had not yet reached them. Again, I would stare at my feet and wonder what to do. And that was my dilemma, of course. Summer was passing and it was all going to kick off any day now.

I would look around the peaceful village at the, if not happy then at least reasonably contented, people living there, their cottages and livestock, their carefully tilled strips of land – it wasn't a rich village, but it was reasonably prosperous. I was getting to know some of them. Enormous John Smith and his countless equally enormous sons, working at their forge down by the stream, near the stepping stones. Miserable Robert Stukely who ran the mill and would cheat you blind as soon as look at you. Nearly opposite, on the other side of the stream, lived Margaret Brewer, whose ale was so good they came for miles around for it. Assisted by her daughter, Big Alice, she lived and brewed almost on the same spot the Falconburg Arms would occupy some six hundred and fifty years from now. And there was William the Carpenter, the two kitchen boys, Roger and Edgar, who might have been brothers. Fat Piers the cook I've already mentioned. And there was Dick, the tall scullion boy, and the other one whose name I could never remember but whose face was an explosion of acne, and Wymer and Cuthbert, the stable boys, who loudly and cheerfully pursued every girl in sight and who would be terrified if they ever caught one.

They were kindly people, hard-working, devout – most of them worshipped daily and even I traipsed off to church on Sunday, significantly failing to burst into flames on the threshold. I would spend the service staring around at the brilliantly painted walls and statues, kneeling and crossing myself at the appropriate moments, always half a beat behind everyone else, as Father Ranulf celebrated Mass.

I had a great respect and liking for them all and I thought – well, I hoped – that that they had some liking for me. I worked hard. I cantered up and down to the village twenty times a day. I was polite and respectful to everyone – and then came the day when I wondered if I'd been kidding myself.

It was early morning. I was delivering today's eggs to the kitchen. Everyone was yawning and stretching, poking the fires back into life, and laying out platters and beakers for breakfast.

I dumped the eggs on the table, turned to go and bumped straight into a man who smelled of urine and onions. Not an attractive combination in any age. It was the gate-guard I'd met on my first day here. The one who had left Pikey Peter in charge while he got his head down. For a couple of days afterwards, he'd walked around with a split lip. Medieval discipline as administered by William Hendred.

'Ah,' he said, taking advantage to run his hands over me. I stiffened. There were very definite rules about touching women. Basically, if a woman wasn't a relation, then you didn't. I, of course, had no relations. There were no men here to protect me. He laughed. I didn't catch everything he said but I did get 'þe womman wiþouten maister.'

Oh God, was that what they called me? The masterless woman? That wasn't good at all. Men come in many shapes and forms. Bottom of the heap is always the greasy, inadequate runt with a sense of entitlement who can't quite understand that all women are not gagging for him. And this one was bottom of even that heap. The sort of bloke you'd use to line your budgie cage. The sort who grabs a woman by whichever bit of her anatomy is most easily accessible and when she struggles tells her he likes a woman with spirit until you kick him in the nadgers and it turns out that he doesn't. Things can then go one of two ways. Either he oozes away and rejoins the primordial slime or he lays in wait until you're alone and far from help.

I was always alone. I could be in trouble here.

I compromised by kicking his shins He hopped backwards cursing and then came back at me with a raised fist. I was preparing to defend myself with a small wicker basket when there was a noise. I can't describe it, but in the silence that followed I looked around to find that it had been the sort of noise made by everyone in the vicinity picking up the nearest implement and assuming a nasty look.

There was never any doubt as to which way things would go and, with a face-saving glare, he seized a loaf off the table and barged his way out of the door.

I picked up my basket and prepared to follow him out.

Dick, the tall skinny scullion, touched my arm and shook his head. I chose to interpret that as a message to let him get clear. He handed me a small beaker and nodded to a stool near the giant fireplace. I put down my basket and sat. My legs were trembling. Good idea.

The beaker was half full of very weak beer which – and you wouldn't think this possible – tastes even worse than beer that isn't very weak. However, I sipped slowly, leaving the traditional small amount in the bottom so I wouldn't have to see what the beer had failed to dissolve.

Yes, that had been one small bad incident among many good ones, but it was the moment I realised I was part of this community. I didn't rank very highly because he was right, I *was* a masterless woman, with all the problems that entailed – but I knew them all, and they were beginning to know me. I was the foreign woman – the one who had lost everything – and they generously forgave my eccentricities and incompetence. They had taken me in and made my life much easier than it could have been, and there was one way I could repay them. I could find someone and make him listen to me. I could repay my debt to them and, if History didn't like it, then that was just tough.

I discounted Walter of Shrewsbury immediately. Even I didn't have that much of a death wish. So it was not without some misgivings that I placed myself in front of William Hendred as he emerged from the stables one afternoon.

Remembering my womanly duty to look chaste, obedient, respectful, humble and dutiful – none of which came naturally – I clasped my hands before me and said, 'God give you good day, sir. May I speak?'

He had been standing in the sun, chewing a straw and, I suspected, just taking a moment to enjoy the day. It wasn't a great moment, but as Walter had pushed off to harass someone somewhere else, it seemed as good a time as any.

William Hendred was a man of very few words but I was beginning to understand his expressions. He regarded me with a familiar mixture of exasperation and faint amusement. Taking the straw from his mouth, he nodded.

I looked around but no one was nearby. It was a hot afternoon – most people were indoors for one reason or another. One of the stable cats was slumped on the roof, fast asleep. The doves cooed peacefully from their dovecote. The chickens had dug themselves little scrapes in the shade and were dozing. There was a faint clatter of pots from the kitchens, but Fat Piers would be fast asleep somewhere. Everyone was off having a reasonably peaceful afternoon.

I took a deep breath and assembled my Latin. 'Sir, I tried to tell you when I first came here.'

I stopped.

He still said nothing, just looking down at me. The sun was behind him so I couldn't see his face. I ploughed on anyway.

'When I was in Rushford – there was an inn – I worked there for two days.'

I stopped again. I could imagine what he was thinking – that if I served ale as incompetently as I did everything else then it was a miracle I'd lasted even that long. Well, that was fine with me.

'Some men were talking. They were drunk. They said something about St Mary's. I did not pay attention to begin with.'

He still said nothing.

'They kept calling for more ale. The landlord made them show him their money. They had plenty of money.'

I paused again in case he wanted to tell me to stop wasting his time and sweep me aside, but he didn't.

'Sir, they were talking of riding here. In force. They said the king is seizing Lancaster lands. That all is forfeit to the crown.'

He knew this. I'd seen those anxious conversations between him and Walter. The lookouts on the road. They were waiting for the arrival of the king's commissioners. Admittedly, this was a very small estate and they would take a long time to get here but, as far as they knew, one day they would come. One day, St Mary's would pass from the exiled Duke of Lancaster and into the hands of the king. The problem was that they were all looking the wrong way. It wasn't the king they had to worry about. Trouble would come from an unexpected direction and I owed it to them to do my best to warn them.

He said, in his slow, deep voice, 'The king is in Ireland.'

'That is why they waited, sir.'

'Why?'

'They plan to take St Mary's before the king returns. To take advantage of both the king's absence and that of Sir Hugh Armstrong. When the king returns, he will have more important things to do than worry about one small manor. They think we are minor and unprotected. That taking us will be easy.'

He stared at me for a while and then gestured with his head. We stepped into the shade.

'When did you hear this?'

'The day before I arrived here, sir.'

'Why did you not speak of this before?'

'I tried, sir, on the day you took me in, but Master Walter was displeased and I did not wish to anger him further.'

I felt a faint stirring at the back of my neck which could have been either a gentle summer breeze or History preparing to wipe me from the face of the earth. Although to be fair, the most threatening thing around at the moment was the stable cat, a terror to the rodent population and a legendary lover, currently flat out on the roof, but more than capable of taking me on.

'How many of them?'

I struck out at random. 'Four, sir.' Four seemed a good number.

'And their badge?'

'I did not recognise it.'

'Describe it.'

Now I was stuck. I had no idea what Guy of Rushford's badge was.

I shook my head. 'I cannot.'

That's one of the best things about being a member of the weaker sex. In modern days, they'd say disbelievingly, 'Oh come on – you must have noticed something about them,' but in these times, we women were subject to all sorts of womb-induced humours that daily deprived us of the ability to think, to reason and, in my case, to notice what had apparently been in front of my own nose all evening. I had to think of something. 'The landlord said I was to serve them quickly because they were Guy's men and used to getting what they wanted.'

'Guy of Rushford?'

'Yes,' I said, apparently remembering. 'They were Guy's men and wanted the best of everything.'

He looked at me, hard-eyed. 'And did they get it?'

I knew what he was asking. Barmaids didn't dispense just drinks.

I lowered my eyes and said in a tiny voice. 'They didn't want it.'

A perfectly reasonable response, I thought. At my age, I was resigned to working my way down men's lists of shaggable women. Without ever having been that high up in the first place. When I looked up again he was smiling his crooked smile. And then he wasn't.

'How many men? And when?'

I racked my brains to remember what Dr Dowson had told me about the history of St Mary's. That the manor of St Mary's had been bestowed by John of Gaunt, Duke of Lancaster, in return for services rendered during the Castille campaign. That the Rushford branch of the family – consisting of the two brothers, Guy and Jerald, and I believe there was a sister around somewhere – had sought to capitalise on the chaos brought about by the king's attempted seizure of Lancaster lands and sought to annexe this manor. They'd been repulsed by – if I remembered correctly – a strategic fire, set by Henry of Rushford's granddaughter. Well, that bit was wrong. Even if Hugh Armstrong was Henry's son or grandson, there was no granddaughter living here. That wouldn't be the first St Mary's legend we'd got wrong – I still had nightmares about 1643 when St Mary's went up in flames

237

and Markham, trapped on the roof, had the choice between jumping and burning. My story was true, but would William Hendred believe me? He was not a stupid man. He'd obviously heard of the king's attempts to seize the Lancaster estates and was expecting trouble of some kind. He had lookouts on the main road – the only road, actually – in and out of the village. He might listen to me. Walter wouldn't, I knew. I could just hear him muttering on about hysterical women, but William might.

He did.

We sat on the bench while he questioned me closely. How many men? What were they wearing? What was the name of the inn? What exactly had I overheard?

Considering I was making it all up, I thought I did pretty well, inventing various villainous-looking characters who goosed the barmaids and raucously spilled their drinks. I remembered not to remember everything because that's always suspicious and after half an hour I think he believed me. He sent me away – and I had to shoot off anyway because it was time for me to sweep out the gatehouse. I left him sitting, deep in thought, on the bench by the door. I know he spoke to Walter of Shrewsbury about what I'd told him because I saw the two of them talking together outside the stables. As I passed, laden with two buckets of water, they broke off and stared at me. I modestly averted my eyes from the sight of two men thinking deeply, making important decisions and doing other things my tiny female brain couldn't possibly hope to comprehend, and went off to be bullied by the chickens again. Medieval life is not all wafting about in a long gown, wearing gauzy veils, and riding side-saddle on a prancing milk-white palfrey, you know. I was growing to hate those bloody chickens.

No one would tell me what was going on – I wondered if Walter still suspected I was some sort of royal spy – but I know William increased the number of lookouts on the road. I'm certain he'd sent men to Rushford as well, to watch and listen.

St Mary's became a flurry of activity and preparation. John fired up his smithy and the sound of hammer on metal echoed around the village night and day as they repaired old weapons and forged new ones. Possessions were gathered up and packed away, including the precious glass from the windows. The tiny corridor between the hall and the solar was blocked off and converted into a strong room. This was where they packed the St Mary's treasures. Wool, plate, glass, documents, spices and so on. When the tiny space was as full as it could be, they bricked up the other end and dragged a heavy wooden cupboard in front of it.

Older children and livestock began to disappear into the woods. The pigs went first, driven off under the trees, then most of the poultry and chickens, crammed into small wooden cages and highly indignant. I think such valuables as the villagers possessed were quietly buried in their gardens for safekeeping. I wondered exactly what items they considered worth saving in this century. In the Great

239

Fire of London, Samuel Pepys buried his cheeses. I can't remember if he ever found them again.

William and Walter walked around daily – William encouraging and urging and Walter finding fault. Men scowled at his retreating back but did as they were told. Walter had lived his entire adult life here and no one could fault his commitment to St Mary's. He was a 14th-century Dr Bairstow. And William Hendred was his Guthrie.

I tried not to think about that – painful stabs of homesickness could still bring tears to my eyes if not firmly kept at bay. And I knew from experience that once I started down that route it was a very short step to Leon and Matthew and panic and disorientation and despair and grief, with tears and snot and all the unpleasant aftermath of a huge crying jag. So I didn't think about it. And it's not as if I didn't have alternative concerns. We were all about to be invaded. I knew the attack would not prevail, but all I knew were history book details. *Attempts to steal the manor of St Mary's were repulsed etc. etc.* I had no idea who would live and who would die. Nowhere was there a list of those who would not survive. People I had come to look on as my friends. Pikey Peter, Father Ranulf, John the Smith, the two stable lads and their incessant but easily rebuffed pursuit of anything in a skirt, Fat Piers and his noisy afternoon naps. And William Hendred, who was all that stood between me and the world. I thrust that thought away as well.

They held weapons practice every afternoon. I could hear the clash of swords outside the gatehouse. All the men were expected to participate. Those who didn't have swords had staffs. There was daily archery practice too.

240

Wandering through the courtyard one day with a bucket of chicken feed, I came upon a solitary staff, propped against the wall. No one was around and I couldn't think who it could belong to. I looked around again. Nope. No one.

Setting down the bucket, I picked up the staff. It was a nice one. Straight and balanced. It was obviously well used – constant handling had worn the hand holds smooth and shiny.

I'm not bad with a staff. I once used a broom handle to knock seven shades of shit out of a really unpleasant bloke called Weasel who was annoying me at the time. This was longer and heavier and deadlier. I flexed my arms a couple of times and then stabbed forward, parried an imaginary thrust, whirled it around at low level, scything the legs out from under my imaginary foe, and then, as he was lying helpless on the ground, stepped in for the kill.

I felt a glow of satisfaction. I wasn't as out of practice as I had thought. Excessive spinning hadn't dulled too many of my reflexes. If I had to, I could defend myself. I had noticed there were fewer and fewer women around every day. I was still here, however, and no one had suggested evacuating me for my own safety. I wondered whether I wasn't valuable enough to be saved or was simply thought too weird to be in any danger. Neither was particularly flattering.

I carefully replaced the staff as I'd found it, picked up my bucket, turned around and found myself face to face with William Hendred. Bollocks. We looked at each other for a while and then I went to walk past him. He blocked my path. We looked at each other a little bit more.

He picked up the staff with a familiarity that told me it was his. Again – bollocks. He held it out to me. I remembered to put down the bucket and took it, my hands automatically taking up the correct position. It was far too late to pretend I thought it was just a stick. He disappeared around the corner, reappearing moments later with another staff. Standing in front of me, he nodded, grunted, and raised it high.

I remembered Guthrie's training but barely had time to get my feet sorted out before he attacked. Not hard and not fast, but he was tons better than me. As he should be.

I held my own for very nearly five whole seconds. Then the first blow caught me gently across the upper arm. I wondered if this was some kind of humiliating punishment for my unwomanly behaviour in touching his staff. His *quarterstaff,* before anyone gets the wrong idea. Drawn by the noise, a couple of men appeared from the gatehouse door and I was walloped across the other arm. Someone laughed.

I stepped back. He lowered his staff. To my right, a man said something. I looked over. He mimed holding a staff, stabbed it forwards and stamped his right foot hard. The man next to him nodded. I looked back at William, who did exactly the same thing. I was doing something wrong.

Slowly, I copied the movement and then he came at me again. I stamped my foot down hard, all my weight was forwards, my staff flew under his guard and swept his own to one side, exposing the front of his body. I touched him gently on the chest.

He laughed. They all laughed. He'd let me do it, obviously. He could have knocked the staff out of my hands any time he wanted. I bowed, handed him back his staff, picked up the bucket and went off to be beaten up by the chickens again.

They came the very next day.

Two young girls – whose job was usually to keep an eye on the geese – came tearing up the hill, shouting breathlessly and gesturing over their shoulders. Someone fetched William Hendred – not that he was ever very far away these days. He handed them each a beaker of small beer, sat them on the bench outside the gatehouse and waited.

Walter of Shrewsbury was plying them with questions which, between gasping for breath and gulping down their drink, they had no chance of answering. William hushed him with a gesture and waited. He was very good at waiting.

The youngest was the first to recover, with a babble of words and gestures I had no hope of understanding.

William listened quietly, gave orders they were to be fed and seen safely on their way, and disappeared with Walter of Shrewsbury.

Ten minutes later, it was as if someone had poked a wasp's nest.

Accustomed as I was to our familiar St Mary's shambles I expected this to be rather similar. I was completely wrong. I wondered afterwards if they'd rehearsed for this. Or maybe similar things happened all the time and it was second nature to them. Whatever it was, William barked a few orders and people scattered back to the village. Women emerged from their houses bearing bundles on their backs and chivvying their children in front of them. Any remaining livestock were herded together and what looked like almost everyone who had remained in the village headed for the forest. Ox-drawn wagons trundled their larger possessions, with those who couldn't walk sitting on the top. Everyone moved quickly but there was no panic. Everyone knew what they were doing and where to go. I was a little ashamed of our shambolic St Mary's fire drills which never seemed to get any better despite Leon's and Ian's best efforts. The last pens were emptied and the long procession of people splashed across the ford, wound their way up the slope past St Marys and into the woods.

Not knowing what to do, I stayed put by the gate and watched them go. They took less than twenty minutes to pass. I looked behind me into the courtyard. All the young boys who served in the castle had joined in the procession. The only people remaining were the two stable boys and a vastly reduced kitchen staff who stood clustered together by the kitchen door. Fat Piers was clutching a kitchen implement in a way very similar to that perfected by Mrs Mack some six and a half centuries later.

I swallowed hard. I'm not sure if anyone's noticed, but wherever I go there's always some catastrophe or other and it's not always my fault. This one certainly wasn't. Although I'd certainly done something to warrant the scowl William Hendred was wearing as he crossed the courtyard to me. I braced myself.

'Why did you not go with the others?'

I fell back on the traditional weak womanly excuse. 'No one told me to.'

He stared up towards the woods. The last stragglers were just disappearing under the eaves.

'Go. You can catch them. Go.'

I stepped back in case he wanted physically to reinforce his argument and shook my head. I couldn't go. It was vital I stayed here and steered events in the right direction. Or so I told myself.

He seized my arm and pushed me up the hill. He was a strong man. I staggered and as I nearly fell, someone shouted. In the silence, I thought I could hear hoofs. They were coming.

I slipped behind him and back into St Mary's, scurrying into the kitchen along with Fat Piers and his gang. Margery the washerwoman was there, too. Well, if she could stay then so could I. We looked each other up and down in silence and I couldn't help thinking that neither of us was a shining example of attractive St Mary's womanhood.

Fat Piers seemed surprised to see me. I assumed he assumed William Hendred had ordered me to stay. We clustered in the doorway and watched. The big gate had been closed days ago, but now the little wicket gate was slammed shut and barred too. If I ever got back to St Mary's – I fought down the by now quite accustomed panic – I must remember to tell Professor Rapson the big gate opened outwards and the little gate opened inwards.

Walter of Shrewsbury withdrew into the hall. I heard the sounds of doors and shutters being slammed both upstairs and down.

William Hendred stood in the courtyard shouting instructions. In this situation, control of St Mary's had obviously passed to him. Men scurried hither and thither, clutching their weapons.

Tam the Welshman, William's second-in-charge, was leading his men towards the walls where they took up their positions. William shot one last look around at the bolted and shuttered buildings and joined them, leaning out over the walls to see.

The walls were crenelated but were no more than fifteen or twenty feet high. There was no moat on the other side although the ground was boggy. I suspected even the smallest army would have no difficulty forcing its way in.

This, however, was not a small army. There were no siege weapons, no – what do they call those people who dig under castle walls? Sappers, that's it – not that it's important because there weren't any here anyway. This was only a hostile neighbour and a group of hastily purchased local thugs taking advantage of the king's absence. As neighbours do.

Once, long ago – before I came to St Mary's and when European travel was much easier than it is today – I worked on a dig in the eastern Med. Four of us were billeted in a very dodgy-looking outhouse on a remote farm somewhere in the Taurus mountains. Once a year, the farmer would summon his considerable family, they would go to his boundary fences, uproot the fence posts, and at a word from him, take five long paces forwards and replace the posts. At a stroke, he would have gained a sizeable tranche of land. They did it every year, apparently. It had acquired the status of a ceremony and there was a giant family knees-up afterwards.

The five-paces-forwards strategy was obviously far too subtle for Guy of Rushford and his brother Jerald. They were going for the whole manor, thinking that when Richard returned, St Mary's would be snugly ensconced within their own boundaries. No one would care and everyone would have more important things to think about anyway. I wondered if this sort of thing was happening anywhere else around the country.

Tam was shading his eyes. Famed for his long sight, he was counting. Around fifteen mounted men and between twenty and thirty on foot seemed to be the total. And no siege engines. I felt absurdly cheerful. Well, that wasn't too bad. We had nearly twenty men here. Good men who would fight for their homes, whereas the Rushford forces must surely comprise either hired men who had no loyalties and would fight for whoever paid them, or sulky serfs who just wanted to go home. All we had to do was hold them off until Richard was overthrown. Henry Bolingbroke must surely have landed at Ravenspur by now. All over the country men would be flocking to his banner. It was only a matter of time before someone turned up here to save us. All we had to do was stay quietly behind our walls, hold on, and not do anything silly. There was no need for any violence at all. All we had to do was wait.

I heard the thunder of hooves grow closer. William glanced back briefly over his shoulder, saw us all clustered in the kitchen doorway and gestured us back inside. Fat Piers chivvied us all into the kitchen and not without some difficulty, because it was never closed during summer or winter, they got the door shut.

We stood in silence, listening. Well, they did. Walter of Shrewsbury appeared suddenly and beckoned to me to follow him. I had a feeling this wasn't good.

He led me back into the hall and pointed to the corner. I went and stood quietly, trying not to feel anxious. He had his doubts about me. I was a stranger. I was odd. I knew things I shouldn't. I'm convinced he was convinced I was some sort of spy – if not for the king's commissioners then for the Rushfords. He said something to one of the men with him who peeled off to come and stand by me. This was bad news. Not only was I to be closely watched, but I was to be closely watched by the onion-smelling gate-guard from the kitchen. The one to whom a masterless woman was a challenge.

I refused to look at him as he stood grinning at me. I folded my arms in an unwomanly manner and stared at the floor, listening as hard as I could. Not that it did me any good. The walls were thick and only the very loudest sounds floated through the shutters. I could vaguely hear shouting so it seemed safe to assume we were being ordered to surrender St Mary's. I wondered if the Rushfords would pretend they were acting under the king's orders, or whether they were just going for out-and-out theft.

I had no details as to what would happen next and the historical records I could remember were not accurate. If they were wrong – what else was wrong? Had my presence, in some tiny but important way, changed the course of events?

I stood quietly in my corner, straining my ears for clues as to what was going on outside. I was certain I'd managed to convince William Hendred of Henry, Duke of Lancaster's return. Obviously, I hadn't told him Henry would be king, but I'd emphasised, over and over again, that Henry would come back, bringing Hugh Armstrong with him. Knowing that, surely he wouldn't surrender St Mary's without a fight.

No, he wouldn't. I heard his voice shouting defiance. Other voices joined in which was reassuring. If they were shouting at each other then they weren't fighting.

The shouting continued for some time and then William appeared in the hall, looking about him.

At the same time, Walter appeared through the other door, and gestured to me.

Onion man pushed me forwards. There was no need – I was already moving but I suppose it was the only way he would ever get to touch a woman.

I stood in front of Walter, entirely forgetting the chaste, dutiful, obedient role of medieval womanhood.

'You – what do you know of this?'

'Nothing but what I have said, sir.'

'How long have you known this?'

'Since I arrived, sir.'

'Why are they here today?'

This is the trouble with knowing things you're not supposed to and then having to lie your head off – you have to think of everything. I had no idea why they hadn't turned up before today. I felt a stab of annoyance. I was trying to help them out here. I shouldn't have to think of everything.

I shrugged. 'I do not know, sir.'

William joined us, saying mildly, 'It might have taken them some time to gather this force. But they are here now and we must deal with them.'

Walter was not one to give up. 'How do we know this – woman – is telling the truth?'

His voice led everyone to believe only an idiot would involve a woman in their schemes.

I looked over to William

'We don't,' he said mildly, 'but she did not have to warn us.'

'She is playing both sides,' said Walter, giving me considerably more credit for deviousness than I felt I deserved. 'And now it is too late to send her away. She will go straight to Guy and his brother and tell them how things stand here.'

I didn't like the way this was heading.

'You should make up your mind, Master Walter,' I said. 'Everyone here will remember that I tried to warn you of this on my first day here. You told me to be silent. You cannot now blame me for the events I did my best to warn you of.'

Onion man went to fetch me a casual slap. 'Be silent before your betters.'

William Hendred knocked his arm away. 'No one touches this woman without my permission.'

I glared at onion man. He glared at William. William glared back at onion man. Walter glared impartially at everyone. There was a long silence. And then – a shout of warning, a long hissing sound and a thunk. I'd heard that sound before. At Agincourt. The Rushfords had unleashed a volley of arrows over the walls. I could hear them clattering off the stonework outside and the roof over our heads. One or two thunked into the wooden shutters. They penetrated to some considerable depth. I remembered a good archer could put a cloth-yard arrow through a church door from one hundred yards away. I don't know why I always remember these things at the wrong moment.

I'm proud to say I didn't move. Actually, standing in my corner, I was probably the safest person in the room – but onion man flinched. He saw me grinning. I just can't help it – I'm lost in time, in the middle of an armed conflict in the Middle Ages, alone, friendless and whichever side won I'd be in trouble – and as if none of that's bad enough, I'm winding up the bloke who's had it in for me since we first met. You can see why I can't get life insurance, can't you?

Over all the shouting I could hear a deep booming noise – a pause – and then it came again. They had a battering ram. They had an actual battering ram. I must remember to tell Professor Rapson. And then I realised that I'd never tell Professor Rapson anything ever again.

The shouting intensified. I could hear William Hendred bellowing instructions outside. He was concentrating his men over the gatehouse. They would be firing at those wielding the battering ram. The noise arose to a crescendo – shouts of warning, shouts of defiance – and the rhythmical boom of the battering ram. Which, I have to say, sounded considerably more effective than poor old Grond of happier days. Whatever William Hendred's men were doing to repel the attack was effective though – the booming noise ceased.

Silence fell. None of us was stupid enough to think they'd given up and gone away. I suspected they'd gone for a fast, surprise attack and now that had failed they were setting up camp for a siege.

It couldn't have happened at a worse time. Early summer is never an easy time. People think getting through the winter is the problem, but that's not true. Winter is usually not too bad. The harvest is gathered in, animals have been slaughtered and salted, and the store houses are full. Then that's all gradually eaten away and everyone crosses their fingers that their dwindling supplies will last at least until mid to late summer, when

251

the crops and fruit are beginning to ripen. A bad harvest in the previous year can cause considerable hardship in the next.

I don't know whether the Rushfords had taken this into account, or whether they were simply taking advantage of events, but, as I said, it couldn't have happened at a worse time. Our storehouses had been almost emptied. The remaining sacks of grain and flour, the stores of salted meat and fish – nearly everything had been taken away. Partly to feed others and partly for safekeeping.

But those of us who had remained behind had enough to get by. And we had strong walls and good men. Best of all – we had water. We would be fine. I looked around again. It was hard to see how anything could go badly wrong. But it would.

Because I knew that the siege of St Mary's ended in fire.

Two days passed and I have to say that after the initial excitement, being under siege is actually quite dull. Perhaps things were livelier on the other side of the wall, but in here … dull. Very dull.

William kept the walls constantly manned. There was even someone at the top of the north tower, with instructions to scan the horizon. Whether for reinforcements for the Rushfords or the possible return of Hugh Armstrong, I don't know.

The shifts were short – three hours only – and then another set of men would take over. Those off-watch ate and slept – as soldiers do. Eat when you can. Sleep when you can. Fight when you must.

And then, on the third day, it all went wrong.

I was still in the hall under Walter's watchful gaze. They fed me – a little – and I was allowed outside to visit our state-of-the-art midden – under escort, of course. At the time, I found it quite irksome and embarrassing and then it turned out to be the best thing that could have happened for me.

I awoke at dawn to find Roger from the kitchen handing me a beaker of weak beer and a bowl of porridge. I thanked him and tucked in. Draining the last of my beer, I stood up and requested a midden break because my guard had changed during the night and this one wasn't onion man. There was no way I would ever go outside and lift my skirts with him in the vicinity.

My guard nodded, yawning, and we unbarred the door and stepped out into the cool, early morning air.

I stretched and looked around. Nothing had changed since my last comfort break. There were still men on the walls and another one up on the tower. Silent buildings huddled around an empty courtyard. Everything was shuttered, or bolted, or put away, or covered over.

I took two steps and then stopped. Something was different. I looked around. What was different?

My guard poked me in the back to get me moving again. This was probably the end of his watch and he was eager to get his head down.

I turned to face him and said, 'Wait. Something is wrong.'

He was only a country boy but he was William Hendred trained. He pushed me against the wall, put his hand on his sword and looked around. We both did.

I pointed. 'There.'

The well was uncovered. Against all instructions – the well was uncovered. I felt a sick feeling in my stomach.

We set off across the courtyard and peered in.

Shit.

Floating in the water, guts trailing like long red ribbons, dead as a doornail, was one of the stable cats. My guard's breath hissed through his teeth. This was a disaster. And it wasn't an accident, either. I looked around. The well cover was nowhere in sight. Someone had been here in the night, removed the well cover, thrown in a more-than-dead cat, and then left the well open so everyone could see the water was no longer drinkable. Everyone could there would be no point in continuing the siege. It was all over.

A stupid nursery rhyme jangled in my head.

Ding dong bell.

Pussy's in the well.

Who put her in?

I couldn't remember who put her in but I knew it wasn't me.

My guard was good. He said, 'Wait here.'

I nodded and watched him set off for William, just now walking the walls and talking to his men. I saw my guard take him a little to one side and whisper discreetly in his ear. He didn't want to start a panic.

The two of them climbed down the steps and leaned over the well. William's face didn't change. He stood staring into the depths, arms braced against the stone lip and thinking.

After a moment, he said, 'Check the other well.' The man nodded and trotted away to the scullery which contained the second, smaller well. We stood together. Neither of us spoke. Around us, St Mary's was waking to its third – and last – day's siege.

I looked around. If the kitchen well was spoiled too, then we were finished. Apart from water drawn the night before, we would have nothing. There was beer in the barrels, but you can't cook with beer. Or give it to the horses. How long could we last without water? Not long enough was my guess. And who had done this? I couldn't help feeling a small measure of relief. No matter who might have done it, one person couldn't possibly be the guilty party and that person was me. I'd been guarded all night. I had an alibi. I was the one person in all of St Mary's who couldn't be blamed for this.

Unless my guard lied, but why would he? If it had been onion man then I wouldn't have fancied my chances of convincing people of my innocence, but he wasn't here. I looked around. No, he wasn't, was he? Men were emerging from the gatehouse and making their way to the walls. Those who'd been on watch throughout the night were climbing down. Those who'd eaten were crossing the courtyard and those who were about to eat were crossing in the opposite direction. Sleepy early-morning greetings were exchanged.

But there was one person who wasn't here. I couldn't see onion man anywhere. I turned slowly – no, no onion man in sight. Unless ...

I tweaked William's sleeve and nodded in the direction of our *plein-air* bathroom. He nodded curtly, his mind elsewhere.

Onion man wasn't there. I walked all around the steaming heap – several times, in fact – before availing myself of the facility and returning to William.

'He is not here.'

His gaze snapped at me. 'Who is not here?'

'The man who was my guard. Not him ...' I gestured to the returning man. 'The one who smells of onions.'

The guard rejoined us, whispering in William's ear. This time William's expression did change and I knew that, somehow, the other well had been poisoned too.

He snapped a curt command and the three of us returned to the hall where Walter of Shrewsbury was waiting.

William took him aside and spoke quietly and I could see immediately who was Walter's number-one suspect.

He took a deep breath to accuse me but before he could utter, William had him by the arm and was propelling him through the doorway into the private family quarters. This was not a matter for public discussion.

They went first, then me, then my guard. We turned left into a large, sunny room I had never seen before. I had no time to notice anything other than the rather handsome red and black clay tiles on the floor before Walter rounded on me.

I saw the blow coming and rode it as best I could, but his clenched fist caught me on the cheekbone and it hurt. It hurt a lot. Stringy he might be, but he packed a hell of punch. I went down like one of those demolished factory chimneys but with less style and more dust. I lay on the cold floor wondering whether I should get up so I could be knocked down again, or stay down so he could kick me more easily. It struck me that if I had an office job then the only decision I'd be making at that moment would be whether to do my photocopying before my filing or the other way around. Office jobs have many hidden benefits.

Ian Guthrie's voice ran through my head. 'Are you going to lie there all day, Maxwell?' He was right. I should get up and put in an honest day's work being their prime suspect. Get it over with, so to speak. If I couldn't convince them of my innocence then in less than an hour I'd be hanging from one of the rafters in the hall as a warning to others.

I climbed to my knees and from there to my feet. I didn't cry, or put my hand to my face, or plead for my life. Bollocks to all that. I was certain the man they wanted was onion man. I was equally certain he wasn't here any longer. He'd climbed out of an upper window hours ago. Nothing I could say would make any difference. All my hope was on William Hendred, who wasn't a stupid man. And, truth be told, neither was Walter. All I had to do was not let him hang me before someone worked out I was innocent.

Walter had rounded on William. The flurry of words was too quick and too hot for me to understand but I suspected the gist of it was that he'd always said I was working for the Rushfords. That I was a spy, planted by them to undermine us. To sabotage the siege. I'd never seen him so angry. There was no stopping him and William didn't even try. We all stood waiting until finally he ran down, chest heaving, eyes glittering with fury and my untimely death looming large on his horizon.

William was questioning the guard. When had he come on duty? Had I left the hall at any time? For any reason? Even for a moment? Had he left me unguarded at any time? Even for a moment? No harm would come to him if he had. He – William – wanted only the truth.

The guard, Owen was his name – a man I knew slightly as one of Tam the Welshmen's cronies – shook his head at every question. He'd taken over from onion man at midnight. I'd slept the night through. I'd barely moved. He'd sat on the window seat, cleaned his sword and mended his belt in the light of a single candle. No, he had never left me alone. Yes, he'd barely taken his eyes off me. No, I hadn't left the hall at any time. I hadn't even woken once.

How could he be so sure, demanded Walter. It was dark. There was almost no light.

'Didn't need it,' he said woodenly. 'She snores. All the time.'

William nodded. 'Yes, she does.'

I nodded too. Yes, I did. Leon had remarked upon it once or twice.

What of onion man? demanded Walter. I say onion man because that's what he always was to me. I think his name was Barden and they referred to him as such but, in my head, he was always onion man. Anyway, whatever his name was, there was no sign of him. He'd gone and his gear was gone, too.

You'd think that would be a clear indication of his guilt, wouldn't you, but Walter, not one to let facts get in the way of a healthy prejudice, leapt back into battle claiming we'd been in it together. A claim so ridiculous I felt safe leaving others to deal with it while I concentrated on my throbbing face.

A rather lively three-sided argument was brewing nicely when Tam the Welshman entered to say a rope had been found tied to one of the upper windows in the north tower. Someone had evidently got out that way.

And, said William Hendred, the door between hall and the scullery had been locked all night. Yes, the scullery door to the kitchen had been open, but to access it, I would have had to leave the hall and cross the courtyard. Someone would have seen the movement, no matter how careful I'd been. And the two scullions slept there. If questioned, they would be able to say whether I'd been there or not.

Owen took the hint and slipped away, returning in a moment. No, they'd said – and I could near the note of regret in their voice – no woman had visited them during the night. Onion man had come in to fill his beaker though.

Walter subsided. Owen was an honest man and believable. And the scullions had no reason to lie. I waited for Walter to accuse me of being in league with them, but

I think the fight had gone out of him. A sensible man, he was now turning his attention to dealing with this crisis.

Both wells were now under guard. Not because it was too late, but to prevent anyone drawing water and topping up any buckets of fresh water that remained uncontaminated. Owen went off to count beer barrels. When he returned, I could see by his face that it wasn't good news.

I ignored my face, stared at the floor and had a bit of a think. I should leave. I should slip quietly away and leave them to do the heavy lifting in the thinking department. I was only a woman. Having a womb probably meant I'd have to use all my powers of concentration just to get down the stairs. They'd forgotten about me so I should just go.

So, obviously, I stayed and pushed my luck.

I've had more than my fair share of coping with disasters. The secret is to find something you can work with and ignore everything else.

I sat in one of the window seats, leaned back against the shutter and listened. They were talking of how many days they could last without water. Even if drinking was kept to a minimum, it wasn't many. And if, as I suspected, onion man was now in Guy of Rushford's camp, they would know what had happened. They would know we didn't have long. They didn't even have to attack – they had only to wait until we surrendered.

Or …

I stepped forward.

'God have you in his keeping, masters. May I speak?'

Walter was still ignoring me but William turned with an air of impatient exasperation. All men have it. Right back to Adam. You expect me to do *what* with this apple?

'Speak.'

'Sir, I believe our best chance of success is to surrender. Let them in.'

I closed my eyes and waited for the other blow. It never came. After a while I opened my eyes again.

Walter turned slowly to look at William. He didn't utter a single word but he didn't have to. We could all feel him saying, 'I told you so.'

No one spoke. I could feel myself losing my audience so I hastened on.

'Sir, they will know our position by now. There is no point in trying to hide it. Therefore, I propose we should invite them in and hold a feast in their honour. With wine. As much wine as we can find. We welcome them with all the good food and drink we can muster.'

I stopped. Make them ask.

'Why? Why would we hold a feast?'

'To give thanks, sir, that the tyrant William Hendred has fled.'

Now I really did close my eyes and brace myself for the blow.

It never came. The tyrant William Hendred was staring at the floor looking thoughtful.

'And then?' persisted Walter.

'And then, when they are drunk, unconscious, unable to defend themselves ...'

'We should kill them all?' I could see Walter's face crease with disgust at my female contravention of the laws of hospitality.

I mustered all my Dr Bairstow managing skills.

'No, sir. I propose we burn St Mary's around them.'

They reeled. Literally. There was a massive babble of protest. Already they were turning away from me. All except one. William Hendred stared at me from under his heavy brows, unspeaking.

Eventually the voices died away.

His voice sounded deep in the silence. 'And then? What of our people?'

'Most are already hiding in the woods. Those who can't fight should join them.'

He folded his arms. An excellent example of intransigent manhood. 'And those who can?'

'Follow you to Rushford, sir. With all speed.'

For the first time ever, I saw him off-balance. 'Why? Why in the name of Christ and all the saints would I abandon this place and ride to Rushford?'

'To take and occupy Guy's castle in his absence. To take from him what he would have taken from you.'

There wasn't even a babble of protest this time. Taking advantage of the stunned silence, I pushed on.

'We let Guy and Jerald in. More than that – we welcome them. We hold a huge feast and fill them with all the food and drink they can consume. While they are rolling in their seats and too drunk to notice, we set fire to whatever will burn and flee to the woods. They will be busy saving their horses, their gear, their lives even. They will be in no state to follow us. We hide deep in the forest. Far from anything Guy or Jerald could do to us.'

I turned to William Hendred. 'You, sir, take every man who can fight – if it pleases you, of course,' remembering possibly slightly too late that I was only a womb-controlled inferior. 'You ride to Rushford and take the castle. I am willing to bet every able-bodied man they have is here now. You will probably be able to walk right in and take it from under their noses. You pull up the drawbridge and sit tight. What can they do, sir? You have their ... their ...' I struggled for an expression other than power base and failed. 'Their power base. There is nothing for them here. Our people and most of our supplies are safely away. The wells are poisoned. Yes, St Mary's will burn, but everything can be repaired or rebuilt. Yes, they can shout and bluster, but Sir Hugh will be here any day now. I promise you that. You have committed no crime. You have done your duty and held St Mary's for the Duke of Lancaster. Who might one day be king. And Sir Hugh is his man. The king will grant him the town of Rushford,' I said, recklessly speaking for the new king who might, of course, do nothing of the sort, but we could sort all that out later. My priority was to save St Mary's. 'The revenues from Guy's lands can pay for the rebuilding here and Sir Hugh will have all their lands and rights. He will have everything and the Rushfords will end with nothing.'

I lowered my eyes and contemplated the floor with traditional female modesty. Folding my hands in a manner I hoped made me look both demure and trustworthy – although I wasn't optimistic – I stepped back again.

What do you think? Not bad, eh?

Still they stared at me. I hoped very much that they were appreciating the brilliant audacity of my plan and not because they were, once again, planning to hang me.

But it all fitted. It all fitted with the little I knew about events in 1399.

'Safe passage,' said Tam the Welshman, thoughtfully.

William turned to him. 'Explain.'

'We demand safe passage for those who wish to depart. In return, we undertake to hand over St Mary's.'

'Without a fight?' he said incredulously.

'Without further bloodshed,' said Tam, whom I began to suspect of being quite bright. A bit like Markham but six inches taller, three stone heavier, dark-haired and Welsh. Otherwise, identical.

264

'And what of Master Hendred?' demanded Walter. 'They will never believe William Hendred would surrender.'

Tam shrugged apologetically. 'Master Hendred's protests were … overcome.'

'How?'

Tam made a graphic gesture and silence fell.

I remained very still and silent because I could do no more and I didn't want to over-egg the pudding.

Walter didn't like it.

Well, no one liked it, actually. William especially didn't like it, but sometimes a man's gotta do ….

Everyone dispersed to make their preparations and then we opened the gates. The big ones. They flung them wide open and stepped back.

Guy of Rushford waited outside on horseback, his men gathered behind him. He made us wait, just because he could, and then slowly passed through the gates and into the courtyard. His horse's hooves sounded very loud in the hot silence.

His brother Jerald rode slightly behind him on an extraordinary yellow horse. I'd never seen anything like it. It looked as if it was carved from butter. He wore a sword – Jerald, not the horse, obviously – but I didn't mind betting he didn't have the slightest idea what to do with it. With his wet blubbery lips and runny eyes, he wasn't the most attractive being in the courtyard – even counting the yellow horse.

Guy was different. He was a big man and dark. Darker even than Tam. His beard was forked – a ridiculous fashion – and his hair close cropped to fit under his helmet. He had a high colour. I suspected he liked his drink. Which was good news for us.

Walter received them formally in the courtyard. Behind him stood Roger, pale and trembling with nerves, with the keys of St Mary's on a velvet cushion. With great ceremony, Walter handed them over and bowed. Not that they were needed. Every door stood open, especially the barns and storehouses, showing the little St Mary's had to offer.

William Hendred's men – all carefully unarmed – stood off to one side, waiting with their horses, all ready to go. I was hiding in the kitchen with Fat Piers and the others, all of us craning our necks to see what was going on. I held my breath. Would they be allowed to leave? Unharmed? I knew a deal had been struck but frankly I wouldn't have trusted either of the Rushfords as far as I could kick them – and believe me, I could kick them a very long way. I'd never seen a more unattractive couple. And I suspected that while Guy looked vicious and Jerald unstable, I wouldn't mind betting that Guy was the more unstable of the two and Jerald the more vicious. I wondered what their sister made of them. Or was she the worst of the bunch?

Guy made no move to take the keys, looking around him suspiciously. He knew who he was looking for. 'Where is William Hendred?'

Walter eased his weight and looked shifty. The expression suited him.

'Gone,' he said, obviously begrudging every word.

I don't think Guy was convinced. Or perhaps that was his normal expression.

'How so?'

'When news of the poisoned well was known, we had no option but to surrender.'

Guy looked even more sceptical. 'Not William Hendred.'

Damn and blast. This was obviously a man who knew his William Hendred.

'No,' said Walter, staring at his feet.

'Where is he?'

Walter contrived to look even more shifty. 'Dead. He was against the surrender. He tried to prevent it and they turned on him.'

I appreciated the subtle 'they'.

Guy looked around. 'Where is the body?'

I held my breath and I suspected I wasn't the only one.

Walter gestured with his head. 'Down the well. You should warn your men – the only fresh water is from the stream.'

Neat. No body to produce. Old Walter was really good at this.

Guy was suspicious. 'And yet, Master Walter, you are alive.'

Walter couldn't meet his gaze. 'William Hendred was living when they threw him into the water. I had no wish to go the same way.'

Who would have thought old Walter could be so inventive? Against my will, I was very impressed.

Guy looked down on him. He was tall enough to look down on most people. 'And you expect me to believe you will serve me.'

Walter drew himself up and gestured to the keys. 'I serve the master of St Mary's.' He paused. 'Whoever he is.'

There was a long moment while Guy appeared to weigh what he had heard, staring around the courtyard at Tam and his men drawn up, all ready to leave. A heavily disguised William Hendred stood inconspicuously at the rear with the old packhorse.

Guy stared again at Walter, standing before him with his head bowed. He reminded me of an animal scenting a trap but unable to locate it.

It was Jerald who tipped the balance. While others had been plotting and planning, Fat Piers had his own way of preparing for disaster. Delicious smells were emanating from the kitchen. Guy and his men wouldn't be starving, but they would certainly appreciate the meal they were about to enjoy.

'Hungry,' he announced.

At a nudge from Fat Piers, Dick and Edgar scuttled out with two goblets of wine. The very best wine in the very best goblets.

Guy sipped, possibly trying to preserve the illusion that, thief and opportunist though he might be, he was still a gentleman. Jerald slobbered his down any old how, a good part of it decorating his front.

I couldn't tell what was going through Guy's mind – I suspect no one ever could – but he appeared satisfied. Draining and replacing his goblet, he nodded dismissal to Tam who wasted not a moment. To the jeers of Guy's men, he urged his horse out of the gates and away. The others followed him. The sound of their hoofbeats died away and we were left – alone and defenceless.

Fat Piers nudged us all away from the doors. We had work to do.

Walter was leading them into the hall, where the tables were already laid out for a massive feast. There was the best linen and the best pewter. Even more wonderful smells pervaded the hall. At the side tables, wine and beer stood ready to be served. We'd pulled out all the stops to impress. To kill them with kindness.

Walter escorted them ceremoniously to high table, seating Guy in Sir Hugh's seat and Jerald in the one traditionally occupied by the lady of the manor. I do sometimes wonder if he had more of a sense of humour than anyone suspected.

He'd judged the situation perfectly, however. I could see the smirks and nudges among Guy's men as they seated themselves and then Fat Piers dragged me away to do some work.

I saw Roger and Edgar run in with napkins and bowls of scented water. I myself had picked the mint leaves and arranged them artistically. My contribution to the downfall of Guy and Jerald. Apart from the original idea, of course. I could hear the rumble and laughter of a large group of men, the scrape of benches on the stone floor. I could hear the toasts and the clink of beakers as they rewarded themselves for a long day's sieging. It was all the best quality stuff, too. We hadn't stinted on the hospitality in any way.

Everywhere, beakers were being filled. And then replenished. Walter had given orders that no one's beaker was to be allowed to run down, let alone be empty. Everyone was encouraged to drink deeply. I saw Roger actually urging a man to drain his cup so he could fill it up again. We were the cowed, defeated villagers hoping that if we were nice to our conquerors then they wouldn't kill us too much.

I peeked through the door occasionally, just to see what was going on – and because I couldn't help myself –

but both Margery and I were very careful to stay out of sight. Neither of us was what you would look for in today's modest medieval maid, but on the other hand, a bunch of drunken conquering heroes weren't going to be that fussy. Fat Piers kept us at the far end of the kitchen, out of sight from the hall, which I appreciated. A bastard he might be on a bad day, but he was a thoughtful bastard.

Sweat pouring down his face and dropping unheeded into the food he was preparing, Fat Piers was working like a madman. Dish after dish was carried up the stairs and paraded around the hall in the traditional fashion, to be greeted with shouts of raucous acclaim.

Some of it was surprisingly sophisticated considering what he had had at his disposal and the time constraints. There was no doubt Piers was an artist. Birds had been roasted. There was a massive amount of fish – carp caught from our ponds. Personally, I think carp is awful – it looks awful and tastes muddy – but he dressed it beautifully and everyone ate it. There were even sweet dishes made of sugar paste, almonds, pastries, and such fruit as they had been able to muster.

I took a moment from finely chopping some green leaves to wonder when it would occur to them they had been eating food cooked in water from a spoiled well. They were going to be horribly ill. Well, the ones who weren't caught in the flames would be. Between burning and barfing, they were going to regret ever coming within five miles of St Mary's.

I don't know whether it was because of the noise in the kitchen – Fat Piers threw several tantrums of massive proportions, just so everyone could see how much of an artist he really was – or the sounds of general carousing coming from the hall where everyone seemed to be having an amazing time, but I never heard everyone leaving. When I stole a brief moment to ease my aching back in the doorway and breathe in some cool air, the courtyard was deserted. Most of the servants, tasks completed, had melted away. There were a lot fewer people than there had been half an hour ago. The two scullion boys had piled up the dirty dishes and departed. There wasn't a soul in sight. Which was odd, considering the guards Guy had left at the gatehouse and the stables. I bit back a smile and returned to the heat of the kitchen.

As I did, Fat Piers stepped back from his last platter, spat soggily and accurately into the sauce, and motioned it away. We were done here. There was nothing left. I was staying well away from the hall, but I imagined the tables must be groaning under the strain. All the best pewter was out there. Roger and Edgar had worn their legs to stumps bringing up the entire contents of the buttery. Wine, beer – it was all nearly gone. Our guests were singing. Always a good sign. I could hear them banging their cups on the table, beating out the rhythm. Now was the time.

Roger and Edgar had left the last full jugs full of wine on the sideboard. If they wanted any more they would have to go off and find it. Not that I reckoned many of them would be that capable. I gathered from Roger's disgusted expression that quite a few of them were already pissing where they sat.

Quietly, people began to disperse. Every time I looked around there were fewer people in the kitchen. Our people were slowly melting away. There was only Walter left in the hall, standing in the corner supervising the proceedings. Now was the time for him to invent a problem in the kitchen that only he could solve and slip

271

away. I hoped he had a horse tucked away somewhere. If Fat Piers hadn't cooked it.

I spared a thought for William Hendred. Where was he now? What was happening in Rushford?

I pulled myself together. I couldn't do everything and he was a capable man who could look after himself. I should concentrate on what was happening here because things were about to get lively.

While we'd been working to get the food out, Margery had brought up the oil. Almost every lamp St Mary's possessed stood on the table nearest the door.

Areas had been allocated. Roger and Edgar would set fire to the upper stories. They went first because they had to get back down again and away before the flames took hold. They would throw oil on the beds, open the shutters and as many doors as they could, strike a flame and run.

Fat Piers would torch his own kitchen because no one else had the nerve.

Walter was to burn the ground floor solar room and whisk himself out of the way.

And Margery and I had the old wooden shed next to the stables on one side and the feed store on the other. From there we would be straight out of the gate and up into the relative safety of the woods.

St Mary's teamwork. What could possibly go wrong?

It was a good job I was with Margery. I'm a modern girl and although I was making a reasonable job of living the life of a medieval woman – well, I thought I wasn't doing too badly – it's the little things that always get you in the end. I didn't have anything with which to make a flame. I snuck into the small barn alongside the stables, flinging oil around the place – including a good bit on myself –

when I realised with dismay that I didn't have the equivalent of matches. On the other hand, I had Margery, who shouldered me aside, made a little pile of hay and straw dust, and breathing heavily, carefully laid a small handful of hay over the top and struck her tinder.

That was when things started to go wrong because she couldn't get a flame going. She tried and tried. I left my station by the door where I'd been hopping from foot to foot, keeping nervous watch, and came to see what the problem was.

Her hands were trembling so much she couldn't get a spark. Drink, nerves, whatever, it just wasn't happening. I stole a quick look out through the door. The courtyard was still empty. But not for long. Roger must have set his fires upstairs, Fat Piers had done the kitchen and they'd both legged it. It was just us and we had to do this.

I put my hand on her shoulder and pressed gently. She nodded, exhaled sharply, took three deep breaths and tried again. I returned to the doorway and stood as quietly as I could, keeping watch and trying not to let my impatience show. Someone was going to notice what was going on at any moment. Flames would be roaring through the kitchen, the solar, and the south tower. I'm sure it was my imagination, but I was convinced I could smell burning.

I looked around. Dry wood. Hay and straw were stored in the loft above. It was high summer. We'd had no rain for several weeks. This barn, the stables next door, the outhouses – everything would go up like a rocket. A small whoomph recalled my attention. She'd done it. Everything *was* about to go up like a rocket.

She nudged me towards the entrance. It was rather like being hit by a soft, warm, beer smelling, heavy goods vehicle, but I got the message.

Not wanting to draw attention to ourselves, we used the unobtrusive back door, intending to skirt the Midden of Happy Memories, nip around the back of chicken house and only emerge into the courtyard proper when we were within sight of the gatehouse. Then a quick dash out through the still open gate and we'd be away.

Margery poked her head around the side of the washhouse. The courtyard was continuing its empty theme. We were both of us very, very cautious. There were fifty drunken men in the hall who would really be in the mood for a little after-dinner entertainment. Anyone would be cautious. But, there was only thirty yards or so between us and the open gate. We were as good as out.

I don't know what made me look behind me, but two men were standing watching us. That they had intended to use the midden was very apparent. They were unlaced and ready to go. Bollocks.

Their faces lit up. One said something to the other – probably the medieval equivalent of 'Don't fancy yours, mate,' and here they came.

It got worse. It was bloody onion man. And he'd brought a friend. I was surprised he had one. And then things got very much worse because the man with him was Jerald, his wet, blubbery lips hanging loose. He caught sight of Margery and gave a high-pitched giggle.

Again. Bollocks. The best that could happen was that we were in for a very unpleasant ten minutes or so. Or, given the state of them, somewhat less than ten minutes. The worst was that they would notice the absence of every other member of the St Mary's household, the smell of burning, the drifting smoke and raise the alarm before we had escaped. Why does this always happen to me? And Margery, of course. I looked around. Margery had gone.

What?

I spun around, disbelieving. I wouldn't have thought it of her. She'd pushed off. She'd left me.

The two of them were striding towards me – equipment hanging loose for ease of access. I looked around for a pitchfork. Or a bucket. Even a bolshie chicken. Anything with which to defend myself. Nothing.

And then Margery reared up behind them both, massive and silent, sleeves rolled up to expose her brawny arms and belted onion man around the head with a wooden bucket. He dropped like a stone. A blow like that could have killed him.

Jerald, never the brightest sword in the armoury, stared down at his fallen friend, and then Margery caught him with her bucket's back swing. Smaller and lighter than his friend, he was knocked clean off his feet and in through the burning doorway.

If he was unconscious he could burn to death. I took one tentative step towards the flames, Margery uttered some exasperated medieval oath, shook her head and seized my arm. With all caution gone, we sprinted for the gate.

I heard a shout behind us. And then another. Whether another midden visitor had discovered the fires or their stricken comrades I didn't know and I certainly wasn't going to stop to find out. I could hear Ian Guthrie, centuries away, telling me to never mind what was going on behind me. I'd find out soon enough if I didn't get a move on.

I could smell burning on the wind. Smoke drifted in the hot afternoon air. I could hear the crackle of flames. And shouting.

We flew out of the gates.

Well, I flew – Margery lumbered a few yards and then stopped, chest heaving, leaning against the wall for support. I tugged at her arm. 'We cannot stay here.'

She shook her head and pushed me away.

I came right back for another go, trying to pull her away from the wall.

Again, she pushed me and gestured that I was to go. Up the hill to the woods to join the others.

'No,' I said, in English, not caring whether she understood me or not. 'I'm not leaving you. We're St Mary's. We never leave our people behind. You can do it.'

But she couldn't and there was no way on this earth I could shift her.

She gestured over my shoulder and at the same time I heard hooves coming up behind me. I swung around, dropped into my best ninja pose and prepared to sell my life dearly. And I might have to. It was bloody Walter of Shrewsbury, astride a snorting, lathered horse, his robe hoicked up around his knees to show his skinny legs. At his heels, on foot, were John the Smith and one of his innumerable sons. Where had they come from?

Walter gestured to me. I gestured to Margery. He gestured to his men. This could go on all day, and all the time I could smell the smoke and hear the shouting. Seconds only had passed but we shouldn't be here. Any of us. Someone had raised the alarm. It wouldn't take them long to pour through the gate and then things weren't going to go well for us. We'd invited them in, tricked them, probably poisoned them, and tried to burn them alive. They weren't going to be particularly well disposed towards any of us and that was before they found out William Hendred was in Rushford, doing the same to them as they were doing to us. But with more success, I hoped.

Again, Walter gestured to me. John and his son each seized a portion of Margery – brave men – and literally ran her down the hill towards the village. I assumed they had some plan to get her to safety. Which left me and Walter. There was a crash behind us. I had no idea what it was but something had obviously just given way. They would be here in seconds.

Walter was reaching down for me.

Not a little surprised, I took his arm, put my foot on his boot, and heaved myself up behind him. I remember thinking again that he was much stronger than he looked. His horse was already springing forwards, foam flying from its bit as we pounded up the hill. I hung on tightly. Obviously, this 'We're St Mary's and we don't leave our people behind' dated from long before the time of Dr Bairstow.

We paused under the eaves of the outlying trees and looked back. St Mary's was burning. The hall and part of the south tower streamed smoke. The stables, chicken house, wash house – all the wooden buildings on the west side were ablaze. Huge orange flames streamed skywards. The courtyard was full of staggering men, all shouting pointlessly.

I let go of Walter's waist because I don't think either of us were enjoying that very much, and slithered off his horse. He went ahead while I assumed my rightful position, staring at his horse's arse, as we made our way by quiet, sun-dappled paths to where the others were awaiting us.

23

We all lived in the forest for a few days. We had to. It was the easily the safest place to be. We guessed the Rushfords would limp back to their former rightful home, only to find that two could play at their game and it had been occupied in their absence. They would not be happy. But that was William Hendred's problem. We'd done our bit by evicting them from St Mary's. I wondered whether, in an effort to make the best of things, they'd return here, but as Roger said, why would they? The water was bad and the buildings were damaged. The villagers had fled taking their possessions with them. The livestock was hidden and the harvest was still in the fields. There was nothing for them at St Mary's. I nodded. He was right.

It was a strange feeling for me to be part of someone else's plan. I was just a cog in the machinery. I didn't know what was going on elsewhere and I wasn't important enough to be kept in the loop. I sat on a log, resting the hand I didn't know I'd burned, and tried to work out what would be happening in the rest of the world. I had no idea of the exact date but we must surely be into August by now. The nights were drawing in. Henry must have declared himself king. It was only a matter of waiting until Sir Hugh returned to reclaim St Mary's.

Some people wanted to return to the village but the homeless Rushfords were out there somewhere and there was always the possibility they could gather more support. I suspected that among their forces, those who could – those who weren't tied to them feudally – would sum up the situation, realise they weren't going to be paid for this one and push off. Enthusiasm for the venture had probably all but disappeared, but that wouldn't make the Rushfords any less dangerous. They were dispossessed and when the king was informed of their attempts to steal a part of his Lancaster lands, they'd be outlawed. Wolf's heads.

Walter despatched a couple of lads to Rushford, to report to William Hendred and inform him what had happened here but, in the meantime, until the situation became clear, Walter insisted everyone remained in hiding. There were four or five sites scattered around the forest and he visited them all daily, alternately haranguing and encouraging. Unlikeable he might be – well, there was no might about it – but he took his duties and responsibilities very seriously.

His resolve was all the more creditable because one of his main concerns must be the harvest in the fields and whether, out of spite, the Rushfords would indulge in an orgy of destruction before they departed. With no second harvest, St Mary's buildings burned and their supplies depleted, it could be a tough winter for everyone, even if Rushford's castle and lands had been captured.

I spent most of my time dozing in the leafy sunshine, waiting for my burns to heal and hoping it wouldn't rain. Living in a forest is all very fine and romantic if you're Robin Hood, but less so if you're a single woman who never remembers to have an adequate supply of dock leaves on her. We didn't eat too badly. There was flat bread and pottage and more green leaves than I would have been comfortable with six months ago, but no one starved.

And then, on the fourth day, we heard horses. More than one horse was approaching fast. The men present – the very old and the very young who had been left behind – pulled out such weapons as they had. We women herded the children together, seized branches from the pile of firewood and waited. I clutched my stick in my unburned hand and stood, tense and still. Who would appear around the corner?

I caught a glimpse of a familiar, big, chestnut horse, snorting as he came, and then William Hendred, heading a group of three or four other men, was among us. Someone gave a cheer which was taken up by everyone.

I let my breath go in a silent sigh of relief.

Walter bustled forwards. They looked at each other for a moment. Walter thrust out his hand, which William ignored and enveloped him in a huge bear hug. People cheered again.

He'd come from the village. The Rushfords were long gone. Most of the village was intact. An attempt to burn down the big tithe barn beside the church had failed. And best of all, Sir Hugh had arrived at the head of a small force of men.

Guy must have realised his world was slipping away from him. That Hugh now occupied his castle in Rushford. That Henry of Lancaster was now king. Or as good as. That this new king would not be kindly disposed towards him. That the future did not hold a lot of promise for the Rushford brothers. He and Jerald had slipped away into the night leaving those who lived in Rushford to return sheepishly to their homes, where they could expect the worst.

Wisely, Sir Hugh did not hold them responsible for carrying out their lord's instructions. There was a pardon for all. A clever move to ensure their future loyalty. He was a clever man. I hoped his benevolence would extend to me.

He was to marry the Rushford sister – Katherine, I think her name was – and live in the much grander Rushford Castle. Walter would go with him to oversee his new lands and properties. Apparently, Guy had mismanaged the estate to such an extent that there would be plenty for him to do and, in so much as he ever could, he looked pleased and excited. I was pleased and excited for him and even more pleased and excited for me. He'd be nine miles away.

William Hendred was to hold St Mary's for Sir Hugh. He would, in effect, be lord of the manor. A stupendous reward for loyal service. I was pleased and excited for him as well. And I would have, if not a friend, a least a familiar face, in a high place. It had been a lively week but it was over now. We could return home.

Our joy lasted until we got back to St Mary's and saw the damage that had been done. They'd wrecked the place before they left. Thatched roofs had been burned, livestock pens wrecked, doors pulled off. Most of the roof was gone from the hall. The ground floor of South Tower, with its lovely sunny room, was badly scorched but, as William said, the curtain wall was intact, as was the gatehouse. A couple of bodies had been found under the stable ruins. Those who hadn't made it out of the fire.

They were quietly buried. Neither Jerald nor onion man were among them.

William took control immediately, allocating tasks and men. Walter was getting stuck into Rushford. Sir Hugh was to return to London to make his name with the new king.

That just left me.

You think I'd be a heroine, wouldn't you? You'd think they'd be falling over themselves with gratitude and flinging me a bit of pork with my nightly pottage. Even a commemorative spot on the midden. Not a bloody chance. There was a lot of muttering – from Walter, obviously – about how, if we'd just hung on for a week, then Sir Hugh Armstrong would have turned up with the king's men and lifted the siege without us actually having to burn the place to the ground. How they would have managed the poisoned well problem wasn't mentioned.

And, as I tried to point out, the place wasn't burned to the ground. Slight exaggeration, guys. All right, the wooden buildings were toast but they could all be rebuilt. And it wouldn't take much to put a roof on the hall. The giant beams were still intact. They could seize the opportunity to modernise it and build in a proper fireplace while they were at it –with a good chimney that my son would approve of, although I didn't mention that, obviously – and in a year or so you'd never know anything had happened. And Sir Hugh had a posh new home in the best part of Rushford. Walter had a spanking new job and a whole new set of people to boss around and William Hendred had been given St Mary's to hold for Sir Hugh. A home of his own with status and responsibility to match. Everyone was a winner. Except me, of course. Never more than two steps from the gallows.

I forgave them the injustice. I could only hope they would forgive me. Because, before he left for London, Sir Hugh had summoned me to appear before him. To account for my actions.

The reason it's called a courtyard is because that's where the courts are held.

They'd set up a table for Sir Hugh, for him to preside over, with Walter of Shrewsbury on one side of him and William Hendred on the other. Father Ranulf sat at the far end. I wondered if he was there to translate. A number of scrolls sat in front of Walter. I was willing to bet he'd itemised the damage I'd caused and costed it down to the last detail. Those scrolls were basically medieval Deductions from Wages for Damages Incurred forms. I sighed. Nothing ever changes, does it?

I was waiting in the gatehouse – in the guardroom actually, which was a little daunting – but I had Tam the Welshman on one side of me and Owen on the other. They were chatting away to each other, bragging about their recent experiences and the parts they'd played, so I wasn't too worried. Not really.

Anyway, it was a pleasant day, the sun shone, nothing was on fire – although the smell of burned wood was still very strong – and I told myself it was just a formality. Obviously, the lord of the manor would want to know the circumstances under which his manor – albeit only a very small part of it – had been burned to the ground.

I was led forward. Unsure which way things were going to go and presumably unwilling to incriminate themselves, everyone else stood well back. I felt very alone as I stood in front of Sir Hugh.

Now that I'd seen Guy, I could see a faint resemblance between the two. You could see they were related, although Sir Hugh – or Lord Rushford as he now was – was fair rather than dark. The nose and chin were the same, though. He had stern, steady blue eyes that missed nothing. I did my best to look like someone with nothing to hide.

He was bareheaded and wore blue, trimmed with dark red. A pair of leather gauntlets lay on the table before him. His boots were good and well cared for. There were no fashionable excesses here. His doublet was a reasonable length and covered his bottom. He didn't wear those ridiculous shoes with the long points and his hair was neat and combed. I thought he looked very smart.

Actually, everyone looked much smarter now the boss was home. William wore a russet doublet with matching hose and his good boots. His beard, as always, was shorter than most and neatly trimmed.

Walter wore an old-fashioned long cotehardie of dark green with his best soft hat and proudly displayed his chain of office. I felt a sudden surge of affection for him. He was old – by contemporary standards anyway – and set in his ways, but he was loyal and brave and did his job to the best of his ability. I found myself smiling at him and hastily looked away before he noticed.

Sir Hugh began to speak. I could understand him easily and he spoke slowly. I wondered if this was out of deference to the foreign woman and shot a glance at Father Ranulf, who twinkled back again. I suspected he knew his translation skills wouldn't be needed but had blagged himself a place at the table out of sheer nosiness.

I was brought forward, named, and invited to explain myself and my actions.

I was certain Hugh would have had an input from William and I was absolutely certain Walter would have shoved his oar in as well, so I kept my improbable background story to a few sentences, while making sure I remembered to thank him for his kindness in taking me in.

It's not easy, this sort of thing. Not only do you have to remember the lies you told in the first place, but in medieval times you were expected to show modesty and respect to your betters at all times, while simultaneously looking them fearlessly in the eye to show yours was an honest and trustworthy character. I compromised by keeping my eyes modestly lowered when they were talking to me, and looking them fearlessly in the eye when I was talking to them. Truthfully, I wasn't sure how well that was working.

I explained about the well while making it absolutely clear the dead cat was nothing to do with me. I mimed my shock and surprise at finding it in the well. I pointed to Owen, who blushed and shuffled and refused to speak, so I told the whole story myself, using exaggerated words and gestures and definitely *not* becoming so carried away that I forgot to stop just before the bit where I recommended setting fire to Sir Hugh's home and livelihood.

Silence fell around the courtyard. Roger leaned over his shoulder and topped up his master's goblet of wine. I was relieved to see the Rushfords hadn't drunk us completely dry.

Sir Hugh sipped delicately, wiped his mouth on his napkin and said pleasantly, 'And then?'

'And then,' I said smoothly, 'Master Walter and Master William discussed how to turn this hopeless situation to your advantage.'

'Really?' He said, turning his goblet around and watching the light fall on it. 'I understood abandoning my manor and burning it to the ground was your idea.'

I stared reproachfully at William Hendred. This was 1399. I was a woman. I had been convinced they would take the credit for my brilliant idea and I could remain safely in the background – unrewarded, true, but not dead, which was always my first choice. I was quite happy for everyone to believe it was someone else's plan and hadn't it worked out well in the end? Especially since what would have been a brilliantly audacious plan when mooted by William or Walter would almost certainly be considered a piece of mindless vandalism when suggested by the weird foreign woman who had appeared from nowhere. I looked around at the piles of charred timbers that used to be the washhouse and the stables. A number of chickens stood atop the black remains of their former home and stared reproachfully at me. I could still hang. I had a vision of them all partying the night away on this very spot, celebrating the accession of the new king and the acquisition of Hugh's new titles and properties while I swung, creaking, overhead.

Oh, sod it. When 1403 turned up I was dead anyway.

I drew myself up to my full inconsiderable height and looked him fearlessly in the eye.

'I mentioned it as an idea, sir, but it was Master William who so brilliantly carried out the plan. It was he who rode to Rushford to take the castle in your name and it was Master Walter who remained here to safeguard your property for as long as was necessary.'

'So if Master William was in Rushford and Master Walter was defending my halls – who lit the fire?'

I didn't dare look at Margery or any of them. I gritted my teeth. 'I did, sir. I set fire to the small barn.'

He turned to look at William Hendred who returned his stare woodenly.

'Are you saying you were only responsible for the barn?'

I wriggled. 'In a way, sir, yes.'

'So the stables caught fire by themselves?'

He was looking at William Hendred again, who picked up his beaker and drank deeply, not catching his eye. I felt a small stir of indignation. Were these buggers winding me up? I suppose there's no reason why people in 1399 shouldn't have a sense of humour. Just not at my expense.

Well, two could play at that game. I channelled Mr Markham.

'Almost sir, yes. The fire travelled from the barn by itself. I didn't set fire to the stables. Or the gatehouse,' I said, gesturing. 'Or the dovecote. Or the …'

I stopped. He waited – as aware as I that the list of buildings that hadn't burned was nowhere near as long as the list of buildings that had.

'Shall we turn to the main buildings,' he said pleasantly and so, because I can't help myself, I turned to the main buildings, granting him a glimpse of my profile.

'What happened to your face?' he said sharply.

I had no mirror but even I could tell the bruising from Walter's blow was still substantial. I could easily say that he'd done it. That his suspicions of me had led him to blame me for the poisoned well and this was his punishment, but for some reason I couldn't do it. Don't ask me why because I don't know.

287

'I fell over, sir.'

'Before or after you set the fire?'

I gritted my teeth again. 'During, sir.'

There was a small disturbance in the spectators and Margery shouldered her way to the front.

Sir Hugh stared at her as well he might. She was a remarkable sight at the best of times. Today, wearing what she regarded as her best attire, she was spectacular.

She wore a green robe that might have fitted her in her youth but not any time since. The cloth was worn very thin in places and over that, she wore a sleeveless surcoat of brown that was stretched to its very limit over her ample frame. Instead of tying her usual linen strip around her head to cover her hair, she wore a stiff wimple that framed her round, red face. With her small black eyes, she looked like a current bun.

She bowed. Something I had forgotten to do. On the other hand, there was no modest lowering of the eyes.

Walter whispered in Hugh's ear.

'Ah, yes. You are Margery Daw of this manor, are you not?'

'I am, Lord.'

Damn. Was he already Lord of Rushford and they hadn't told me? Or did she address him as lord because he was lord of her manor? You see – this is what happens when you don't get the chance to prep your assignment properly. Ignorance and arson abound.

'You wish to speak?'

She nodded. 'I set the fire, Lord.'

He frowned at me. 'You said you set the fire.'

William intervened. There was a whispered conversation the subject of which, I guessed, was my uselessness in general and my fire-lighting abilities in particular.

'And I would have,' I said, doing my best to divert attention away from Margery. Although to be fair, in her get-up that was never going to work.

'But you didn't.'

'No, Lord,' said Margery. 'I did.'

'But I would have,' I said, determined to shoulder the blame.

'But you didn't,' he said.

'Well, no but …'

'Why did you say you did?'

'Sir, I am the foreigner here. And it was my idea. The blame for all this should lie at my door.'

'But you didn't set the fire.'

'But I would have, sir.'

'Then why did you not?' he shouted and I could see William was wearing his *welcome to my world* expression.

I said meekly, 'I had nothing with which to make a flame.'

He turned to Margery. 'So, you started the fire.'

She nodded. 'I did, Lord.'

'Which spread to the stables.'

We nodded.

'And the kitchen.'

We both stopped nodding. If we were outside setting fire to the barn then we weren't inside setting fire to the kitchen. Or the South Tower.

William, who knew perfectly well what had occurred that day, whispered in Hugh's ear.

'Step forward, Piers of Wem.'

289

Fat Piers materialised beside me. So that was three of us now.

'You burned down the kitchen.'

He bowed low. 'No, an it please you, my lord.'

'You deny it?'

'No, Lord. I burned down the kitchen *and* the scullery *and* the bakehouse.'

Roger, seeing where this was going, quietly set down his flagon of wine and began to ooze backwards into the hall.

Without even turning his head, Sir Hugh said, 'Step forward Roger, son of Peter of this manor.'

So that was the four of us standing there.

William Hendred was still staring off to his left. I had no idea what could be interesting him so much.

Sir Hugh stood up. I know I expected the worst. I don't know about the others. Walter stood with him and they marched around the table to stand in front of us. I closed my eyes.

Hugh raised his voice so all could hear. 'Piers of Wem.'

Piers fell to his knees.

'For your loyalty and your service to me at no small risk to yourself, I give you this token of my gratitude.'

I opened my eyes. He was handing Piers a small leather purse.

Piers gasped, muttered a few words of thanks and kissed his lord's hand.

'Roger, son of Peter of this manor.'

Roger too fell to his knees and was awarded a similar purse.

'I thank you both.'

They murmured something and kissed his hand again.

Which left me and Margery. I wasn't comforted. What was commendable and proper behaviour for a man was not necessarily so for a woman. Either of us could still go to gaol. Or undergo a beating. Margery belonged to Sir Hugh but I could be marched to the borders of his lands and evicted.

'Margery of this manor.'

Margery knelt massively.

'You have served me well. Master Walter tells me you are unmarried. Take this for your dowry. With my thanks.'

He passed her a small purse. Smaller than Roger's and Piers', I noticed.

She kissed his hand and managed to say, 'God save my lord.'

That left me.

'Joan of Rouen, step forward.'

I stared for a moment and then thought, shit, that's me.

I knelt and not very gracefully, either.

'Master William tells me yours is a sad tale.'

'Sir, I have endured much misfortune and I must thank you for the sanctuary you have offered me. If I have offended your hospitality by my actions then I sincerely beg your pardon.'

He looked down at me. 'You are an educated woman?'

'Oh no,' I said, horrified at this accusation of unwomanliness, 'but I helped my father at his work.'

'His trade?'

'A scribe, sire,' I said, hacking yet another path through the Land of Make Believe. 'When his sight failed, I read to him and wrote his replies.'

He nodded. 'And your husband?'

'Leon of Rouen sir. Recently dead.'

'I am pleased to offer you a home here, Joan of Rouen. And a woman should not be without a husband. I offer you a dowry in gratitude for your part in … recent events.'

I was nearly overcome. Not only was he not going to hang me but I was being rewarded. I would have money. I could buy a comb. And a warm cloak for the coming winter. And I would have a home. I would be safe.

I did as the others had done and kissed his hand, words being beyond me.

He stepped close to the four of us and said in a low voice. 'Never do that again.'

We all fervently promised never to set fire to St Mary's again. Piers and Roger scuttled back into the crowd, who cheered and applauded. Margery lumbered to her feet, clutching her purse and grinning fit to burst. I noticed several men sidle up to her as she rejoined Little Alice. I suspected they had suddenly discovered she was a fine figure of a woman. With the gratitude of her lord. And a dowry.

This seemed to signal the end of the proceedings. Hugh moved off and was joined by Walter. People milled around. I stayed on my knees tightly clutching my little purse as if I feared it would be taken from me.

A voice murmured, 'At last – you seem bereft of words. I can scarce believe it,' and William walked past me to join his master.

As soon as I could, I took myself off to a quiet corner to examine my purse. I tipped the coins into the palm of my hand and turned them over curiously. Some were so worn I couldn't make out their denomination. Not for the first time, it occurred to me that my short-sightedness was going to cause me some problems, sooner or later. For instance, I was never going to be able to thread a needle. You don't have a needle to thread, said my common sense. So stop worrying.

I strained my eyes and brain to work out their value. A labourer would earn around 3d a day. One shilling and sixpence a week – no one worked on a Sunday. Well, they did – they worked their own land on a Sunday. So that brought in five or six shillings a month. Working around three hundred days a year – and paid less in winter because of the shorter days – he'd come home with about three pounds a year. A woman would get around half of that.

As far as I could see, thirty minutes of arson had earned me four farthings, four ha'pennies, four pennies and a tarnished and clipped silver shilling. I think I had about one and sixpence. Two weeks' wages. Good for Hugh. Although I suspected the tarnished and clipped silver coin came from Walter and would turn out to be worth considerably less than face value. Never mind. I had no intention of buying myself a husband, although chance would be a fine thing. Whereas the acquisition of a dowry had rendered Margery considerably more attractive to the opposite sex – she had quite a small crowd around her now – it was obviously going to take more than a few dubious coins to convince a man I was worth taking on.

Never mind. You could get a gallon of not very good wine for around 3d, so a few pennies should be more than enough to buy me a knife to eat with, a comb for my hair, some linen to cover my head, a second-hand dress from somewhere, and if I was really lucky, a good thick cloak for the winter. Things were looking up. I would walk to Rushford market to try my luck.

A thought struck me. I would need permission to leave the village. Well I wasn't going to ask Walter. I would approach William.

All this sounds very exciting. And funny. And some parts of it were and I've told you about them. What I haven't mentioned are the long dark nights when I lay alone on my stone floor weeping quietly into my stole. Trying to push away soul-crushing thoughts of fear and loss and loneliness and failing utterly. Seeing Leon's blue eyes every time I closed my own. Feeling his arms around me. Listening to his breathing as he slept beside me at night. Feel the touch of his hands. And Matthew, with his shock of dark hair we couldn't persuade him to have cut. The way he slid his hand into mine when he wanted comfort but wouldn't admit it. I heard his oddly deep voice.

'Mummy shouted at Ma Scrope and she died. Mummy's *awesome*.'

And Peterson with his gentle kindness and pain-filled eyes. And Markham with his new-found sense of responsibility. And Dr Bairstow with his beaky nose, peering at me over his desk as he found something to complain about in one of my reports. Even Rosie Lee and our daily – sometimes hourly – skirmishes over who would make the tea. I missed them all. They were gone forever. As I was gone from them.

And with that thought I would curl up even more tightly and feel the tears run down my cheeks as I waited for another day to dawn without them.

We embarked on busy rebuilding. Tarpaulins were secured over the hall which reminded me of my own time. William the Carpenter was permitted to bring in extra labour. The sound of hammering and sawing echoed from dawn till dusk. The smell of new wood was everywhere. No one was hanging around. Winter would be here soon enough. And there was what remained of the harvest to get in. Livestock to fatten up. Houses to make weatherproof. Firewood to be collected. Every cottage began to sprout enormous piles of wood that would last hardly any time at all.

Being the most unskilled of all the unskilled labour, I was on firewood-collecting duty. The rules were simple – if it was on the ground then it was mine. I was forbidden on pain of death and worse to touch living wood. I spent days lugging back old bits of wood salvaged from the forest floor. The pile by the kitchen door never seemed to get any larger.

Autumn began to happen. One night I awoke and I was freezing. The first frost is no fun if you sleep on a stone floor. When William had finished with his pot the next morning, I ventured into his room to make a request.

'God give you good morning, sir.'

He grunted, pulling on his boots. His chattiness plumbed new depths in the early mornings. 'Pack your gear.'

What? Why? Now what had I done?

I said cautiously, 'Pack my gear? All of it?' As if I had trunks full of clothes and combs and mirrors.

He finished with his boots and got to his feet. 'Today we move to the solar.'

That was news to me. I mean, I knew he was moving out. As almost lord of the manor he was entitled to better accommodation than this. And a toilet without a weird foreign woman sleeping in it, too. I hadn't realised it was today. And I certainly hadn't realised I was going with him. I'd rather hoped for a little corner all to myself. Still, at least I wasn't one of the fittings, to be passed on to Tam the Welshman when he succeeded to William's position.

I said cautiously, 'I have no gear, sir.'

He was on his way to the door. Now was a good moment to ask.

'Sir, I crave leave to travel to Rushford.'

He stopped with his hand on the latch and looked at me. 'You are leaving us? You are unhappy here?'

'No, sir. Not at all. I am much beholden to all here for their kindness and care.'

'Then why? Do you have news of relatives there?'

'No, sir.' I gestured at my by now very well-worn Persian tunic. 'Sir, winter draws near and I would go to Rushford for a warm cloak.' No need to burden him with the rest of my shopping list.

He seemed to see what I was wearing for the first time.

He nodded. 'I go there today. Be ready at the third hour. Terce.'

I nodded and retreated back into my toilet.

I made sure I was early. I didn't want to keep him waiting. He was my ride.

They led out his horse, the big chestnut beast, Theobald. He snorted in the crisp morning air and tossed his head. William Hendred reached down for me. It seemed I was to ride pillion.

He didn't speak at all, but it was a pleasant ride. Theobald was a good horse, strong and easily able to carry both of us. We crossed the ford and trotted up through the village. Once away from the buildings, we broke into a canter, eating up the miles. Most of the path was through dense woodland although at one point I saw what I took to be the village of Whittington away among the trees.

The sun was warm on my back. It was hard to believe that winter would be here soon. The trees were just beginning to turn gold.

I heard Rushford before I saw it. The peal of the church bells carried across the river. That and the smoky haze over the town told me we were getting close. It's always a surprise to see how low the buildings were at the time. There was nothing above two stories apart from the church towers and the castle itself, glowering down at everyone from its position on top of the hill.

The Rush was wide here and shallow, fast flowing over a gravel bed. We slowed and splashed through the ford.

The town walls weren't high. Not much higher than ours at St Mary's, and the gates stood wide open. There was only one guard and he was leaning against the wall, his pike leaning with him. It was market day and everyone was welcome. Their money even more so.

Once in through the gate – where the guard greeted William respectfully by name – he disappeared into the first inn we came to. The old wooden sign denoted it as *The Cider Tree*. I stood out in the street for a while, feeling like an idiot, unsure whether he expected me to wait or not, decided I wasn't getting any younger, and pushed off to see what I could see.

Rushford was so much smaller than I remembered. There were very few buildings on the other side of the river. The majority of the buildings crouched around the base of the castle.

Today was definitely market day. Stalls filled the narrow streets leading up to the castle. I took a tight grip on my purse and made my way slowly past metalworkers, haberdashers, furriers, shoemakers, gold merchants, spice sellers, butchers and bakers, all yelling their goods at the tops of their voices. I fought my way through a gaggle of geese, spitting and honking at everything in their path as they were driven down the street. Beggars sat or lay in the road, palms outstretched. Many of them were children.

Finally, I came across a tiny stall, rammed into a corner between two buildings. I liked the look of this one because it was run by a young woman. I examined her merchandise, looking for what I needed.

I found a tiny comb I suspected was part of a much larger original. It was made of bone or ivory, I wasn't sure which, but it was just what I needed.

I did my best to haggle. To look like someone who could easily walk away if the price wasn't right, but I was rubbish. I had to have a comb and this was the only stall I'd seen that sold the sort of tat I could afford. I held out a coin. She shook her head and went to take another. I shook my head. She shrugged and stepped back. Bugger –

this wasn't going well. And I really had to comb my hair. It was driving me insane. In the end, reluctantly, I nodded and smilingly, she handed me the comb. I had a nasty feeling I'd paid well over the odds and I think perhaps she felt a little guilty about it because she included a small piece of hard, grey soap in the deal. It wouldn't lather, but maybe I could use it to scrape my skin clean.

I picked over some lengths of ribbon. I could really do with a touch of colour in my life – the red and green silk stole was fading fast under the bashing it was taking these days, but I couldn't afford to waste what might be the only money I might ever have in my entire life. I sighed and went to move on.

She really was the most persuasive saleswoman I'd ever met. Unerringly she picked out my favourite colours, holding up a handful of blue and green ribbons. And yes, she was right and they would have looked wonderful – even on me – but no, I couldn't afford them. Shaking my head and smiling regretfully, I backed away.

Now I needed to find a clothes stall which, in an age when people made all their own clothes, could be difficult. Clothes were worn almost until they fell apart and then had a new lease of life when they were cut down for the kids. I was ranging up and down the stalls, looking for someone who looked as if they sold second-hand clothes when a heavy hand fell on my shoulder. I jumped a mile, spun around and found myself face to face with William Hendred.

He stepped back, slightly astonished at my reaction. You could tell he'd never been kidnapped in his entire life. Not even once.

I pulled myself together and greeted him politely.

'God's greeting, sir.'

He nodded curtly. 'Come.'

Wondering why I always attracted the chatty ones, I followed him closely as he worked his way through the crowds. He stopped at a stall under the shadow of a large house. The front of the house was let down to display bolts of colourful cloth. I hung back. All of this was far too expensive for me. He pushed his way past the displays and we entered the house proper. A man bustled forwards – well fed and well dressed – obviously the shop owner. They greeted each other. I stood quietly, looking around me.

This small room also seemed part of his shop. More bolts of material were stacked around the walls, but in the corner, hanging from pegs, were items of clothing – male and female, but mostly female.

The man stepped away and spoke to an underling who immediately cleared a space on one of the tables and began to unhook items of clothing and bring them over.

I've never actually bought clothes when surrounded by men before and I was quite embarrassed about it. I think William Hendred must have realised this because he muttered something and took himself off out of the door. I made myself concentrate.

Here were second-hand clothes of all types. I had no idea if they'd been traded in for new material or what, but I was grateful. I would never have found this on my own and certainly wouldn't have known what to ask for. The owner, whose name was Robert Sutton – or Sugden, I wasn't sure and no one actually introduced him – and his man eyed me up and down, measuring my size, I hoped, and began to lay out various bits and pieces.

Carefully sorting through the pile, I pulled out something in dark brown – a good, practical colour. The length was too long, but Margery would help me cut some off. It had obviously been discarded because of a large stain all down the left-hand side. I sniffed it carefully. I think it was an oil stain. Still, I couldn't be choosy. If it didn't have the stain I probably wouldn't be able to afford it. I laid it carefully to one side and then saw something blue.

This was the one. It had once been a very good dress. It still was, if you discounted the fact it had faded almost to grey over the years and had been ripped down one side. Again, Margery could help me mend that. I suspected it had been someone's pride and joy once. Dark patches showed around the neck where an original piece of fur or embroidery had been removed and transferred to another garment. But the wool was good – soft and warm. This would do me well.

The servant, murmuring respectfully, pulled out something in brown and held it up. A sleeveless surcoat, hopelessly old fashioned, but again, good quality, and just what I needed as an extra layer for the winter. And not too long, either. It was perfect. I nodded my thanks.

William Hendred returned, spoke again to the owner, Master Sugden – or Sutton – who barked a sharp command and someone found a cloak. A wonderful cloak. Thick and full, it was made of felted wool on the outside to make it waterproof and with a soft lining on the inside. There was enough of it to go around me twice. It even had a hood. It was wonderful. It was a cloak in which I could confidently face the winter. I could even sleep in it. Again, it wasn't perfect – the hem was ripped and ragged and the hood needed a repair – but if it had been perfect then it would have been too expensive for me. I was thrilled, wrapping it around me, again and again, feeling the weight and the warmth.

I piled up the three garments and took out my tiny purse.

I'm not sure what happened next. There was a great deal of talking, I know that. They went at it hard and fast. Initially I thought they were having an argument and stepped back, worried that all this wonderful clothing would suddenly disappear and I'd have to get through the winter in a thin linen tunic and a battered and rapidly shrinking piece of silk stole. I reckoned I'd last until the end of September at the very latest. The servant, carefully folding the dress and surcoat and wrapping them in the cloak, winked at me, and carried on with his task, completely unperturbed.

Eventually, Master Sutton – or Sugden – made a gesture indicating he was ruined forever and to leave his premises forthwith before he was reduced to begging in the streets.

William Hendred grinned and clapped him on the shoulder. Unsure of the outcome, I timidly produced my purse and shook the contents into my hand.

Master Sutton was far too grand to handle money. His servant sorted through the coins and showed me what he'd taken. I nodded my approval – I still wasn't sure how much I'd paid for the whole lot but this was not the time to argue – and was handed the surprisingly neat bundle.

They said their goodbyes, good humour restored now that business was concluded. It seemed likely Master Sugden's – or Sutton's – business would survive at least until the next market day after all, and I found myself back out in the noisy street again.

I would have thanked Master Hendred, but he shook his head and I couldn't tell if he was embarrassed or irritated, so I let it go.

I was so excited by my purchases. I wasn't a beggar any longer. I wasn't relying on the goodwill of other people – well, I was, but I could pay my way now. I had a change of clothes. I could finally wash the ones I was wearing – and not a second before time, let me tell you. I could comb my hair properly. I had possessions to lay out on my stone shelf in toilet. Or wherever I ended up.

A pieman stood on the corner with three or four people queueing before him. An historian tip. Always buy your pies from the vendor with the queue. If the locals are eating his wares then they're probably OK. I nipped over, and juggling purse and bundle, bought two golden pies. I handed William Hendred one.

He seemed so surprised that I wondered if I'd done something wrong. I probably had. I wondered if an unmarried woman buying an unmarried man a pie in public constituted forward behaviour, but I was grateful for his help and this seemed an appropriate way to thank him.

We walked away, eating and being jostled by the crowd.

He said, 'Give me your purse.'

I chewed, swallowed, and said thickly, 'Why?'

He sighed. 'Cutpurses.'

'Oh.' I handed it over and he tucked it in the front of his doublet for safety. Not that I thought anyone would rob him anyway. He was obviously well known in the town. Men saluted him courteously or stepped back to give him room.

I wanted to look around, to compare the Rushford I remembered with this older version, but the steep streets were too narrow and crowded and I had to spend my time looking where I was going. The cobbles were slippery, badly laid in some places and not at all in others. And there were people everywhere, shouting, arguing, selling things, buying things, greeting each other. Children ran in and out of groups of chattering people. Occasionally a man would try to push his horse through the throng. Men stood outside the taverns, talking, doing business, socialising. There were all sorts here from street beggars clothed in rags and sitting against a wall, their hands held out for alms, to rich merchants striding through the streets as if they owned them – which they probably did. Women with baskets bought spices, inspected poultry, sniffed disparagingly at whatever was being held up for their pleasure, gossiped and displayed their best dresses for admiration.

We rounded a corner and there was the castle, but not as I remembered it. In my day, the outer ward was gone, but here the walls were intact. I could see the drawbridge was down. A stream of people made their way in and out. Somewhere in there, Walter of Shrewsbury would be bustling about, full of importance, doing his master's business and thoroughly enjoying himself.

I glanced up at William Hendred who grinned at me. I suspected he'd had exactly the same thought.

And then it was time to go home.

I had another stroke of luck. We had returned to *The Cider Tree* where he had stabled his horse and waiting outside was William the Carpenter, complete with his family and cart. I was offered a place in the back along with all the little carpenters. I hopped in. William Hendred walked his horse with us back through the gate and then, once on the road home, broke into a canter and disappeared in a cloud of dust. I passed the journey home showing off my purchases and admiring theirs. For me, it was a happy day.

There was one more thing to come.

They took me to the ford. I jumped down from the carpenter's wagon, clutching my bundle of new clothing, eager to shake it all out and hang it up. I wanted to lay my comb on the stone shelf, along with the little piece of soap the stallholder had given me, but I wasn't given the chance. When I arrived at the gatehouse, Owen directed me across to the solar. I had forgotten. William was moving into the main building today.

The door to the solar was to the left of the hall. I crossed the courtyard and stepped down into the sunny room where I'd first met Master Walter. It still smelled of burned wood. William Hendred was there. He nodded his head toward the stairs. I found my way up, wondering whose toilet I would be sleeping in this time.

There was a good bedroom up there. I could see William's stuff scattered around as young Roger carefully carried his belongs up the stairs. This was a comfortable room. Not as grand as the rooms in the newer North Tower, which is where the family would lodge when they visited, but much more pleasant than the gatehouse. There were larger windows through which the sun streamed – hence the word 'solar' – the floors were of wood, the walls plastered and painted with a swirly feather design in dark red.

Roger pointed to a partitioned corner. Ah – I was in the toilet again. I felt a stab of resentment. They still didn't trust me. After everything I'd done they still didn't trust me.

I stepped behind the partition. It was a proper room and it was lovely. There was a window with a view out over the carp ponds. There was even a niche in the wall in which someone – Roger probably – had put a little rush light. Someone had placed a palliasse on the floor with a new blanket folded neatly on the top.

And curled neatly on the blanket were two blue ribbons and two green ribbons.

Christmas was much jollier than I thought it would be.

The hall and staircase were decorated with holly and ivy woven into swags. The red berries looked cheerful amongst the greenery. The Yule Log was brought in amid much laughter and ceremony and even more drinking.

William Hendred, Tam the Welshman and a couple of others took the dogs and went hunting for hare, deer, or boar. We had a falconer, known as Nob although I was sure that wasn't his real name, who took his birds out for rabbits. Someone slaughtered a pig kept especially for the occasion and any number of geese didn't make it through December. Fat Piers and his kitchen crew went into overdrive. His language became so fiery that either the dishes he was creating were truly magnificent or he was auditioning for the medieval equivalent of a TV-chef programme. Whatever the reason, we all benefited from the results.

They'd also caught massive quantities of carp which were now spending their days in barrels of fresh water, rather than the liquid mud of the carp ponds outside, the reason being, it was explained to me, that this would filter out the mud and we'd all have lovely fresh carp over

Christmas. Baked according to Fat Piers's special recipe, they said.

We ate until we were stuffed. It was all delicious. And fresh. Most of what we were eating had travelled food yards rather than food miles.

These were the days when people made their own entertainment. Yes, there were jesters, strolling minstrels, troupes of acrobats, conjurors and so on, but few of them ever made it past Rushford to our remote manor. So we did it ourselves. There were songs and stories. Everyone already knew the story word for word, but that was the point. Breath was held at the exciting bits. Even children sat silent and enthralled. King Arthur was a special favourite. Everyone took part. Even me. Somewhat nervously, I gave them the hastily edited story of Sir Luke Skywalker, Jedi Knight of great renown, and the wicked dragon Darth Vader, complete with asthmatic breathing and hollow voice. I'll admit I did get a little carried away during the final duel, as the wicked dragon fell, pierced by the sword of the true knight, Sir Luke, to perish in his own flames. It seemed to go quite well. People nodded. Evil is always vanquished in the end.

But not for me. For me, evil won every time. I sat by the hearth, staring into the flames and trying not to think of last Christmas, when Leon, Matthew and I had been together. I kept hearing Matthew's voice, 'Mummy's *awesome*.'

I truly felt I had begun to make some progress with him? Where did he think I was now? What had the Time Police told him? Had he even noticed I wasn't around? And Leon? What of Leon? I'd been gone seven or eight months. For him it might be even longer. Had he moved on? Worse – had he moved out of St Mary's altogether.

He was always threatening to go and work on the Mars Project – especially when the History Department had been even more rigorous than usual in their treatment of one of his beloved pods. And then I'd tell myself not to be so stupid. Leon would never top looking for me. There was every chance he'd walk through the door any moment now, heading up a rescue party. Peterson would be there, too. And Markham, shambolic and scruffy, and with a better handle on what was happening than anyone else.

Sometimes I would actually raise my head and look at the door and, of course, nothing would happen and I would sigh and carry on with whatever I was doing.

Twelfth Night came and went with all the usual festivities. The decorations were taken down on and, reluctantly, we all went back to work.

We'd had a white Christmas. No one got excited about it. There had been a mini Ice Age in the 14th century and most Christmasses were white. Snow fell every night as the weather worsened. As the snow fell, the need for firewood rose. There were a lot of us out in the woods these days. William was a liberal master who saw no reason why anyone should be cold but there was never enough wood. Temperatures dropped. The snow became crispy and sparkled in the weak winter sunshine. Trust me, snow is no fun when you have no dry shoes to change into. I dried mine in front of the fire ever night and it wasn't doing the leather any good at all. They would probably last out the winter, but a pair of shoes was the next thing on my list. I missed my old boots – lifelong companions who would almost certainly outlive me.

On one cold, sparkling day I was tramping through the snow under a deep blue sky. It was so cold even the birds weren't singing. I was following William the Carpenter's flat wagon down a snowy track, as we picked up more firewood. Every day we had to range further and further afield. I had an armful and was hastening to catch him up when, on my right, a bush waved violently, shedding snow in all directions and someone said 'Pssst'. Or the medieval equivalent anyway.

My heart soared. I couldn't believe it. They'd found me. Somehow, St Mary's had found me. At last. I had no idea how, but they'd found me. Checking no one was looking, I put down my wood, stepped off the track and someone dropped something over my head and held it tightly. I kicked out, but he was very strong. I struggled like a madwoman, but my arms were pinioned. I tried to shout but I had a mouthful of what tasted like old sack. I was literally helpless. My feet were off the ground and I couldn't get a purchase. I couldn't see, couldn't hear ... couldn't breathe ...

I think I was only out for a few moments. When I was able to take notice again, the wood was completely silent. No voices called to each other. No patient tramp of William Carpenter's aged horse. No creak of wagon wheels. Nothing. As far as I could ascertain, I was hanging, limp, in someone's arms. I stayed that way while I tried to work out what was happening. It seemed safe to assume this wasn't a St Mary's rescue mission.

The second thought was Ronan. That somehow, he'd wormed the truth out of my two pleasant but very incompetent kidnappers and turned up in person to finish me off. That didn't seem tremendously likely either.

And then he shifted me slightly in his arms – I'm not light – and I caught a forgotten but familiar scent. Onions and urine.

Shit. Shit, shit, shit.

Now I was in trouble.

I kicked out again and began to struggle. I had to tear myself free while William Carpenter was within earshot although whether he would hear me over the clump of his horse's hooves and the creak of his ancient cart I had no idea, and every step took him further away from me and into the white, misty, sound-swallowing woods.

My captor cursed and changing to a one-handed grip, he punched me hard in the kidneys which shut me up for a while as I was carted off through the woods.

He didn't have it all his own way. I'm not light and the going was rough underfoot. He stumbled several times, once falling almost to his knees. I could hear his laboured breathing and the occasional curse.

In all too short a time I heard a muttered exchange and I was chucked into the back of what I presumed was another cart. Someone climbed in after me and passed the time trying to put his hand up my skirt. I kicked out hard and something connected somewhere because he gave a sharp cry of pain. Someone else told him to keep quiet, chirped at his horse and we bumped our way along a rough track.

The journey seemed over with very quickly. I wasn't sure if this was good or bad. I was dragged from the cart, set on my feet with a jolt and pushed forwards.

Ahead of me, I heard a door open. I tripped up a step and knew by the sudden changes in sound and temperature that I was inside. Someone pulled off my hood and finally, I could see.

I shook my hair of my face and stared around, no little outraged. In fact, I was absolutely bloody furious. Seriously? *Seriously?* How many times could one person be kidnapped? It was like those Russian dolls. This was a kidnap inside a kidnap, for crying out loud. Bloody bollocking hell – a lot of people would suffer for this and not one of them was going to be me.

Two men stood in front of me and as far as I could make out, another two behind me. My heart sank. The two I could see were Guy and Jerald, formerly of Rushford. This was a revenge kidnapping, rather along the lines of Greeks snatching each other's princesses, as described by that shit-faced bastard, Herodotus. Of course, again according to Herodotus, that all ended with the fall of Troy and death and destruction on a massive scale. Well, that would give me something to aim at. Because I was bloody livid. I'd had enough. I was sick to bloody death of bloody men swanning into my life, picking me up and dumping me somewhere else. Well, no more. I might not be able to do anything about Ronan, but this lot were bloody well going down and I would be the one to do it. They would live just long enough to regret the day they ever clapped eyes on me.

Looking at them now, I could see that neither was as sleek and prosperous as they'd been six months ago. Before they'd tangled with St Mary's. Their clothes were worn and smelled none too fresh. I was guessing neither of them knew how to use a needle or mend their own gear, so they were beginning to look very shabby. Guy was paying off onion man and his friend so I guessed the Rushford boys lived here alone in what was probably some sort of hunting lodge. We were in a square, stone room quite snugly fitted out with a blazing fire, two chairs, and a table with several flagons of wine. A couple of faded tapestries hung on the wall and had done so for some considerable time by the looks of them. I wondered if this had once been a favoured meeting place for the

313

Rushford men and their mistresses – or boyfriends, of course. Or, looking at Jerald, a favourite sheep. This was somewhere deep in the forest – quiet and private. Just like the Rushford boys themselves, however, it had seen better days. Yeah, well, that's what happens to people who tangle with St Mary's – things never end well. And they were about to get a lot worse and *not* for me. I really was feeling quite belligerent.

Over in the corner, a door led to what I guessed was some sort of kitchen because they had to have had somewhere to prepare the results of their day's hunting. And in the other corner, a rickety – a very rickety –flight of stairs that wasn't much more than a ladder led up to God knows where. At least one other room – possibly two. Maybe even three, depending on how many guests they were in the habit of entertaining.

I wondered if William Hendred was aware of this place. Or even Hugh Armstrong. If I was looking for the Rushfords this was the first place I would have looked.

Oh, of course. Guy and Jerald had hidden, waited for the place to be searched, and then moved in. Once it was all clear. Very few people think to go back and search a place twice.

Guy tossed the two men a small leather purse, jerking his head at the door. They were to get out. Onion man sent me one last knowing leer and the two of them filed out of the door, slamming it behind them.

I didn't bother to watch them go. I moved to the fire and held out my numb hands to the flames.

To be honest, I was at a bit of a loss as to why I was here. If they wanted someone to keep them warm these long cold nights, there were younger and prettier women than me around. For Jerald, there were younger and prettier sheep around than me, and surely I wasn't important enough for a bit of petty personal revenge. I suppose it was possible they knew it had been my idea to take their castle, but this was 1400 – women didn't have ideas and if they did, some man was usually able to persuade them that the idea had been his all along. A wise woman would nod, smile, think *cretin*, and go off to feed the poultry.

The fire crackled. Behind me I could hear Jerald pouring wine. Bet there wasn't one for me.

I was wrong. He poured three beakers and Guy passed one to me. I sniffed it suspiciously.

He smiled at this but said nothing.

From the brief glimpse I'd had of Guy back at St Mary's, I'd had the impression of a dark, powerful man. Now I'd seen Hugh Armstrong as well, I could see there was a vague resemblance around the mouth and nose. Other than that, there were no similarities. Hugh was tall, fair and built like a whippet who hadn't had a good meal for a month. Guy was a bulky bully. A part of my mind said, 'Norman.'

And then we were joined by joined by Jerald the Gormless who didn't look like anyone in particular. For which the rest of the human race was probably very grateful.

The last time I'd seen him had been on the end of Margery's bucket when he'd fallen into the burning shed. She should have let me fish him out. One side of his face was red and shiny and a large patch of his hair had burned away revealing puckered skin. I was betting it wouldn't ever grow back. That had been a bad day for the Rushfords. Guy had lost his title and his lands and Jerald had lost what little looks he'd had to begin with. Now he was something to frighten small children.

They stood together looking at me. I was determined not to speak first. Nothing undermines your position as much as hysterically demanding an explanation for this outrage. I turned to look at the flames and pretended I didn't care.

'The foreign woman,' said Guy, in Latin. So he knew all about me.

I said nothing.

'The masterless woman.' He sipped. 'No one's property.'

I wondered if I could get away with pretending I didn't understand him. On the other hand, if he was busy talking then he wasn't doing anything more unpleasant to me.

I nodded and said in English. 'Yep – that's me.'

He frowned at these strange words. Jerald finished his wine and poured another. His brother told him sharply that he'd already had too much. Defiantly, Jerald tossed it back.

Guy was waiting for me to have hysterics, demand to be released, burst into tears, plead for mercy, and so on. I sipped my wine. It wasn't bad. Better than I usually got, anyway. I sipped some more. I have some of my best ideas when I've had a few drinks. Or so it always seems at the time.

'Do you understand me?'

I nodded with my *'of course I understand you – do you take me for a complete idiot?'* expression, and still didn't ask why I was here. I suspected he was dying to tell me anyway.

'Revenge.'

Well, yes, I'd gathered that.

316

'Yes,' I said, slowly so he could understand me. 'That is obvious. It is my role in your revenge that is not clear.'

'I seek to destroy Hugh Armstrong. To get to him I must break his good friend and ally, William Hendred. An almost impossible task, I thought, until someone told me of the foreign woman he so dotes upon. And so, to break William Hendred, I must hurt you.'

My heart began to thump but I pretended to consider this. 'Yes, I see. A good plan. May I have some more wine, please.'

His mouth crooked in a rather unpleasant smile. 'Do you think that is wise?'

'I rather suspect I am going to need it.'

He nodded an acknowledgement and poured it himself.

Jerald, the one who was causing me the most concern, was alternately staring at me and then at the fire. Unconsciously he reached up and touched his burned face. I had to get out of here.

Guy was speaking again. 'I confess I have never had any love for Master Hendred, and now I find myself harbouring a desire to do him as much damage as possible – starting with you.'

'Yes,' I said slowly. 'I think you should be the one to start with me.'

He frowned.

I nodded at Jerald. 'If you want your share of revenge then you should go first. I suspect once Master Jerald starts, then for me, it will all be over with very quickly. We both know he is not always in control of himself.'

It was a shot in the dark but not a wild one. I had heard enough gossip about Jerald.

I drained my beaker. The wine was really rather good. I watched the corners of the room blur in a way that

317

wasn't completely because I can't see that well these days. I wasn't sure whether the wine was a good move or not but at this precise moment, I needed all the courage I could get.

He ran his hand down my breast. 'You seem strangely … amenable.'

I don't know why people think I'm not amenable. I really don't.

I sighed. 'I have been the property of William Hendred for six months. He has not used me well.'

He stood very close. 'I shall not use you well either.'

I moved even closer to him and looked him in the eye. 'William Hendred is … overrated. Are you?'

We were chest to chest. 'Ah – now that is a word that has never been used to describe my … performance.'

I made a small sound of contempt. 'That is what all men say.'

He went to speak but was interrupted by Jerald banging his beaker on the table. 'Stop talking all the time. You promised me.'

His brother broke eye contact and turned to him. 'Drink more wine, Jerald. Leave us to … talk.'

I gave him a small half smile. 'Oh. More talk. Always more talk.'

He looked down at me. 'I wonder about you.'

'Many do.'

'I wonder whether you are the very clever woman I think you might be.'

I drank more wine. Bloody hell, this was good stuff. 'I am clever enough to see the flaw – the enormous flaw – in this great plan of yours.'

It broke the spell. He stepped back. 'What enormous flaw?'

I too stepped back. Ignoring Jerald as if he didn't exist, I picked up a flagon and two beakers and set off for the stairs.'

Guy caught me in two long strides. 'Oh no. I do not let you out of my sight.'

I sighed theatrically. 'Two minutes is all I need.'

'For what purpose?'

I sighed again. 'Preparations. Women's things.'

You can get away with murder simply by citing 'women's things'. The phrase 'women's things' implies all sorts of dark and dubious female mysteries than men don't have a clue about. Especially in this medieval day and age. But also in the future too. Pre-Dr Bairstow, I'd once had a boss who was a complete moron and he'd demanded, at the top of his voice, in front of an entire roomful of men, exactly why I'd made a simple mistake on some paperwork. I let the silence gather and then boomed, 'Pre-menstrual tension, I expect,' in a voice that bounced off three continents. He left me alone after that.

Guy and I locked eyes. I forced myself not to look away and then he said, 'Let me show you the way.'

Jerald set up the wail of a petulant child. 'What about me?'

Guy spoke to Jerald but looked at me. 'Your turn will come. This is but a short interlude.'

A chill ran down my back. I hadn't fooled him at all. But if I could just have a few minutes on my own. A few minutes to sum up the situation. A few minutes to have a bit of a think …

There were two doors at the top of the stairs. One left and one right. He opened the left-hand door and pushed me inside. The cold room was empty apart from a bed. Not even a stool to wallop him round the head with.

He walked to the window. 'Too high to jump. You would almost certainly injure yourself quite badly. And you should know – I would not let that stop me. It might even add to my enjoyment.'

I swallowed hard and pushed away thoughts of broken legs and ruptured spleens and Guy of Rushford's excruciating weight and fought to keep my voice steady. 'I understand.'

'I do wonder about you,' he said again, looking at me.

I said nothing.

He backed out of the room. I waited for the sounds of a key turning, but he had a bar across the door instead. I'd had some thought of pushing the key out of the lock, pulling it under the door and escaping that way but there's no escaping from a barred door.

I ran to the window. It was indeed too high. There was no point in jumping and breaking both my legs.

I stared around the room. Nothing.

Yes, there was. There was a bed. With covers. I pulled them back. Sheets. Yes!

Have you ever tried to tear a sheet? It can't be done. Yes, easy enough if you can start it off with a pair of scissors or a knife but my knife was back at St Mary's. I tugged and tugged. Panic gave me a strength I didn't know I had but I couldn't do anything. And they were too bulky to knot together. And this wasn't a four-poster. There was nothing I could tie them to anyway.

I ran to the window again. A dark courtyard. A dim building opposite – stables, probably. Snow covered everything. And a bright moon. When had it got dark? How long had I been here?

I ran back to the door and stood listening. Voices. They were talking together.

And back to the window again. I stared down at the snow. And then I had a brilliant idea ...

I ripped off my cloak and dress. Not without some reluctance – the night was bloody freezing. Seizing the big feather bolster, I stuffed it inside the dress and wrapped my cloak over everything.

I went back to the window and pushed the shutter wide open. I had to do this right. I would only ever get one chance.

I remembered to brush the snow off the window sill, then I leaned out as far as I could go, screamed so long and loudly that I hurt my throat, and let the bolster fall.

It plumped into the snow below. I was staggered. It looked amazingly realistic. My cloak covered a pathetic little mound in the snow. You could just see my dress underneath. It looked for all the world as if a terrified woman had risked everything by jumping from an upstairs window – and it hadn't worked.

I ran back and hid behind the door.

As I hoped, I could hear footsteps pounding up the stairs. I was in luck. Both of them burst into the room.

Guy took one look at the open shutter, at the snow-free window sill, cursed horribly and ran to the window, closely followed by Jerald. My instinct was to run now – to get out of here as quickly as possible, but I made myself wait until they were at the window and leaning out – as far away as possible, and then I whisked myself through the door and out onto the landing. They'd left the bar. I pulled the door shut, fumbled for a horrible moment and then slammed the bar into place just as Guy reached the door and tugged. The door shifted slightly but the bar was solid. I was safe.

He rattled the latch and banged furiously on the door. 'Open this door. I order you to open this door.'

Why do people do that? Was it likely I was going to open the bloody door? Silly sod.

I scampered back down the stairs, stumbling over the last few because:

    a) They were very steep and very rickety and swayed every time I went near them.

    b) Yes, all right, I'd had a few and the alcohol had gone straight to my legs.

    c) Actually, the whole world was swaying around me in a manner probably not unconnected with b)

Back in the downstairs room, I took a moment to give the place a quick survey, mentally sorting the contents into:

    a) Things that would burn

    b) Things that probably wouldn't burn unless helped on their way

    c) Things that definitely wouldn't burn

I kicked over the table, scattering wine everywhere. I added the wooden stools to the pile, tugged at the tapestries which fell off the wall at my first touch, enveloping me in a dusty, musty darkness. Coughing, I fought my way free and added them to the pile. They'd burn – I was sure of it.

Picking up every oil light I could find, I emptied the contents over the heap and laid a trail to the fire. I think I might have misjudged things slightly because there was a kind of whoosh noise coupled with a sudden blast of heat and I might have lost my eyebrows.

I opened the doors to give a nice through draft and left everything to find its own path through today's events.

There was a torch burning by the front door which was thoughtful of someone. I yanked it from its sconce and stepped out into the yard.

Jerald was leaning out of the upstairs window, shrieking with fear. I felt a moment's compassion. He'd burned once … on the other hand, this is what happens when you kidnap an historian. We don't like it, you know. He shouted over his shoulder and Guy appeared, bellowing commands for me to let him out immediately. Yes, he really hadn't thought that one through at all, had he?

I ran to my pile of clothes and yanked the bolster free. The night was freezing – I had to have clothing or I'd be dead in an hour.

Guy and Jerald were both leaning dangerously far out of the window. I paused and frowned. How long before they stopped shouting and started thinking? If Guy – the stronger of the two – dangled Jerald from the window he'd be a good six feet or more nearer the ground. Dropping from that reduced height might mean nothing more than a sprained ankle. He'd be straight up the stairs to free Guy – and then I'd really be in trouble. I'd be lucky if they only killed me. But there might be something I could do about that.

I shot over to the stables and yes, I was running around like a headless chicken, but I was terrified they were going to get free and I had to use the little time I had to make sure they weren't able to come after me. They were going to free themselves at some point and I couldn't see my little fire doing a lot of damage to a stone building. There were two horses currently in residence. One I ignored completely. A huge destrier with a nasty look in its eye, already restless at the smell of smoke, and about

323

the size of a three-story block of flats, rolled an eye at me. I pulled on his tether to free him – from a safe distance obviously – because although I had no problem with toasting Guy and Jerald, it didn't seem right to do it to their horses.

The other occupant was Jerald's seriously yellow horse. It looked back at me. Even at this stage I could see our relationship was going to need a lot of work.

There was a pile of straw at the far wall. I held the torch there for just long enough for a flame to catch and then I was off. No time for a bridle. The yellow horse was haltered and that would just have to do. I dragged it out into the yard, stepping smartly aside as Big Boy thundered past me and down the track. I did panic that the yellow horse might follow him but, as I was to discover, the yellow horse did not do thundering.

I turned for one final look, Jerald was indeed being dangled from the upstairs window. Guy was bellowing at him to let go and Jerald was whimpering and kicking and clinging on for dear life.

I carefully tugged the heavy bolster into position directly beneath them. They both stopped shouting and stared at this suspicious piece of consideration. And they were right to do so because I tossed the torch on top of it. Feathers aren't particularly flammable but anything will burn if you hold a flame to it for long enough.

Jerald's whimpering turned to a shriek as the flames grew higher.

I no longer cared. I scrambled aboard the yellow horse and took one last look around. Flames were licking around the front doorway. The interior was a roaring nicely. The stables were well ablaze. Even the bolster had joined in the spirit of things. Guy and Jerald were blaspheming into the uncaring night. I gave them an historically inaccurate finger.

My work here was done. Time to go.

I'd like to say I thundered out of the yard and into the night. I mean, on the strength of my performance so far, you'd think a good thunder would be the least the god of historians could grant me, wouldn't you?

That bloody horse. That bloody, bloody horse.

I thundered out of the yard and out into the night at a gentle canter. Slow, sedate and majestic. Not what you look for in a getaway horse. I should have stuck with Guy's destrier. Yes, it would have dumped me in the nearest ditch and then eaten me, but at least I might have been a mile or so away before that happened.

Even if I'd never seen him before, I could have told you this was Jerald's horse. He could no more ride a destrier than fly to the moon. Or stop picking his nose in public. It was just right for him. Slow and sedate. A horse with only one gear. In vain did I drum my heels against his sides. He ignored me. I lashed him with the end of the halter rope. He ignored me. I shouted at him. He ignored me.

Glancing back over my shoulder, the whole area was ablaze. People would come to investigate. Perhaps the trees would catch fire as well. Oh God, this might burn down the entire wood and what would Hugh Armstrong would have to say to me then? Perhaps I could offer him the yellow horse as payment.

We cantered gently down the track and through the trees. The moon was up and full and the yellow horse seemed full of purpose and direction so I left him to his own devices while I had a bit of a think.

I didn't have the slightest idea where I was in relation to St Mary's. I wondered if anyone was out looking for me. If anyone was out on this freezing night they'd head straight for the burning glow amongst the trees. Should I hang around to see if someone turned up, or should I get as far away as possible in case Guy and Jerald had managed to free themselves? That's the problem with being kidnapped. Escaping is the easy bit – it's what to do afterwards that's the bummer. For all I knew I was cantering majestically in the wrong direction. In fact, I probably was.

And I was freezing. I had to get my clothes on again. And as soon as possible. This was no night to be out in just my tunic. The yellow horse was warm enough so my bum was OK, but the rest of me was numb with cold. The heavens above were clear and scattered with bright stars. The moon hung in the cold sky, casting long blue shadows over the white snow. The thick, white snow. If the yellow horse lost the track, stumbled and came down, or if I fell off, it would be a disaster. I needed to get as far away as I possibly could, find some shelter, get dressed, wait for the sun to come up, and then get myself back to St Mary's. I had to warn William Hendred so he could warn Hugh Armstrong, but all I had was this bloody yellow horse so I sat quietly and allowed him to find his own pace and his own path.

We seemed to travel for a very long time although I'm not sure it was. Eventually the yellow horse began to pant and then the track emerged from the trees. We stopped, our breath puffing around us. It was hard to tell under all that snow, but I think we'd joined a road. I looked left and right. No clues. Just a blank and empty snowscape. Away on the horizon, to my right, an eerie glow lit the sky.

I turned left, saying, 'What do you think?' to the yellow horse. He seemed happy enough with left. He was certainly the closest thing to a satnav I was going to get.

We trotted for a while. I bumped up and down, keeping my eyes peeled and my ears open for any sounds of pursuit. If Guy was free and had managed to recapture his horse, they could be on us in minutes. Struck by a sudden thought, I twisted around and looked behind me. Yep, a lovely set of hoofprints, sharp and clear in the bright moonlight. Bollocks.

There was nothing I could do about it, however, so I urged the yellow horse onwards. Its shoulders heaved unnervingly but I gathered this was its precursor to moving up a gear. I wondered who on earth would be stupid enough to own a horse like this. Other than Jerald, of course.

We cantered merrily along. Me rapidly sobering up in the cold and slowly turning blue, and the yellow horse apparently quite enjoying his night out, until finally, I couldn't stand the cold any longer. I had to get my clothes back on as quickly as possible.

Note to anyone interested. Don't try and get dressed while riding a horse. I am aware it can be done. Just not by me. I fell off. And now, because I'd fallen into the snow, I was wet as well as cold. The only good thing was that the yellow horse stopped and looked back at me with an expression of mild enquiry. I was beginning to hate that bloody horse.

Actually, my fall turned out to be a good thing. In the sudden silence, I could hear hooves. Coming up behind me. Coming up fast.

There was a small copse off to one side of the road and I set off at top speed, slipping and tumbling on the rough snowy ground. The yellow horse, which I'd intended to leave on the road as a decoy, trotted happily along beside me. I told it to bugger off and it ignored me.

We reached the copse. I dragged the horse in beside me, hid behind a tree, shivering violently, and tried to see the road. Two riders appeared around the bend, both bending over the clear as day hoof marks they'd obviously been following. They reached the spot where I'd fallen off. One said something to the other and they both laughed. I gritted my teeth. They'd pay for that. I was just in the mood.

The one in front, sitting easily on his big chestnut horse, rested one gloved hand on his hip and called for me to come out.

I seriously considered spending the rest of my life in that copse, but there was no real choice, was there? Clutching my bundle of clothing in one hand and the ridiculous yellow horse with the other, I scrambled down the bank and confronted William Hendred and Tam the Welshman.

Again. Bollocks.

I stood, clutching my pathetic bundle of clothing, and shivering so hard it was a miracle I didn't shake something loose.

He looked at me, trembling in my underwear, at the yellow horse, at the glow on the horizon and said, 'What have you done?'

It was too much. His tone was mild – there was no blame in his voice, but it was still too much. Much too much on this crowded night. I didn't mean to but I burst into tears. Blame the drink. I did.

I heard him say something to Tam as he dismounted. I was shaking with cold, trying to disentangle my clothing – which was as wet as I was – sobbing like an idiot and blaming everything on the yellow horse, which was looking at me as if I was its new BFF. Well, anything was an improvement on Jerald, I suppose.

William Hendred took my clothing off me and passed it to Tam. The next minute, I was up on his horse and he was swinging himself up behind me. The saddle was easily big enough for two of us. He pulled me in close, carefully wrapped his cloak around us both and urged his horse forwards.

We covered the ground a lot more quickly than the yellow horse had managed and yet, when I looked, there he was, cantering along behind us, apparently determined not to be separated from me at any cost.

I know his horse was warm – as was he. I could feel the heat coming from both of them. I could feel their warmth on my skin, but nothing seemed to penetrate. It was as if I was made of ice and nothing could touch me. I shivered and shook. Only now that there was warmth did I realise how cold I was. I should have stopped and dressed long before this.

He held me tightly against him and I clutched at his doublet with both hands.

Words and pictures danced through my brain. The foreign woman he so dotes upon. Dancing flames that froze in the moonlight. A yellow sea that rose and fell. Rose and fell ... the foreign woman ... dotes upon.

I think I whispered something. He clasped me harder and I felt Theobald's muscles bunch. We bounded forwards, adrift in a world of blue and white shadows. Something touched my icy cheek. There was a world of warmth under this cloak and I wanted to stay here forever but I was slipping back into the icy flames. Nothing could touch me. Nothing could warm me.

Dawn was breaking as we reached St Mary's. I heard the bell ringing, cutting through my dreams. We swept into the courtyard. I could hear Tam shouting for the grooms. His voice was a long distance away.

I was lifted down. I thought I heard Margery's voice somewhere and then I was back in William Hendred's arms again and he was striding towards the solar. Someone threw open the door. The heat hit me like an oven and then we were up the stairs and into his chamber. I could hear his voice, issuing instructions. There was a fire lit, but someone brought in a brazier as well. And then I was in a bed. I could hear a babble of voices. Someone held a beaker to my lips. There was a warm, sweet drink. The door banged. Silence fell. I felt him climb in behind me. The covers closed over me like the sea. I could feel the heat from his body seeping into mine. I remember giving brief thanks that at least someone knew how to treat hypothermia. And then I slept.

I awoke once to the sound of the shutter rattling in its fastening. There was a violent storm out there. I could hear the wind shrieking around the walls and rain against the walls. I however, was warm and safe. I shifted a little and something moved beside me. He was still here.

I woke again and both the wind and William Hendred had gone.

I woke a third time and I was a new person. Something had changed. I didn't know what, but inside my head, something was different. No longer was I a modern historian half in this world and half in my own. I knew I was here for good. No one was ever going to find me. I would never go home – because this was my home now. I was Joan of Rouen – I really wished I'd chosen a more interesting name – and this was my world. These people were my family. I needed to stop regretting what could not be changed and look ahead. This was my future. For a few years, anyway.

The weather had changed drastically. Things were a little soggy underfoot after the rain washed the snow away – not that I noticed. Every time I stood up I swayed like one of those wobbly toys that don't fall over. Margery, who would burst in through the door in a gust of beer and enthusiasm, would laugh her head off at me, deposit some food, exhort me to eat it all, and depart again.

I did my best to comply.

After a day or so I wobbled my way downstairs to see what was happening in the world. I knew there had been a huge storm and the ground was littered with fallen trees and broken branches. As Firewood Supremo, I should be out there, tucking half an oak tree under one arm and an old elm under the other.

William Hendred looked up from his table by the window, smiled slightly, and then ordered me back upstairs. I was bored and shook my head. We looked at each other for a while. I don't know if he was worried about my reputation or his. The whole world knew I'd been in his bed for the last week. Although I suspected he hadn't been in it with me. From something Margery had said, I think he'd gone back to the gatehouse. Great – he'd rather sleep with Tam the Welshman than me. Understandable, I suppose. I do snore.

I wouldn't disobey him in front of other people, but we were alone, so I tossed my head and went to sit by the fire. He sighed and scowled heavily at the records he was perusing.

People were in and out all morning, doffing their caps and bowing. It was all business as usual. Around mid-afternoon, when the light was going and I could hear them banging around with the tables in the hall, he put down his parchment and said, 'Weather permitting, Lord Rushford comes tomorrow.'

I jumped, looked up from the fire and enquired why, although I thought I knew the answer to that one.

'To question you on the matter of Guy and Jerald, formerly of Rushford.'

There was no information I could give him on their whereabouts. They were long gone. Tam the Welshman had taken a party of men to search the burned remains of the hunting lodge and reported there were no signs of them – living or dead. The hunting lodge had only partly burned away – the stairs were gone but they could see up to the landing and the chamber door was open. A sodden sheet was found in the yard and they'd come to the conclusion Guy had used it to lower Jerald out of the window. Having done that, he would have rushed up the stairs, freed his brother and then the two of them had vanished.

'If they're still alive,' said Tam. The storms had been severe. One or both of them had probably incurred minor injuries. There was no sign of Guy's horse so, if they'd both been on foot, their first priority would have been shelter. No one around here would offer them aid, he said, and everyone was assuming they'd left the area as fast as they could. Sir Hugh – sorry, Lord Rushford – was offering a reward for their capture.

And he was coming here – ostensibly to question me about my kidnapping, but almost certainly to enquire why I'd found it necessary to set fire to even more of his property. I sighed. Once might have been moderately acceptable. Twice …? I sighed again.

He came the next day. There was no thought of holding court outside so it was all set up in the hall. Half the roof was on, the other half still covered in canvas, but a fire was burning cheerfully on the hearthstone. Behind the high table, I was pleased to see the beginnings of a fireplace. A big one. Life would be a lot more comfortable with a crackling log fire and the smoke going up the chimney in a civilised manner instead of taking the long way around.

Sir Hugh – sorry, Lord Rushford – sat at the high table with William on one side and Walter of Shrewsbury on the other. I was none too pleased to see that Walter had felt the need to attend today. He'd have me hanging from one of the new beams as quickly as he could knot the rope.

Warm for the time of year it might have been, but it was still colder here than the solar. I wore my tunic, with the wool dress over that, the surcoat over that, and my cloak over everything. Margery had cleaned and dried my clothes, to my eternal gratitude. I sat on the stool someone had placed for me. As always, everyone crowded around, all eager to hear the latest instalment of the foreign woman's adventures. Seriously, there was a lot they could have got on with – firewood to be gathered, livestock to feed, ditches to clear, roofs to put on – you'd think they'd have better things to do, wouldn't you?

'Joan of Rouen.'

I started. That was me. Again, I really wished I'd chosen a more exciting name. I could have been Griselda. Or Laurentia. Or Hildegarde. I became aware people were speaking to me. I sat up and did my best to concentrate.

Walter was holding a pen and looking at me. Something was required of me and I'd missed it.

He sighed loudly so everyone could hear. 'Your name, please. For the records.'

He knew my name. It probably haunted his darkest dreams. He was just being difficult.

I straightened my back. 'Joan. Formerly of Rouen.'

And now?

'Just … Joan.'

He sighed again. A man at the end of his endurance. 'Where were you born?'

'York,' I said, trawling the Seas of Untruthfulness again.

His pen scratched. 'Joan of York,' he said slowly.

Lord Rushford interrupted, rightly realising we'd be here until teatime at this rate.

'You were in the woods?'

I went to rise but he motioned me to remain seated so I did.

'Yes, Lord.'

'Alone?'

'No, Lord, I was with others.'

'Did you wander off?'

'No, Lord. A man called to me and I went to see what he wanted.'

That sounded bad. You could argue I'd been picking up firewood with one hand and touting for trade with the other.

'You had no suspicions he might mean you harm?'

'No, Lord.'

'And then?'

'And then he put something over my head and carried me away.'

'You did not struggle?' he said, in tones that indicated he found that hard to believe.

'I did, Lord,' I said indignantly. 'I kicked him. Several times.'

Every man present looked as if he could well believe it.

'And then?'

'And then I was taken to a small house. I do not know where.'

'Describe it.'

I described it. Walter's pen scratched and scratched. A weak sun shone through the open door. The fire on the hearthstone warmed me nicely.

'And then?'

'Guy of Rushford announced his intention of revenging himself upon you. To do this he said he needed to hurt William Hendred. To do that he needed to hurt …' I stopped for a moment, ostensibly to cough, and then continued, '… his people. He would begin with me.'

I waited for him to ask why me but he didn't. He didn't even look at William who was staring thoughtfully at the table. No one said a word. I appreciated their discretion.

'What did you do?'

I answered truthfully. 'I drank a great deal of wine to give me courage, went upstairs, threw my clothes out of the window and locked Guy and Jerald in the bedroom. Then I went downstairs and set fire to the lower rooms.'

A stir ran around the room. Hugh raised an eyebrow at William Hendred who closed his eyes and shook his head slightly.

I forged on. 'I went out into the stables and released their horses. I set fire to the stables. Guy and Jerald were trying to climb out of the window so I placed the bolster in the place where they would fall and set fire to that. Then I mounted the horse and rode away.'

He sat up.' What horse?'

'The horse I found in the stables, Lord.'

The destrier?' said Walter, trying to catch me out.

'No, Master Walter, Jerald's horse.'

William whispered in his ear. They exchanged a look.

'Describe this horse.'

'Yellow, Lord.'

A whisper ran around the hall and not a few smiles. I gathered the yellow horse had made a name for himself in this part of the world.

'You brought this yellow horse here?'

'No, Lord.'

'And yet it is here in the stables,' said Walter, swift to catch me in a lie.

'It may be, sir, but I did not bring it. It followed me home.'

Now it was Hugh's turn to stare at the table while William appeared to be finding something interesting over to his right.

Walter, always happy to put things in the worst possible light had a question of his own. 'Why did you throw your clothes out of the window?'

'It was too high to jump, sir.'

I could see him sit back to work that one out.

Lord Rushford hadn't finished. 'And you set fire to my hunting lodge?'

There was no point in denying it. 'I did, Lord.'

'You could not have just locked them in and escaped without any further loss of my property?'

He was right. I could have. Quite easily.

'Yes, Lord. I could.'

'Then why?'

I didn't stop to consider my reply. 'I was angry, sir. Bad men caused me to lose my home and my husband. I am penniless. I came to St Mary's and, of your kindness, I was allowed to remain here. Just as I was beginning to be happy I found myself being used by another bad man to revenge himself upon you, Lord. I was angry.' I was drunk as well but probably best not to mention that. 'If you had been there you would have drawn your sword and run them through,' I said virtuously, with no idea whatsoever of his sword skills, but it never does any harm to flatter a man. 'I am not a man. I have no sword. So I used what came to hand, Lord.'

339

'But your clothes,' persisted Walter, a man with a one-track mind.

'What of them, sir?'

'You took off your clothes. What were your intentions.'

'To throw them out of the window, sir.'

'But why?' he said impatiently.

'Because it was too high to jump, sir. I would have hurt myself badly.'

Heads were swinging from Walter to me and back again.

'But the window was too high to jump from whether you were wearing your clothes or not?'

'Yes, sir.'

He struggled. 'Then ... why?'

William interrupted. I think he felt sorry for him.

'You threw your clothes out of the window so they would think you had jumped.'

'Yes, sir.'

'And while they were looking for you out of the window you locked the door behind them.'

'Yes, sir.'

'And then you set fire to my hunting lodge.' The heads swung back to Lord Rushford again. He did keep bringing that up.

'Yes, Lord.'

'When last we met, did I not instruct you, very clearly, never to set fire to my property again.'

'You did, Lord. You said, "Never do so again.".'

'And yet ...'

Sometimes you just have to bite the bullet. 'I disobeyed your instructions, Lord. I wanted to injure them. For what they had done to us last summer.'

340

William Hendred raised an eyebrow. Was I pushing my luck?

I lowered my eyes, remembering, far too late, about maidenly modesty. 'I disobeyed you, Lord. I am sorry.'

'And yet because of you, Guy and Jerald are far away. Without shelter. Without friends. And possibly badly injured.'

I said gravely, 'If we are very lucky, Lord,' lowered my eyes and stared demurely at my lap.

There was a very long silence. I resolved to say no more.

'Joan of ... ?'

'York,' said Walter.

'Joan, formerly of Rouen, now to be known as Joan of ...'

'York,' said Walter.

'Joan of York ...'

'Lord?'

'Will you accept my judgement?'

I rose to my feet. 'I will, Lord.'

'I find myself at a loss,' he said. 'That you were taken from the safety of this manor, against your will and to your detriment is a matter of concern to me. That you did your best to defend yourself is understandable. That you set fire to my property – again – is slightly less understandable, but I accept that your actions were well motivated. I am unsure whether to reward or punish you, so I shall do both. Let all here listen to my judgment. The woman Joan of ... Joan ...'

'Of York,' said Walter, never giving up.

'... shall receive into her ownership the horse, formerly the property of Jerald Wolf's Head, as compensation for the injuries she has sustained and punishment for the injuries she caused. Say now if anyone does not accept my judgment.'

He was a clever man. People were laughing. Even William had a half smile on his face. Walter – who was obviously as familiar with the yellow horse as anyone else – was smiling grimly to himself as he wrote the judgement.

And I was now the proud owner of the worst horse in the county.

I was the proud owner of one comb, four hair ribbons, two dresses, a winter cloak, a surcoat, a linen tunic in the Doric style, an extremely battered silk stole, a piece of rock-hard soap that despite regular use was no smaller and looked set to last me till the end of my life, and a yellow horse. I'd been here nearly twelve months. At this rate, by the end of this year I could be a substantial landowner.

I had everything I needed. Everything except a husband. I could be ordered to marry – Lord Rushford could order me to do so, even to the extent of picking out a luckless victim – or husband, as they're often known – but so far, no one had put the moves on me. Or even shown the slightest interest. Not even to gain possession of the yellow horse. I was unsure whether to feel relieved or slightly miffed.

And then, one day, I found out why.

One lovely morning, my tasks completed earlier than usual, I bunked off. I nipped out of the gate, down to the ford and then walked upstream, past the mill and the storehouses and the barns, out of sight of St Mary's completely. I followed the bank until I found a pleasant spot, sunny and sheltered, where the stream formed a small pool. Iridescent turquoise dragonflies buzzed around at head height. Sometimes they can be quite aggressive, but I sat quietly and they left me alone.

Summer was nearly here. The weather was so warm I'd reverted to my linen tunic and Persian stole. It was hard to believe I'd been here nearly a year.

I took off my shoes and dangled my feet in the cold water. Once I got over the initial shock it was rather pleasant and looking after your feet is important. I carefully put my shoes to air, and had a go at making a daisy chain – something I hadn't done for years.

There were flowers everywhere and I wished I knew their names. You don't see flowers like that in modern times, but here they grew wild, peeping out from under bushes, or just scattered through the meadows.

I lay back, squinted up at the sky and watched a lark hover.

I heard the man before I saw him and, given my recent track record, had a hefty branch within easy reach, just in case someone hadn't heard what happened to the Rushford boys.

William Hendred appeared on the other side of the stream with a couple of trout dangling from a line. We caught sight of each other simultaneously. He stopped dead and I tried inconspicuously to throw my branch into the bushes. I thought I saw him smile and then he splashed through the shallow part of the stream and came to sit by me on the bank.

Uncertain how erogenous bare feet might be in this day and age, I curled my feet under my skirt.

Having made it this far, he seemed content to sit in silence. Well, why not. He was a busy man. Time alone must be as welcome to him as it was to me. And it's not as if he talked much anyway.

344

I picked up my half-completed daisy chain and busied myself. He didn't have to speak if he didn't want to.

The morning wore on. My daisy chain grew longer. I knew he was watching me. I remembered that time under his cloak. When I had been in his world. When I held on to him and he to me. Had he kissed my hair? Or had I dreamed it?

I stole a glance at the man sitting next to me. He looked just the same as he always did. Quiet. Unemotional. Undemonstrative. But I had felt his heart race in his chest.

We sat for half an hour or so and then he got up and began to make a small fire, feeding it with twigs and small sticks. His movements, like everything he did, were sure and steady. I tended the fire as he took the trout to the stream and carefully cleaned them.

They took only minutes to cook on two flat stones. When they were ready he shovelled one on to a large leaf – I was delighted at this refreshing new use for broad-leafed plants – and offered it to me.

I looked at it and then up at him. His face was expressionless, but I could see a tiny pulse beating at his temple. And then I nodded, smiled, took the fish, and we sat together, picking the flesh off the bones.

Right out of the blue, he said to me, 'You no longer cry in the night.'

I hadn't realised he'd heard me. I'd struggled to be quiet, stifling my sobs as best I could.

I said, 'No,' and we left it at that. No more words were spoken, but I was under no illusions. This man had brought me food and I had accepted it. This had been a significant moment.

And then, as the sun neared its highest point in the sky, he got to his feet, cleaned his knife in the water, nodded at me, and disappeared down the track.

I watched him go.

Noon was approaching when I returned to St Mary's and there was a real warmth in the sun today. I strolled in through the gate and headed for the solar, to wash my face and hands and get stuck into my afternoon duties.

He was waiting for me.

Taking my hand, he led me into his room. He closed the door behind us. I felt no alarm, even though my heart was trying to bang its way out of my chest. I could hear a faint clatter in the kitchen and, not quite so faintly, Fat Piers giving someone hell. This quiet room seemed a long way away from all that.

Retaining his clasp, he said, with no preliminaries, 'Will you be my wife?'

It wasn't unexpected. I'd spent long hours thinking about this when I should have been concentrating on chickens or spinning, but it was a shock finally to hear the words spoken.

Typically, having spoken, he fell silent. Not for him the outpourings of a man in love. No talk of wild desire or unbounded passion. Just a simple request.

I let my hand lie quietly in his, cast down my eyes and made myself think. Because the moment had come.

I had no man to give me status. I had no relatives, no property, no skills of any kind. I couldn't brew, or raise livestock, or churn butter, or make cheese. I still couldn't spin. Every woman in the country, from the highest to the lowest, knew how to spin, except me. I'd never be able to get employment. Yes, the guilds permitted widows to work, but you had to have been married to a guild member in the first place. I couldn't set up a business. No one would trade with me.

There was only one way for me to earn a living and if I had to do that then surely it was better with just one man than many. Besides – he was a good man and I was never going home. I'd never see St Mary's again. Or Leon. Or Matthew.

I'd made up my mind to commit to the 15th century. There would be problems in 1403, but that was two years away and I'd be lucky to last that long. I should say 'yes'. I wanted to say 'yes' but, deep inside, the tiny part of me that never lost faith flickered one last time. To say 'yes' would be to give up hope forever.

As you should do, said the rest of me. *Close the door on hope and get on with the rest of your life. While you can.*

I took a breath and looked at him. If I said 'yes', then we were as good as married. Yes, there could be a church service if we wanted one, but in these days for a man to ask a woman and for her to say 'yes' bound both parties. To all intents and purposes, we would be married.

If I said 'no', then that would be it forever. He would never ask again. He wouldn't throw me out, but he would move on. There would soon be someone else. He was a very eligible man. Could I bear seeing another woman have what I could have had? I should say 'yes'. I wanted to say 'yes'. I don't know what held me back.

Clasping his hand tightly, I said, 'Sir, must I answer now?'

'No.'

'Sir, I … I …'

347

'I understand. Your husband is not long dead. Perhaps it is too soon.'

I nodded. That would do. 'Sir, I must ... say "goodbye" to my husband. In my heart. He was a good man.' My voice wobbled. I swallowed hard. 'Tonight. I will answer you tonight.'

He nodded. 'Tonight.'

I don't know what happened next. I don't know who moved towards whom. I had my eyes closed.

He kissed me.

I've never been so thoroughly kissed in my life. He brought the single-minded concentration he brought to everything he did. Slow, gentle and very, very long. People say their senses swam – well, mine certainly did. I leaned my head against his chest for support and listened to his heart race again and struggled for breath.

He stepped back and the world felt suddenly strange and cold, so I lifted my face to be kissed again. I had to. I wanted to. The second kiss was even better than the first. At the finish, I had to clutch the front of his doublet for support. I couldn't catch my breath. He was a very thorough man. I imagined his hands ...

He kissed me again. Even longer this time. We stood alone in his sunny chamber, the world silent around us, and I was conscious only of him.

Eventually, I stepped back. It was that or pass out from lack of oxygen. He stepped back too.

'Tonight,' I said hoarsely, and whether I was talking about giving him my answer or something else entirely, I couldn't have told you.

He nodded. 'Tonight, then.'

He crossed to the door, put his hand on the latch and looked back at me over his shoulder.

I whispered, 'William,' and he was across the room in two strides and I was in his arms again. I could feel his urgency and his desire. And my own. I could kiss him forever.

Now he was the one to step back. He laughed a little, and said again, 'Tonight,' which was just as well, because if he'd whispered, 'Now …' I would have been a lost woman.

Then he opened the door and I could hear him running down the stairs.

I spent a few minutes trying to pull myself together. It wasn't that I was dishevelled. Not externally anyway. Internally I was extremely dishevelled. I was all over the place. I smoothed my tunic, checked my stole was still covering my hair and splashed my face with a little water from the bowl on his wooden chest. Then I made my way downstairs.

There was no sign of him anywhere, but Fat Piers was bellowing for me in the kitchen. Good God, was it that time already? For how long had I been in his room? Well, never mind that now.

I shot in at a less than stately walk and snatched Father Ranulf's basket off the table. It struck me that if I did say 'yes' to William then this would be the last time I would ever do this. Not that there wouldn't be a whole new set of duties and responsibilities, but I could be – I would be – lady of the manor.

I sailed out through the gate, my basket over my arm and my head full of thoughts and dreams and plans and ideas. Hopping over the ford, I waved to John Smith and the several of his many sons who were helping him that day and set off up the hill. Pikey Peter's mother,

Eadgytha, sat outside her door, spinning and keeping an eye on the oven. The smell of fresh bread temporarily overrode the smell of turned earth and manure.

Three or four women were drawing water from the village well, tiny children running around under their feet, trying to help and only succeeding in getting in the way. A dog rushed out from William Carpenter's house, sniffed around my skirts – no idea what he was looking for there – and rushed off again, nose down, intent on his own business.

I didn't hurry. The day was fine and sunny and my basket wasn't heavy. I was looking forward to sitting with Ranulf and Rowena on their bench, practising my very improved medieval English. These days there were many more words and much less miming.

And then my mind ran back to this morning, sitting by the stream with William Hendred and then afterwards in his chamber and my pace slowed even more. I replayed the scene. His words. His touch. That kiss. All those kisses. If I said 'yes' to him, my life would be hugely improved. I would have status. The same status as my husband. As lady of the manor, I would never again have to rise before dawn on a winter's morning and go in search of eggs laid by absent-minded hens. No more breaking the ice on the water trough to wash my face. I would sit at the high table. Near the fire and out of the draught.

And if I said 'no' ... it didn't bear thinking about. Even if I survived, in only a few years I would become another Maud, toothless and old before her time, with no man to support her, always dependent on the charity of others.

I shivered. I didn't want that. Not in a million years. I knew what my answer was going to be. Tonight. Tonight would be something magical …

I was so lost in pleasant thoughts I nearly missed it.

I was just about to turn off for the church when a voice behind a bush said urgently, 'Hey. Maxwell.'

You don't catch me twice. Unless you're Clive Ronan, of course.

I moved to the far side of the road, assumed an aggressive stance and said, 'Bugger off. Whoever you are.'

The bush said again, 'Maxwell. Here.'

I took a few paces further away.

The bush panicked. 'Don't go. For God's sake, don't go. I need your help.'

'Who are you?'

The leaves rustled and cautiously – very cautiously – out stepped the old man – Ronan's old man – the one who had left me here nearly a year ago now.

I was too surprised to speak. Then I thought – Ronan's here – and looked around for the nearest help.

'No,' he said, quickly. 'Don't run. For God's sake, wait. He's hurt.'

'Who's hurt? Ronan?'

'No. Rigby. The lad. You were right. We should never have gone back. He shot us.'

Now that I peered at him I could see a dark patch on his shoulder. He looked very pale.

'I think he's dying. And the pod's about to blow. You have to help us.'

Did I? These men had kidnapped me. On the other hand, these men had saved my life. They hadn't killed me. They'd brought me here and given me a fighting chance.

As far as they could help me, they had. I should help them.

I took a quick look around but no one was watching. 'Lead on.'

I followed him down the familiar forest path and there – exactly as it had been before, stood their pod. It looked no different. In fact, for them, it might only have been minutes.

But it was a pod. My ride home.

He said, 'Door.'

Nothing happened.

More loudly he said, 'Door.'

Nothing happened for a second or two and then it jerked open, taking two or three seconds to open fully. A small fug of acrid smoke rolled out with it.

I pushed him to one side and stood in the doorway.

The console was smoking. I could hear a fizzing and crackling behind the panels. Several live wires hung from the ceiling, sparking. The entire console was covered in red lights and I guessed the slurring noise was the computer trying to tell them all was not well.

The young lad – Rigby – lay against the far wall. The old man had obviously performed as much first aid as he was able to – the medkit lay almost empty nearby. He too was very white and there was a great deal of red, shiny blood.

The old man went to enter the pod but I held him back. This pod was about to blow. It might only have minutes left. The only reason we weren't enveloped in a wall of sound as computers, klaxons, warning beeps and God knows what went off full blast was that there wasn't enough power. I was certain the computer was trying to advocate immediate evacuation to a safe distance.

A safe distance meant a good long way away. When a pod blows, it doesn't mess about. Anyone in the vicinity, walking their pigs, or looking for firewood, or indulging in a spot of hanky-panky in the woods would not survive.

I took a moment to think. I needed to prioritise. First was to get this pod away from here. Second was to get the young lad some urgent medical attention. Third was the same for the old man. There were lives at stake here. My personal feelings were not important.

I pushed the old man inside ahead of me. 'Stay with him.'

Crossing to the console, I tried to clear my mind. I needed to make sense of the readings. There was power – otherwise the wires wouldn't be shorting out like that, but was there enough power? Would attempting to initiate a jump be the final straw that finished the pod, the people inside and the immediate area?

There was only one way to find out. I set familiar coordinates, guessing at the date I wanted because there was no time to double check – or indeed check at all. A rather nasty hum was filling the air, rising in tone and volume.

A single thought pounded inside my head. I could come back. I could always come back.

I had a sudden thought and forced the door open again.

I caught the panic in the old man's voice.

'Where are you going? You can't leave us.'

I had to leave something of myself behind. I couldn't just disappear. If I could come back then it didn't matter but if for some reason I couldn't ... I ripped off my stole – the brightly coloured one from the Persepolis assignment, now sadly faded, but very recognisable as mine, folded it neatly, and placed it, with the basket, in the middle of the path. I pulled the ribbons from my hair, coiled them up and left them for him as he had left them for me. I couldn't take them anyway. I couldn't take anything from this time. This was all I could do. I couldn't write to him. This was the only message I could leave for him. If I left these things here – clearly visible – carefully folded ... then, surely, he would know nothing bad had befallen me. I was terrified he would think I had run away. That I had disappeared as abruptly as I came. He would search for me. He would look everywhere and he'd never find me. What would he think? What would he do?

This is why we never get involved with contemporaries.

I turned and ran back into the pod. I'd done what I could and my duty now was to concentrate on the immediate problem. My hands flew across the console. I shut everything down, including life support. Whatever happened, we wouldn't need it five minutes from now. There was no time left. We had to go now.

I said, 'Brace yourself.'

He did.

I said, 'Computer, initiate jump.'

Something, somewhere went bang. The lights flickered and went out. Apart from the red light show on the console, we were completely in the dark. I could only hope it was because the computer had shut down all inessential systems.

The floor heaved beneath my feet – it really shouldn't do that – and the world went a kind of sludgy grey.

Worst. Landing. Ever. Worse even than the one made by Dieter and me all those years ago when we were caught in a Cretaceous landslide and fell off a cliff. It made Peterson's worst efforts look like a fairy's footsteps.

We hit the ground with a crash that threw me out of my chair and onto the floor. Locker doors flew open and the contents fell on top of us all. I rolled into a ball and the old man threw himself over the young lad. The only thing we could do was protect our heads and wait for everything to settle. Hanging wires spat sparks. Black smoke poured from underneath the console. Something else went bang. And then there was silence – which was most worrying of all.

I staggered to my feet, groped my way around the wall and threw the trip switch. The last few lights died. The pod was dead and now we were completely in the dark, but at least we weren't about to blow up. At least, we *probably* weren't about to blow up.

I said, 'The door's on an emergency circuit, but if I don't get it open now then it may never open again. Stay put. Don't make any hostile moves. We may have survived the crash only to be shot dead by the Security Section.'

I wasn't joking.

355

I had no idea when we'd arrived. I'd aimed for about a month after Persepolis but haste, fear, panic, wonky pod – we could be anywhere at any time.

I hit the manual switch for the door.

It jerked open a few inches. I got my hands into the gap and heaved. It jerked another few inches. Just enough for me to squeeze through.

It was hurling down with rain. Typical. But I really hadn't done too badly. It could have been a lot worse. I was quietly proud. We'd landed just outside Hawking and I was surrounded by a ring of security guards. All with weapons raised and none of them looking very friendly.

Evans shouted, 'On the ground. Hands on your head. Now.'

I said, 'It's me.'

Markham said incredulously, 'Max? What the hell?'

Behind me, black smoke was billowing from the open door. The old man was shouting for help.

I gave up. There's only so much you can do in one day.

I sat down on the tarmac, put my hands on my head and said, 'Medical emergency. Two men in there. Both wounded. Neither armed. No chance to decontaminate. Full medical precautions.' And let the cold rain fall on my head and run down my face.

Markham was brilliant. He had men inside rendering first aid in seconds. He had Dieter inside the pod checking its status. He had me picked up and whirled off to Sick Bay before I could ask when I was, about Leon, or Peterson, or Matthew, or anyone.

Hunter met me at the door, suited and booted in the medical gear that always makes it very clear that if, by any chance, you have contracted anything unpleasant, you're completely on your own.

'Bloody hell, Max, where's the rest of you?'

I had no idea what she was talking about. I looked down. Yes, two arms, two legs, everything seemed intact. I put that to one side.

I said, 'Can I come back later? I need to jump again.'

'Not a chance.'

'But ...'

I was wasting my breath. She shoved me in the scanner, perused the printout and shoved me in again.

'Why didn't you decontaminate?'

'Unsafe pod.'

'Well, there doesn't seem to be anything terrible here. You'll be in isolation for at least a week and I shall want blood and stool samples. Usual thing.'

She stopped and took in this year's fashionable look in 1400. 'Have you seen yourself at all recently?'

I shook my head.

There was a full-length mirror on the wall by Helen's office. I'd often wondered why and assumed it was so you could check you were departing with the same number of limbs you came in with.

She pulled me over and I looked at myself. *Bloody hell*.

'I don't see the problem,' I said, in a vain attempt to stem the medical onslaught. 'You've been on at me to lose ten pounds since the day I walked through the door.'

'Yes, ten pounds. Ten pounds would have been good. Max, you've lost stones.'

I had too. Whether through fresh air and exercise, or bloody hard work as I'd always thought of it, or a healthy vegetable-based diet and a complete absence of heavily sugared tea, I'd lost stones. Even my loose-fitting tunic couldn't conceal it.

I looked at my plaited hair, slowly unravelling because I'd left my hair ribbons behind in 1400. I'd left a lot of things behind in 1400.

I said, 'Bloody hell – there's more of me back in the 15th century than there is here,' and I wasn't joking.

I could hear Dr Stone's voice approaching.

'Come on,' she said, 'let's get you into isolation.'

I asked if I could have a bath. Partly because, after a year, I really needed one, partly because I really wanted one, but mostly so I could be alone for a while. No one would begrudge me an hour in the bath after being away for so long and I needed time to think. I'd been catapulted into 1399 and now I'd been catapulted back home again.

They'd all be up here any time now – Leon, Peterson, Dr Bairstow. There would be questions to answer, reports to write and I couldn't do it. I had to have some time to sort things out in my mind so that I could get my act together and face this strange new world.

When Hunter came in I said, 'I don't want any visitors.'

'Just as well,' she said cheerfully, laying out pyjamas and a dressing gown. 'You're not allowed any.'

I was unreasonably annoyed because that was supposed to be my decision. 'Who said so?'

'Dr Stone. He's waiting for you if you want to go out and argue with him.'

I humphed. I've argued with Dr Stone before. It's like trying to fill a bath without a plug. There's an enormous amount of effort and when you finally pause to get your breath back, absolutely nothing has happened and you realise you've been wasting your time.

When I exited the bathroom, he was waiting for me. Of course he was.

'There you are,' he said cheerfully, his eyes smiling at me over his mask. 'How are you feeling?'

I mumbled something.

'Jolly good,' he said cheerfully. 'Well, you have got yourself into a bit of a state, haven't you?'

I had the strangest feeling he wasn't talking about my physical state, but said nothing.

'You'll be wanting to know about those two men,' he said sunnily. I wished he'd bloody stop that. Especially since I'd completely forgotten about them. 'All patched up and the Time Police took them away.'

'The Time Police are here?' I said, trying to focus on something tangible.

'Not any longer. Been and gone.'

'Captain Ellis?'

'Sends his regards.'

I dragged my mind back to what had been, for me, a year ago.

'Ronan never showed, did he?'

'No.'

'He came straight after me in Persepolis.'

'He took us all unawares, Max.'

'I should have known. We're all looking for him in one place and he pops up in another. It's what he does. How was I so stupid?'

'Not your fault.'

'Yes, it was.'

'Look, we're no worse off. Which, from what I've seen of St Mary's, is a bonus. Everyone got back from Persepolis all right. There's some great footage of Alexander. No golden-inked books, sadly, but one or two

359

small objects were saved from the flames. Thirsk were pleased.'

'You're sure everyone got back OK?'

'I'm sure.'

'They're all safe?'

'They are.'

I looked around. 'Where is everyone?'

'All out looking for you.'

'Still? How long have I been gone?'

'Just under a week.' He looked closely at me. 'How long have you been gone?'

'Just under a year.'

There was a long silence as my mind struggled to cope. I'd been gone a year but I'd only been gone a week …

He regarded me carefully, his head on one side. 'Be aware, Max, you may experience one or two minor difficulties in … readjusting …'

There was no 'may' about it. My brain was struggling to get itself around two timelines. One where I'd been gone a year and many things had happened to me during that time, and one where I'd only been gone a week and none of it had happened at all.

'The crown?'

'Arrived in London yesterday. Safe and unharmed.'

'*Yesterday*?'

'Max, you've only been gone five days.' He hesitated. 'You're a little disoriented. It's only natural. Have something to eat and we'll talk tomorrow.'

'Wait,' I said stupidly, trying to find something on which to fasten, because my mind was operating like finely honed cotton wool and all I could see was the sun-dappled world I'd just left. 'They're all safe? You're absolutely certain?'

'Absolutely certain,' he said. 'Everyone got back except you. They're all there now, looking for you.' He looked at me carefully. 'Including Leon. Who isn't well enough to travel but insisted on going anyway. Mr Clerk's nipped off to tell them you're back.'

I would have to see Leon. What would I say to him? It struck me that if Ronan's men had arrived even twenty-four hours earlier my life would be a hell of a lot less complicated. I wanted to see Leon and I didn't want to see Leon and because I didn't know what to say, the best I could come up with was, 'Ummm …'

'Hasn't Hunter told you?' he said, still manically cheerfully. Maybe his mask was depriving his brain of oxygen and he didn't know he was doing it. 'No visitors for seven days. Not until we're quite sure you haven't brought back anything unpleasant. Other than yourself, of course.'

He and Hunter fell about. I shouldn't have to put up with this.

'Now then,' he said, apparently pulling himself together again and bashing away at his scratchpad. 'Six meals a day. Small ones. We need to build you up again, Max. Get some rest. We'll start tomorrow.'

'Start what?' I said, but he was on his way out.

There was a tray on the table. Chicken soup, a bread roll, scrambled eggs and an orange.

The soup tasted too salty. As did the eggs. The bread roll was rubbery with no texture. I ate the orange. I poured out the tea, automatically adding three sugars. I couldn't drink it. They obviously hadn't made it properly.

I wandered over to the window. It was dusk. Daylight was fading fast. I yawned. Time for bed.

361

The bed was too soft and too warm. I couldn't get comfortable. I tossed and turned for half an hour and then got up, pulled a blanket off the bed, wrapped it around me and lay down in the corner, back to the wall. That was better. I lay in the dark silence. There was no sound of William Hendred's breathing to comfort me through the night. Nor mine to comfort him.

I stared into the darkness.

The next day began badly.

'Leon is here,' said Dr Stone, still masked and gowned.

I smiled and nodded. I'd been awake since before dawn, overcome by a sudden need to get up and collect eggs. I'd lain quietly until the clock showed a more reasonable hour, but I was sure the medical staff knew that not only had I barely slept at all, but that I'd spent the night on the floor.

He nodded at the observation window, and there was Leon.

We stared at each other for a while. It's never easy, talking through a large observation window and knowing that every word can be heard over the intercom system.

'Hello,' he said. 'How are you?'

All right, a little unemotional for someone whose wife had been missing for a week – or a year – but I couldn't have coped with drama just at that moment. I wondered if Dr Stone had had a word with him.

'Absolutely fine,' I said. 'How are you?'

'I'm fine.'

I persevered. 'Are you taking all your meds?'

'Yes, of course.'

'And walking? You don't seem to be walking very easily and you look tired.'

'I've been in and out of Persepolis half a dozen times in the last week, looking for you.'

'I wasn't there.'

'Well, we know that now.'

I moved the conversation to neutral ground so we could do our usual thing of not talking about the important stuff.

'The two men and their pod?'

'The Time Police took them away.'

'Were they still alive?'

'They were. And very cooperative too.'

'How's everyone else? I understand they all got back from Persepolis OK.'

'They did. A little scorched, but we have some good footage of Alexander. I'll have it forwarded to you.'

'Anything from the Treasury?'

'A few bits and pieces. No old manuscripts written in golden ink, I'm afraid.'

Bugger. No treasure and no Ronan. What a washout.

He stepped nearer to the glass. 'So ... Max ...'

I interrupted. 'When are you next due back with the Time Police for more treatment?'

'Not for some time. There's not a lot more they can do. It's all up to me now. Physio and light duties mostly.'

'Half a dozen visits to Persepolis doesn't sound like light duties to me.'

He frowned. 'Why are we talking about me when we should be talking about you?'

'I told you, I'm absolutely fine.'

Dr Stone turned up. I had the feeling he hadn't been far away. 'That's it for both of you. You're both still on the sick list. Go and get some rest, Chief. Come back again tomorrow.'

He disappeared again.

Leon looked at me. 'I'll say "goodbye" then'. He put his hand on the glass. I covered it with my own. It was the closest we could get.

'Goodnight, Leon. Sleep well.'

'You too.'

He paused a moment and then limped away. I watched him go and then turned back to find Dr Stone entering the ward.

'Now then,' he said. 'The usual question. Have you opened your bowels recently?'

'Not for the last six hundred years,' I said, trying to be funny.

'Thought as much,' he said, offering me one of those little plastic beaker things with two enormous tablets the size of golf balls. 'Take these.'

I recoiled. 'You're kidding. I'll never get those down.'

'Actually, they go up.'

I folded my arms, channelling more female intransigence.

He sighed. 'Max, I don't know what you've been eating, but you appear to be harbouring nearly every parasite known to man. You're riddled with God knows what and you've certainly smashed all Markham's previous records. Please do as you're told.'

I stamped off into the bathroom and was unavailable for the rest of the day.

I can hardly find the words to describe how very much not in this world I was. My body was still on medieval time. I kept waking just before dawn and then dropping off as the sun sank below the horizon. Accustomed as I was to a day of hard –ish – physical labour, my confinement in the isolation ward was driving me insane. I was restless. I couldn't concentrate. I had problems with food. Everything tasted either too sweet or too salty. I couldn't drink tea with sugar and I didn't like it without. And, all the time, on the very edge of hearing, was an all pervasive electronic hum that nearly drove me insane. I really was all over the place.

And as if that wasn't enough I was seeing things. I looked out of the windows and saw, faint and undetermined, the shadowy outlines of buildings that hadn't been here for six-hundred-and-fifty years. Sometimes I thought I would see the shape of someone disappearing through a door or around a corner that no longer existed. I seemed to be partly in one world and partly in another. I was torn between the two and this world was less real to me than the one I had just left. I should talk to Leon— ground myself. But what could I say to him? He wasn't well himself. He already felt himself to be less than he had once been. I couldn't add to that. And so it went on – around and around – while I sat on the floor in Sick Bay and tried to find something I could hang on to.

I was disoriented and confused. And guilty. And angry. I was guilty because of William Hendred and what we had had. And what we had nearly had. And angry because I felt guilty. I kept telling myself I had nothing to be guilty about. I had done nothing wrong. I stared out of the window and wished Helen Foster was here.

One morning, Dr Stone came to see me. He sat himself by my bed, smiled, and said quietly, 'Why can't you talk to me, Max?'

I shook my head but smiled, so he would know I meant no offence.

'Or Leon?'

It should be Leon, of course, but what could I say to him? What should I say to him? My thoughts circled around me like vultures around a dying donkey. I should talk to someone, if only to get this awful weight off my mind, and if Helen was still here it would probably have been her. She'd have lit a cigarette, puffed the smoke out of the window, said something acid but appropriate, and sent me on my way. I added Dr Stone guilt to Leon guilt. I know there are people for whom the unburdening of themselves is a relief, but that's not me. I open my mouth to speak, but somewhere a brake is applied and a voice says, 'Whoa there, Neddy – do you really want people knowing your weaknesses? Do you want them to know what makes you vulnerable?' and all the doors slam shut and that's it.

He sat silently for a while and some of that must have shown in my face because he said, 'OK then, try not to worry too much,' put his hand on my shoulder and walked away.

I remember being surprised he gave up so easily. I really should have remembered what a devious bugger he was, because the next day I looked up and there was Kalinda, staring at me through the observation window.

I recoiled. She's not something you want to come upon unawares.

'Dear God.'

'What ho, Max.'

He must have telephoned and she'd come roaring down the motorway from Thirsk to sort me out. It was a bit like being hit by an academic version of the Imperial Storm Troopers.

'What are you doing here?'

'Come to see you. Do you know you look like shit?'

'How did you get in?'

She shrugged. 'I walked in through the front doors. What did you think? That I abseiled down the chimney?'

'I don't know what to think. Why are you here?'

'I told you – I'm visiting the sick. Let's go for a walk.'

I shook my head. 'I'm not allowed out.'

She stared. 'OK, I give up. Who are you and what have you done with the real Maxwell.'

I opened my mouth and closed it again. She was right. I'd torched St Mary's. And a hunting lodge. I'd wreaked dreadful revenge on those who'd meant me harm. I'd even opened my bowels – two months ahead of schedule but let's not go there. The person who'd done all that didn't sit around bleating about not being allowed out.

She didn't bother to wait for me, simply saying, 'I'll meet you outside by the lake.' She slapped the door control and walked away.

I eased open the door and peered cautiously up and down the corridor. There was no one in sight and all the doors were shut, so I just walked out. The lack of people telling me to get back inside again wasn't suspicious at all.

I slunk down the stairs, nipped along the corridor, climbed out of a window and set off across the grass. She was waiting for me near the willows where I'd hidden when Leon first brought Matthew home.

368

It wasn't that long since I'd last seen her, but she never changes. Kal is tall, blonde, looks like a Disney princess and drinks the blood of ... well, anyone who doesn't move fast enough. She and Dieter were still together and trust me, if you think Markham and Hunter are weird, you don't even want to start on those two.

'Come on,' she said, and we set off around the lake.

The weather was soft and warm. We walked along the bank, she enjoying the sunshine, and me resisting the urge to cram my pockets with big-leaved plants.

She didn't beat about the bush, either. 'So, what's this all about then, Max?'

I tried to assemble words to communicate just how I was feeling.

'I'm lost,' I said, fumbling and stumbling as usual. 'I'm neither here nor there. I see things that aren't here. I'm ... unanchored. I'm just drifting in the wind. Sometimes ... sometimes I wish I could just blow away completely.' I imagined climbing to the top of a mountain and letting the wind carry me away until there was nothing left. Which would solve so many problems.

'And then what?'

'What?'

'Well, you've blown yourself away on the wind – then what?'

'Does it matter?' I stared back across the grass. To the stables and the henhouse and the dovecote that were no longer there. If I closed my eyes I could hear Fat Piers shouting ... 'I didn't belong there and now I'm beginning to think I don't belong here either. I don't know where I do belong. Or even if I actually belong anywhere. And then there's Leon ... and Peterson ... and there's always Matthew ... Kal, I just don't seem able to rouse myself and make the effort. Sometimes I think it would be so nice just to close my eyes and ... let go.'

There – it was out at last.

'Yes,' she said thoughtfully, 'That's very understandable.' I blinked at her in surprise. I've said before, Kal does sympathy like Hitler did Stalingrad. 'But,' she continued, 'I do think it's very important that you ...' she paused. I leaned towards her so I could hear more easily and she pushed me into the lake.

People underestimate the weight of wet clothes – even just PJs and a dressing gown. I lost my slippers immediately.

Icy water closed over my head as I floundered around, swallowing vast quantities of lake liberally laced with pond scum and swan pee and probably topping up all my parasite levels again. I kicked out, struggling to reach the surface, eventually breaking through, coughing and gasping and going straight back under again. I was really glad Major Guthrie wasn't around to see all his careful training going up in smoke. Or sinking to the bottom of the lake in this case.

It was embarrassing. We're supposed to be prepared for this sort of thing. During my training days, we regularly practised rescuing each other and being rescued ourselves. It generally went quite well until one day the tensions between the History Department and the Security Section boiled over and Sussman – a fellow trainee and a bit of a hothead – accused Big Dave Murdoch of trying to drown him and Murdoch proved him wrong by actually trying to drown him – just so he would know the difference in future – and it all got a bit out of hand with quite a lot of other people jumping in, 'to assist', they said at the subsequent disciplinary hearing.

I came up for the third time coughing and gasping and frozen. Managing somehow to overcome my waterlogged dressing gown, I disentangled myself from the clinging pond weed and crawled out of the water onto dry land, getting absolutely no help at all from Kalinda who simply stood back and watched me struggle.

I clambered to my feet, wrung half a lakeful of smelly water from my dressing gown, raging and furious. 'What the hell?'

She shrugged. 'See – you do want to live after all.'

'Chance would be a fine thing. I've just swallowed half the bloody lake. Thanks to you, I'll be lucky to make it to lunchtime.'

She looked at her watch. 'Sorry, kiddo, can't stick around that long. Meeting Dieter for a meal, prior to rogering him senseless.'

I stormed off, squelching my way back to Sick Bay, ignoring everyone who stared at me.

Dr Stone was waiting for me.

He looked me up and down and said, 'This Kalinda Black – I haven't met her before, have I?'

I shrugged off my sodden dressing gown, let it fall to the floor with a splat and wiped my face. 'Do you still have a full set of working testicles?'

'Er … mostly, yes.'

'Then no.'

The downside of Kal's visit – apart from my near-death experience – was that I was now open to visitors.

'You're not going anywhere for a few days yet,' said Dr Stone, 'but I have quite a long list of people who, inexplicably, would like to visit you. Do you perhaps owe them money?'

I'd been scowling at the wall and hoped – really hoped – he hadn't caught my sudden flash of panic.

'One of whom is your husband.'

Now was the moment when I should say something. Tell him I needed a few more days to acclimatise myself. Just a few more days before facing the world. But what could I say? I opened my mouth. Nothing came out and, once again, I took refuge in silence.

He sighed and sat on my bed, squashing my feet and, accidentally or otherwise, preventing my escape.

'The fact is, and I may as well tell you, Max, I'm considering leaving St Mary's.'

'What? Why?'

'Don't think it's not hard for me to admit this, because I thought I was a fine fellow when I first came here. I was flattered that Dr Bairstow sought me out. And it all sounded so exciting but, well … I think you'll be the first to agree, I'm not Helen Foster, am I?'

I was overcome with guilt and took refuge in indignation. 'Who said that?'

'No one. But they don't have to, do they? It's what everyone's thinking and, let's face it, although you haven't said anything, I rather think that's what you've been thinking too.'

I shook my head, suddenly feeling terrible. 'You mustn't go. Not just because of me.'

'Well, not just because of you, of course.'

'I'm sorry …'

'Look,' he said kindly, 'don't worry about it. If you don't want to talk about anything then that's fine with me. If you like, we'll give it another day or so to see if anything unpleasant crawls out from behind your eyeballs and if it doesn't then I'll discharge you and you can pick up your old life as if nothing had happened. But, Max, I really wish you could find it in your heart to trust me.'

So did I. I knew that I needed help now more than ever before in my life and all I had to do was ask for it. I groped for words, forming and dismissing phrases and sentences, trying to fish coherency out of the logjam of emotions inside me and, as usual, despaired and gave up – and while I was thinking about how useless I was, I caught the sharp and unmistakeable tang of cigarette smoke. As if, somewhere far away, a door had opened. Just for one second. One very brief second.

I don't know why, but, unbelievably, after everything that had happened to me, that was the moment when my train came off the rails. Tears ran down my face. Without looking at him, I reached out my hand and grasped his sleeve.

He put his warm hand over mine. 'OK,' he said. 'Understood. To quote someone not a million miles from here – I've just had a brilliant idea.'

I never before realised how irritating that phrase is.

'You need to talk to a doctor.'

He hadn't understood after all. I tried to pull my hand away. There was no chance. His ears might have the wingspan of an albatross but he was very strong.

'So, how about Dr Dowson?'

I stared some more.

'Of course, if you have him then you'll have to have Professor Rapson, too. I might as well tell you, Max, the pair of them have been camped outside your door since you arrived back, clamouring for a debrief. So that's what you'll give them. Look at it as not so much a girlie psychiatric session, but more in the nature of a professional debrief. They've even offered to bring their own crumpets.'

The crumpets might not have been such a good idea because the professor brought his own patented two-storey six-seater toaster with him. His thinking was that there were three of us and no would want to have to wait for their crumpets, would they? Nothing is worse than watching others tucking into their own butter-sodden taste explosions while having to wait for your own to finish browning, he said. Therefore, he said, dumping his enormous machine onto my bedside table after first having swept aside my few personal possessions, he'd knocked up a little something to solve the problem and what did I think?

I knew exactly what I thought, but what the hell.

374

The first six crumpets were fine. We should have stopped there. The second batch obviously placed an unreasonable strain on the professor's precarious circuits – and those of the toaster, as well – and the bloody thing emitted a noise like a dying donkey, fired six charred crumpets in eight different directions, burst into flames and toppled over onto my bed which also began to burn. I attempted to put beat out the flames with the pillow from the next bed and that went up too. I tried to remember a time when I wasn't setting fire to something. I was still in isolation and the door doesn't open from the inside so I was trapped in a room with two idiots, a blazing toaster, crumpet-peppered walls, a burning bed and a smouldering pillow. Or, as the two idiots later attempted to explain to Dr Stone, *they* were trapped in a room with a compulsive arsonist.

Somewhat to everyone's surprise, the alarms went off which at least meant we couldn't hear each other screaming. The door was kicked open by Nurse Hunter bearing a fire extinguisher. She dealt ruthlessly with the fire while we cowered at the far end of the ward. Dear God, did she ever shout. Anyone would think it wasn't an accident.

Dr Stone came to see what all the noise was about, watched through the window for a few minutes and then abandoned us to our fate. So much for prioritising the welfare of his patients. Hunter's voice was stripping paint of the walls and she was waving the extinguisher around like a Scud missile.

Flames out, she turned and kicked her way back out again, colliding with Markham and his team, also in full fire-fighting gear, and disappointed at not being granted the opportunity to showcase their skills; closely followed by Leon, torn between concern for his wife – he said – and astonishment that the fire alarm contained a working battery; and Major Guthrie who limped out of the men's ward to see what all the noise was about, took one look at me, rolled his eyes and said of course, who else would it be, which I thought was a little unfair since none of this was actually my fault; and Mikey, whom I'd forgotten all about, emerging from the female ward, still a little white and wobbly and worried the Time Police had found her.

Obviously, everyone talked at once, the isolation ward was smoky and uninhabitable and, since, inexplicably, nothing medically horrible had emerged from any of my orifices, they decided I could be released into the custody of my husband. I didn't have a lot of choice and so Leon took me away while everyone else was engaging in the blame game.

I turned at the door to look back at the confusion and was almost certain I saw Dr Stone and Leon exchange a glance. I glowered suspiciously, but Leon put a gentle hand under my elbow and my eyes were still smarting from the pillow smoke, so probably not.

Actually, the debrief idea – *sans* crumpets – was genius. Neither Professor Rapson nor Dr Dowson gave a rat's arse about any personal issues I might have. We moved into the library and every morning, after breakfast with Leon, I wandered in to find them, datastacks open and ready to get stuck in.

They were, as usual, single-mindedly insatiable. I can't believe people actually fall for their, *'Oh, I'm just an absent-minded academic, don't mind me,'* routine. I'd once seen the two of them put together a lethal flame-thrower in about thirty seconds flat, using nothing more

376

dangerous than a vacuum cleaner and a stirrup pump. And rumour had it that, at their first meeting, the professor had nearly blown up Dr Bairstow with just a bottle of urine and a toadstool.

We began with the village. They produced large-scale Ordnance Survey maps and I drew in the village – the houses, the church, the barns, the smithy, the ovens, everything. From there, I listed the occupants of each house, described them and their relationships to those around them. I listed occupations and livestock. I described the fields and the crops, the agricultural year, who did what and for whom. I sketched what I could remember, each page being ripped from my pad before I'd barely finished.

Moving on to St Mary's, I took a deep breath and began. I drew a floor plan. I labelled and described each room and its function. I described the kitchens, the food we ate, Fat Piers and his team. I talked about Margery and Little Alice, and about Walter of Shrewsbury. I drew very good sketches of Tam the Welshman, Owen, and all the others.

I described the siege – if you could call it that – of St Mary's, the dead cat down the well, the taking of Guy of Rushford's castle and Sir Hugh Armstrong. I described Rushford itself, the main buildings, the position of the market, its prominent citizens. They were particularly excited to know the medieval bridge had not yet been built and that the bulk of Rushford was still on the other side of the river.

Yes, I managed to describe nearly everything without once mentioning my relationship with William Hendred. Make of that what you will.

At the end of three days, we were finished. I had talked myself out. The library was littered with files, papers, whiteboards and maps. Datastacks twisted gently in the sunlight. We sat back, exhausted. They would pull it all together and put it into coherent form, but my part was done. I felt a hundred years younger, but now I had to deal with Leon. I couldn't put it off any longer. I shouldn't put it off any longer. None of this was his fault. None of it was mine, either, but that didn't stop the guilt.

First, however, was Dr Bairstow. He'd been to see me on my first day, staring in through the observation window and we'd had a brief conversation.

'I am pleased to see you have returned, Dr Maxwell. I am becoming very bored with organising your funeral.'

'Sorry, sir.'

'Never mind. Mrs Partridge tells me she has filed the paperwork away for easy access in the future.'

'Very sensible, sir.'

'The Time Police have removed your … captors? Rescuers? Travelling companions?' He consulted a note. 'Messrs Rigby and Lorris.'

'Can you request they be treated fairly, sir? They saved me. Twice, in fact.'

He nodded his head. 'Noted.'

'Thank you, sir.'

He shifted his weight and prepared to depart. 'Come and see me on your discharge, Max.'

'Yes, sir.'

And here I was, returning the visit, sitting in his office, watching the sun make patterns on his faded carpet. Mrs Partridge brought tea. I stared at it.

'Welcome home, Dr Maxwell.'

'Thank you, Mrs Partridge. It's nice to be back.'

She handed me my tea. 'Is it?'

I had no words. I stared at her.

'Drink your tea, Dr Maxwell.'

'I … um … I'm sorry but don't think I like tea any longer.'

'I understand, but I have made this just the way you like it only with less sugar. I think you will like it.'

I had no thought of refusing. I sipped it gently. She was right. She was always right. I nodded my thanks.

She took up her usual position behind Dr Bairstow and took out her scratchpad.

He cleared his throat.

'Max, have you never wondered why we don't permit solo jumps?'

'I always assumed it was so there would be at least one person to bring the bodies home, sir.'

'Well yes, obviously, but there's slightly more to it than that. There's a reason, Max, why we don't send people out alone. Or why we break long assignments into shorter periods. If you remember, even at Troy, there were frequent breaks and you had your colleagues around you at all times because, as you have discovered, it is very easy to become lost, mentally, as well as physically. The problem manifests itself in several ways – some people report they see one world superimposed on top of another – I believe you have made several attempts to walk through doors that no longer exist. Others are disoriented – experiencing something akin to jet lag, I believe. Dr Stone tells me the most common complaint is that the patient is convinced there's absolutely nothing wrong with her and that the problem lies not with her but with the real world. It is the real world which is out of step.'

I nodded.

'In your case, Max – although time is the problem, time is also the solution. Make an effort to re-enter this world and I assure you, everything will pass.'

'Yes, sir.'

'Now,' he said, briskly, 'I believe young Matthew will be joining us for a visit very soon.'

'Yes, sir.'

'Excellent. It will be good for all three of you to spend some time together again.' He smiled slightly. 'I know both you and Leon have had a lot on your plates recently, but have you given any more thought to his future?'

'Well, nothing has really changed, has it, sir? We failed again with Clive Ronan and, as things stand, neither Leon nor I are in a position to protect Matthew should any further threats be made against him. We both agreed – or we did the last time we were together – that he's probably better off where he is for the time being. As long as we can see him regularly we're both ... not happy, but content, for things to continue as they are, short-term.'

He nodded. 'A wise decision.' He closed the file. 'Welcome back, Max.'

'Thank you, sir.'

He hesitated. 'I have to ask this and forgive my bluntness, but what are your feelings about getting back into a pod.'

I understood the question. We'd experienced this before with Elspeth Grey. Her reluctance to re-enter a pod had never been overcome. We'd given her time but we couldn't give her the confidence. Dr Bairstow was now enquiring whether that was the case with me. How reluctant was I to get back on the horse?

I didn't make the mistake of airily assuring him that everything was absolutely fine. I took a moment to think seriously, staring at my hands clasped in my lap. How *did* I feel about getting back into a pod?

I opted for the truth. Always a wise move with Dr Bairstow. 'A little apprehensive, sir.'

'Good. I would not have believed you if you had said otherwise. A little apprehension is perfectly normal and I am pleased to discover you do have at least a tiny drop of self-preservation left. So, your return to the active list, Max – sooner or later? Your choice.'

I took a deep breath and met it head-on. 'Sooner, sir, if you please,'

He made no comment, merely making a note on his scratchpad.

'Very well, Dr Maxwell. That will be all.'

'Thank you, sir.'

Back in her office, Mrs Partridge turned to me. 'I understand you have a few days leave due to you.'

'Yes. I return to work on Monday.'

She looked at me. 'Use the time wisely, Max,' and pulled her keyboard towards her.

I waited, but she seemed to have forgotten me. 'Um ... yes, Mrs Partridge.'

Leon was waiting for me on the gallery. 'Fancy a walk?'

I stopped dead and said darkly, 'I'm not going anywhere near that bloody lake.'

He laughed, suddenly looking so much like his old self. 'I don't have her balls. Besides, I can't run fast enough.'

We settled ourselves in the sunken rock garden. The afternoon was warm and drowsy. I was tempted to sit back and close my eyes and just enjoy the afternoon with Leon. It was so long since we'd had the chance to do anything like this. Just be together. By ourselves. It seemed such a pity to spoil it, but the longer I left it, the more difficult it would be. I'd talked to Dr Stone. I'd talked to the professor and Dr Dowson. Surely, I should be able to talk to my own husband.

'Leon, I have something I must tell you.'

'Yes, I rather thought you might.'

'I ...'

'Lucy, you can say anything to me. You know that.'

I swallowed the urge to rest my head on his shoulder and cry.

'I do know that. It's just ... I don't ... I don't want you to be disappointed in me.'

He didn't make the mistake of rushing to assure me that could never happen. We'd both knocked around too long and seen too much to make rash promises to each other.

'You and I used to be able to say anything to each other, Max. What's happened to us? I don't understand what's happened to us.'

'I don't know what to say. I haven't done anything wrong and yet I feel as if I have.'

'Well, why not tell me and then we can see.'

'All right. Except I don't know where to start. I think you're going to be unhappy which will make me unhappy. And if you say it doesn't matter then I won't believe you, and if you say you forgive me then I will never forgive you.'

'I don't seem to have a lot of options, do I?'

'Well, we could always walk away from this conversation.'

'Or we can face things as we always do. Together.'

'Leon ...' I couldn't go on.

'I think I already know,' he said, heavily. 'There's someone else, isn't there?'

'Well, yes. But no. Not really.'

He gave a shaky laugh. 'I see your answer covers all bases, as usual.'

I smiled sadly and shook my head.

'Just tell me, Max.'

Well, he'd asked for it. I said carefully, 'I was lost, Leon. I don't just mean lost without you – which I was – or physically lost – although I was that as well – I was cast adrift, if you like. They meant well. Those two men. They let me live. I sometimes wonder if it would have been better ... but they just left me there. I know I was lucky to be alive. Ronan had given instructions I was to be killed and my body – pushed out of a pod somewhere. Anywhere. Anytime. He didn't care and he didn't want to know. St Mary's – you – would have been tied up for years looking for me. And you'd never have found me.

'Anyway, you know what happened. I did end up at St Mary's but about six hundred and fifty years ago. No supplies. No prep. Nothing but the clothes I stood up in. And they weren't the right clothes. It all looked very bleak. I'm not excusing the choices I made. I'm giving you the reasons for them. I needed a man. For protection. For status. For a home. You know how these things go. I had no relatives. No income. No skills. No one to support me.'

I took a breath. 'His name was William Hendred. He was marshal of St Mary's. Head of Security, I suppose we'd say. He was a good man. A very good man. He took me in. He protected me. He treated me with respect and made others do the same. He saved me when I torched St Mary's and again after I was kidnapped and had to burn down the hunting lodge.'

'I begin to feel a certain sympathy for this unfortunate man. Did he have any choice in the matter?'

I smiled reluctantly. 'Yes, of course. But my choice was of being used by many men or just one. I chose the one.'

There was no expression on his face. I knew what he was thinking. There had been a connection between William Hendred and me. Another man had had what Leon held so dear.

'I have to tell you, Leon – he never forced himself on me. I told him I'd just lost my husband. He was sympathetic. He ... I suppose you could say he courted

384

me. He brought me ribbons for my hair. He gave me time to heal. And then ...'

I took another breath. 'And then the moment came and he asked me to marry him. I had to decide. Did I take a chance and hold out for an impossible rescue? Or did I commit to my new life and everything it entailed?'

Leon stood up suddenly, took a few paces in one direction, wheeled about, took a few more, and then sat back down again. 'Go on.'

'I was walking through the village, thinking about my future and half way up the hill, someone called my name. My real name. It was one of the two men who'd left me there. Ronan, presumably wanting all traces of me eradicated, had turned on them. I'd warned them not to go back, but they hadn't listened. They were both injured. They'd barely escaped. They couldn't operate their pod very well and it was faulty anyway, so they jumped back to me for help. The pod was in a terrible state. I estimated we had just enough power for one last jump. And it had to be then – that moment or never.'

I stopped and stared at my feet.

'What is it? What's the important thing you're not telling me?'

And here it came.

'I left him, Leon. Without warning. Without a word of farewell. I just disappeared. As far as he's – he was – aware, I walked out of the door and vanished. We never got the chance to say goodbye. He's an honest man with honest feelings. What is he thinking? That I've run away – that I've abandoned my home rather than be with him? That the Rushfords have had another go at me? He'll spend weeks looking for me – to no avail. I've vanished into thin air. How will he recover? I'm not big-headed

385

enough to say I've ruined his life but how will he move on from this? He'll look for me in every face he sees. He ...'

He pulled me into his arms. 'Hush.'

I was sobbing. 'I can't ... I can't just ...'

'Hush,' he said again.

'Leon, I didn't ... we didn't ... but I would have. I would have married him and been a wife to him and ...'

'And a very sensible decision that would have been,' he said calmly. 'You would have been safe. You would probably have been happy. I'm not selfish enough to deny you that. I'm glad you found a good man. He sounds as if he deserved you.

I wiped my nose on something. I've no idea what. Leon, probably. 'We didn't ...'

'You don't have to tell me that,' he said. 'You have the most transparent face in the universe.'

'But I would have,' I said, determined to make a clean breast of everything.

'But you didn't,' he said, determined to be considerate and reasonable.

I sighed.

He sat staring at his feet for a long time and then said, 'Listen Max, you should go back. You're talking about him in the present tense. You spent nearly a year there. Part of you is still there. This is your problem. Part of you is still there with him. You need to go back and say what is necessary for both of you.' He tightened his grip on my hands. 'And then come back to me.'

My heart swelled with gratitude. Why had I thought he wouldn't understand? I should have known. And then I remembered what Mrs Partridge had said.

'Come with me.'

'What?'

'Come with me. If I can tell him my husband has found me again he will accept my leaving him. He's a good man. He would never come between a husband and his wife. Knowing I'm back with my husband will give him the strength to move on.'

He nodded slowly. 'All right. Yes, I will.'

I spent the remainder of the day in Wardrobe with Mrs Enderby, and then in the library, carefully calculating the coordinates. Because I had no clear idea of the date on which I'd left, Leon insisted on at least one clear month between my leaving and our arriving.

'I think it was June or July,' I said. 'So August or September.'

'Beginning of October,' he said, 'just to be on the safe side.'

We set off for the first week of October, 1400.

We were almost too late.

We landed in the woods at the top of the village, opposite the church. We picked our way up the path, through the russet woods, and emerged opposite the church.

I stood very still, absorbing the sights, the sounds, the smells. I was back. Looking around, nothing seemed to have changed.

'This way,' I said, and we turned right to make our way down through the village towards the ford.

Leon wouldn't have been human if he hadn't stared around him, comparing what he was seeing now to the village he knew. He touched my arm.

'Do you see that cottage over there. The one with the sprouting thatch and the oven outside?'

'That's Pikey Peter's mother's house,' I said.

'That's the one I would have rented for us after Matthew was born.'

'That will still happen,' I said. 'I haven't given up.'

He looked down at me. 'Neither have I.'

I looked away and blinked back the tears. More tears. I really had to stop bursting into tears every ten minutes. I'd wash myself away at this rate.

Curious faces appeared over hedges and in doorways. I smiled and nodded, hoping curiosity would win over hostility. Leon and I had dressed well for the occasion. He wore a thick, woollen robe in a rich dark red, matching hose and good leather boots. His cloak was fur-trimmed despite the autumn sunshine, because he was making a statement. I am a wealthy merchant and this is my wife. Who was also better dressed than anyone here would ever remember seeing her. I wore a long, green dress with a blue surcoat. My headdress was as elaborate as Mrs Enderby could contrive and I could legally wear. We were both almost as well dressed as Hugh Armstrong. In these new times, there wasn't a lot of difference between a wealthy member of the middle class and a not-so-wealthy member of the aristocracy. The boundaries were beginning to blur and we were exploiting that.

We crossed the ford – neither of us lost our footing, but the water was very low anyway, and set off to St Mary's.

There was something wrong.

Just as on the occasion of my first arrival, there was no guard.

Leon was busy taking it all in, so I rang the bell.

There was a long delay and I looked around. That strange sense of something not quite right had returned in force. I knew what it was. There were no men. I looked

388

back down to the village. All the faces I had seen were female. No men were working the land. No man answered the bell. In fact, no one answered the bell at all.

I rang again. There was a tremendous curse off to my left and Margery appeared from the washhouse, sleeves rolled up, arms bleached white with the harsh soap. Her jaw dropped when she saw me and then she lumbered towards us.

Leon said afterwards that I stepped in front of him but that wasn't strictly true. He definitely stepped behind me.

She stopped a few paces away, taking in our fine clothes and prosperous air. I would have to go to her. I stepped towards her, ignoring the smell of lye and urine and God knows what, and put my arms around her. She was stiff for a moment and then I was enveloped in a bone-crushing bear hug.

Extricating myself with difficulty, I introduced Leon. She looked him up and down and then bowed. She'd obviously pegged Leon as being more socially respectable than his wife. Most people make that mistake.

I took a breath to still my heart. 'Master Hendred? Is he here?'

I already knew the answer to that one. If he hadn't turned up to investigate the noise Margery was making then he wasn't here.

I was wrong.

She gestured towards the solar. 'In there. This way.' She set off for the door.

I caught her up. 'Where is everyone?'

'Gone with Lord Rushford.'

'Where?'

She shrugged. 'Wales. Shrewsbury. Somewhere there. Fighting the rebels.'

Had Owain Glyn Dŵr's rebellion begun?

'Are all the men there now?'

She halted at the door to the solar. 'Most, yes. Except for the wounded. They've come home.'

I swallowed, already knowing the answer. 'Master Hendred is here?'

Leon, who had already worked it out, took my arm. 'Max ...'

I nodded. 'I understand.'

'Shall I go first?'

'Please.'

He motioned to Margery to lead the way and I followed on behind them. We were met at the top of the stair by Roger, a tray of uneaten food in his hands. His face went slack with shock when he saw me.

'How is he, Roger?'

He shook his head. A tear ran down his cheek. 'I do not think he will last the day.

I made a small sound and turned away.

'No,' he said. 'It will be a mercy, mistress.'

We went in.

I didn't need the smell of death in the air to tell me William Hendred was dying. I barely recognised him.

Father Ranulf, sitting on the stool by the bed, rose to his feet. I don't think he recognised me until I spoke. His eyesight was getting worse.

He took us aside. 'The wound has gone bad. There is nothing we can do other than give him the poppy juice. I am glad you are here. Sometimes, when the pain is bad, he calls for you.'

I introduced Leon and they greeted each other, gravely.

'How did it happen?' I asked

'When you left ...'

390

'My husband found me,' I said quickly.

'When you left, he searched for you. Mistress, could you not have left some message?'

'I tried to. I left my basket where it could easily be found.'

'And then the rebellion began. Lord Rushford rode with the king and Master Hendred raised a force from St Mary's and went with him. He was injured. Not seriously, but it would not heal. It kept breaking open. He could not fight so Owen brought him home with the other wounded. By the time he arrived, the wound had gone bad. We had hoped that with rest and prayer ... but it was not God's will.'

I nodded, blinked back tears and went to stand beside his bed. Roger pushed the stool for me and I sat where he could see me, putting my hand over his. The smell was sickening, but I smiled. 'Master Hendred. I am here.

He smiled, caught his breath with pain, and smiled again.

I felt Leon move up behind me.

'Master Hendred, this is my husband. This is Leon of Rouen. He found me. I am sorry we had to leave so quickly. We looked for you. To say "thank you" and "goodbye".'

He made a tiny sound.

Leon stepped forwards, saying in his deep voice, 'Thank you, Master Hendred, for your care of my wife. She means everything to me and I could not bear to lose her. I do not tell her that often enough.'

I knew he was really talking to me.

I translated that, speaking slowly for him. William nodded, sucked in his breath again and cut his eyes to the goblet of poppy juice by his bed.

Leon and I looked at each other and then I got up, took Father Ranulf's arm, and led him away to the window. 'Father, my husband travels widely. He has many medicines. He can perhaps do something for the pain.'

'Of course,' he said quickly. 'If you think it will help.'

'It will,' I said gravely. 'You understand nothing can save him …?'

He nodded.

Behind me, I heard Leon rummaging in his pouch. He'd brought a basic medkit – I'd brought pepper spray. Between us we had all the bases covered.

I distracted the good father with queries about Rowena while Leon prepared the shot. We stood at the window until I heard Leon say, 'There.' When I turned back, he was refastening his pack.

He said quietly, 'I'll wait downstairs.'

He and Father Ranulf disappeared down the stairs. Roger had already gone. It was just William Hendred and me.

William died a gentle death. I sat with him the whole time. He was unable to speak, but he knew what was happening. I talked to him about our time together. I started from the day we met outside the gatehouse. The haymaking. Walter and his bad temper. The raid by the Rushford brothers. The night he found me in the snow. The yellow horse. Which was, apparently, still here. The moment by the stream. All our adventures together. I brought out old memories and relived special moments. He couldn't speak but that was all right because I could talk for both of us. I leaned in close because he couldn't see very well. Sometimes he drifted away and I sat patiently until he came back again. Occasionally, he caught his breath in a faint hiss and I knew he was laughing.

As I finished, he lifted his hand. I followed the movement across the room to his wooden chest. Where he kept his belongings. And his treasures. I lifted the lid and there, on the top, neatly folded, lay my stole. Now faded almost beyond recognition, but I knew it. As I lifted it from the chest, blue and green hair ribbons fluttered to the floor. I picked it all up and gently placed it under his hand.

His fingers scrabbled feebly at the stole. I carefully unfolded it to find my purse. The one I'd given him for safekeeping the day we went to Rushford. He'd kept my purse for me.

I couldn't speak.

He sighed and closed his eyes.

I looked around. Leon was coming through the door. The sun had moved on. I'd been talking for more than an hour. William's face was creased in pain. Sweat beaded his brow. Leon's painkiller was beginning to wear off already. In a few minutes, he would be in agony again. And I would depart, leaving him with nothing but an old stole and a slow and painful death.

Leon looked at me. I knew what he was saying.

I looked down at William. A spasm twisted his face. He would not recover. He would die soon. In agony. I closed my eyes and saw that vigorous man striding up the hill to St Mary's. Standing in front of me with his hands on his hips. Riding towards me in the snow. Keeping me warm. Buying me hair ribbons. He deserved a better death than this.

I nodded at Leon.

It took only a moment. I looked away as he did it. William's breathing began to slow. I went to the door and shouted for Father Ranulf whom I knew would not be far away.

I heard him call a response and the next minute his bald head appeared below me on the stair. He pushed past me, his attention all on William, who was gently fading away.

I closed my eyes and bowed my head as Father Ranulf began the last rites, and, when I opened them again, William was dead.

We refused all offers of refreshment. I said a final word of farewell to Margery who was waiting in the courtyard.

Everything was as it was before. The chickens still pecked between the stones. A stable cat still dozed on the roof. The doves cooed. And William Hendred was dead.

Leon took my arm and we walked back up through the village to the pod and jumped away.

We returned to St Mary's and sat in silence as the cold blue decontamination lamp played over us. Leon shut things down. We still hadn't spoken.

Finally, he said, 'Max, how do you feel?'

'I'm fine,' I said. I wasn't, but I'd deal with that later.

'He's dead.'

'He was always dead, Leon. He died six and a half centuries ago.'

I pushed away the memory of him lying helpless and in pain. That wasn't William Hendred. I would always see him striding up the hill towards me, standing with his hands on his hips with that expression of mingled exasperation and amusement. That was William Hendred. And he'd been dead now for a very long time.

Silence fell again. I don't know why neither of us made a move to leave. Perhaps because there were still things to be said and something told me that this was the moment to say them. To talk to each other properly. This wasn't the time for smart remarks or dodging the issue or changing the subject. There were things that must be said.

I turned to him. 'You would have done the same, Leon. If you found a woman – anyone – alone and lost and afraid, you would have taken her in. You would have sheltered her and protected her from others. Yes, you would probably have become fond of her. You might even have loved her, although you wouldn't have been "in love" with her. But you would never have forgotten me or done anything to betray the memory of me – as I never did to you.'

He turned away. 'You know I wouldn't have blamed you if you had.'

I pretended to be stupid. 'Had what?'

He looked at his feet. 'You know.'

Long lines of bitterness etched themselves across his face.

'Leon, I told you. Nothing happened.'

He turned away abruptly. 'Not with William Hendred.'

I was bewildered. 'What are you talking about? No – hold on – *who* are you talking about?'

He turned back to me. 'Peterson.'

The unexpectedness took my breath away.

I think I've said before that I'm shallow. That I can only do one emotion at a time and that's usually hunger. At that moment I was so taken aback that I don't think I actually felt anything at all. I just stared at him. Probably my mouth was open. Once upon a time, before life had knocked me about so much, I think some sort of red mist would have enveloped me and I'd have felled him to the ground, or ripped off his head. Or something.

I didn't do any of that. Not because I'd grown as a person or matured or anything daft like that but simply because I was too gobsmacked to move. And then there was a tiny spurt of anger. Not the familiar, red, all-encompassing destructive rage, but the cold, sharp, white, laser-focused rage that picks its target and kills quickly and cleanly.

'What did you say?'

'You know what I said. I said Peterson. It didn't take the two of you very long to forget me, did it?'

Surely he didn't mean …? He did. He meant the night Peterson plucked up his courage and asked me out, and I plucked up mine and said 'yes'. And then it never happened. Because that was the night they told me there was a tiny chance that Leon might still be alive.

A small part of me knew this wasn't Leon talking. This was pain and frustration and the fear of losing everything he held dear. I wanted to tell him how mistaken he was. Because he hadn't seen Peterson in his smart jacket and with his neatly combed hair, putting aside his own feelings and trying so hard to be pleased for me.

'I never stopped thinking of you, Leon. Not one single day – not one single hour passed when you weren't in my thoughts. I never forgot you. You, however, appear to have forgotten that when I first came to this world, you had taken up with Isabella Barclay. Peterson and I turned to each other for comfort, but you took up with the woman who murdered me.'

His head jerked up but I swept on. 'I can't tell you how disappointed I am in you, Leon.'

I was out of the pod, out of the paint store and into the long corridor before I even thought to draw breath.

Six steps later I stopped simmering with resentment. Six more steps and I remembered that I myself hadn't reacted that calmly on discovering that Leon had taken up with Bitchface Barclay. In fact, I'd walloped him with a blue plastic dustpan.

Six more steps and remorse began to set in. This is my problem. I can't hang on to the anger. It's a bit of a nuisance actually. I mean – what's the point of being married if you can't harbour a grudge until the end of time, or maintain levels of red-hot resentment throughout fifty years of marriage?

The first person I ran into – literally – was Markham, who stood squarely in front of me so I couldn't get away, took one look and said, 'Everything all right?'

I made a huge effort to pull myself together. 'Of course.' A thought occurred to me. 'Could you do me a favour?'

He looked wary. He'd been caught like that in the past.

'I've left Leon … near the paint store.'

He nodded his understanding.

'Could someone just make sure he's … OK.'

He didn't ask a single question, saying amiably, 'I'll go myself,' and disappeared down the corridor.

I went to my room and spent some time looking at myself in the mirror. I was still wearing my medieval gear. My wimple-wrapped face looked back at me. This was the face that William Hendred had seen. I smiled and whispered, '*Requiescat in pace*, William Hendred.'

I stood for a moment. Then I closed another door in my mind, changed my clothes, washed my face and hands, and wondered what to do now. I knew what I couldn't do. No matter how much I wanted to, I couldn't stay in this room for the rest of my life, so I shrugged my shoulders to give me courage, stuck my chin in the air, and clattered back down the stairs again.

The second person I ran into was Markham, trotting around the gallery.

'I found him,' he said, in answer to my unspoken question. 'And he's fine. I left him with Peterson.'

I think I might have stepped back, saying, 'What? How? You can't … no. Wait. What?' Before pulling myself together.

'I left the two of them deep in some sort of discussion,' he said sunnily and with absolutely no idea of the effect his words were having on me. 'It looked a bit serious.'

I might have uttered some sort of dreadful oath.

'Everything OK?' he said with the perspicacity for which the Security Section is famed.

'Absolutely fine,' I said.

He caught my arm as I tried to push past him. 'They're all right, you know, Max,' and I should have listened to what he was trying to tell me, but instead I shot off round the gallery.

'They're on the front terrace,' he called after me.

I found an appropriate window through which I could see and not be seen and peered out. Yes, there they were, walking slowly along the terrace. Peterson was talking, with Leon, now back in his familiar orange jumpsuit, limping slowly along beside him, head bent, listening. They strolled out of sight and I galloped to the next window to pick them up again. And then on to the next and so on, all down the corridor until, eventually, I ran out of windows.

I cursed and craned my neck and then had a brilliant idea. I heaved the window up – carefully, because some of our sash windows are linear descendants of Madame Guillotine, and leaned out. I could just see them if I stood on one leg and hung precariously out of the window. They were still walking and talking, deeply involved in their conversation. I watched anxiously. Leon was making some point with short, emphatic gestures and Peterson was nodding. What was that all about?

I leaned out even further and fell out of the window.

Apparently, these days, it's heart disease that's the killer. And cancer, of course. And stress. Falling out of the

399

window doesn't do you a lot of good either, even if you only fall three feet or so onto the flat roof underneath and the window slams shut behind you, narrowly missing taking your leg off.

I sprawled, winded, on the dirty roof littered with gravel and odd bones and bird shit and thought, *why me*?

Dragging myself to my feet, I brushed myself down and looked around. I was on the low flat roof between the main building and the Staff Block. The window behind me had locked itself shut – of course it had. Why wouldn't it? – and I couldn't get back in.

There were three windows opposite me. One, I was almost certain, was Markham's. Not that it mattered, because it was shut and locked. The other two belonged to Peterson. One was open. I could wriggle in through the window, whisk myself out of his door – no one ever locks their doors at St Mary's – and be away down the stairs with no one any the wiser.

I heaved myself into his room, dropping heavily to the floor on the other side, but I knew he wasn't in, so no problems there. I didn't hang around either. I had the door open in seconds and just as I thought I'd got away with it, I heard their voices on the stairs.

Bloody bollocking hell. Does nothing ever go right? I could just imagine what Peterson would be thinking if he found me here. And I didn't even want to think about what Leon would be thinking. *For God's sake, Maxwell – do something.*

I stepped back, closed the door quietly and took a panicky look around. There was nowhere to hide. Well, there was his bedroom through the open door over there but I wasn't going anywhere near that.

There was a bookcase with a picture of Helen. Nowhere there.

Under the table? Don't be stupid.

Behind his chiller cabinet? The one with the Portable Appliance Test Failure sticker. In all of St Mary's, only Leon's doesn't have one of those. He used to go around cutting the plugs off the failures in a well-intentioned effort to save everyone's lives until he realised people were just twisting the wires back together again, covering the join in a giant wart of duct tape, keeping calm and carrying on. I know he did once attempt to remonstrate with Bashford about this but, as Sykes had pointed out, the man had replaced his girlfriend with a chicken. Electrocution was the kindest thing that could happen to him.

Concentrate, Maxwell. There was an armchair. Yes. Behind the armchair in the corner.

Their voices were very close. I heard the door handle rattle. They were coming in.

Fear lent me wings – as the saying goes. It also lent me a jetpack and super booster. I was across the room at only just under the speed of light and squeezing behind the chair as the door opened.

'... need to get this sorted before it becomes a problem,' Peterson was saying.

'I quite agree,' said Leon. 'Prompt action, I think and ...' he stopped and there was a short pause.

I held my breath, hugging my knees and making myself as small as possible, telling myself they hadn't seen me.

'Anyway,' said Peterson, in a slightly different tone of voice, 'I've got the report here. I don't have to tell you ...'

'No, indeed. I'll take a look and let you have it back this afternoon.'

There was another pause and then Peterson said, 'Was that …?'

'It very much looked like it, don't you think?'

'Why?'

'Your guess is as good as mine. Anyway, I'll get right on this.'

'Thank you, Leon. For your eyes only, obviously.'

'Of course.'

'Thanks. Do you fancy a spot of lunch?'

'Why not?'

There was another strangely odd pause and then Peterson said, 'You coming, Max?'

Oh God. Oh God. Oh God. Oh God …

'Um … no …' I said, as casually as I could from behind the armchair. 'I think I'll just hang on for a bit.'

'OK then. See you later.'

'Yes,' said Leon, and I could tell by his voice he was grinning. 'See you later, Max.'

'Mmhm,' I said, channelling all the nonchalance I could muster.

The door closed and I heard them moving off down the corridor.

I sat, on fire with mortification, hugging my knees, eyes squeezed tight shut, and I then toppled slowly to one side and lay among the dust bunnies.

As soon as I could, I took refuge in my office, where no one would ever know what had just happened and everything was just fine until Rosie Lee returned from lunch.

'Why are you so dusty?'

'I'm not.'

'Yes, you are. You're all black down one side.'

'No, I'm not.'

'What have you been up to?'

'Nothing.'

'Looks as if you've lain down in a bed of dirt. Have you lain down in a …?'

'No, of course not,' I said, foreseeing I was going to have to make my own tea for at least a month to shut her up.

'Because that's what it looks like.'

'Well, I haven't,' I said. 'Why would I do such a thing?'

'Well, if was anyone else I'd agree but …'

'I must have brushed against something,' I said desperately.

'Brushed? Rolled in it more like.'

'Look, could we just …?'

'I mean, you look as if you've been under someone's bed.'

Surely there must be circumstances under which murder is legal? Or even qualifies for a small reward?

She was probably going to go on forever – or at least until I sent her home early out of sheer desperation – when Peterson stuck his head round the door. I felt myself begin to go red all over again. The only good thing about this situation was that Leon wasn't here.

'Can you spare a moment?' he asked. 'Meeting with Leon and the Boss. In his office.'

'What, now?'

'Why are you so dirty?' he asked, grinning.

'Just what I was asking,' said Miss Lee triumphantly.

I felt myself get even hotter. I must be glowing like a dust-covered Belisha beacon.

'Yes, Max,' he said, leaning against the wall and grinning again. 'What have you been up to?'

Something snapped.

'Actually, I was hiding in Dr Peterson's room as I do every Wednesday morning as part of a complicated and long-standing ritual, the purpose of which I have sworn never to divulge to a living soul on pain of death, so I'm going to have to kill you both now, and it's all Peterson's fault because if he swept his room occasionally then no one would have been any the wiser and ...'

Rosie Lee returned to her desk with her *'Now you're just being silly'* expression.

I subsided. 'What does Dr Bairstow want?'

'Tell you when we get there.'

It was serious. I could tell by their expressions. This morning's nonsense was put aside for the moment.

We sat at his briefing table. Dr Bairstow said heavily, 'We have a problem. Our new Number Four has returned from its test jump.' He turned to me. 'With Mr Clerk, Miss Prentiss and Mr Cox.'

'Yes, sir?'

'Apparently, they have experienced some difficulties.'

'In what way, sir.'

'A disagreement arose during the assignment.'

Well, that wasn't unusual. The collective noun for a group of historians is an argumentation. An Argumentation of Historians.

He went on. 'A disagreement of such magnitude that blows were exchanged and Miss Prentiss and Mr Clerk have separately informed me they will leave St Mary's rather than work together again.'

I goggled. Clerk and Prentiss had been together for years. After Peterson, then me, they were our longest-serving historians. Clerk had been on the intake behind me. In the days when we had intakes. The thought of losing either of them was frightening. Both of them leaving would be a disaster. Clerk was calm and quiet, and Prentiss's good nature was almost legendary. I couldn't, for one moment, even begin to contemplate an argument of such ferocity that would preclude them ever working together again.

'And Mr Cox?' said Peterson.

'Will never go out with either of them.'

Leon stirred and said, 'Do we know the cause of this disagreement?'

'No. None of them will say.'

'But blows were exchanged?' I said, resolving to get down there and bang their silly heads together. 'Who hit whom?'

'Mr Cox punched Mr Clerk. Mr Clerk returned the blow. Miss Prentiss hit both of them.'

There was only one explanation. 'Were they drunk?'

He hesitated. 'According to Dr Stone, that might be a possibility.'

I inhaled sharply. We don't drink on assignments. We don't even drink the night before. It's clearly understood. Yes, we carry medicinal brandy. And medicinal vodka, too. And medicinal wine. Even medicinal beer. But that's for afterwards. *After* a successful assignment. Never before and never, ever, *ever* during.

I stood up. 'I'll talk to Mr Clerk and Miss Prentiss, sir.'

'If you would, please, Dr Maxwell. Mr Markham is debriefing Mr Cox. Chief, I'd like you to run diagnostics on Number Four as quickly as possible, please.'

Leon bristled. 'Are you saying there's something wrong with the pod rather than the occupants?'

'I don't know,' he said frankly, 'but I think we should investigate every eventuality, don't you? Report back here in one hour, please.'

I got nowhere with any of them. Cox was in the men's ward, sitting on his bed, staring at something only he could see. I left him to Markham.

Clerk was in isolation, staring out of the window with his back to the room. I stared thoughtfully and then went off to try Prentiss.

She was curled in an armchair pretending to read a book.

'Hey, Max.'

I didn't bother with preliminaries. 'What happened?'

'I don't want to talk about it.'

'Paula ...'

'No, I mean it, Max. I'm not saying a word. Do what you will ... put me on a disciplinary ... sack me ... I'm not saying anything.'

'But you must see – this must be investigated and ...'

'I'm not pressing any charges so it's not important.'

'Charges?'

She stopped abruptly.

'Paula, give me something.'

She shivered but said nothing.

I waited, but there was nothing more. And it was the same for Clerk. Hostile silence and folded arms. In fact, he turned his back on me. I got nothing from either of them.

I talked to Dr Stone.

'All their injuries are consistent with a fairly lively punch-up.'

'Wait,' I said, sharply. '*All* their injuries? Are you saying Cox and Clerk hit Prentiss?'

'It would appear so, but before we jump to any unpleasant conclusions, let's wait for the results of blood tests and so on.'

I couldn't believe it and said so.

'There might be many innocent explanations, Max. They might have been trying to prevent her from doing something dangerous. Or self-harming. We just don't know.'

'But surely an explanation like that raises more questions than it settles.'

'It does indeed.'

'What did the scanner say?'

'Their readings were all over the place. Extreme agitation, elevated heart rates. As I say, I'm waiting for the test results. Not long now.'

'Don't let them leave Sick Bay,' I said.

He smiled grimly. 'Not a chance.'

I reported my lack of success to Dr Bairstow. 'None of them will say a word, sir. And there's no chance of any written reports.'

He frowned. 'Guilt?'

I took a moment to think. 'No, I don't think so.' I cast around for the appropriate word. 'More like ... shame, sir.

Leon looked up from his scratchpad. 'There's nothing wrong with the pod. Dieter has already been over everything and I've checked his findings. Number Four is functioning perfectly. It landed exactly where and when it was supposed to. All the readings were spot on. Whatever happened, you can't blame the pod for it.'

Dr Bairstow thought for a moment. 'Very well. Dr Peterson, put together a repeat assignment. The three of you together. Doctors Peterson and Maxwell will report from an historian perspective and Chief Farrell will monitor pod performance. Because if it's not the historians then, somehow, it's the jump or the pod.'

He picked up a file and limped to his filing cabinet.

'I want this jump reproduced as accurately as you can. Not the same date, obviously, but as close as pod protocols will allow you to get. And make sure the internal cameras are on this time. Report directly to me on your return. I want this nipped in the bud. The last thing we need are unfounded rumours flying around the building. That will be all. Dr Maxwell, a moment please.'

The door closed behind them and he turned to me. The silence was a little unnerving.

'Sir? Is there a problem?'

'I don't know, Max. Is there?'

'I have many problems, sir. Could you be more specific?'

'How are you?'

I opened my mouth to say, 'Absolutely fine,' and closed it again, because I wasn't and he knew it.

'I'm not at my best, sir. This world is still … a little unfamiliar to me. I'm improving every day, but if you want to send someone else may I recommend Miss North.'

'And Leon?'

'Oh, he's recovering well, sir. He doesn't always need his stick now.'

'And Dr Peterson?'

'Also well, sir.'

None of that was what he meant and we both knew it.

'Sir, we'll get it all sorted out.'

I wasn't referring to this new assignment and we both knew it.

'I would be grateful for some reassurance that my unit is not crumbling around my ears.'

'And you shall have it, sir.'

He nodded. 'I hope so. Why are you still here, Dr Maxwell?'

'I'm waiting for you to instruct me to see to it, sir.'

He smiled. 'See to it, Dr Maxwell.'

'Yes, sir.'

Number Four's inaugural assignment had been a small one. Nothing too strenuous for what was, literally, its first date. Rushford, 1815 – the post-Waterloo celebrations. Napoleon was no longer at large; the Iron Duke was a national hero; relief and jubilation were sweeping across a country no longer at war. We would be on home ground and I would be interested to see Rushford again, four-hundred and fifteen years after my last visit. We'd jump there – monitor all the readings very carefully, take a quick tour around town and come back out again, reproducing the conditions of the first jump as closely as possible. Then I'd push off to interview Prentiss and Clerk again, and Leon and his team of techies would evaluate the pod and its performance. Easy-peasy.

We were dressed well. I wore a silk gown of pale blue with a matching bonnet. The same one I'd worn to George IV's coronation, when Markham pimped me out to a clergyman. Cream gloves and matching half boots of kid completed my get-up. And my pepper spray, of course, tucked away in my pretty girlie reticule.

Peterson and I walked down to Hawking together. It was on the tip of my tongue to ask him whether this was what he and Leon had been discussing earlier, thus cunningly ascertaining how things stood between them, but that would mean bringing up other topics of conversation as well – such as what exactly I'd been doing behind his armchair – something for which I had yet to think of an acceptable and believable explanation that didn't involve massive toe-curling on my part and hilarity on his, so I left it.

Leon looked very handsome in a navy coat and biscuit-coloured breeches, while Peterson struck a slightly dandified note in a high crowned hat, green coat and cream waistcoat. He also carried a cane. All the better to whack them with, presumably.

It was Peterson's mission, so he seated himself in the central seat and wriggled his bum a little.

'Problem?' said Leon, in what I hoped was normal defence of one of his beloved pods.

'Not in the slightest. Hold tight everyone. Computer, initiate jump.'

'Jump initiated.'

The world went white.

The date was late July. Most of us had been to Waterloo and Dr Bairstow had insisted we leave a clear month between then and this jump.

We landed down by the river. The dock area was downstream from the town itself, because upstream from Rushford, the river widened abruptly and became unnavigable. The port was considerably busier than in modern times. Tall-masted ships lined the quays, surrounded by swarms of shouting men either loading or unloading their cargoes. The warehouses were hives of activity with bales and barrels being carried in through one door and out through another. Horse-drawn wagons waited in line to be loaded and, everywhere, rope makers, chandlers, sailmakers, carpenters and sailors all surged about, shouting, gesturing and generally getting on with the business of the day.

Peterson turned from the screen to Leon, already tapping away at his scratchpad and frowning at the results. 'Anything?'

'Mm? No. Nothing. As I anticipated.'

'Well, according to their mission programme, they were to make their way up into town to suss out what was happening there. We'll leave you to it.'

'Mm,' said Leon, barely looking up. And they say we historians are obsessed.

'Five-minute progress reports,' persevered Peterson.

'Mm.'

We left him to it.

The smell of tar was overwhelming. Even the people reeked of it.

'Jolly Jack Tars,' muttered Peterson.

I nodded and did as other women were doing, and rummaged in my reticule for a handkerchief to hold over my nose.

We left the docks and emerged into the town. It was lovely to see the medieval bridge back in place. I wondered exactly when it had been built. After my departure, obviously, and now the town had spilled over the river and up the hill on the other side. The market was now held up near St Stephens.

Many medieval buildings were still here – I recognised the Guildhall, almost completely unchanged – but now they were interspersed with Jacobean and Elizabethan buildings too. There were some imposing stone houses lining the streets. Rushford was obviously booming. Because of the docks, I guessed. In modern times, the docks had dwindled, the warehouses had been converted into smart flats, trendy coffee shops had spawned where the chandlers and rope makers once worked, and right in the middle of all of it, the council had commissioned a block of modern apartments, all plate glass and blue plastic so everyone could see that Rushford was happy to throw away its heritage in favour of modern tat. Peterson always muttered under his breath and averted his eyes – as did most people who had to pass near it.

The streets were still filthy though. That hadn't changed at all. The dirt was knee high in places. For a penny, small boys would sweep a crossing for their betters. Not having a penny, Peterson and I took our chances, dodging the very much increased volume of wheeled traffic which came at us from all directions. You really needed your wits about you here.

There were even more inns than before. I put that down to the mail coaches. *The Cider Tree*, where William Hendred had stabled his horse the day we went to Rushford, was still here, although it was now greatly enlarged, and the frontage was different, with a huge archway through which the mail coaches swept in and out, blowing their horns for a change of horses. I smiled to myself and moved on.

The crowds were thickest here and we were jostled from all sides. Peterson linked his arm with mine to avoid us being swept apart. There were people shouting, drivers roaring at pedestrians to get out of the way, street cries, and the rumble of wheels on rough paving. We could hardly hear ourselves speak.

It all happened very suddenly – but then, unexpected things usually do.

We had paused to listen to a street preacher – all wild eyes and waving arms – when a ragged street urchin, barefoot and terrified, burst out of the crowd, followed by a bellow of startled rage. He swerved, collided with a portly gentleman with a red face and a fancy waistcoat who shouted with alarm and swung at him. His cane caught the boy around the head. The boy staggered and dropped something before disappearing back into the crowd.

413

Whatever it was fell almost at my feet and, like an idiot, I let go of Peterson's arm and picked it up.

It was a gentleman's pocket book. The urchin had attempted to steal it, been caught in the act and had fled the scene, getting rid of the evidence as he went. This was not something in which I should get involved. I dropped it and kicked it away. Too late.

Someone seized my arm, shouting, 'Got her. Over here.'

Cries rose up around me. Apparently, I was a thieving doxy and transportation was too good for me.

I was surrounded in no time at all. I strained for a sight of Peterson who had been swept away in the turmoil, but my view was blocked by angry citizens at every turn.

Someone pushed me. I fell against someone else who pushed me the other way. My bonnet was knocked over my eyes and then I couldn't see at all.

At some point I dropped my reticule, but it left my hands free and I began to struggle. I kicked out and caught someone's shins. There was a muttered oath and someone hit me across the face.

For a brief moment, I heard Peterson's voice in my ear. 'Max, stay …' and then another blow knocked out my earpiece. I didn't hear it fall but it seemed safe to assume it had been trampled by the crowd. I was protesting my innocence. Loudly and at length. From far away, I thought I could hear Peterson shouting at me, telling me to stay put. He was on his way.

Too late.

I was hustled away. I couldn't see where. I couldn't see anything. I remember slipping and sliding on the cobbles and then being hustled down a flight of steps. A door slammed ominously behind me, shutting out the sounds of the angry crowd.

I would have fallen down an unseen stair, but they held me tightly. I could tell I was inside a building, but the smell was dreadful. The sharp smell of urine and unwashed bodies stung my eyes and nose. It was underlaid with something else that turned my stomach. I remembered, when I was at school, reading a report on the reforms of Elizabeth Fry, which described the women's wing of Newgate Prison as hell on earth. This wasn't Newgate, thank God, but it still wasn't a good place to be.

My bonnet was dragged off my head, bringing my hair down with it. I looked down at my dress, splattered with the filth of the streets and torn where I'd caught my foot in the hem. It was going to be very difficult to convince the authorities I was a respectable wife and mother.

A man in a shabby dark coat stood at a high wooden desk, inscribing something in a book. His tongue protruded as he laboriously constructed his letters. His teeth looked like splayed tombstones on a dark night.

I said, 'I think there has been some mistake,' and the man on my right, a fat old bugger with a straining waistcoat said, 'Yer don't speak.'

Turning to the man at the desk he said, 'Thieving jade – caught in the act.'

The man dipped his pen in a cup of brown, muddy ink and began to write, slowly and with great precision.

'What was stolen?'

'Gennelman's pocket book.'

'Does she still have it?'

That, of course, was their cue to run their very grubby hands all over me. They knew I didn't have it but any excuse ...

'Passed it on to an accomplice. Saw her do it.'

'Wosser name?'

They shrugged. 'Take yer pick.'

I said quickly, 'My name is Mrs Farrell. My husband is Leon Farrell Esquire, of St Mary's Priory.'

When they'd stopped laughing, they took great pleasure in informing me St Mary's was let to Captain Jessop and his family, currently sojourning in Bath for the summer. Then they realised that if I was part of a gang they'd just told me the house was empty and clipped my ear, presumably to induce deafness. And indeed, on top of the blows I'd already received, my head was beginning to ring. I'd been out of Sick Bay less than a week and look at the state of me already.

Tombstone teeth – obviously the thinker of the outfit – was regarding me dubiously. 'Are ye sure? Seems a well-dressed mort to me.'

'Likely stole those as well.'

'Anything else on her?'

Back they came with the hands. Time to put a stop to this. I drew myself up and summoned every ounce of hauteur that I could muster.

'You, sirs, will kindly desist. When my husband hears of this outrage it is you who will be answering to the magistrates – not I.'

The hands paused. 'Cor, listen to her,' said someone. 'Good as a play.'

But I noticed the hands did not recommence. I told myself a seed of doubt had been sown. And Leon and Peterson were out there somewhere. They'd get me out.

I was hustled down some more steps. Someone ahead jangled their keys and there was the sound of a wooden door scraping across a stone floor.

I was pushed forwards, slipped in something slimy, and fell onto my knees in a pile of wet straw.

Behind me, a man laughed and said, 'Not so hoity-toity now are you, my fine lady?' and the door slammed shut behind me.

Darkness and silence enveloped me.

I waved my hand around but couldn't see anything. There was no window and no light. I crouched and felt around, which wasn't pleasant. You'll never guess what I put my hand in. I wiped it as best as could on my skirts. Mrs Enderby was not going to be pleased with me.

My outstretched arm found a wet wall. Brick, I guessed. I took a tentative step forward, and then another.

There's no direct evidence for a sixth sense, but we have it just the same. I don't know what made me stop and stand still, but I did. I stood stock still for a long time, uselessly turning my head from side to side trying to discover what wasn't right, why I'd stopped ...

A blast of cold air lifted the short hairs around my face. Cold, foetid air ...

Surely not ...

I felt around with my feet. Very, very carefully.

Even though I was expecting it I very nearly overbalanced, and that wouldn't have done me any good at all. Because there was nothing there. Just a nothingness from which an evil smell arose.

The floor gaped before me. I stood on the brink of a pit. God knows how deep it was and I certainly wasn't going to check. I didn't think it was that deep. At least I hoped it wasn't that deep because I suspected this was a bit of a joke. Payback for me doing the posh bint thing. That was why they hadn't left me with a light. I would grope my way around, fall down the hole, flounder around in whatever lay at the bottom – going through the motions, as Markham would say – and present myself at the next sessions dripping with God knows what and earning an automatic one-way ticket to Australia. I wouldn't be surprised if this wasn't a cell at all. This might be somewhere they shoved the stroppy prisoners to teach them a lesson. Was this why I was here alone when 19th-century prisons were famous for their overcrowding?

I shuffled very carefully to one side, found the wall again, kicked aside what I hoped was wet straw and lowered myself slowly to the floor. I made myself as small as possible, drawing up my knees in much the same position I'd been in behind Peterson's armchair only a few hours ago. Another place. Another time.

I suppose it was some form of primitive sensory deprivation. I sat in the silent darkness and lost all sense of time and space. I had no idea how long I'd been there. It could have been anything from twenty minutes to several hours. I tried to count my breaths to give me an idea of passing minutes and kept losing count.

I told myself it didn't matter. As soon as it was dark – if not before – Leon and Peterson would be here. They'd get me out and we could return to our investigations.

Despite the damp stone, it was very warm in here. Every time I moved, I felt my clothes sticking to me. My forehead prickled with sweat. I kept wiping it away, forgetting to keep my dirty hands away from my face, but it was so hot … I leaned my head back against the cool, wet wall but it didn't help. I was going down with something. The symptoms had come on too quickly for gaol fever, although that would be something to put on my CV – and would certainly stop Peterson in his tracks every time he started on about his twinge of bubonic plague.

Time passed. My head began to throb. And then I felt sick. Whether because of the headache, I don't know. I stared into the darkness and tried to tell myself this would soon be over. Leon and Peterson would come.

They didn't. And then the doubts crept in. Suppose they couldn't find me. Suppose Peterson hadn't followed me back to this gaol. Suppose he and Leon only took a cursory look around, decided I was somewhere else, and went off and left me here. I'd been locked up for hours and hours. Surely they should have been here by now. Either bribing the gaolers, or if that didn't work then intimidating them, or if that didn't work then blowing the place sky-high, and pulling me out from under the rubble.

And then I had an even worse thought. Had Peterson been arrested too? Were we both incarcerated in this place and Leon didn't have a clue where we were? Would I ever see them again? I stared into the dark. Would I ever see anything again? A tiny voice said, 'We're St Mary's and we never leave our people behind,' but I'd been left behind in 1399. I'd only been back at St Mary's for a week and now I'd been left behind again.

Unbelievably, I think I might have dozed off. I'm not sure. Just for a few seconds, anyway. I only know I woke with a jerk.

I hadn't even thought of it until it actually happened. I'd been sitting here for hours and in all that time there hadn't been a single sound so I'd assumed I was alone.

Somewhere to my left, the straw rustled. I held my breath. Someone was in here with me.

Fresh sweat broke out all over my body, prickling my hair and running down my back. My instinct was to stand up. To face whatever it was and defend myself.

419

Second thoughts kept me where I was. It was equally dark for both of us. Sitting here against the wall, I was a smaller target than if I was standing. I kept very, very still and listened until my ears nearly fell off.

Nothing. I heard nothing. Was it possible I'd imagined it?

And then I thought – idiot. It's a rat. Of course it is. The place would be riddled with them. They probably nipped in and out through the hole in the floor which was probably some sort of open drain. I leaned back against the cool wall and closed my eyes in relief. I wasn't old or infirm, or sick. I was in no danger. I could deal with a rat or two.

The straw rustled again. In exactly the same place.

I froze and held my breath, straining all my senses. And then it happened again. A little closer this time. This was not a rat scuttling around my cell. This was something slowly drawing nearer – an inch at a time.

I'd lost my reticule with my pepper spray inside. I had no means of defending myself against whatever was in here with me. I don't know why I thought some*thing* rather than someone, but I did. My eyes were stinging. Sweat was pouring off me. I was dreadfully thirsty. My head ached fit to burst. And something was in here with me.

The straw rustled again. Very close this time. I was convinced I could hear breathing. This was no rat.

I had a sudden picture of something climbing out of the hole in the floor. Silent and menacing. Something that could see in the dark whereas I was blind. Something that would stalk me around this tiny space. Something from which I could not escape.

I was gasping for breath. Panic. Fear. The heat. I couldn't breathe properly. My head was throbbing. If I'd had time to eat before I left then it would have been all across the floor by now.

I could hear breathing. I swear I could hear breathing. Long, slow and heavy. And I could smell something. Even over the robust aromas of a 19th-century prison cell, I could smell decaying earth.

My mind flew back to another small space. When I was trapped in a pod with Kal and we were fighting something that would not die. Had it found me again?

I couldn't sit still any longer. I struggled to my feet and stood swaying, keeping one hand on the wall for support.

The straw rustled again and a voice breathed, 'I see you ...'

I screamed and at exactly that moment, the cell door opened. It was only a feeble light, but it stabbed at my eyes and did my splitting headache no good at all. I heard men's voices and Leon said, 'I've got you, Max.'

I tried to warn him. 'There's something here. Something dangerous.'

'Yes,' he said grimly. 'Me.'

I was convinced I had gaol fever.

'No, no, no,' said Peterson. 'Nothing as classy as gaol fever. You've just picked up some horrible nameless infection that will probably kill you. Nothing to worry about.'

He was fussing around with the med kit. Leon was laying a welcome cold cloth on my forehead. My temperature was about a hundred and eighty. You could have boiled the kettle on me.

Our medications are colour coded for safety. It's quite simple really. Blue and green can be used with each other. Orange can be used with green but not with blue. Red can only be used on its own and not with any other colour. Simple. We have to do this because we carry a bewildering array of drugs to counteract the bewildering array of diseases an historian can contract if she really puts her mind to it.

I had two blues and a green.

'Pretty,' I said groggily, admiring the colours.

Peterson rolled his eyes.

'How are you feeling?' asked Leon.

I looked around. I was back in the pod with no memory of how I'd got there but I wasn't in gaol so I didn't really care. Speaking of which …

'Did you see it?'

'See what?' said Leon, reapplying the cloth.

'See what was in the cell with me?'

'There was nothing in the cell with you.'

'Did it escape through the hole?'

'What hole?'

'The hole in the floor,' I said impatiently.

He said quietly, 'There was no hole in the floor.'

'Yes, there was,' I said, becoming quite cross with him. 'I felt it with my foot. Or rather I didn't feel it with my foot if you know what I mean.'

'Max, there was no hole and no one else. You were on the floor in a perfectly normal ten by four room.'

'No, I wasn't,' I said, trying to sit up so I could put him right.

'Yes, you were,' said Peterson, putting the medkit away. 'You were on the floor rabbiting on about God knows what and as high as a kite.'

'No, I wasn't,' I said again, getting angry now because they were both completely wrong. 'I wasn't there all that long.'

They exchanged glances. 'You were there overnight.'

'No, I wasn't. Was I?'

'Yes. It took us that long to get you out. They wouldn't let you go without a magistrate's signature and it took us all night to track one down.'

'I thought you'd blow up the gaol,' I said, disappointed.

'That was Plan B,' said Leon gravely.

'And they let me go?'

'Once they realised you were the wife of a respectable citizen, they couldn't wait to get rid of you,' said Peterson. 'My heart went out to them.'

'I don't feel very well,' I said plaintively.

'No,' said Leon, 'but the antibiotics will kick in and you'll be fine in the morning.'

He got that wrong.

We all spent a lively night.

I awoke with a fit of coughing and couldn't stop.

I remember Peterson running his long fingers over the medkit before saying, 'I think we'll try ... this one. And this one.'

Shadows came and went. I asked Leon if he'd found the problem with the pod and my mind slithered away before he could reply. I drank vast amounts of water. Dark dreams danced before my eyes before, at long last, the meds kicked in and I fell properly asleep.

I awoke to a silent pod. Peterson was stretched out in a sleeping module and Leon was sitting at the console, scratchpad in hand, frowning at a readout.

Everything was peaceful and quiet. My fever had gone.

And then, to my right, a locker door swung open and there stood Clive Ronan. Fresh from the Egyptian desert. I could clearly see sand caught in the creases of his jeans and T-shirt. A little pile of it had collected around his feet. He was still wearing his bandana. He was standing there – in the locker – with my baby in his arms. Matthew was holding out his little arms to me. I had to save him because, somehow, I'd been given a second chance. A chance to save my little Matthew. I tried to kick my legs free so I could get up. A huge weight bore down on me. Someone was shouting. They wouldn't let me get up and I had to save Matthew. I was shouting. Someone was shouting back again. I couldn't move.

Clive Ronan grinned at me and the locker door closed. He was gone, taking my baby with him. I screamed and kicked. Something pricked my arm and I went back to sleep.

I opened my eyes. Leon and Peterson were sitting at the console, talking quietly.

I said, 'Hey,' and they both turned around.

Leon got up and knelt stiffly at my side. 'Max, do you know where you are?'

I tried to get up. 'Did you see him? Did you see Ronan? We have to get after him.'

He gently pushed me back again. 'You're hallucinating, Max.'

I had to make him understand. 'No. He was here. He was in the locker over there. He had Matthew. We can still catch him. We can get our baby back.'

At the console, Peterson made a sound and turned away.

Leon pushed my hair out of my eyes. 'Sweetheart, you're dreaming. It's not real. You have a fever.'

'No, I don't,' I said, coughing up a lung. 'I'm fine.'

He passed me some water.

'We're going to get you back to St Mary's and let Dr Stone take a look at you.'

'No, we're not,' said Peterson, quietly.

Leon turned impatiently.

'It's no good looking like that, Leon. We've been over this. You know the rules as well as I. Whatever Max has – we can't take it back with us. We wait until she's better.'

'It's been two days – she's not getting any better.'

Two days? Really?

'She will. We just have to find the right meds.'

'I tell you – we should go back, declare a Code Blue and let Dr Stone sort it out.'

'Out of the question,' said Peterson quietly, and turned back to the console.

There was a rather nasty silence and then Leon said, 'Just because you've lost Helen doesn't mean I'm going to lose Max.'

Peterson turned slowly from the console and his face was … no. No, no, no. This wasn't happening.

He took a deep breath and his voice was too calm. 'Leon, I am not risking St Mary's – and possibly the rest of the world – for just one person. The rules are clear. We stay put.'

'Until she's dead or better?'

'Until she's dead or better, yes.'

I lay still and watched them argue, hoping – praying – this was another hallucination. But it wasn't. I watched their mouths open and close. There was the strangest sense of déjà-vu. Had I done this before? Had this happened before? I tried to kick my sluggish brain into action.

Yes. Yes, it had. A long time ago in the future, two men had argued over a sick woman with catastrophic results. People had died. And continued to die to this very day.

I tried to speak and was overtaken by yet another coughing fit. Peterson brought me some water. Leon snatched it off him. I remember sipping something cold and closing my eyes. Just for a minute …

I awoke to raised voices. They were shouting. Two men who never shouted were shouting now. Shadows

426

danced before my eyes. Did we carry a gun? There's a lockbox in one of the lockers for any weapons we feel we might need. Which we don't very often. We're not allowed to shoot contemporaries. Although the rules about shooting each other are less stringent. I should do something. I should ignore my temperature, my sweats and shakes and double vision and deal with the situation. Before it got out of hand. Before someone died …

Too late. I heard the sounds of a scuffle. Something broke. A mug, I guessed. There was grunting and the sound of a blow. This was a nightmare. A waking nightmare. What might they do to each other? Could an event repeat itself before it had actually happened? They fell against the locker in a tangle of arms and legs. I rolled out of the way before I was trampled. Under the console seemed a good idea. I could see feet and legs and everything was slipping away again ..

'Max? Max talk to me.'

I opened my eyes.

It was just me and Leon. Peterson was nowhere to be seen. I peered out from under the console, but it wasn't that big a pod. Peterson definitely wasn't here. I'd been hot and now I turned cold.

Leon tried to help me out. 'What are you doing under there?'

'Not being trampled. Where's Peterson?'

'Outside.'

I froze and then tried to squeeze further back under the console. 'What have you done?'

He sat back in surprise. 'Nothing. What do you think I've done?'

427

A long time ago in the future, a man had shot his friend, thrown him out of the pod and abandoned him to die.

I opened my mouth to give utterance to the unthinkable and then stopped.

'Leon, what's this?'

'What's what? Will you come out from under there?'

'Leon, there's something under here.'

'Yes, you. Come out, Max. Please.'

I was almost completely entangled in my sweat-drenched sheet. I struggled feebly and got nowhere.

'Here.'

He pulled me out. I was too weak to be of any assistance and even not assisting brought me out in another sweat.

The door opened and Peterson appeared in the doorway. He had a cut on his cheekbone and, now I could see Leon clearly, his lip was split and he had a slight bruise over one eye. They looked at each other.

Leon said, 'Come back for more?'

His tone was ugly. Peterson's lips curled. 'Beating up a sick old man is just too easy.'

I said, 'What's going on?'

No one was listening to me. The atmosphere was thick and toxic. Yes, it was, wasn't it? Toxic was exactly the word to describe it.

I rolled back under the console. 'Leon ...'

They still weren't listening. At any moment they'd start circling each other. I reached up and pulled. It came away with a slight reluctance that told me it might be magnetised.

Leon said, 'What are you doing?' And at the same moment, Peterson said, 'What's that?'

I held it up. Leon snatched it off me. 'For God's sake, Max, it could have been fitted with an anti-tamper device.'

'It's an air freshener,' I said woozily. 'Surely blowing up is slightly counter-productive.

'Actually,' said Peterson, scooping me up and dropping me back on the sleeping module. 'When it comes to thinking, Max, you might want to leave the heavy lifting to us men.'

'Yeah. You've both been such a stunning success at it so far, haven't you?'

Leon laid it down carefully and disappeared under the console again.

'Open the door.'

'Why?'

'Because I'm shutting down the ventilation system.'

'Why?' My turn this time.

'Because we're being drugged. I suspect my feelings of dislike for Peterson, justified though they are, have been chemically induced. As was Max's Ronan hallucination.'

'You mean I'm not ill.'

'No, you're very ill, but you've been drugged too. We all have.'

Even as he spoke, the little air freshener gave a tiny squirt, releasing something into the air.

'Peterson, get a container. Something airtight.'

Peterson seized the medkit and upended the contents onto the floor. Leon dropped the air freshener inside and sealed the lid. We all peered at it as fresh, cool air blew gently into the pod.

Peterson went to stand by the door – we never leave an open door unguarded – and breathed deeply. No one spoke for a very long time until he said, 'Well, what do you know. My very reasonable desire to strangle Leon is slowly beginning to fade.'

'That's good,' I said, 'because my urge to bang your stupid heads together is increasing with every second,' and closed my eyes to let them sort things out between them.

We stayed for another twenty-four hours. I didn't do a lot. I just lay around looking feverish.

'I think,' said Leon, reading the temp tape, 'It's safe to take you back.' He showed the reading to Peterson who said, 'I agree.'

There was no hostility or aggression. They were exactly as they'd always been. Leon caught me watching them and put his hand on mine. 'It's fine, Max. Really.'

I was too tired to argue.

At least if you've had gaol fever you're excused report writing. Both Leon and Peterson said anything I reported would be wildly inaccurate anyway. Apparently, I'd been in my own world most of the time. Imagining all sorts of things, they said, not looking at each other and I agreed that, yes, I'd imagined all sorts of things.

The canister was sent off to Professor Rapson who reported that it contained a mutated form of DMT, or 'Dimitri' as he called it, a drug quite easy to manufacture and known for its abilities to induce hallucinations. To give nightmares shape and form, he said. They had to restrain him from knocking some up there and then just to demonstrate. And yes, before anyone asked, there were fingerprints all over the canister – mine, Leon's and Peterson's, so that wasn't very helpful.

Dieter gave Number Four a clean bill of health. Every other pod was rigorously searched by both the techies and the Security Section. No one found anything at all.

The three of us were shoved into the isolation ward together, which was, apparently, to be known in future as the Maxwell Ward.

Dr Bairstow spoke individually to Cox, Prentiss and Clerk and then left them alone together. I've no idea what their personal crisis had been – they never said and no one ever asked. We didn't say much about ours, either. I know that Leon and Peterson had a long and quiet talk together one night when they thought I was asleep. I'm not saying anything about that, either, so don't ask. Incident closed.

Mostly.

Peterson was discharged first, Dr Stone informing him that he appeared to be disappointingly normal and he would therefore appreciate him ceasing to lower the tone of his Sick Bay and to regard himself as expelled.

Leon was also given permission to depart, but offered the option to remain with me since I was detained at Dr Stone's pleasure for another twenty-four hours. It was up to him.

He took up the option, returning to his own corner of the ward, not looking at me.

When you have so many things to talk about, where do you begin? And who makes the first move?

I watched the door close behind Peterson and then got off my bed and went over to him. My poor Leon, wounded in just about every way it was possible to be hurt.

I said very gently, 'Leon, how are you feeling?'

431

He stayed silent, looking everywhere but at me before finally saying, 'Not wonderful.'

'Great. Now I've made my husband cry.'

'Yes, well, he's not doing that well these days.'

'Oh, I don't know. He's not doing too badly.'

'He's a bit of an idiot.'

I snorted. 'He's a complete idiot,' and took his hands.

Eventually he cleared his throat and said, 'I have something I want to say, Max.'

'There's no need.'

'I think there is.'

'OK then, off you go.'

'I was thinking about the first time I ever saw you.' He smiled slightly. 'My heart fell right out my chest and I've been looking for it ever since. Do you remember those days? They were good times, Max.'

He paused for a moment, not looking at me. 'I'd give anything to have those days again. I don't know how things could go so badly wrong between us. It's my fault. I know. I'm not completely recovered from my injuries and things aren't ... good for me, but I can't blame everything on that. You know me, Max, I don't always have the words to say what I should be saying, but I think ... what I'm saying is ...'

He fell silent.

'Yes?' I said, wondering what revelation was about to smack me in the face this time.

'I think we should reboot to the factory setting.'

I wondered if I was having some sort of relapse. 'What?'

'I think we should go back to that day, the day we first met. We remember how we felt about each other and I ask you to be generous and forget everything else. Because it's not important. We're what's important. What do you say?'

I couldn't say anything so he lifted me onto his bed, thereby contravening every rule known to man and Dr Stone. He rested his head on mine and we held on to each other because sometimes you don't need words.

Twenty-four hours later we were both discharged. Apparently, they were sick of the sight of us. We were given to understand that we were never to darken their doors again. I had a compulsory forty-eight hours' leave imposed upon me – as if it was some sort of gift.

We nodded meekly and departed.

Leon escorted me back to our room, with me complaining every inch of the way. I'd only just begun to touch on the world's injustices in general and to me in particular, when we met Peterson and Dottle on the gallery on their way to a meeting. I stiffened warily, but he and Leon greeted each other normally. Miss Dottle was clutching an armful of files.

'We're putting together a new funding proposal,' she said, looking excited and happy at the prospect because, of course, being with Peterson had nothing to do with it. We wished them luck and watched them disappear into his office.

Leon said, 'What do you think?'

I sighed. 'I don't know.' I suddenly realised I had mixed feelings. 'She's not Helen.'

'No one's Helen.'

'I know, it's just … she's so … different.'

'That may not necessarily be a bad thing. And does it matter as long as she makes him happy?' He looked down at me. 'We can't help who we fall in love with.'

433

I broke our self-imposed rule about not touching if we were in uniform and took his arm. 'I know. And if she does make him happy …'

'I think she does. She's soft and gentle and earnest and she worships him. I'm not saying it will last, but I think that as the person to help him to get over Helen, he couldn't do better.'

I looked up at him. What was he saying?

'People take comfort where they can, Max. We've both done that. There's no blame attached. No one blames anyone for it.' He looked at me. 'Do they?'

It was as if a great weight had fallen away. 'No,' I said. 'No one blames anyone for anything.'

Leon made me a mug of tea before pushing off.

'Thank you. My husband is wonderful.'

'Your husband has had it made abundantly clear to him that his duties are manifest and varied, and not confined solely to rocking his wife's world on a regular basis.'

'Nevertheless, his wife is grateful.'

'Enjoy your leave,' he said, limping towards the door. 'Stay here. Don't break anything. In particular, don't catch anything. Just sit quietly and recover. Drink your tea, read a book and stay out of trouble.'

I sighed, but he just laughed and disappeared out of the door, promising to meet me for dinner.

I picked up a book.

Seventeen minutes later I was bored stiff. Don't get me wrong – it was a pleasant morning. The sun was shining through the windows and I could hear the gentle background hum of others working. It was just ... I don't know. My book was failing to grip me. I could go for a walk – a healthy way to spend a morning and with the additional bonus of annoying all the people who'd been telling me to take things easy. Tempting, but I couldn't be bothered.

I looked around. Matthew would be back with us soon. I could get his room ready.

I'd been away so long and so much had happened. This time last month I'd been discussing setting a trap for Ronan and he'd set one for me instead. I pushed that thought away because I was supposed to be convalescing, and tried to remember if Matthew had clean sheets or not. I changed them anyway, dusted his room, made sure his Time Map plug-in was working, and tidied his drawers – because he'd really appreciate that, wouldn't he?

Back in our bedroom, I sorted my own clothes, which didn't take long because I don't have many but, on the other hand, I hadn't seen them for quite a long time. Moving into our sitting room, I tidied briefly, even though there wasn't much to do. Both Leon and I are very neat. I straightened our books, plumped a few cushions and that was it. I looked at the clock. That had taken twenty-three minutes. Long hours stretched ahead of me. I'm not good with time off. I flung myself onto my very recently plumped cushions and looked around for something else to do.

Two teddies grinned at me. Bear 2.0, Leon's gift to me during a very dark time, and Matthew's blue teddy, looking slightly the worse for wear and rather letting the side down. Now would be an ideal opportunity to clean him up ready for Matthew's visit.

I filled the washbasin with warm water, added a tiny drop of shampoo, and dropped him in. The water turned a horrible murky brown. He was a lot dirtier than he looked. Pale blue, while pretty, is not a good colour for a child's teddy.

I left him to soak while I chucked some cleaning stuff down the loo, wiped down the bath and put out some clean towels.

Job done, I went back to Matthew's teddy, lifting it, dripping, from the basin and because there's something disquieting about treating a teddy bear like an old dishcloth, I closed my eyes before squeezing hard.

Ouch – that hurt.

I wrung it out again and, yes, there was definitely something there. Gingerly, I felt around. There was something inside his head. Something sharp.

I held him up to the light. His eyes weren't level, but they never had been. Now that I looked more closely though, they weren't the same. One was slightly darker than the other. The slightly darker one was ... not an eye.

I didn't hesitate. I found an old scalpel in my painting gear and set to work. It didn't take long. Something small, round and dark rolled into the basin. A good job I'd put the plug in or it would have gone straight down the plughole.

I stared at it because I'm an idiot. All I could think was that Matthew had had this as a baby and it was a stupid thing to put in a teddy bear destined for an infant. I wouldn't have thought it of Dottle.

There was no blinding moment of revelation. I wasn't Saul on the road to Damascus with a donkey and a bright light. I was a small, tired, unintentionally underweight, emotionally battered historian staring at something I didn't understand and struggling to get myself together as random thoughts and impressions and memories all ran together like pools of mercury.

This was how Ronan knew Matthew was in Sick Bay the day he killed Helen and stole him away. As a baby, Matthew had loved his teddy. It went everywhere with him. Ronan would have known exactly where he was at all times. And murdering Helen had been a snatched opportunity to harm us all. Me and Peterson in particular.

This was how Ronan knew when and where to intercept me the day I left St Mary's on maternity leave. I saw my little box of possessions, the pale blue teddy sticking out of the top.

This was how Ronan knew he would find me in the reed beds that day I went running. I heard her voice asking me, 'Where are you off to?' I'd told her where I was going and guess who turned up thirty minutes later with his offer of an olive branch. He'd said, 'I've met someone.' Was it her? Was it Lisa Bloody Dottle?

This was now Ronan knew I'd had a boy. What had he said? He'd said, 'And how is the little lad? Does he look like his father?'

This was how Ronan knew we were waiting for him at Persepolis. Leon and I had discussed my plan here in this very room.

This was how Ronan had been able to stay one step ahead of us all this time.

I looked again at the device lying in the basin and I knew. I just knew.

Lisa Dottle.

Lisa. Bloody. Dottle.

There had been that incident in the canteen. When she first arrived here. When her supposed boss, the idiot Halcombe had publicly humiliated her. We'd sympathised with her and hated him. How easy it would have been for her to organise that and make herself the victim. We'd all felt so sorry for her. And again, when her hamster died. Was it even possible she'd killed it herself? As part of her cover? What sort of a person would do that?

Then there was the night we'd been burying King John's treasure up in the woods. When something very unpleasant was right behind us and we couldn't get into the pod because every time we opened the door, she slapped it closed again, claiming later it had been panic-stricken inexperience.

And the time in the Sunken Garden, when Ellis and I had been discussing our plan to trap Ronan here. Dottle had overheard every word and then, unable to get away quickly enough when she heard me coming, had flung herself over a bench and burst into tears. She'd been lucky enough to have Halcombe to cry about, but it could easily have been something else. Peterson and her unrequited love for him, perhaps.

And that was why she hadn't pressed to accompany us to Persepolis. Because with no historians or Dieter around, and Leon only part-time, that would have been the ideal opportunity for her to plant the canister of gas in Number Four. Magnetised, so no fitting skills required. She'd just wandered into Hawking one day, files and excuses all prepared in case anyone challenged her, but no one ever did because it was only Lisa Bloody Dottle. She'd waited until the busy techies were looking elsewhere, nipped into Number Four and just shoved it under the console. Ten seconds, tops. All ready to go as soon as the pod was in service. If I hadn't rolled under the console and discovered it ... who knew what damage it would have done. Had already done. Clerk, Prentiss, Cox, me, Leon, Peterson, techies servicing the pod ... dear God, no wonder nothing ever went right for us.

I was pacing about like a madwoman. Was it possible that the only reason Matthew was still safe at TPHQ was because I'd accidentally left his teddy behind and he'd

439

been too busy with his new life to ask for it? His teddy had been sitting on the window sill ever since. Our window sill. In our room. There's little enough privacy at St Mary's but this room was *our* space. The place we could be together.

I thought of some of the things Leon and I had said to each other in this room, some of the things we'd done in this room, and felt hot, purple rage in my heart. My instinct was to get rid of it – as quickly as possible, so I did. I crossed to the front window and hurled it as hard and as far as I could, slamming the window closed again afterwards – as if that would make any difference, because the damage was done.

She'd played the victim and we'd fallen for it. We'd taken her in, included her, made her welcome and talked in front of her. Typical St Mary's – a bloody great threat hanging over us like the Sword of Damocles and all this time we'd been looking in the wrong direction. Bloody typical. She must be laughing her bloody socks off because the biggest threat wasn't the idiot Halcombe and never had been. I wondered if the two of them were working together or whether he'd been as used as we had. She'd never been working for him, but had he been working for her?

He'd wandered around the building making himself obnoxious on every possible occasion. Far too obnoxious. He hadn't made the slightest effort to build a working relationship. He'd gone at it with all the delicacy of a bull in a china shop. He'd deliberately sabotaged the Caernarfon jump, trying to convince a bunch of historians – all of whom knew better – that he might have contracted leprosy. How eagerly we'd seized on what we saw as an opportunity to lock him in the isolation word and count ourselves safe. Threat neutralised.

And all this time he hadn't been the threat. He'd never been the threat. Knowingly or unknowingly, he'd been working for Dottle – someone clever enough to lead from the back. Someone discreet. Someone who presented herself as slightly pathetic and very definitely non-threatening. Someone we regarded with a very unhealthy mixture of affection, pity and slight contempt. Someone who'd been laughing her head off at us ever since she walked through the door.

Lisa. Bloody. Dottle.

We'd been so taken in by her pink nose, her shyness, her apparent ability to blush at will and her schoolgirl crush on Peterson. We'd separated her from Halcombe, welcomed her into our ranks, talked in front of her and never for one moment thought …

Overcoming the urge to hunt her down and kill her in the most painful way possible, I made myself a cup of tea and sat down to think.

Barely had I taken the first sip when someone knocked at the door. I was in such a state that for one moment, I was convinced it was Dottle herself. Had she discovered my discovery?

I wrenched the door open. It wasn't her. It was Markham. Aggrieved and slightly wet.

'I was walking along minding my own business,' he said indignantly, 'and this fell on my head. Don't we keep Bashford for that sort of thing?'

He held out Matthew's now one-eyed teddy.

I thought quickly. 'Oh my God, are you all right?'

'No, I'm bloody not. It gave me a nasty shock.'

441

'I was talking to the teddy. But while you're here, come in a moment.'

'Why are you hurling teddies out of the window anyway?' he said, closing the door behind him. 'Who does that?'

'I washed it,' I said, ever so casually because anyone might be listening, 'and when I put it on the window sill to dry, it fell out. I'm so glad you're here. Can you ...' I had a quick think '... get the lid off this for me? It seems to be stuck.'

He's really not an idiot, you know. 'O ... K,' he said slowly. 'Show me.'

I led him into the bathroom and pointed. 'Look at that. Can you do anything?'

He bent and peered closely and then looked back at the one-eyed teddy he was still clutching. He worked it out considerably more quickly than I had done. I saw him remember who gave me the teddy, put two and two together and arrive at the correct answer. Waggling his eyebrows, he made a winding motion with one hand. 'Oh, yes, I think so.' He grabbed a can of air freshener, grunted realistically, and pulled of the cap. 'There you go. Another triumph for the Security Section. Anyway, I thought I'd take you for a spot of lunch. I expect you're having a really boring morning, aren't you?'

'Worst ever,' I said. 'Let's go.'

I picked up the device, wrapped it in a thick towel, shoved it and the teddy into my sports bag and we left.

Out on the landing, I whispered, 'Do you think it's still working?'

'Well, dunking it in water won't have done it a lot of good, but assume it is.'

'What is it? Is it a camera?'

442

'I don't think so. And even if it was then the field of vision would be very limited. But it's definitely a listening device.'

'Range?'

'Unknown, but the techies will be able to tell us. Deep breaths, Max.'

'I'm ... slightly annoyed.'

'Suck it up.'

'OK. Is she still with Peterson?'

He pulled out his scratchpad and tapped. 'According to her diary, she's with him for another thirty minutes. Let's leave her there. You talk to Dr Bairstow and I'll get my team together.'

I clutched his arm. 'She mustn't get away.'

'She won't,' he said reassuringly. 'Go.'

Mrs Partridge was sitting at her desk.

'Good morning, Mrs Partridge. May I leave this here please?'

I waited for her to assimilate my scruffy bag and say no, but there must have been something in my face because she said immediately, 'Of course.' She opened the bottom drawer of her filing cabinet and I stuffed it in, slamming the drawer shut afterwards.

'Please don't let anything happen to that.'

She nodded.

'I need to see him urgently.'

She nodded again and I went straight in.

I gave it to him in as few words as possible. When I'd finished, he said, 'Where is the device now?'

'Mrs Partridge has it safely stowed away.'

He nodded and then sat silently for a very long time, staring at his desk. I too sat quietly. The urge to do something violent now – right now, right this very minute – was slowly subsiding, to be replaced by the urge to get it right.

'She is with Dr Peterson, I believe.'

'Yes, sir.'

There was a tap at the door and Markham entered.

'I've cleared the Hall, sir, and locked the doors to R&D. The front doors are secured. Chief Farrell has Hawking on lockdown. We're ready to go whenever you give the word. Where do you want her?'

'In here, I think, Mr Markham. With no less than two of your men with her at all times – armed, of course – and another two men outside.'

'Agreed, sir. One in Mrs Partridge's room – with her permission, of course, and the other out on the gallery guarding the outer door.'

'Very well, Mr Markham. Go and get her. I have a letter to write.'

I went with Markham and his team out to the gallery and was all set to follow him to Peterson's office when he drew me aside. 'No.'

'What?'

'I don't want you there, Max.'

'But ... it was me that ...'

'That's true and I'm grateful, but you've done your bit. I've no idea how this will go down, but you will keep your distance. I don't want her grabbing you as a hostage, or anything like that, and if she shoots you, then Leon will come looking for me. You can wait and watch, but from the other side of the gallery. No closer than twenty feet, Max. If you won't agree then you can wait with Dr Bairstow – who, incidentally, trusts us to get on with the job ourselves.'

I reluctantly stepped back. 'OK.'

They waited while I trailed around the gallery until I was opposite Peterson's office. Then they pulled out their weapons and moved in.

Markham went in first, closely followed by Evans and Cox. Gallacio and Keller covered them from the door and the rest waited on either side of the corridor. They were quick and professional.

I heard her scream. 'Oh my God, oh my God, what's happening?' and through the open door I watched her attempt to jump out of her seat. Markham pushed her back again, his gun in her face. 'Dr Peterson, sir. If you would be so good ...'

I caught a glimpse of Peterson as he stared at this invasion in astonishment. Then he pushed back his chair. Keeping his distance, he edged away along the wall, taking care to stay out of their line of fire. He was three-quarters turned away from me and I couldn't see his face.

The next minute they had her out of the chair and she was face down on the carpet while they secured her hands. Then they had an arm each and were dragging her out of the door.

I was very good. I stayed safely on my side of the gallery, but she turned her head and saw me standing there.

It was astonishing. This wasn't the same Dottle at all and now I realised what a very clever woman she was. Suddenly – don't ask me how – she wasn't so hunched – her nose wasn't so pointed – her hair wasn't so ratty. She straightened up, tossed her hair out of her face, looked across at me ... and smiled. All my former rage boiled up again. I could actually feel acid rising in my gullet. I so badly wanted to hit her. Again and again. To wipe that smile off her face. For good.

They jerked her along towards Dr Bairstow's office. I watched them go in. Mrs Partridge's office was empty. Markham was leaving nothing to chance in the hostage-taking possibilities – although frankly, you'd have to have the biggest death wish in the world to try anything with

446

Mrs Partridge. Then the door closed behind them and I was alone on the gallery.

I was suddenly conscious of a very great need to see Leon. I called him up. 'Are you all right?'

'Yes,' he said. 'Have they got her?'

'They have. Quick and quiet.'

There was a pause. 'Max, I can't come to you. We're still on lockdown.'

'I know,' I said. 'I'm fine. I was worried about you.'

'I'm fine, too, but you should go and talk to Peterson. Find out how he is.'

Shit. I'd forgotten about Peterson. It was too late, anyway. I don't know where she came from, but as I looked across the gallery, Miss Lingoss was just closing his door behind her. On any other day, I would have found that quite interesting.

Whatever was happening in Dr Bairstow's office was happening without me and I found I didn't really care. In lieu of Leon, I headed towards the other place I felt safe.

Rosie Lee looked up as I entered. 'What's happening? They told me to stay in here and I'll be wanting to go home soon.'

I looked at the clock. 'Ten past two. I'm astonished you stayed this late. You're usually out of the door by now so as to make your five o'clock finishing time.'

'My life was a lot easier when you were trapped in 1399.'

'So was mine. Stick the kettle on.'

'It's your turn.'

'Stick the kettle on or I'll make sure you're still here this time next week.'

There was a lot of kettle banging for the next few minutes but we got there in the end.

447

I took my mug to the window to wait for the appearance of the Time Police. Dr Bairstow must have finished his letter by now. They could be here any minute.

They were late. I'd finished my tea and was considering embarking on negotiations for another when a squat black pod appeared. This one was much smaller than usual. It looked what it was. A prison. Four armoured men marched out. Their visors were down. That and the antennae sprouting from their helmets gave them the sinister look of blind insects. This must be one of their clean-up squads. The ones you never want to meet.

I watched Evans go to greet them. They talked for a few minutes and then set off around the outside of the building. I couldn't see from up here, but I could imagine faces lining the windows. Everyone would know something was up.

I watched them disappear from sight, round to the front of the building. Faintly, I heard the front doors opening.

I don't know what made me do it, but I set down my mug and left the room. Promising myself I'd stay well out of things, I leaned over the bannisters and watched them emerge through the vestibule.

Evans led them through the Hall. They marched in two pairs of two – in step, even as they climbed the stairs. I watched them pause at the outer door and knock. Cox let them in.

Everything went quiet again.

I stood in the corner of the gallery, just outside R&D. Everything was silent. I had no idea what was going on in Dr Bairstow's office. I could imagine her somehow breaking free, killing eight armed men, overcoming Dr Bairstow and his canon and escaping out of the window. Had anyone even thought of that? Just to put my mind at rest, I trotted around the gallery and peered out of a window.

Of course someone had thought of that. An armoured and visored guard stood silently on the steps looking around him. For God's sake, Maxwell, get a grip. I retired back to my corner and waited. I don't know for how long.

And then the world started up again.

Mrs Partridge's door opened. Evans and Cox appeared.

Everything went smoothly. I could barely see her for armed figures around her. Evans and Cox were in front, going on ahead. Then two Time Police officers. Then Dottle – or whatever her bloody name was – sandwiched between the other two officers with Keller and Gallacio bringing up the rear. Markham ranged up and down, checking this way and that.

Below, the vestibule door opened, and the remaining officer crossed the Hall and began to climb the stairs, weapon raised in case of trouble. He paused at the top of the stairs, checked one last time and nodded the all-clear. The procession marched past him and he fell in behind.

I stared, feeling the hairs on the back of my neck lift. Something was wrong. Something wasn't right. And suddenly I had it. Only four officers had left the Time Police pod.

It wasn't anyone's fault. Or it was everyone's fault – take your pick. The Time Police thought he was one of ours. We thought he was one of theirs.

I wasn't stupid enough to burst out of the shadows shouting, 'Wait,' because that would just get me shot. Many, many times. I remember I eased my weight onto the balls of my feet, prior to uttering a warning – I can't remember what I was going to say because subsequent events pushed it out of my mind – but it was too late anyway.

He had his weapon switched to single shot. Without seeming to take any aim at all, he fired at the two officers on either side of Dottle. They went straight down.

He fired again and Gallacio and Cox dropped to the floor. Markham was racing around the gallery shouting instructions as he came.

Someone was returning fire but I wasn't watching. I was watching Dottle. She didn't hesitate, breaking free and running down the stairs to the half landing, taking them two at a time and then straight up the other side. Turning left, she disappeared into the gloom.

I went after her like a greyhound. Bullets were flying everywhere but I knew for a certainty that none would hit me. Because Lisa Bloody Dottle was escaping and there was no way I could allow that.

Behind me I could hear shouting. All the alarms went off. And then I was through the fire door and standing on a hot, dusty, dead-fly-speckled landing. The door slammed behind me, cutting off all sound. It was a hefty door. All our fire doors are hefty, but this one was at the end of the R&D corridor and could survive a nuclear blast. And, for all I know, had done so in the past.

I stood in the silence, listening. Had she fled up? Or down? Down, surely. There was nothing up there but the roof. Down the stairs led to the car park, fresh air and freedom.

I turned to my left and began to descend. Three steps later I stopped. I don't know why. I stopped moving, but I also stopped reacting and started thinking.

We'd caught her unawares. I'd seen the shock on her face. She'd been taken completely by surprise. She had no

450

idea the device had been discovered. So the device wasn't transmitting to her. And if not to her – then to whom?

Well, I think we all know the answer to that one.

So – never mind who. Where? Markham had said he thought it wouldn't have a long range, so somewhere quite close then. The woods above St Mary's would be good. Someone could easily hide up there and remain undiscovered. But was it close enough for a rescue to be attempted at such short notice? Barely an hour had passed since I'd made the discovery. And how had he got into the grounds unseen. Yes, Markham had a full team escorting Dottle, but he wouldn't have left the monitors unattended. Someone would have noticed.

I had a sudden vision of Dottle with an enormous plateful of sandwiches and other goodies, telling me some rigmarole about pulling an all-nighter so she could impress Thirsk and Halcombe. She'd stood in front of me, her pink face radiating earnestness and an anxiety to do well and I'd swallowed it. Hook, line and sinker. She'd lied over and over again and I'd believed every word she'd said to me. On that occasion, she'd been heading towards the stairs. She'd been going up. To the roof.

And that was where she was heading now. Ronan would be covering her retreat. Was it possible one man could overcome Markham and his team? To say nothing of the Time Police? Even with the element of surprise – could he do it?

Not my problem. I closed my mind to everything else. Markham could handle all that. That was his job. My job was to prevent Dottle getting away.

I turned, discarded speed in favour of stealth, and crept up the stairs towards the roof.

I had no idea what I was going to do when I got there. I was completely unarmed and a trifle wobbly because even the equivalent of gaol fever can do that to a girl. On the other hand, Dottle was still in restraints. Her hands were tied behind her back so she couldn't run fast, climb up or down, or throw anything at me, and she wasn't armed. I told myself the odds were on my side.

The fire door to the roof was wide open. I could see bright sunlight and blue sky. There might have been birds singing – I don't know. I could hear only my own quiet footsteps and the thump of my own heart.

I reached the door and stood to one side, thinking. If it was me, I would stand behind the door, wait until my pursuer was crossing the threshold and then kick it shut with all my might. With luck, the metal door would catch them in the face, possibly render them unconscious, break their nose and even knock them backwards down the stairs.

Two could play at that game.

I stood listening. Complete silence.

I took two steps forwards, raised my right leg, and kicked the door as hard as I could. It slammed back, rebounded off the wall and I had to jump aside before it hit me. Bugger. She hadn't been hiding behind the door. She was out on the roof somewhere.

And the slamming door hadn't been quiet. She would know I was here. What could she do to me?

She could conceal herself behind the chimneys and play hide and seek. But why? The longer she was up here the greater the chance of recapture. What was the point? Unless this was just the result of blind panic – the urge to run as far and fast as possible – she was trapped up here. All I had to do was close the fire door – there's no access from the outside – and wait for reinforcements to turn up.

The answer came hard on that thought.

Oh my God. Was there a pod up here? Was it possible – was it actually possible that someone who might have a small pod with a camouflage device could have been living on our roof? I had no idea how long Ronan could have been up here, but long enough, apparently.

I couldn't believe it, but it made perfect sense. He'd been up here all the time. No one ever came up here – he could have spent his days lolling around in the sunshine as she brought him tasty snacks. Like a bloody holiday. The Time Police had been scouring the timeline for him and he'd been here all along. Was this was the reason Rigby and Lorris – the two most incompetent pod operators in History happened to have St Mary's coordinates programmed in? I'd wondered at the coincidence and then forgotten it.

So Dottle had been spying and he'd been up here listening. Between them, they'd got just about everything covered. No wonder he couldn't be found. He was on our bloody roof. Any trace of his pod would have been lost among the signatures of our own pods and even if it hadn't, everyone would have assumed it was only an echo. Now, far too late, I remembered the Time Police officer looking for Adrian and Mikey. He'd reported echoes everywhere. Including on the roof.

Ronan had probably been up here the whole bloody time. We'd been sheltering Clive Ronan. We'd even bloody fed him. I was a cauldron of fury. Hideous things were bubbling to the surface. She would suffer for this. This was for Helen.

I took a deep breath and stepped out.

The heat hit me immediately. The familiar long roof stretched out in front of me. I saw clumps of chimneys at regular intervals. They'd been put in when St Mary's was rebuilt after the Civil War. Except for the big one over there. The original chimney for the big fireplace in the Hall. The one I'd watched being built six hundred odd years ago. It was blocky and massive. That's where she'd be hiding.

I wanted her to know she was trapped so I slammed the door closed behind me. Keeping well away from the parapet – because it's not high and I didn't want her jumping out at me and pushing me over – I set off to find her.

I was actually feeling quite confident. There were twigs and small stones and all the debris dropped by birds over the years, but Mr Strong was efficient and conscientious. There was nothing up here that could be used as a weapon and she still had her hands tied.

So – the burning question – where was his pod. And would she have access? If she did then she might already be inside and that would be a bit of a bugger because all she had to do was sit tight. And if, somehow, Ronan had got away downstairs, he could be pounding up the stairs at this very moment. And he was very definitely armed. I might actually have only seconds before he turned up.

Throwing caution to the winds – I'm an historian and it's in my job description – I ran across the roof, straight towards the big, central chimney.

She'd anticipated me. I was only half way there when she shot out from behind a smaller chimney stack, cannoned into me and sent me flying. I rolled across the hot roof. Something kicked me in the back. And again in the side. I tried to roll away but she followed me, kicking and stamping and shrieking at me.

The only thing that saved me was that she was wearing those sensible court shoes so beloved by women who like their footwear to be stylish yet practical during their working day. I on the other hand was wearing my boots. Beloved by women who like to kick the living shit out of people during *their* working day.

She was kicking out so hard that one shoe flew off and landed a good distance away. It didn't stop her. She just swapped legs.

I stopped rolling away and rolled towards instead, grabbing her foot and twisting. She fell on top of me and now I had her because she couldn't get up.

I heaved myself painfully to my feet and refrained from returning the favour boot-wise. The mood I was in, I would have killed her.

Careful to keep my distance, I wiped blood off my lip and told her to stay still.

She managed to push herself into a sitting position and we both glared at each other.

I thought I was remarkably restrained. 'I really don't like you.'

She was dirty and dusty and yet she still managed to smile. 'Well, that doesn't surprise me in the slightest. You don't like me because I'm exactly like you, aren't I? Manipulating every situation to my advantage. Lying and deceiving to get what I want. Sacrificing others. Just as you do. We're actually very alike, you and I, don't you think?'

Even her voice was different. Lower in pitch. More confident. The voice of someone who knew the next person through the door would be her accomplice and I'd be dead.

'We're not alike in any way.'

'Oh, but we are.'

'No, we're not. I could kill you for what you've done to Peterson.'

She shrugged. 'And yet another similarity. I *will* kill you for what you've done to Ronan.'

'What? What I did to him? How deranged are you?'

Suddenly she was furious, struggling up onto her knees.

'He trusted you. I warned him you were a slippery two-faced bitch and he wouldn't listen. He trusted you. Do you know how difficult that is for him? He never trusts anyone. Bairstow was his friend and he killed Annie Bessant. Ronan broke his heart over her. He *grieved* for her. He came to you. He trusted you and you betrayed him as well. Everyone betrays him in the end.'

I felt an astonishing need to defend myself.

'It wasn't me. It wasn't St Mary's. It was the Time Police.'

'You were the bait. You were the trap. You're a dishonest, deceitful bitch who uses everyone around her and doesn't care about the cost. How many people died over the years because of you. You let Helen Foster die ...'

'Ronan killed Helen Foster. Don't you put that on me. I was there ...'

'You were there and you did nothing. Everyone said so. Even Peterson said it. You do nothing and people die all around you.'

'Not as many as die around Ronan.'

'Because you betrayed him. He was the one who wanted to end it all. We wanted to be together. We would have been and ...'

I spoke quietly to get her attention. 'Is that what he told you?'

She stopped suddenly, panting with emotion. 'What did you say?'

'Did he never tell you about Isabella Barclay?'

'What about her?'

I pretended to hesitate. 'Well, if he hasn't told you then it's probably better if I say nothing. He'll tell you if he wants you to know.'

'You're lying.'

'I'm not. I swear I'm not. Look, obviously I don't want to say too much if he hasn't mentioned her ...' I am never going to heaven '... but you should definitely ask him about Izzie Barclay.'

'Why, what happened to her?'

'She died, too. They all die in the end.'

She was struggling to get to her feet. I had no means of stopping her and I certainly wasn't going to within touching distance. Every second I had her attention was a second nearer her recapture.

'This is not the same at all. We want to be together. That's all we ever wanted. He came to you. He trusted

457

you. I told him. Over and over, I told him not to. And I was right. He should have listened to me. You betrayed him.'

She was on her feet now and we were screaming at each other but even over the noise we were making I heard it. I heard the door open behind me and realised what she'd been doing. She'd been doing the same as me. We'd been keeping each other occupied until reinforcements arrived.

And now, of course, the question was, who had opened the door? Who was standing behind me?

I turned slowly, confident it would be Markham.

It wasn't Markham.

Bollocks.

He pushed the door closed with his foot, wedged it shut, and started to edge across the roof. It gave me a shock to see half-healed scratch-marks all down one side of his face. I'd done that. At Persepolis. Only a week or so ago. And now that I looked more carefully, his wrist was bandaged, too.

My one thought was that I could do nothing about Ronan but I could and would prevent Dottle escaping. She was obviously privy to his plans and the Time Police would make her talk. If they couldn't then I was prepared to have a go myself.

The same thought had obviously occurred to him. He pointed his gun at her.

'Sorry, Lisa.'

She was backing away. We both were. Because that makes such a difference when confronted by a maniac with a high-powered weapon probably capable of disabling an aircraft carrier.

'Clive? What are you doing?'

458

'I'm sorry, Lisa. As they say – it was good while it lasted.' He was striding across the roof, gun pointed towards both of us, heading towards his pod, presumably. He was going to get away. Where were Markham and the security team? I could hear shouts and footsteps pounding on the stairs. They'd be here in seconds.

But he'd be gone in seconds.

He stood in a patch of empty roof and said, 'Door.'

The door opened.

She screamed. 'Wait for me. What are you doing?'

'Can't afford to hang about. See you around sometime.'

'You can't leave me here.'

'You underestimate me, my dear, of course I can.'

Her voice was that of a little girl. A bewildered little girl. 'But ... why?'

He paused in the door, turned and smiled. A nice smile. Not his usual sneer, or a mad grimace, or an unpleasant smirk, but a pleasant smile, warm and friendly. 'Because, my dear, you're not Annie.'

He raised the gun and fired at her.

I heard the shot.

The impact knocked her back hard into me. I staggered against the low parapet which caught me mid-thigh. I flailed wildly for a moment, but her hands were tied, she could do nothing to save herself and her weight carried us both over the edge.

The last thing I saw was Markham bursting out onto the roof.

Too bloody late now ...

459

They say your life flashes in front of your eyes. Or is that only when drowning? I never know, although I'm sure I'll find out one day. Anyway, I can categorically state that my life did not flash in front of my eyes. It didn't have time. There was only just enough time for me to think, I'm falli – when I wasn't. I was crashing through a tree. My world was suddenly full of the smell of conifer.

Fortunately, my body is a great deal better at self-preservation than my brain, which is generally left to fend for itself on occasions like this. I instinctively clutched at things – branches, I assume. I got a broken finger for my trouble, but the tree was soft and whippy and it slowed my fall to some extent. Most importantly, it turned me around so, as I slithered downwards, I could land more or less on my feet.

I broke both my ankles.

I fell forwards and broke my collarbone.

I lay quietly for a while, thinking of Actium, sideways and bracelets.

It took me a minute to get myself together again. I kept thinking, bloody hell, I've fallen off the roof. I've actually fallen off the roof. A large piece of yellowy-green conifer lay beside me. Squinting up at the tree, I could see I'd torn away a huge piece as I fell. I could see the scar where it had ripped away. Mr Strong would not be pleased with me.

The rest of the tree seemed to be occupied by Miss Dottle who hung, motionless, head downwards, not looking that healthy.

I thought I saw someone leaning over the parapet. They were silhouetted against the sky and it could have been anyone. I heard a far-off voice shouting, 'Medical emergency,' and wondered who was hurt.

It was rather nice, just lying here. I found the smell of conifer to be pleasantly soothing. I seemed to have landed in some sort of flower bed. I was betting there were any number of plants and bushes crushed beneath me and I was grateful to every one of them.

There was something important I had to do and I really should get up and deal with it. Or – a much better option – I could leave it to someone else to sort out. My conifer branch and I would just lie here … in the sun … not doing anything very much … I closed my eyes.

And opened them again to find Dr Bairstow kneeling beside me and carefully crossing my arms over my chest.

I couldn't let that go. 'A bit premature, sir, surely.'

'Alas – the pitfalls of wishful thinking.' He paused. 'I think you may have a broken bone here, Max.'

'What's happening?'

'At the moment, I have no idea. There was a great deal of gunfire but traditionally you appear to be the only casualty.'

'But the security team?' I was too dazed to remember their names. 'How are they?'

'Armoured', he said shortly. 'Their pain is not sufficient to prevent enough bad language to curdle milk.'

'There's another casualty, sir.' I nodded over his shoulder to the tree-borne Miss Dottle.

'Ah. Do we know her status?'

'He shot her and she fell of the roof, sir, so utilising my wide-ranging medical expertise, I'd say she hasn't survived.'

'I hesitate to contradict your wide-ranging expertise, Dr Maxwell, but I feel I should point out that if you did then so could she.'

'But I haven't been shot, sir.'

He raised an eyebrow and I squinted down. My shoulder was stained with blood. Mine. And I should know. I've seen it often enough.

'Bloody bollocking hell,' I said, mildly aggrieved. 'The bullet went straight through her and into me.'

Markham turned up, shouting over his shoulder, 'I've found her.' He holstered his gun. 'Max?'

I said good afternoon, because now he's head of the Security Section the power has gone to his head and he insists on standards being maintained.

'Wotcha,' he said, and I decided I was too injured to cope.

'What's the damage?' he said, crouching beside me.

'I think I may have broken a finger.'

'I'll say. And you have one foot pointing in a refreshingly original direction and the other pointing backwards.'

'What?' I tried to sit up and hurt my arm.

'And your arm as well. All minor injuries.'

I found his casually dismissive tone quite irritating. 'I fell off the bloody roof, you know.'

He shrugged. 'Been there. Done that.'

'*And* I've been shot.'

'Boring. I get shot all the time.'

I closed my eyes. 'I can see why.'

He stood up and began to circle the tree, gun in hand, just in case.

'She's dead,' I said helpfully.

'She certainly is. She looks well and truly wedged to me. God knows how we're going to get her down.'

I closed my eyes again. 'I wouldn't bother, if I were you.'

'We can't just leave her up there.'

I didn't see why not. 'I don't see why not. I'm sure Professor Rapson would relish the opportunity to investigate an authentic sky burial.'

'Well, for a start, we'll have every vulture in Rushfordshire circling overhead.'

'There are no vultures in Rushford.'

Dr Bairstow climbed awkwardly to his feet. 'Dr Maxwell has obviously never had dealings with the Parish Council.'

A thunder of boots announced the arrival of miscellaneous groups of St Mary's and Time Police, some more mobile than others, but all determined not to be excluded from anything that might be happening. I was in grave danger of being trampled. Dr Stone, following on behind, took one look at me and pulled up short. 'You again.'

'Who were you expecting?'

'For God's sake, I only discharged you an hour ago. We haven't even changed the sheets yet. Is it too much to expect even a morning to go by without a member of the Farrell family occupying one of my beds?'

Dr Bairstow intervened. 'Ah, Dr Stone, I wonder if we could have your professional opinion here, please.'

Dr Stone looked up and squinted in the approved medical manner. 'Dead.'

Dr Bairstow sighed. 'Not that one. This one.'

'Sorry, sir.' He bent over me.

Dr Bairstow hadn't finished. 'Mr Markham, I would be grateful if you could arrange for the body to be removed.'

'At once, sir. Mr Evans, remove the body.'

'Yes, sir. Mr Cox ...'

'What? How?'

'I don't know. Ropes?'

'What do you mean, ropes?'

'Lower the body down.'

'Wouldn't it be easier to lift it back up to the roof?'

'Or across and through the window. Whose window is that?'

'Professor Rapson's.'

Dr Bairstow frowned. 'Under no circumstances ...'

'No indeed, sir.'

I closed my eyes. One of the advantages of being a shattered wreck is that no one expects you to get the body out of the tree. I lay quietly and listened to the war of words going on over my head. Promising to be as much trouble in death as she had been in life, Miss Dottle appeared to be well and truly wedged. I had no idea how they were going to get her down and neither, it seemed, did anyone else.

So, to sum up. There was good. Leon was safe. Matthew would be arriving in a few days. Peterson was ... after Dottle, I wasn't sure what Peterson would be, but no one was dead. Apart from Dottle, of course.

The bad, of course, was very bad indeed. Ronan had escaped. Worse – he might have been on our roof for weeks. Months even. That was going to take some explaining and now he was back in the game. What sort of condition was he in? He'd looked fine to me. And, most importantly, where would he go next?

I heard Captain Ellis again. 'A good hunter works out where his prey will be, goes there and waits.'

I lay on my back, half listening to the turmoil around me and half thinking about other things. One thing seemed very clear – the Time Police, Leon, Guthrie – they'd all had a go at capturing Ronan and got precisely nowhere. We – they – were doing it all wrong. A new approach was required. Away to my left, someone was shouting for an axe – whether to dismember the tree or the late Miss Dottle was unclear, but obviously a drastic solution was called for.

Yes, it was, wasn't it? A drastic solution was definitely called for. A couple of neurons blinked in the daylight and got to work. I can only assume my fall had jolted something loose because I'd just had a brilliant idea. A truly, truly, incandescently brilliant idea.

I thought a little bit more and came to a decision. I didn't know what Dr Bairstow would say about it. Or Leon. Or the Time Police. It seemed safe to assume that no one was going to be happy, but enough was enough. They'd all tried and failed.

Now it was my turn.

THE END

Acknowledgments

Thanks to Tina Rowles of Gloucester Libraries Enquiry Service who provided information on Alexander and Persepolis.

Thanks to Scott who so patiently answered all my questions on denial of service attacks and never allowed the fact that I didn't understand a word he said to put him off.

Thanks to Dr Webster of Longlevens Surgery who took the time and trouble to answer all my questions about sewing people's legs back on again.

Thanks to Accent Press and everyone there.

Thanks to Rebecca, my long-suffering editor.

Thanks to Karen and everyone else who assisted with the medieval English.

Thanks to Kieran Bates of the *Coach and Horses* who generously allowed me to use the name, *The Cider Tree*, for the inn at Rushford.

All these people did their best for me, but I'm certain I've managed to get most of it wrong somehow. Sorry, guys.